WHIPPED UP

RYAN CHAISE BOOK 2

STUART G. YATES

Published 2021 by Terminal Velocity – A Next Chapter Imprint

Edited by Jayne Southern

Cover art by CoverMint

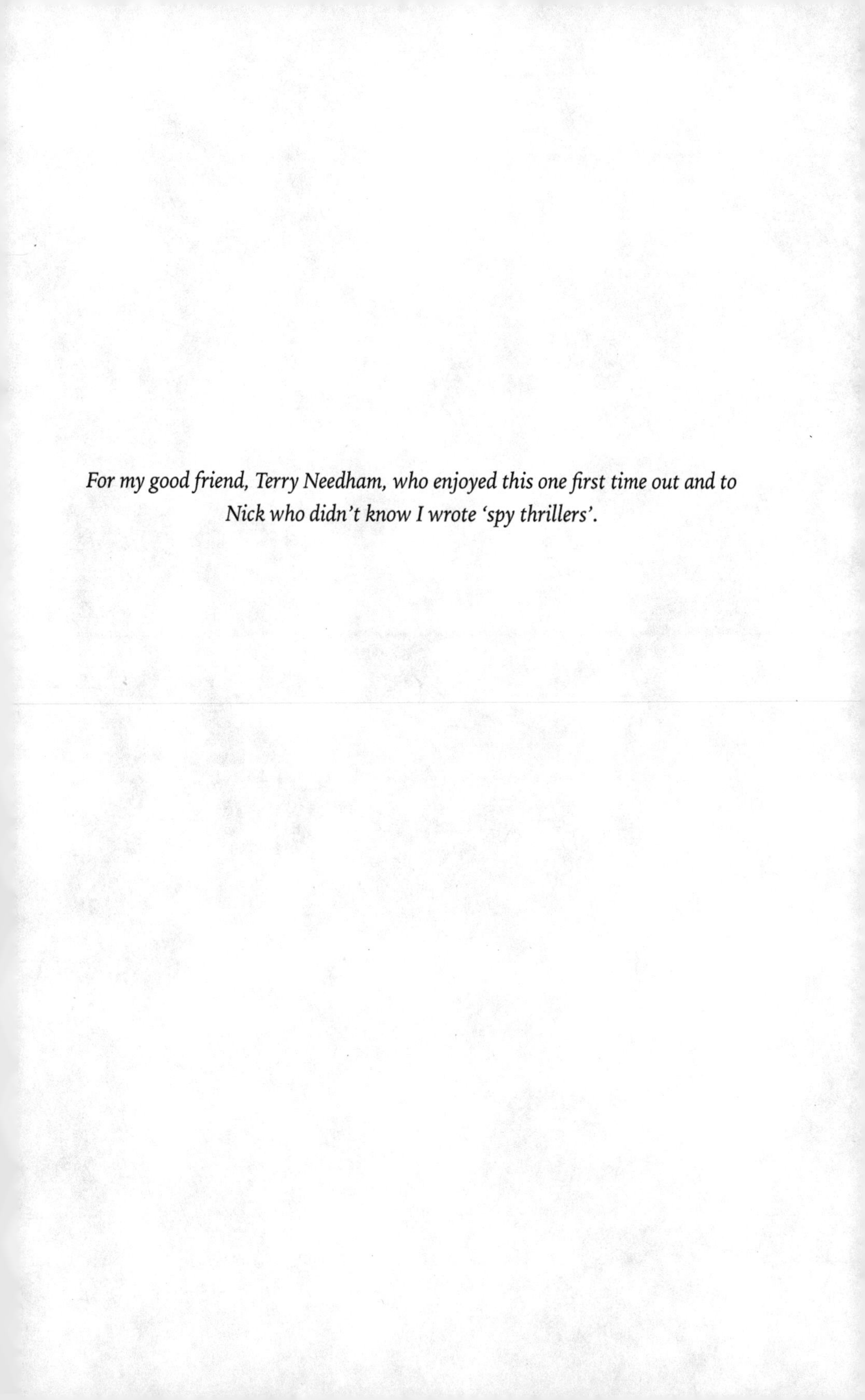

For my good friend, Terry Needham, who enjoyed this one first time out and to Nick who didn't know I wrote 'spy thrillers'.

PROLOGUE

IN THE DEBRIS OF EAST CONGO ...

For two days now, Esteban had holed himself up in the almost demolished apartment block overlooking the main highway that snaked through the rubble of this shattered suburb in the eastern part of the Democratic Republic of Congo. Highway was perhaps too exotic a word for a rutted track, interspersed with rocks and boulders and the occasional unexploded shell, which led to the still beautiful city of Bukavu. Vehicles rarely travelled its length.

Throughout the many long hours, Esteban waited, only three broken-down carts, pulled by scrawny looking oxen, had trundled by.

Alongside this track stood the remains of shattered buildings, once inhabited by a lively, cheery populace. Now, most of them dead, only piles of broken, blasted masonry remained, sad, vague memories of homes and families. Jagged twisted steel rods burst through splintered concrete, whilst next to them scorched thatch collapsed inside shattered mud-brick huts. An eclectic mix of the old and the new, devastated by a war proving impossible to win by either side.

A dog barked from somewhere in the distance, but no human activity encroached. The immediate area remained desolate. The stillness suited him; the heat didn't. Nor the humidity which left his clothes soaking, clinging to him like a second skin. Dark grey stains of stale sweat covered the upper half of his t-shirt, and the reek of his own stink turned his stomach. He stretched out his legs as far as possible, easing out the cramps. He dragged the back of his hand across eyes burning with sweat and concentration.

He ignored the discomfort, blocking it, except for the stench. He didn't like being dirty. He needed a shower, or better still a luxurious hour in a deep, hot bath, music softly—

Something moved.

Esteban switched off all extraneous thoughts and squinted down the sight of his Barrett-M82 sniper rifle as two figures emerged from the entrance to the underground bunker.

The entrance looked just like any other gaping hole amongst all the crumpled rubble, but Esteban knew it was there. He had always known it was there.

The first man appeared tense as he scanned the surrounding buildings. A bodyguard, an AK-47 slung across his chest, a Kevlar helmet painted dark brown with sunglasses perched above the rim. The dark green combat jacket and matching trousers, tucked into high-laced boots, completed the picture of a soldier on high alert. A big man, shoulders rounded, bare arms bristling with muscles, he moved his head from left to right, surveying the immediate area. Esteban sensed his stress level even from this distance.

Next to him, and slightly behind, the second man stood tall and angular, his camo gear hugging a hard, rigid physique. His boots glinted in the sunshine, black and highly polished, the silver automatic in its holster suspended from a new-looking ammunition belt. Bareheaded, a youthful face belied what lay behind his eyes: the cold, clinical single-mindedness, the obsessive desires, the endless capacity for violence.

Known to the world as Jimmy Spooks, Esteban did not know his real name, nor did he care. He'd waited here for days, out of sight, knowing that finally the target would appear. The only requirement patience, of which Esteban had an endless supply.

He was almost six hundred metres away. An easy shot. Jimmy Spooks, wanted by virtually every government agency on Earth. A feared warlord, deranged many said, who recruited children from as young as eight, nurtured them, taught them how to kill. And they had killed: tens of thousands of people brutally massacred in a guerrilla war many believed would never end.

Nobody even knew where to find him, this Jimmy Spooks.

Most thought he lived in the jungle, moving from one ramshackle camp to the next, a phantom, never leaving any clues as to his next stop. Special Forces scoured every tree, but nobody found any sign of Jimmy Spooks.

Except Esteban, and not in the jungle. His instincts had brought him to this area; a few interviews with barely alive locals, the handing over of American dollars, had paid off. He had what he wanted, and so had they; the promise of Jimmy Spooks' death. Still fearful, the informers had left the country on what Esteban had given them. None believed that Esteban would succeed.

Elsewhere, the search continued. No one uncovered any clue as to Jimmy's whereabouts, nevertheless, they carried on searching in all the wrong places.

Rumour had it the Russians were out there, the French. Certainly the Americans. The British had kept their distance, none of this anything to do with them.

Except they had employed Esteban.

He shot Jimmy Spooks in the forehead, the high-calibre bullet blowing off the back of his head as it exited his skull, a plume of blood following bone and brains. The guard jumped with shock but before he could even turn, Esteban shot him in the throat. A snapshot, the man ducking low. Jimmy Spooks, the main target, lay dead but Esteban didn't want anyone to know what had occurred here, or how. He hit the guard a second time, just above the left eye, as he pitched backwards to the ground.

Before the blood had even started to congeal, Esteban slipped away from his hideaway, unseen and unheard.

The hum of the air conditioner proved a faint distraction as he sat in the exquisitely furnished office just around the corner from St. James's Park. It was what he had always imagined Edwardian to be; soft, plush leather chairs, deep-piled carpet, hand-woven wallpaper hyphenated by watercolours of rural scenes. All of them genuine. All of them worth a small fortune.

Beyond the wide, deep desk, a large green door opened and Harper entered. He barely looked at Esteban as he sat down and picked up the manila file in front of him. He tapped the photograph of Jimmy Spooks and pressed his lips together.

"Good work."

Esteban shifted position in his chair, the heat inching up from his shirt collar, feeling uncomfortable. Although he loved the opulence of this room, the intensity of the occasion disturbed him a little. He would much rather be on the other end of a gun than have to sit here under this man's gaze. "Thank you."

Harper flipped through the file. "Everyone is up in arms, of course, shouting State-endorsed murder, but no one can prove anything, not even those snoopers from the various television channels." He smiled. "All in all, a most professional and satisfactory outcome."

Esteban said nothing.

Harper slapped the folder shut and pulled out another. He turned it so Esteban could see the face.

"This man. He is returning to the UK, at our behest."

Esteban frowned.

Harper ignored him and carried on. "An incident, in Spain. Didn't go too well, and he rather took things into his own hands, with a little too much enthusiasm. Caused us some concern. Still does. He's what might be termed a rogue."

"A rogue? What is that?"

"Someone who works alone, without orders. For the most part it goes fairly smoothly, but ..." He shrugged. "Sometimes, like now, we have problems. It is an inherent trait of the beast itself."

"*Pardon?*"

"The beast – the rogue. It is in his make-up to be difficult, unpredictable. Often, giving so much freedom to an operative can lead to ... excess."

"I don't understand."

"Do you need to?" Harper leaned forward, clasping his hands together in an attitude of prayer. "We've recalled him, and now we want to try to slow him down a little. Give him the opportunity to conform. But, I'm not so sure." He chewed at his lip. "This is where you come in. You are to be his shadow, his invisible nemesis."

Esteban's frown grew deeper.

Harper raised his eyes for a moment before he continued. "Follow him wherever he goes and target him. Make his routine your routine. Be fully prepared, Esteban, because when he goes off the rails – and I believe he will – I want you to be there and to kill him. Understood?"

"Absolutely." Esteban flicked open the file and read the information, which was scant, and gave no hint why Harper thought this man so dangerous. He closed the file and stared at the photograph, paper-clipped to the cover, the face of a hard-jawed man of indeterminate age. "Who is this man? His name?"

"His real name is of no importance." Harper sat back in his chair and let out a long sigh. "The name he lives by now is Ryan Chaise."

ONE

He stood at the top of the aircraft steps and took a moment to look around. The grey sky matched his mood, and the fine drizzle didn't help either. Not for the first time he wondered about the rightness of his actions.

Coming back home.

There was Linny, of course. She figured largely in the decision, rather more than the coercion perhaps. Being told what to do was not something that came easily to Ryan Chaise.

The air stewardess touched his arm and smiled. She beckoned him to continue; some disgruntled passengers wanted to disembark as quickly as possible. Lost in his thoughts, he hadn't noticed. He gave a nod of apology and descended. Overhead a plane soared into the sky, all around the noise of jet engines and the smell of kerosene invaded his senses. The steel steps clanged under his shoes, each one sounding like a death knell. Back home. Blighty. He sucked in a breath, hating it as much now as he ever did.

He'd been in the Costa del Sol for a long time, building up a comfortable little niche for himself selling real estate to the ex-pats. He'd done well, managed to earn enough to buy a beautiful villa, which Linny loved. Life was good, at first. Everything came tumbling down when he became involved with gangsters and drugs. None of it of his own making, but that hadn't prevented Linny from leaving him.

She was sick of the lies, she'd told him. Sick of the way he kept his past so secret. She'd never understood; how could she? He'd created a protective layer of deceit and for a few years, it had remained intact, with no hint of who he really was.

Nothing about his life as a covert killer in Iraq, the follow-up operations in Bahrain, Kosovo or Pakistan. He couldn't reveal anything. He'd signed the papers, and the men in grey suits had him under their thumbs.

The shit hit the fan in Spain when he'd killed one of their own. Since then he had become an undesirable, a threat. They'd recalled him, leaving few options other than to acquiesce. The alternative meant death – his own.

He went through the various exits and down an endless stream of corridors. When he finally arrived at the passport desk – or should that be *control,* he wondered – he felt tired and hot. Some idiot had put the heating on.

A smiling security guard in navy blue uniform guided him towards one of the queues. Hundreds of people milled about. Britain, gripped with paranoia over terrorist activity and the continuing pandemic, had up-graded its passport controls. Chaise couldn't work out whether it had more to do with illegal immigrants than bomb threats.

The politicians vied to hit the right nerves; preventing anyone not 'British' from trying to enter the country was always worth a few votes, with Eastern Europeans in particular blamed for the nation's ills. Strange how all the hotheads kept quiet when a 'white Anglo-Saxon' committed an outrage. None of them grasped the simple truth that good and bad resided in everyone, regardless of colour or creed.

He took a breath, sick to the back teeth of such thoughts. He'd never been able to get inside the heads of racists, nor did he wish to. His own troubles monopolised his time now, chief amongst them being how to get in touch with Linny.

Finally, his turn arrived and he stepped up to the little cubicle. Chaise presented his passport and the customs officer scanned it. She stopped, pulled a face and studied her monitor. He knew what would come next. He watched her turn to a colleague standing with arms folded some way behind her. She motioned him to approach. An exchange of whispered comments, followed by a quick glance towards Chaise. The colleague stepped away and pulled out his mobile.

Chaise stood and waited, his breathing shallow and controlled. This was what he'd expected, but it irked him nevertheless.

After a short while, two more uniformed men arrived. These were a different species: big, serious looking, with automatic rifles strapped across their chests. Another brief exchange and they came up to him, one on either side. "Can you come with us, sir?"

Stupid question. Chaise shrugged, accepting there was little gain in taking the men apart. He nodded to the customs clerk and went wherever the men with guns wanted to take him.

He didn't know how long he sat in the tiny, clinically-clean room in which they'd deposited him. Before leaving, they'd taken his watch, trouser belt, wallet and passport. He wore slip-on shoes, otherwise, he felt sure they would have taken the laces from them as well. Now, alone, he sat and waited. Lacking a window, the room felt claustrophobic, with nothing but a small table and the strip light for company. In the corner, high up, a security camera. A little green light blinked underneath the lens. Did that mean it was operating, or not? Chaise didn't really care. He closed his eyes and slept.

When the door flew open, he woke with a start, turned around. Two men came in, one of them moving behind the opposite side of the desk. He sat down, dropped a manila file on the top and leaned forward on his knuckles. He didn't look happy. "My name is Commander Mellor," he said.

This revelation failed to impress Chaise. He merely gave Mellor a blank stare.

The Commander scowled, somewhat put out by Chaise's lack of reaction. "I have a message," he said. "From London."

"Where are my things?"

Mellor blinked. "What?"

"My things. My passport, my watch. Why did you take my watch?"

Mellor shook his head. "Didn't you hear what I said? I have a message for you, from *Control*."

A heavy silence descended. Chaise looked from Mellor to the other man and back again. "And?"

"You're a surly sod," said the man positioned against the wall. Chaise gauged the distance and knew he could be at his throat before anyone could react fast enough to stop him. He noticed the man had a gun in a hip holster, and he filed it for later. He might need it.

"Don't waste your breath, Simms," said Mellor, his eyes narrow. "Our Mr Chaise doesn't like authority, do you, Mr Chaise?"

"Why don't you just tell me what the message is, then give me back my things."

"We keep the passport."

"Like fuck you do."

"Listen, Chaise, you're here at the behest of Her Majesty's Government. You don't make the rules, Chaise – we do."

"So tell me what the rules are."

"We have a flat for you. Simms here will take you, help you settle in. Someone will be in touch. Until such time, you stay quiet, keep your nose clean. You crossed the line over in sunny Spain, now it's time for you to toe it."

"Jesus, where the hell did they find you?"

"I told you, Chaise, I'm a commander in the Royal Navy. You'd do best to remember that."

"And you'd do best to remember that I am also a commander ... at least I was, last time I checked."

"London wants you to stay at the flat, keep low. They will want to talk to you about a few things. In particular, why you killed Embleton."

"He was about to rape my girlfriend."

"Well, that's as maybe, but London will need to get it all straight, with no misunderstandings on either side. Until then you do as you're told."

"I need to find her. Linny. My girlfriend. She left. That's the only reason I'm here, not to answer questions or kiss the arse of anyone from *Control.*" He stood up. "Now, if you'll give me my passport, I'll be on my way."

"Sit down, Chaise," said Simms, sounding bored. "You heard what the Commander said; you're coming with me to your new flat."

"No," said Chaise and looked deep into Mellor's eyes. "Tell London that I'll be in touch, when *I'm* ready, not before."

Mellor straightened and tapped his finger on the cover of the manila file. "It says in here you can be difficult."

"Does it really? Where's my passport?"

Mellor reached inside his jacket. Chaise spotted the gun.

The passport fell to the desktop. "I'll do a deal," said Mellor. "You can keep the passport, if you go to the flat."

"I'm going up to Liverpool," Ryan said quietly. "To find Linny."

"London won't allow that."

"London can kiss my arse."

Simms moved, reached for the gun at his hip. He probably thought it would intimidate Chaise, cause him to rethink his approach.

The elbow hit Simms under the chin, snapping his head back, stunning him. In one easy movement, Chaise twisted behind him, locked Simms's arm, wrenched the gun free, and pointed it directly at Mellor, who sat and gaped, everything happening too fast for him to react.

"Now," said Chaise, applying more pressure on Simms's wrist. The man squealed, Mellor closed his eyes and sighed. "I want you to put all my things on the table then take off your shoes and trousers whilst Mr Simms and I go for a little drive."

"You're being bloody stupid, Chaise."

"It's in my nature. So is killing people who don't do what I ask."

It took only a few moments for Mellor to comply. With his few belongings secured, Chaise left the airport with Simms. In one hand he held his suitcase and Mellor's bundled up clothes, in the other the trim Walther automatic relieved from Simms. Simms himself didn't appear too happy and spent most of the stroll across the car park rubbing his swollen wrist.

When they reached the car, Simms handed over the keys and Chaise hit him very hard in the solar plexus. The man folded and fell to his knees, groaning loudly. Chaise pushed him aside, opened the car door, threw his bag in the rear seat and slid in behind the wheel.

On the way out, he saw Simms in the rear-view mirror, still down on his knees, taking time to recover. For a moment, Chaise thought that perhaps he should have killed him. The man would almost certainly come looking for him. But it had been a bad start to the day. Chaise didn't really want it to become so much worse.

TWO

By the time Chaise reached the motorway, Simms was back at the airport interview room. He found Mellor still there, looking sheepish.

"Well?"

"He took the car."

Mellor nodded and reached for his mobile. He punched in a few numbers and waited, arching a single eyebrow towards Simms and motioning for him to sit down, before he spoke into the phone. "He has flown." He listened, winced, switched it off and steepled his fingers. "Don't suppose you got my trousers back?"

"No, sir. He kept them."

"Maybe he liked the colour."

Simms's face registered not a flicker. "Maybe. He also took my gun."

"That was to be expected. I'll need you to go out to Burtons or somewhere and buy me another pair. Brown will do. I'm a thirty-eight waist, twenty-nine inside leg." He pulled out some banknotes from his wallet and pushed them across the desk to Simms.

"I'm going to kill him when I find him." Simms put the money into his pocket.

"No, you won't." Mellor leaned forward. "You'll do your bloody job, understand? He's gone, just as we planned. He doesn't know we'll be watching his every move, and that's good. It's worked. He's duped."

"He hit me, and nobody does that."

"This is not a suggestion, Simms. It's an order."

Simms stiffened. "Yes, sir. Sorry."

"If he steps out of line, then you can do what you need to do."

Simms allowed himself to relax, and a tiny smile fluttered around the edges of his mouth. "Let's hope he does."

"Just go and get me the trousers."

Not so very far away from where Mellor and Simms sat, in another small office a few metres from Westminster Palace, Harper rapped his fingers on the telephone receiver for a few moments before he buzzed his secretary. "I'm going to see the Minister."

It was a short walk through the underground corridor linking Harper's office to Whitehall. He enjoyed the few moments of solitude along this subterranean system Winston Churchill ordered built during the Second World War. It had served its purpose then, and still did, especially when the rain beat down as it did today.

The secretary barely glanced at him and pointed her pencil towards the Minister's door. Harper stopped, straightened his tie, and went through, giving a tiny knock as he did so.

The Home Secretary sat reading a file as Harper entered. He'd been in this room many times, having served under several ministers, some of them vagaries of international affairs, others couldn't give a damn. This particular one fell somewhere in the middle, a man with an agenda, out to make his mark. So Harper sat, looked around the modern, Spartan room, and waited. And waited.

"This Chaise is quite a character," said the Home Secretary at last. He took off his reading glasses and folded them very carefully. He held them in both hands as he stared hard at Harper. "You think you can control him?"

"I believe so, Minister. But we have the back-up, just in case."

"The idea of somebody out of control, roaming our streets is not a comfortable one, Harper."

"I know sir, that is why we—"

"Nor is the idea of employing ... what word did you use ...?" He flipped open the file and scrolled down the tightly printed words using the ear-stem of his glasses. "Yes ... using a *freelance.*" He slapped the manila folder shut. "I don't like that, Harper. I want our own people for this type of work, not outsiders."

"He's very good, sir. He took care of dear Jimmy for us."

"Yes, but *dear Jimmy* was shot in a Central African backwater, not on the streets of Britain. I don't want any unpleasantness if this all gets out of hand. We've had enough of answering awkward questions in the House, and God help us if some over-ambitious journalist got hold of this. I would prefer us not to be likened to Mossad, Harper."

Harper shifted uncomfortably from one foot to the next. "I doubt it will come to that, Minister."

"So why hire this *Esteban* individual in the first place?"

"Insurance, Minister. You can never be too careful with the likes of Chaise."

"One of the best it says here," he stabbed at the file with his index finger. "And now he feels hard done-by. We need to reassure him, not alienate him."

"I'm keeping a close eye on him, Minister. I'm confident things will not get out of hand."

The Home Secretary narrowed his eyes, taking note of Harper's tone when re-using his own phrase. He grunted. "If they do, you'll use this Esteban?"

"That is the plan, yes ... but ..." he spread out his hands, "... I think everything will be all right."

"I can't take the risk, Harper. I want our best man on this."

"Esteban *is* our best man, sir."

"No. For all the reasons I've mentioned, it simply is not acceptable. I've been talking to MI6."

Harper's face drained of colour. "Minister, I'm not sure if that's such a good—"

"They have provided us with an operative, and he will be working undercover to shadow Chaise. He's already on his way to Liverpool where he—"

"Minister, I really must object to—"

"I've given him *carte blanche,* Mr Harper. He is good, low-key, and experienced. Most importantly," he gave an oil slick of a smile, "he is answerable to me. But I'm not an autocrat, Mr Harper. Naturally, you can continue to keep your man on the ground, so to speak, but all operational decisions will go through this office, and then to *my* man. I want that clearly understood. Your job is to ensure these instructions go down the line, Mr Harper. I will not tolerate any *unsanctioned* actions from officers ignorant of my wishes – or who *claim* to be. All clear?"

"Perfectly Minister. Is the Prime Minister aware, sir?"

"I'll ignore that rather inane question, Mr Harper." He stood up and wandered to the window and, hands behind his back, stared out across the expanse of Horse Guards Parade. "All being well, as long as we remain in the shadows this Chaise character will be unaware of our close proximity, and simply live a normal, quiet life. But if he should begin killing people, Mr Harper ..." he turned, "... in that instance, we could use Mr Esteban. Until then, we keep it very much under wraps and out of sight. Agreed?"

"It was never my intention to use Esteban in any other way but to—"

"Are we *agreed,* Mr Harper?"

"Yes, sir. Absolutely."

"Good. I want weekly updates, Mr Harper. I shall pay you the same courtesy."

The interview was over.

Harper went out and closed the door behind him. He leaned back against the woodwork and let out a long breath. What he'd experienced was akin to the worst excesses of Adolf Hitler's administration, when he ordered two or three different departments to do the same job, with each remaining in ignorance of the other. Hitler would then sit back and enjoy the ensuing chaos.

Harper wondered if the Home Office operated in a similar way, because this plan would lead to disaster, and Esteban was out there, difficult to contact depending on his location. Part of the beauty of using freelancers such as Esteban was that they were anonymous, invisible. Whoever this agent from MI6 was, he had better be careful, because going up against Chaise *and* Esteban was not something to be advised.

"Are you all right, Mr Harper?"

It was the secretary with the pencil, with which she was drumming her perfect teeth.

Harper sighed and shook his head, "No. I most definitely am not."

THREE

When Frank came through the door of the club, two couples writhed around the small stage. He gaped. Johnny Stokes watched intensely, his eyes glued on the bald, skinny black guy who had a cock as big as Frank's forearm. The girl beneath him had her knees pressed back against her breasts as the guy drilled her with long, deep thrusts, rotating his hips to grind into her. Covered in sweat, her moaning constant and very loud, Frank thought she sounded in pain.

The more he watched, however, the more he realised her cries were those of pleasure.

His gaze shifted to the other couple, and the girl bouncing up and down on another guy's cock. She seemed bored and he didn't appear very interested either, both of them going through a well-rehearsed act. She had difficulty keeping his flaccid cock inside her.

Frank stepped up behind Johnny and breathed into his ear, "What the fucking hell is going on here?"

Johnny, who wore a grey flannel suit, with a satin shirt also in grey, and a bootlace tie, almost jumped out his skin, upturning the stool on which he sat in his surprise, stood up and gaped at his boss. "Jesus, Frank, you scared the fucking life out of me."

The girl under the black guy screamed, "I'm gonna come, I'm gonna come," and Frank noticed Johnny was close to doing the same, his erection tenting his trousers. "I asked you what the fuck is going on."

"I'm auditioning, Frank. Live sex show."

"Oh shit, I'm gonna come!"

Frank glanced towards the stage and at that moment, she orgasmed, arching her back, going into some form of fit, legs thrashing, arms flapping around as if she were trying to fly. The black guy gently withdrew his enormous member and she squirted all over him.

"Get rid of them."

"But, Frank, I—"

"Now."

Johnny immediately clapped his hands twice. "Okay, okay, thanks everyone ..." He went up to the black guy and said something to him as the other 'performers' gathered up their clothes and crossed the dance floor towards the exit. The girl who had orgasmed so demonstratively took her time, looking shaken and breathing hard. "You, darlin'," said Johnny with a lewd grin, "This Friday, eleven o'clock."

Frank didn't give them so much as a glance as they trooped out. He went around the far side of the bar and poured himself a whisky. He drained it in one and poured a second. "I asked you to do something for me, Johnny, not conduct some sort of private peep show."

"Frank, I told you, it was a—"

Frank held up his hand, "Yeah, you said. An *audition.* I'm not interested, Johnny, I just want to know what you've found out."

Johnny took a handkerchief out of his breast pocket and dabbed his forehead. "Not a lot, sorry to say."

With great care, Frank put down the glass on the counter and rotated it three hundred and sixty degrees, "You better not be joking, Johnny, because I want to know where that little shit is and I want to know *now.*"

Johnny looked as if a wasp had stung him, his face twisting up in discomfort. He shook his head, "He's gone."

"Gone? Gone where?"

"Back to the UK."

Frank took a few seconds to mull over the news. His voice held a hint of menace when he said, "And his girlfriend?"

"The same. He's left Spain and has gone looking for her."

Frank thought for a moment, chewed his bottom lip, then gave Johnny his finest Clint Eastwood, "Well, you get yourself over there and fucking well find them." He picked up the glass and studied it. "I want him *dead,*" he yelled and brought down the glass with a solid crack on the counter. It was a heavy glass and didn't smash, which was fortunate for Frank's hand.

"But what about the club, Frank? Who's going to look after everything?"

"I couldn't give a flying fuck about any of that, Johnny. That bastard is responsible for the murder of my wife and I want him *dead,* his girlfriend *dead,* and anyone who knows him or even looks at him across a crowded room *dead.* I want his head on a silver platter, delivered to me in a fortnight, or I'll fucking have you killed too."

"Frank, you can't—"

"I've sorted it. You fly over there and you'll have all the help you need. You find him and you kill them both. You do the girl first, and you make sure he sees and knows why. You understand?" Johnny nodded without a word. "You ask her friends where she's gone, and then you go and do it. I'm holding you personally responsible for this, Johnny, so you better not make a balls up."

"I won't, Mr Leonard, I promise."

Frank nodded and fixed himself another drink. He took a few deep breaths before staring Johnny straight in the face. "Now, before you go, you tell me how the black guy managed to make that girl squirt."

FOUR

Colin Brace often spent Friday afternoons in the public library. He had never completely embraced new technology and despised the idea of seeking out information on the Internet. Instead, he preferred to scour through encyclopaedias, maps and other reference materials to find what he needed.

The librarian was a pleasant-looking woman of around forty-five, with a trim figure and sparkling eyes. One of the main reasons for Colin visiting the library was not only to use books but to see her. He gained a lot of pleasure knowing she would be behind the desk, usually with her spectacles perched on the end of her cute nose as she studied the computer screen. A little thrill of expectation always ran through his tummy as he bounded up the steps to the reference section. Today, however, she was not there, and at once he felt deflated.

"Where's Miriam?" he asked.

The sour-faced replacement looked up from her work and frowned. "Sick."

Shocked, Colin swallowed down his concern, "It's not … you know …"

She gave him a filthy look and an emphatic, "No."

He sighed in relief and leaned forward. "I need some books about Spain."

"Geography section," the woman said and pointed in a vague direction. He bristled, knowing if it were Miriam behind the counter he would have lingered longer, asked her to accompany him in his search, her scent filling his nostrils, stirring his loins. But this woman brought no such urge and so, without another word, he went over to the bookshelves and found what he sought. He pulled down several large books.

One other person sat in the huge reading room, immersed in a newspaper, and Colin had no problem finding an empty table. He put down the selected volumes and sifted through the contents.

The hours drifted by and, with the desired information gathered, he returned the books to their places and went out, giving only the briefest of nods to the librarian.

Once outside, Colin scanned the grey, featureless car park before getting into his old, battered Clio. He took a route out of the busy town and headed towards the river and an anonymous-looking brick blockhouse some five miles away.

The sign said 'Her Majesty's Customs and Excise', the worn, battered sign echoing the tired, uncared-for exterior of the building. He paused and peered up at the closed-circuit camera before running his security card down the sensor on the wall beside the door, which gave a small sucking sound and whispered open. He stepped inside.

At a cramped desk, a pair of brutish-looking security guards nodded and waved him forward. They knew him well. Without a word, Colin went down the narrow dimly lit corridor and took the last door on the right into a large, gloomy, airless space, weak lights casting insipid pools onto the floor. As he walked on, sensors flicked on the ceiling lights and he stopped and winced at the sudden glare. The padded room, partitioned by a low wall with a narrow entrance between, was deathly quiet.

Colin stepped through the gap and peered down to the far end where life-size targets of various sizes waited, suspended by thin wires. Most were of men holding Kalashnikovs.

"Hello, Colin," said a voice.

Colin squinted and saw Norfield, the armourer, emerging from a dark corner busily cleaning the cylinder of an old but dependable Smith and Wesson hammerless snub-nose. He checked his watch and smiled. "Aisle three, please."

Colin took off his jacket and draped it over the back of a chair. He wandered to aisle three to a trestle table with several firearms laid out: two automatics, a six-round magnum and a .38 calibre Colt. A pair of earphones hung from a hook and Colin put them on. He checked the magnum was loaded, brought it up, and fired off four quick rounds.

Even with the ear protection, the noise was tremendous. As the cordite dispersed, he squinted down the aisle to the cardboard figure some twenty-five metres away. At four bullet holes, neatly spaced around where the heart would be.

Without a pause, he moved to the Colt, checked it and went through the same operation, followed by each of the automatics. His ears were ringing by the time he'd finished. He glanced sideways to find Norfield at his shoulder, who handed over the tiny snub-nosed gun. Without a word, Colin squeezed off two rounds at another target. Then, he pulled off his earphones and gently put the gun on the table.

"It's untraceable."

"So it should be." Colin smiled. "It's crap compared with the others."

"Yes. But it's yours."

Colin sighed and picked up the gun and weighed it in his hand. "When was this made, eighteen hundreds?"

"Nineteen fifties. It's a good gun which won't let you down and packs one hell of a punch." Norfield reached across and pressed a button on a small console against the wall. A tiny electric hum and the target drew closer on its metal line. When it finally stopped some six feet away, Colin saw where the two bullets from the snub-nose had obliterated the area around the head. "Nobody will be getting up from that."

Colin grunted.

Norfield produced a shoulder holster and two cartons of bullets. "Not that you'll need this many, I shouldn't wonder."

"I'll need a back-up."

"Sorry, Colin. The powers-that-be have been pretty strict about that. If you are arrested, all they will find is the Smith and Wesson. Nothing else."

"I always have a back-up."

"Not this time. Sorry."

Colin shrugged, took the shoulder holster and put it on. Then he reloaded the snub-nose and dropped it into the holster. In a flash, he drew the gun and aimed it directly towards the target. He grunted again and returned the gun to its holster.

"It's smooth and virtually indestructible," explained Norfield, watching Colin moving over to where he had thrown his coat.

Colin pulled on his jacket and flexed his shoulders a few times. "It feels fine. Can you notice anything?"

"Nothing. Nobody could tell it was there. That's one of its advantages. And because it's hammerless, it won't snag whilst being drawn. It's a good gun, like I said."

"All right, I believe you. I still prefer a Glock."

"That's because you're an ignoramus, Colin."

"That's because I'm careful. And that's why I'm alive."

Norfield smiled and moved to clear away the assorted guns from the table. He watched Colin shuffle towards the exit. An old man, knocking on the door of sixty. Yes he was still alive, but Norfield couldn't help wonder for how much longer.

FIVE

A nondescript street with a row of terraced houses on either side. Each had a red brick wall enclosing a tiny garden, a narrow path running up to the door, and a single bay window on the ground floor. Above, two more windows, one frosted. Every house the same, except for the front doors. Here, the residents exhibited some individuality by having the paintwork applied in different colours.

The one Ryan Chaise approached was blue. He looked down both ends of the street then pressed the bell.

At this time in the early evening, the sunlight bathed the houses with a honey glow, which made them appear almost welcoming. Chaise might have hoped some of this ambiance would permeate inside too, but when the door opened and a surly looking teenager stood before him with limp greasy hair and down-turned lips, hopes faded.

"Yeah?"

Chaise did his best imitation of a caring, sharing family member. "Is your mum home?"

"Who wants to know?"

"Tell her it's Uncle Richard, come to bring a little sunshine into her life."

The kid frowned, clicked his tongue, and disappeared down the hall. “Mum, some weirdo’s here saying he’s your uncle.”

After a moment, she emerged from the kitchen at the end of the hallway, drying her hands on a brightly coloured pinny.

Emma Bennet, Chaise’s stepsister, had been stunning once, auburn hair tumbling to her slim shoulders, dimple-cheeked, smooth-skinned. Before he drifted off to the Forces he had often fantasised over her. Now, standing with her waist thickened, her hips broad, he had to concentrate hard to find any hints of her past loveliness. Vestiges lingered still in her eyes, sparkling gold, sprinkled with flecks of green, and his stomach lurched as a wave of nostalgia hit him, making him go weak.

Her mouth dropped. “Oh, my God,” she gasped. A brief moment of shocked surprise before her face split, and she rushed towards him, tears mixing with whoops of joy.

He caught her in mid-charge and spun her round as he used to, all those decades ago. She was lighter then, and younger. Not yet a woman. As she kissed him full on the mouth, Chaise realised the child had gone, and he held her close, the years disappearing in a breath. He prised himself free of her lips and grinned. “Hi, Emma.”

She stepped away and reached inside the pocket of her pinny. She pulled out a shredded tissue and dabbed her weeping eyes. “Oh, my God,” she repeated, then laughed and sniffed loudly. “Richard. I ... I had no idea. Why didn’t you phone?”

“It was all a bit spontaneous. Sorry. Is it a bad time?”

“Bad time?” She punched him playfully in the chest. With an exaggerated wince, he made as if the blow hurt. “God, you look amazing,” and she threw herself into his arms again and he held her for a long time.

When at last she extracted herself, she took him by the hand and led him down the hallway into the front room.

The television was on, and the same teenager who had opened the door lay sprawled out on the carpet, back against the sofa, pressing the buttons of a game console. The sound of squealing tyres and crashing vehicles erupted from the screen, so loud and convincing it seemed real. "Reece, will you switch that off, please?"

Reece glared at them both, and blew out his cheeks. For a moment, Chaise thought the teenager would ignore his mother's request, but after another loud sigh, the youth threw down the console and busied himself with pulling out various leads from the back of the television. He stomped out, face grim, eyes downcast, unhappy. Emma smiled self-consciously as she brushed off some crumbs from the sofa. "Sorry, it's a bit of a mess."

The room was tiny, barely big enough to contain the matching sofa and armchair crammed inside. A single radiator running along the wall beneath the window served as the only heat source. Above the television, which stood on a well-worn cabinet, hung a large painting of a Lancaster bomber flying through thin clouds, the one attempt to break up an otherwise drab and soulless interior. Chaise sat down.

"I can't believe you're here," Emma said, pressing herself into him again, kissing his cheeks and mouth. More tears came, taking her by surprise. She looked embarrassed, face reddening as she untied her pinny and twisted it around in her hands. "I'm such a mess, Richard. You should have warned me."

"Sorry. Like I said, everything was a little rushed."

"Well," she said, then stopped as a sudden thought came to mind and her eyes widened. "Oh God, I'm so bloody rude. That was Reece by the way. My son. He's off sick from school. He's a bit, you know ..." her voice faded away, "... a teenager."

Explanation enough thought Chaise and nodded. He put his hands on his knees and gave the room another scan, a rueful smile on his face. "I've never had that pleasure, but I can empathise ..."

"Not sure if 'pleasure' is the right word." She leaned across, clutched his hand in both of hers. "I can't believe you're here! My God ..." She laughed, clearly not knowing what more to say.

"I called on Great Aunt Doris, but ..." he shrugged, "... she died. I didn't know."

"Well, not to worry, I didn't know either." She sat back, squeezed the tissue in her fist. "I've lost touch with almost everyone. She was your dad's sister wasn't she?"

"His *mum's* sister."

Emma had never had many dealings with any of Chaise's family. Her mother, and his father, had been married only briefly. It was something of a disaster. But she had remained close to Chaise, always loved him. He could see that she still did. "It's lovely to see you again, Emma. I just wish I'd had the chance to get in touch, give you some sort of warning, but things sort of ran away from me."

She frowned. "It's all right, really. I'm so thrilled you're here."

"I, er, I'm in a bit of a fix. My plan was to stay with Doris, but now that's ... you know, what with her dying, it's ..."

"Please," she squeezed his hand, "don't worry. If it's somewhere you need to stay, Richard, I'll—"

"It's Ryan, Emma." She stopped, blinked, not understanding. "That's the name I use now. I'm no longer Richard." Her bemused expression brought a lump to his throat and it was his turn to hold her hand. "I'll explain later. I promise. Can I, er, use your bathroom?"

"Of course! I'll make us a cup of tea. Darren will be home soon, then we'll ... Yes. A cup of tea. That's what we need. I'll go and do it right now."

At the top of the stairs, he went through into the tiny bathroom and locked the door. The overwhelming smell of soap and disinfectant brought him a curious feeling of comfort. A waft of childhood. He stood in front of the mirror and studied his face. Tanned, lean, hard. A face he knew well, but rarely took notice of. The face Linny so often held, kissed, but never truly knew. What the scars and granite jaw didn't reveal was the real man underneath. The killer.

From below came the sound of sugar stirred in cups and saucers clinking, Emma's voice raised to scold Reece. Reece replying with a grunt. Normal, everyday. Chaise leaned his forehead against the cold of the glass, closed his eyes, thought back to the days when he and Linny had a taste of peace living in Spain, selling property to the Brits. A good life, free from anxiety and after a few years the nightmares stopped, things became normal and settled into a mundane and contented sort of existence.

And now this.

The normality of Emma's life was in such sharp contrast to his own, to what he had allowed it to become. He tried to escape, put everything behind him, to find a new path in the foothills of the Axarquia in southern Spain. It hadn't worked. The old ways refused to go away, and when he came face to face with threats and intimidation, he'd resorted to type, to the things which came so naturally. He was who he was, no matter how hard he tried to shake off the shackles.

They'd approached him whilst stationed in Iraq, the memory seared into his brain. Three men, white shirts, ties pulled down, dark jackets thrown over their shoulders. One suffered badly with the heat, his face awash with sweat, a developing patch of grey running around his collar. All three wore sunglasses as they stood behind Major Clifford's desk like statues.

Called a 'command tent', the interior resembled something more akin to a well-furnished mobile home, with all the comforts found in any affluent house in the UK. Clifford relished it. Drinks on a glass-topped table, television, music system, books, numerous framed photographs of family arranged across an oak display cabinet. Inside this impressive piece of furniture resided a host of awards, citations, and a collection of beautifully painted model soldiers, which followed the history of the regiment from Blenheim to the present day. A 'Persian' rug broke up the drab floor, and despite the hard-packed naked earth, the place gave off a certain warmth that made it feel cosy and welcoming.

But it wasn't a home at all. It was a war zone and outside, in the heat, men were dying. Chaise had been in the thick of the operations, mainly at night. In one of Saddam's many palaces, he'd painted the walls and sent the Intel. As soon as the dictator showed signs of becoming suspicious of the group of Liverpudlian interior decorators, Kuwait having fallen and the Arab coalition mobilising, Chaise had disappeared into the desert.

Soon afterwards, an old man had shouted at him near a crossroads and Chaise had killed him, the knife sinking deep and easily into the carotid artery. He'd watched the light go out of the old man's eyes and from that moment something inside changed for Ryan Chaise.

To live so simply, herding goats, getting up every morning, each one the same as the last; to have fathered sons, daughters; to have laughed and cried. A life without ever thinking, even for a nano-second, it all would end on a deserted dirt track, with an Englishman's knife in his throat. The more Chaise thought about it, the more he wished it had never happened because from the moment he'd killed the old man, he'd set out on a path impossible to deviate from.

They'd listened and liked the story, those men in sunglasses. They smiled and said he was a 'valuable asset' and they wanted him to work for the government.

"You should be honoured," said Clifford, sitting back in his swivel chair, hands interlaced across his stomach. If it wasn't for his immaculately pressed camo-jacket he could have been a financial director in a prestigious business rather than what he was: brigadier, British army, veteran of the 'troubles' in Northern Ireland. A career soldier, efficient, cold-blooded, and as distant as the Malvern Hills were to the men fighting in the arid death-hole that was Iraq.

"Can I have time to think about it, sir?"

Clifford's brows furrowed, and the others exchanged looks. Tension rose, tangible within the canvas walls, and Chaise knew he was close to overstepping the mark. This was not so much an invitation, as a demand. There would be no question of him refusing, so he'd better get used to his new role. He had no choice, except to say 'yes', or find himself face down in a lonely *wadi*, his own throat cut this time.

Men like Ryan Chaise only ever received one option, usually a permanent one – a 'job for life' – but without any of the usual company benefits. No, he was who he was. A killer. It would never go away, never leave him entirely. He knew stories of men like him, who had 'retired'. Those nameless, stoic men in suits reminded him. "People like you don't 'retire'," said the one in the middle, the tallest, expression hidden behind mirrored black glass, "they simply go away. Nobody knows where the gravestones are. Nobody cares."

Chaise had paid scant attention to such tales in the past, never believing they would apply to him. Not until now, with those men patiently waiting for his reply.

Clifford gave him twenty-four hours, but ended the interview with, "You had best make the right decision, Chaise. These gentlemen have come a long way. They don't take kindly to having their requests ignored."

Recently, images of the dead old man at the crossroads had faded, but they returned that night as he lay on his barrack-room bed, and when he stepped back inside the command tent and told Clifford, his commanding officer put his chin in his hands and listened. Nightmares. A nightly ritual of the old man's craggy face coming towards him out of the darkness, eye sockets filled with writhing worms and maggots, mouth toothless, open, a putrid stench trailing from withered, pale gums.

He explained and Clifford listened. "I want to go away, sir, start a new life." Clifford raised a single eyebrow. He lifted his phone, told his secretary to send for the men in black suits. They trooped in and stood in stony silence whilst Chaise said what he had to say. None of them appeared happy, mouths downturned. Perhaps they didn't believe him; perhaps they thought he was too great a risk, a threat to their meticulous plans for the future.

"A new life? That's not really what we're offering you, Chaise. A *different* one, perhaps."

He looked at the tall one again. No use of rank. These were civilian personnel. Security. The silent, invisible guardians of the sovereignty of the United Kingdom.

So, reluctantly, Chaise agreed. He underwent prolonged psychological tests, and afterwards everything went into slow motion, a sort of delaying tactic for what they had in store for him. He fought men twice his size, used weapons of every kind, and sat through endless interviews, tests, role-plays.

"You'll get over it, Chaise," said a grey-suited administrator as

Chaise put his face in his hands and released a loud breath. "I know it is long, probably boring, but it is essential you are tested to the very limits of your endurance. It happens to many men such as yourself who have seen combat. You feel that nothing can get worse, like being on a conveyer belt to nowhere and you can't get off. Give it time."

Time, however, proved too much of a luxury. He arrived back from one particularly dirty, mismanaged mission one morning some years later, packed his bags, sold his car, and went to Spain. There he met Linny, and a life, a *real* life actually seemed more than a possibility.

"Richard, your tea's here."

He snapped open his eyes and stared into the face of the man in the mirror, the man he had become. No longer Richard Parry. They'd taken away even that.

SIX

Nowadays, fewer and fewer people were around to talk to; most of them had returned to the UK, dreams of the good life shattered in the wake of spiralling prices and diminishing exchange rates. Johnny sat under the shade of a beachside terrace, watched the girls go by, and wondered what the hell to do. He twirled his fourth vodka and tonic in his palms and tried to concentrate on staying cool. The alcohol didn't help, but he needed it after what had happened. And when Frank found out, the shit really would hit the proverbial fan.

None of it panned out well from the start. Alex Piers, the one name which kept coming up every time Johnny mentioned Ryan Chaise, had returned to the old country and disappeared. In pursuit of his wife, so the story went. Johnny couldn't give a damn about Piers, but as the only link to Chaise, it was imperative to find him.

Johnny walked into the Estate Agent's office just off the main drag at Fuengirola. The girl at the desk smiled, brushed away a strand of light-brown hair and sat up to reveal a t-shirt stretched tight over her well-toned body. Johnny's throat went dry and he stared for a moment too long, caught her look, felt the heat rise to his cheeks.

"Can I help you?" Lancashire accent, eyes that danced.

Johnny gave his finest disarming smile. She remained unimpressed. "I'm looking for Ryan."

She didn't flicker. "Ryan has left us. Are you a client?"

"More of a friend, but yes ... a client. He sold me a house."

A tiny crease in the smoothness of her brow. "Oh, which one?"

Slight panic, the question not one he had prepared for. Johnny scanned the wall plastered with numerous posters of properties for sale, neatly arranged in price order. "I just need to talk to him."

"I could pass you over to one of our other agents." Johnny turned to her again, her face a perfect mask. Inscrutable, immovable. "Mr Chaise has gone back to Britain."

"Do you know where exactly?"

The shutters came down even further. Information padlocked inside. Johnny made his excuses and left. He stood in the street, looking out across the beach to the Mediterranean. All he wanted was a scrap, a tiny clue to Chaise's whereabouts.

Even though Johnny knew Chaise had returned to the UK, he didn't have the exact location. The more he searched, the more desperate and frustrated he became. The locals he spoke to claimed ignorance of Chaise's background, and when Johnny went to the office of another estate agent where Chaise sometimes operated from, he found the building boarded up. Times were hard and businesses were falling like harvested wheat.

One last hope remained. Chaise's girlfriend was popular, had many friends and Johnny knew the address of one, recognising her name as soon as a weedy barman down in Fuengirola told him. Cindy. He'd put off going to see her because of the husband, Vinnie. A monster, well known down in Marbella, who worked the doors of the clubs. A man's size was not something about which Johnny usually worried. Tough, Johnny knew how to hurt people and enjoyed doing so up to a point. But this guy came from a different league. Johnny had seen Vinnie at work, so he had to be careful, approach the situation quietly, with grace and patience. So Johnny drove up to the house and tried his best to be pleasant. The husband remained unmoved, wondered what Johnny was doing, 'asking all these fucking questions'. He recognised

Johnny, had done so as soon as he pulled up in the driveway of the lovely little villa perched up on a hillside overlooking the town. Far enough away to be private but close enough to be convenient for work.

Vinnie filled the doorway with his frame, his great bullhead glaring down. Clearly, this guy was good at his work, with hands like whole hams and a scowl intense enough to crack eggshells from forty paces. "It's my day off. Come to the club tomorrow evening, we'll talk then."

"I'm in a hurry."

Vinnie gave a sardonic grin. "Yeah, well, it can fucking wait. I'm fucking tired and need some kip, now piss off."

He went to close the door but Johnny's foot got there first. The bouncer didn't like that; his shoulders tensed, the great head grew red. Johnny experienced a surge of disappointment. He wanted nothing more than an agreeable outcome, so he tried a smooth smile. "I really am in something of a hurry."

It was a hot day, and the sweat collected around the rim of his collar. In contrast, the bouncer looked cool in his Bermuda shorts and thin cotton t-shirt. Apart from his face, which looked less cool by the second. When Vinnie growled and his bunched fists came up, Johnny had had enough.

Johnny shot him in the throat. From that short distance, the result was a hell of a mess, the guy falling back into the hallway, arms flapping, the blood spouting. A blonde girl, whom he assumed was Cindy, came around the corner, saw it all, screamed, and dropped to her knees to cradle her husband's head as he died, the blood leaking all over her top. Johnny stepped inside and shot Cindy in the shoulder, blowing her back into the lounge. He followed her, ignoring the big bouncer sprawled on his back, hands pressed into his throat, the blood frothing up over fingers totally inadequate for staunching the flow. Johnny stooped down next to her and put the barrel of the gun against her head. "Where's Linny?"

Cindy's eyes rolled, pain overtaking her senses. He gave her a moment, allowing the shock to recede a little, then he jabbed the muzzle of the automatic hard against Cindy's skull. "Where has she gone?"

She groaned, the colour drained from her face, mouth trembling, salvia drooling. Not comprehending where she was or what had happened, Cindy blubbered and wept. Johnny had seen this many times, the total disbelief, the struggle to come to terms with the idea life had changed, might even end.

He sighed, pressed the gun into her head again.

Cindy whimpered, muttered, "Liverpool", then he shot her through the temple and went out.

Vinnie still lay in the hallway gurgling. Johnny shot him again and all movement stopped. Some blood splashed onto his chinos and he swore. Why couldn't things ever be simple?

Now, here he was, trying to stop the shakes with the vodkas and they weren't working. He'd killed before, of course. It wasn't that, it was the fact he had nothing more to go on. Linny had flown off to Liverpool. Liverpool. Jesus. Of all the places in all the world.

Frank would not be happy about the killings. Johnny squeezed his eyes shut. It was a fucking mess, and he had barely begun. He drained his glass, put twenty euros under the saucer with his bill and stood up. Light-headed, he held onto the table for a moment to steady himself, took some deep breaths, tried not to let the heat get to him too much. He straightened, adjusted his tie and stepped out into the sunshine.

No, Frank wouldn't be happy. So Johnny decided not to tell him.

SEVEN

After dinner, Darren helped Emma with the washing up, whilst in the front room, Chaise engaged Reece in virtual tennis.

"So, he just appeared on the doorstep?"

Emma nodded, stacking the plates. "I had no idea he was coming. He told me he was going to stay with his Aunty Doris, but of course she's no longer with us, so he had no choice I suppose."

"I thought you said he was working in Spain?" She nodded, wiping her brow with the back of her hand. "So, how did he find our address?"

"I don't know, Darren. Why? What's the problem?" She put her dishcloth down on the draining board and glared at him. "He's my brother, I can't just say, 'Oh hi, haven't seen you in ten years, but you can't stay for long'."

"But he *can't* stay for long, can he? We haven't got the room."

"I don't think he plans to stay. Maybe a night or two. Until he's settled."

"Settled? What does that mean?"

"It means, until he finds somewhere more permanent to stay." She blew out a breath. "He's looking for his girlfriend. There was some trouble over in Spain. He didn't tell me much, but he had to change his name ..."

"Change his name? Jesus Christ, Emma, what is he – a gangster or something?"

"Don't be bloody stupid."

"Well, why else would he change his name? That's not an easy thing to do, and you'd only do it if it were serious. Shit." He put his face in his hand and took some deep breaths.

"Don't get all stressed, Darren. I'm sure it's nothing. He said he'd had a problem with his taxes. That was why he went out there, because he owed money. He changed his identity to keep the Inland Revenue at bay, that's all."

"He told you that?"

"Yes. It's no big deal, Darren. People do it all the time."

"Not me, Emma. I've never changed my bloody name."

"*I* did."

She gave him a look, which meant the conversation was at an end.

Emma made coffee, brought it into the dining room, and placed the tray on the small table, which stood against the wall of the cramped room. Chaise was at the other end, from where he looked out through the patio doors to the neat rear garden. In the early evening gloom, little solar-powered lights gave off a blue haze, lighting a narrow pathway to a raised area of decking in the corner. He felt a twinge in the pit of his stomach for a life he had never known, that had passed him by. Suburban normality.

"Are you all right, Richard?"

Chaise turned, thoughts flitting away, and shrugged. She handed him a coffee. He took a sip, smiled. "Yes. Thinking."

From where he sat, at the table, Darren chirped, "You're here to find your girlfriend?"

Chaise snapped his head up and gave Emma a quizzical look. She shrugged. "I had to tell him, Rich. I didn't think it was a secret."

Chaise let it go. She was right; searching for Linny wasn't a secret.

It was the main reason he had come, if he ignored the gangsters and the SIS. He took another sip of coffee, smacked his lips and stared into the cup. "I realise coming over here is a long shot, but it's all I've got. She still has some friends living on the Wirral, so ... tomorrow, I'll ask around a little, see if there's anything to go on."

"You must love her a lot," said Darren, unable to keep the lack of conviction from his voice.

The silence hung heavy in the air and Chaise studied the coffee dregs in the bottom of his cup, straining to remember this man was his sister's husband. It wouldn't do to break his jaw. After a while, he looked up and stared Darren straight in the face, knowing what ate away at the back of the man's mind. "I won't be in your hair for long, Darren, so you needn't worry."

Darren blushed and shifted position in obvious discomfort. "No, it's not that ..."

Emma reached across and squeezed Chaise's hand. "You can stay as long as you like."

He forced a smile, not wishing to be the cause of any domestic strife. "I know, and thanks, but I'll go to an agency tomorrow and find something as soon as I can. I'll only be here for a couple of nights, if that's okay."

He could see her eyes glaze over. She was upset. "I don't want you to think—"

"It's all right, Em ... I'll find somewhere."

He lay in Reece's bed and stared at the ceiling. Downstairs, the television blared. The disgruntled teenager had objected at first, but soon changed his mind when he realised a night or two on the sofa meant he could continue with his video games well into the early hours.

Right now, Chaise heard muffled explosions and the rattle of machine guns. The modern-day opium for the masses. Virtual reality. He turned over, tried to sleep, but failed.

At around three-thirty, he crept downstairs and went towards where he thought the kitchen was. He groped along the wall, but due to the smallness of the house, it wasn't long before he found his bearings, despite the gloom. A tiny green light above the fridge door guided him forward.

He took out a jug of iced water from inside, poured himself a generous glassful, and closed the fridge. Whilst he stood in the darkness, sipping his drink, he looked out of the window into the garden. The solar lights had all but gone out now but he still made out the back wall, the shrubs, the back gate. He frowned, focused, leaned forward and felt his gut tighten.

The gate, unlocked, yawned open a few inches before gently slapping closed again. He watched, not daring to move, the drink forgotten.

He placed the half-finished water on the draining board and stepped farther back into the kitchen, never taking his eyes from the gate. He waited, but nothing stirred until the gate gently opened and rapped against the latch. He turned and ran up the stairs to his room.

It might be all innocent of course, but he couldn't afford to take the chance. He reached under the bed and pulled out his overnight bag, drew back the zipper and delved inside. His fingers closed around the cold, comforting metal of the Glock and he took it out. He checked the action, careful not to make too much noise, and went over to the window, eased open a small slit in the curtain and peered into the garden below.

He waited, giving himself time to allow his eyes to adjust to the night. Soon, objects came into focus, and he held his breath, concentrating. Nothing, no movement, no sign of any forced entry, loose bricks, broken lamps. But then, he mused ironically, there wouldn't be.

He cursed himself for not changing the car, abandoning it somewhere and replacing it with a hired one. His anxiety to get to Merseyside to try to find some clue about Linny overrode everything, even his common sense. He'd been out of the game too long, he realised. Getting himself back in might prove a more demanding process than he first assumed. He needed to take things slowly, be extra cautious, diligent, observant. God knows how much he had already missed.

Of one thing he was certain: Mellor and Simms had set him up, the farce at the airport proof positive. Everything too easy, taking the Glock the way he had, the car, the drive north. He never thought, however, they would follow him so quickly. Why the hell hadn't he changed the damned bloody car?

Pointless thinking about all that now. He stepped away, padded down the stairs and went back into the kitchen. He took a breath, listened again. He turned the key in the lock, moved to the side, and pulled the kitchen door open. Another wait before he dropped down on one knee.

He trained the gun ahead of him, scanning the tiny garden from one corner to the next. If anyone were there, they would die. He'd face the consequences later.

The back gate creaked open and he tensed, bringing his left hand to join the right, steadying the Glock. The seconds ticked by, breath held. The gun began to shake, so he lowered his hands, steadied his breathing, and brought it up once more.

Time stretched out. Cold air fluttered across his face, and far away an owl hooted. The silence of the night pressed in all around and still he waited.

Images of a man in black slipping through the door loomed large. The bullet would sound loud in the stillness, a massive explosion, waking everyone within a hundred metres. Chaise put the thought aside. Someone had followed him, picked up his trail, and they were here to do him harm. Choices already made.

Damn them. Damn Mellor, damn Harper. They were all the bloody same. Cold, humourless automatons, their sense of duty the only trait that mattered. They couldn't be bargained with, appeals would fall on deaf ears. He hated them, and if this was the game they wanted to play, then so be it.

The gate creaked open wider and Ryan took a bead on the approximate location of the intruder's chest.

A cat, blacker than the night, slipped through the crack of the door, looked around and when Chaise's breath came out in a loud blast, it froze, saw him with huge, startled eyes and bolted.

He fell back against the kitchen doorwell, the gun so heavy in his hands, closed his eyes and took in several gulps of air. He lowered the Glock to his lap, told himself what an idiot he was and then the light came on and he jumped.

Reece stood in the kitchen entrance, looking gaunt and pale, dressed in his underpants, mouth open, eyes fixed on the gun.

Chaise stood up. "I think I may have disturbed a burglar."

But Reece didn't speak. He seemed in shock.

Without another word, Chaise went into the garden, strode across the damp grass and quietly pressed the gate closed. He slid the bolt into place and gave everything a final scan. No signs, as before. Maybe Emma or Darren had simply forgotten to lock it.

Maybe.

He came back into the kitchen, closed the door and turned the key. Reece still stood rigid, in the same position. Chaise smiled, whispered, "All clear." He tapped the side of his nose, "Not a word to Mum, eh?"

Reece gave the smallest of nods. "Who the fucking hell are you?"

Chaise shrugged, weighed the Glock in his hand. "Special forces." With a grin, he pushed passed the teenager, whose face had drained of colour. If Reece knew the whole truth, he would probably have fainted.

EIGHT

The mobile phone trilled into life. Esteban pressed it to his ear and waited.

"I'm pleased you have your phone switched on," said Harper. "There's been a slight complication."

"What sort of *complication?*"

"Nothing to be unduly concerned about. Another interested party has become involved, that is all. So, plans may have to be adjusted accordingly."

"I see."

"Until you hear otherwise, you continue as originally discussed. Find him, stay close to Chaise, watch his every move and—"

"I have located him."

A silence. Harper's voice, when it returned, had lost something of its previous edge. "Ah. Good work. Does he know?"

Esteban inhaled loudly. "No one ever knows."

"Yes. Sorry. Stupid question. Don't underestimate him, however."

"He is rusty. Easy to follow."

"Perhaps too easy?"

Esteban ignored the implication. "No. I know a great deal about him, his capabilities. You must not concern yourself over that."

"I have no concerns about you, my friend. Only this other unlooked-for intrusion. Details are not important, but our target is of interest to others and, therefore, might prove something of an inconvenience. So, as I said, a subtle change to our plan is required."

"I see. How subtle?"

Harper told him. When he had finished, which did not take long, Esteban drummed his fingers on the arm of his chair. "Forgive me, but what you suggest is far from subtle."

"Perhaps not, however you will implement the change when it becomes necessary. In its entirety. You understand?"

"Absolutely. I take it there will be an alteration to my payment, given these developments?"

"Ah." A pause. "I'll see what I can do, but I can't foresee any trouble."

"No, of course not." Esteban grinned, "And it won't be so *subtle* either. My payment."

Esteban switched off the phone before Harper answered and put his head back against the back of the chair and considered what Harper had told him.

The changes would not cause much of a problem. In fact, they would bring an added layer of interest to the entire assignment. Variety. The key to job satisfaction. He yearned for variety, it kept him on the edge, concentrated. The alterations as laid out by Harper seemed to offer Esteban the chance to enjoy himself.

He smiled.

He was more than happy because in the end, of course, there would be death and above all else, the prospect of killing pleased him.

NINE

The few friends of Linny's he managed to track down had not heard from her for ages, apart from the occasional message on Facebook. Chaise had no reason to believe any of them lied. He sat in the lounge of a nearby public house a little way from Church Street in the City Centre. He'd strolled through the centre, shocked at how much everything had changed.

Not only did the cold bother him, but the development of shops, businesses, all of them had received endless face-lifts. Gone the hard, featureless buildings of his younger days, replaced by clean, bright, modern edifices, efficient and somewhat sanitised, although the soul remained. The people were cheery, as always, and they lightened his heart.

He'd spotted the shadow as he stepped out of the station at Moorfields and wandered down to the City. He headed towards where one of Linny's friends worked in a fashion boutique, remaining as natural and as calm as possible.

The slightly built tail, if anything, made Chaise more cautious. Some of the deadliest men he had ever known had been well under six feet and slim.

He took the shadow on a circuitous route, just to make sure. And

Chaise was sure. Of course, he always knew they would come. Over breakfast, he'd asked Emma if she had a problem with the back gate because it banged in the night and woke him. Darren looked shocked, as he checked it every night. Last night the same. Chaise made no comment.

Of course, he could have killed the shadow there and then, but another would arrive in his place. And another. So he walked and the shadow followed.

The girl in the boutique didn't know anything. Like all the others.

He had no choice but to contact Linny's mother, not an attractive prospect. She had never liked him, making her feelings clear every time they met, which wasn't often, thank God. The idea of meeting her pressed down on him like a lead weight, but he had little choice if he wanted to find Linny and talk some sense into her.

Before returning to Emma's house, he called into the Job Centre on a whim. He used the computer console to scroll through the vacancies, not thinking anything would show up for estate agents.

He was wrong.

There was a job, a real opportunity. He wrote down the contact number and left. Later, at Emma's, he sat in the dining room and read the number again. Beccles, Suffolk, a place he had never heard of, as far away from Liverpool as he was likely to find without leaving the country. And that he didn't want to do, not yet.

The guy on the other end of the line sounded interested, wanted Chaise to fax his CV. As the conversation progressed, it developed into an interview. Could he come for something more formal in two days time? Taken aback, Chaise hastily agreed, closed his phone and noticed Emma standing in the doorway. "You're leaving? Already?"

Her voice trembled and Chaise crossed over, put his arms around her and held on tight. She cried into his shoulder.

Later he took the car and drove to visit Linny's mother. Before he got halfway up the path to the door she was there, arms folded, face set hard.

"She doesn't want to see you."

The rain pounded down but she still kept him on the doorstep. He managed to get his head under the porch. The house stood in a quiet cul-de-sac, an affluent area with driveways big enough for three cars, landscaped gardens boasting ornamental water-fountains, all the usual stuff. Five bedrooms at least, the pebbledash sparkled. Everything manicured and well-maintained, like the people who lived behind the solid walls.

Linny's mother looked the same as he remembered her. Slim, attractive, possessing a natural beauty requiring no make-up or expensive trips to the hairdressers. Perhaps she visited a gym, to keep herself so trim and firm. It was clear from where Linny got her good looks.

"You know where she is?"

She shrugged. "You've hurt her, Ryan. Deeply. It's going to take some time, and you have to give her that. Space too."

"I just need to know she's okay, Brigit. That's all."

"She's fine. I'll tell her you called. She still has your number, so she'll contact you when she's ready, but not before. Respect her wishes, Ryan."

"I never meant ..." He sighed, resigned himself to defeat, returned to the car, and got in. The rain hammered down on the roof and when he glanced back towards the house, the front door stood closed. Like a chapter in his life.

TEN

At John Lennon airport, two large guys wearing jeans and white t-shirts met Johnny and escorted him to a waiting car. From their thickset necks and the size of their arms, they looked like bodybuilders. One pulled open the door to the big Ford, and smiled. Johnny settled into the back and they drove him into the City.

He sat and watched the changing panorama streak past his window. Soon, the no longer busy but still magnificent waterfront came into view; Albert Dock well scrubbed, the Liver Building gleaming pristine. He knew little about Liverpool save for the obvious, and nobody spoke to enlighten him further.

The car turned into a side street and pulled up in an enclosed car park at the rear of a grubby building well past its best and, Johnny believed, should be condemned. Again, the same silent one as before opened his door and waved him towards a nondescript entrance, covered with chipped, peeling green paint.

The man who greeted him was also huge, but very different from the bodybuilders. For one thing, he was older, and the scars on his coarse, chiselled face spoke of a lifetime of fistfights. He sported a grey goatee and filled the tweed jacket he wore with his massive shoulders, the holstered gun under his arm plain to see.

"I'm Tony," he said, his voice a deep boom and he nodded to the bodybuilders. "Thanks guys. See you at eight-thirty." He moved aside and motioned for Johnny to step inside.

Johnny took a moment and allowed his eyes to adjust to the dimly lit corridor. Tony squeezed passed, and Johnny got in behind him and followed the big man deeper into the building.

Through a door, another corridor stretched ahead, with further doors on both sides, all closed. Two, one to the left, the other to the right were labelled 'Toilets', each with a picture of a man and woman respectively. A nice touch for the clients who could not read. Johnny guessed there might be plenty of them.

Tony opened the door at the far end. Johnny stepped into a large, rectangular floor space, with tables and chairs laid out on the perimeter. A nightclub, trimmed to appear as much like the Eighties as possible, with mirror globes suspended from a ceiling of dark blue, speckled with tiny lights. A flight of stairs led to the upper storey with more tables from where customers had a good view of the dancers. The place stank of stale beer and sweat. Johnny had visited a hundred places like this one and as he walked across the dance floor towards the big bar dominating the far end of the room, the soles of his shoes snagged on the sticky residue of innumerable spilled drinks. The familiarity brought him a certain degree of calm. He already felt at home.

"Would you like a drink?"

"Vodka and tonic."

Tony went around the bar and found a glass, filled it with ice, and positioned it under the optic. He released a generous measure, brought out a small bottle of tonic and opened up the cap, which fell to the ground with an audible clatter, the sound amplified in that quiet, lifeless place. Tony used a long cocktail spoon to give the drink a quick stir, then slid it across to Johnny. "Lemon?"

Before Johnny answered, a door behind the bar sucked open and a callous-looking guy wearing a dark pin-stripe suit appeared. Considerably shorter than Tony, he was about twice as wide. When he smiled, Johnny saw the glint of gold teeth, sparkling in his flat, tanned face. The man stuck out his hand, wrists rattling with a gold-chained bracelet. Johnny knew for certain that beneath the crisp, white shirt, the man wore a gold medallion.

"I'm Alfonso. You must be Johnny?"

Johnny took the hand and almost instantly regretted it. Alfonso's grip was like a vice and when he squeezed, Johnny wanted to cry out. He gritted his teeth, aware of the prickles of sweat on his brow, and then the big man released him. Johnny felt his shoulders drop, but he managed not to sing out in relief.

Alfonso beamed and slapped Tony hard on the shoulder. "Tony, this is one of Frank's best men. His name is Johnny. Frank and me, we go back a long way, to the old days before Albanians and Lithuanians and all those other shit-shovellers muscled in. When Marbella was a good place, a *clean* place, when the only thing we had to worry about was not upsetting Sean Connery." He slapped Tony again and winked. "You give him everything he needs. You hear?"

"Loud and clear, Mr Calderon."

Johnny could not suppress a laugh. "*Calderon?*"

Alfonso arched an eyebrow. "I have to maintain a certain mystique, Johnny, something I'm sure you can appreciate."

Calderon was an affluent suburb of Malaga. The Spanish connections continued unabated, even here in the backstreets of Liverpool. Johnny took the point, raised a hand in surrender. "Sure. No problem." He drank the vodka.

"Tony will take you to a nearby hotel, settle you in. Tomorrow your search for this guy you're after can begin. Frank and I had a long conversation the other night, before you flew out. This man, this Ryan Chaise, has caused you a great deal of trouble, yes?" Johnny nodded. It seemed Alfonso already knew the full story. "Okay, my friend. But not for much longer, eh Tony?"

Tony grunted and pulled out a buff envelope from his inside pocket. He opened it and laid out several sheets of typewritten paper. "I've been doing a lot of searching, Johnny. Land registry, Poll records." He ran an index finger along the first few lines. "There's not much here at all, Johnny. Not a single clue as to where your guy might be. Except," he looked up and smiled, "his wife's mother."

"He hasn't got a wife. A girlfriend."

Tony shrugged. "Wife, girlfriend, boyfriend, mother, what's the diff? She's known as Brigit Lonsdale. It took some searching, as she changed her name after her split from the girl's father. He was Spanish. Did you know that?"

Johnny didn't, but he nodded anyway and finished the vodka.

"We'll go and talk to her tomorrow."

"I'd prefer today. No point in letting things slide."

"Nothing is going to slide," put in Alfonso. "We have plenty of time."

"Frank has given me two weeks. That's not long."

"Yeah, he told me. But don't worry, Johnnyboy, you'll have this dickhead in the bag before the week is out."

"If the mother knows where he is."

"She'll know where the girlfriend is, and that's all we need. For now."

Johnny couldn't argue with the logic, so he allowed himself to relax. Tony fixed him another vodka, and it tasted even better than the first.

ELEVEN

Ryan Chaise's plan was to drive across the country to East Anglia a little later on in the day. He calculated five hours, six with a stop for lunch. The big Audi would eat up the miles but being a large car, sticking out like a sore thumb, he'd have to ditch it, perhaps just outside Norwich, and hire another one. That way he might lose the tail, but he doubted it. The thought of someone following him did not cause him undue concern. He always knew they'd be there, somewhere, as soon as Mellor, the messenger boy at the airport with shit for brains, reported in. The amateurish way in which they had set up Chaise meant, perhaps, to wrong-foot him, the heavy Simms proving ridiculously easy to take down. Being out of the business for so long Chaise had forgotten how galling everything was, the duplicity, the unending weaving of lies and deceit the chief reason why he had turned his back on it all. And the killing, of course.

He woke up early. The previous day, after a number of phone calls, things had begun to move forward. Job-wise, at least. Nothing about Linny. Not a sniff, but then he had no idea where to begin. Old friends might be worth talking to, but the thought of rekindling past relationships made his guts twist, so he decided to wait, think, and get it straight in his head. And ignore idiots like Mellor.

Darren stood in the kitchen, scooping ground coffee into the cafetière. He looked up briefly as Chaise came in before returning to what he was doing. "Sleep well?"

"I'll be leaving fairly soon, as I told you last night. Is Emma still asleep?"

"She doesn't want to get up. She's upset." He turned and leaned back against the worktop. "You turning up like this, unannounced, it's thrown her. She's happy, of course, but now …" He shrugged. "Now you're going to go away again, and she doesn't know how to take it."

"It's what you want, Darren. Don't try to kid me otherwise. Nor Emma."

Darren glanced down. "You're not her *real* brother. She told me. Your dad married her mum."

"We're as good as brother and sister. We were always close." Chaise stepped past him as the kettle boiled and the switch clicked off. He poured the water over the coffee and positioned the cover, preparing to lower the plunger.

"Yes. She said."

Chaise caught something in Darren's voice and he arched an eyebrow. "Please. There's nothing … you know … it was never my intention to hurt her. And I'm sorry if I have." The awkwardness riled him and he bit down on his lip. He did not need to explain anything. Yes, Emma and he were close. They had *connected* almost as soon as they had met, a hundred years ago. Nothing more. No reason to analyse it any further. And besides, whose business was it but his own? Except for Emma, of course, and now she lay upstairs in her bed, no doubt reliving the good times, football in the park, climbing trees, running along the beach. If he listened hard enough, he might be able to hear her sobs.

"So, will you be coming back?"

He sighed. "I don't know." He pressed the plunger down. "If I get the job, who can tell?"

"But you'll keep in touch? With Emma I mean."

"Unlike I have done these last years, is what you really mean."

Darren shifted position, his turn to feel uncomfortable. He

watched Chaise pouring out the coffees. "I just know she was happy to see you, and she hasn't been happy for a long time. Things aren't easy. Money, or the lack of it. All the usual bullshit."

"Married life." Chaise slid over a cup and took a sip of his own. "I had a taster of the matrimonial life back in Spain, which I thought was the natural way to be. Find someone, fall in love …" He smiled, without any humour and shook his head. "Like you say, it's all bullshit."

"I didn't mean being married was bullshit. Just everything that goes with it." He blew over the surface of the coffee before taking a drink. "What are you going to do about your girlfriend?"

"Think, get settled, make some money, find her. For the moment, I have little choice. I can't rush things as everything is still very raw. Maybe later, when things are more settled, we might try again. Who knows?" He drank his coffee.

"You're an estate agent, so Emma says. This job in Norfolk, it could be just the thing."

"Yes. Just the thing."

"But you will keep in touch?"

"I said I would."

They drank. Chaise looked out of the window and studied the garden, catching no clues of anyone having returned, no repeat of the other night. Perhaps he had made a mistake, tired brain playing tricks.

Darren gave a nervous cough. "You're not an actual estate agent are you?"

Chaise, in the process of lifting the cup to his mouth for one more mouthful, stopped.

"I know you're not. I've watched you, the way you move. Like a cat. And your arms," he nodded towards Chaise. "Don't think I've seen anyone with arms like that, not outside a gym."

"I keep myself fit."

"That's more than fit."

"What is it then?" Anxiety spread, turning blood to ice, muscles and tendons becoming rigid. He wasn't sure he liked Darren, but that was no reason to kill him. If he continued on this route, however and became insistent for answers, he may have to die. But how to do it, with Emma upstairs in bed, and Reece flat out on the sofa? Slowly, Chaise put his cup down and ran a forefinger around the rim and when he spoke, his voice was low, calm. "You said it, I'm an estate agent. Nothing more."

"I don't think so," pressed Darren, voice also controlled. "Emma told me you served in the army, over in the Gulf."

"I was in the navy, before they transferred me and I went to Iraq twice."

"Transferred you? From the navy to the army? That's unusual, isn't it?

He turned his face towards Darren, held his eyes. "It wasn't quite like that. I was ... it was a long time ago."

"But it changed you?"

The question caused Chaise to do a double-take. "*Changed* me?"

"Yes. What do they call it – post-combat stress disorder? Something like that. Shell-shock, that's the common parlance isn't it?"

"Common parlance? I wouldn't know a *common parlance* if it jumped up and bit me on the arse." His eyes narrowed. "Post-traumatic stress disorder, like you say. It's not the monopoly of the services and can happen to many people, after all sorts of events. Car crash victims, survivors from accidents, earthquakes. Not just squaddies on the front line, although they probably suffer more than most. I know, I've seen it."

"But you were in the navy, didn't you say? So, nothing ever happened to you on the front line?"

"I didn't suffer, if that's what you're getting at. Not in the sense you mean."

Darren frowned, looked into his coffee cup. "I don't understand. How can you be in the navy *and* the army?"

"There's much you don't understand, Darren."

"I get the feeling that there is a lot more to you than you let on. You changed your name. Why would you do that?"

"I had to. I told Emma about it all."

"Yes, but that takes some doing, not simply crossing out one name and replacing it with a different one. What about National Insurance numbers, how did you change them?"

Chaise's stomach twisted another notch. This was dangerous. If Darren maintained this line of constant questioning, the inevitable would follow. He examined the alternatives, but there weren't any. Not that he could see.

"I mean, you can't get a job, can you, without your National Insurance number? And once that is checked, your real name would come up."

"Not in Spain. That's why I went. To start again. I went through their system, applied for and got their own version of National Insurance. I had a passport in my new name. It was simple."

"Simple? I'm not sure I would have the wherewithal, or even the balls to do that."

"Well, then it's a bloody good job I'm not you, isn't it?"

Chaise held his eyes, and a cold detachment spread inside, as it always did when he had to do what he needed to do. He should strike now, three fingers, just above the breastbone. It would only take a second or two. Reece might be trickier, but nothing like as hard as putting Emma away. He turned his feet slightly towards Darren, allowed his hand to hang free.

Darren pushed himself away from the worktop, finished his coffee, and put it down with a resounding smack. "Ah, well, what's it to me, eh? As long as Emma's happy, then I am. And if you stay in touch, she will be. So …" He shrugged. "*C'est la vie.*"

He walked out of the kitchen and Chaise stood stunned, hit by a wave of relief mixed with terror as the tension dissipated. He had actually considered killing them all. He turned and looked out into the garden, forced himself to relax, not wanting to psychoanalyse right now. When he saw the cat, he smiled.

TWELVE

Frank hated doing anything he himself had not arranged. This, however, was a little different.

Sarah's mother had come to Spain as soon as she heard the news, taking over all the arrangements for the funeral. What remained of the body they laid in an ornate coffin, with brass fittings, ivory laminate sides and padded purple interior. Sarah was to be buried, not cremated, her mother insisted, not wishing to mock the horrific manner of her death by a repeat process, no matter what anyone else said or thought. Her daughter Sarah deserved some respect at least.

Frank sat beside her in the car following the hearse, grateful for all she had done. Since she'd arrived, barely a half dozen words had passed between them. He wondered what he would do now, without Sarah there, to smile and laugh. His companion. His friend. He watched the world go past the window and thought of the meeting he had had the day before.

He had been in his club, finishing off some tortilla and aïoli when the doors exploded open and Burmese Bill came in. Bill was a huge man, with a waistline to match. His olive-coloured face, creased in agony, oozed sweat from every pore. "We have a problem, Mister

Frank," he said through clenched teeth before he fell flat on his face and didn't move.

Neither did Frank. A piece of tortilla dropped unchewed from his lips as two men approached, holding guns. They weren't smiling.

A third followed, short and thin, dressed in a black satin suit which shimmered every time he took a step. He did smile. "*Mister* Frank?" He prodded Burmese Bill with the toe of his shoe. "Is that what all your redundant staff call you?"

Frank dabbed at his mouth with a napkin, struggling hard to stop his hand from shaking. The man's voice held a distinctive Eastern European twang, so no doubts why he had come.

The one in the suit sauntered over to the bar and pulled up a stool. He reached across and helped himself to a portion of tortilla. "I won't waste any of your time," he said, dipping the corn bread into a bowl of salsa beside Frank's arm, "So I'll get straight to the point." He popped the food into his mouth and munched it down. "I want to buy your nightclubs, Frank. Together with your restaurants, beach-side cafés, car-hire business and ..." he grinned, "your prostitution operation. I will make you a good offer."

Frank gaped, in shock. "*Make me a good offer* ..." His voice slipped away as he struggled to bring his thinking up to speed. He threw down the last dregs of his gin and tonic as his temper threatened to boil over. "Hold on a fucking minute, you piece of oily shit, just who the bloody hell do you think you are, bursting in on me like this? Get the fuck out of my club, you shithead before I have your balls served up on a plate!"

"I don't think so, *Mister* Frank."

Frank's frown cut deep. "Just fucking watch me." He reached for his mobile on the bar counter.

"No point calling anyone, Mister Frank. They are all ... how can I say this without sounding like an extra from a cheap gangster movie?" He pursed his lips, thought, then shrugged. "No, I can't. Your men, Mister Frank, they are all *retired.*" He ignored Frank's open mouth. "My name is Kabac and I have a business proposition." He nodded at the goons with guns, and they drifted over into the corner, out of sight.

"What the fuck do you mean *retired*?"

Kabac shrugged. "I think you know." He gestured towards Burmese Bill. "You have been away a little too long, my friend. Your business has become shoddy. Your associates in Malaga, for example, they did not handle recent events too well. Business is not so good, eh?"

"What the hell do you know about that?"

"I know a lot about everything, *Mister* Frank. I know that one man takes out your entire operation and fucks you deep. How is that possible?"

Kabac's voice was low, almost friendly, but beneath lay veiled mockery, as if he knew who was in control, who held all the cards.

Frank shifted uncomfortably on the stool, turning away from Kabac's slightly amused gaze. "I'm sorting it, don't have any worries on that score you little—"

"Please," Kabac held up his hand, "no more insults. I want this to be *professional,* Frank. Make your phone calls if you wish, but you will receive no answer. Not from anyone."

Frank grimaced. His initial thought was to ram his fist into this upstart's face, but something flicked on inside his head and prevented such a reaction. Common sense perhaps. For a long time now he had considered jacking it all in. He was tired, not getting any younger, and Sarah's murder had caused him to revaluate life, family, his own mortality. Perhaps he should go back to the UK, disappear, live on whatever he had managed to save. Kabac's proposition may not be so unwanted after all.

"I want to make an offer of seven-hundred and fifty thousand *pounds,"* said Kabac, breaking into Frank's thoughts.

Frank snorted. "That's a little short." Kabac smiled even more sweetly than before. "But I'll accept."

Not how he'd envisaged handing over the business, but the thought of a protracted dispute, which would almost certainly end up in violence and death irked him. Those days had gone and he no longer had the muscle. Ryan Chaise had seen to that. Besides, the Chinese were taking over now, in huge numbers. No one could survive against the Chinese, not even these tough hard-nosed Ukrainians, or whatever they were. Soon, they'd all be eating chop suey through a straw.

"I have a little business to sort out," said Frank. He eased himself off the barstool and went around the counter to fix them all drinks. Vodka, he guessed. Kabac motioned his men forward, where they took their drinks, neat, and swallowed them in one. Frank grunted and poured them another. "If we could postpone everything for a few days, I'd be grateful."

"Certainly," said Kabac with an oily grin as he drained his vodka. "I understand some bastards murdered your wife."

"Yes. The funeral's tomorrow."

"Animals," said Kabac with a shake of the head.

"I have colleagues over in the UK who will tie up the loose ends for me. The guy you mentioned who had caused me some grief? He's at the root of everything. And he's going to die."

"He is the one who murdered your lovely wife?"

Frank felt his throat tighten and he suddenly realized he hadn't spoken to anyone about any of it. And yet, here he stood in deep conversation with a perfect stranger, a man who wished to take everything he had built up, lived and breathed for most of his adult life. He put a finger and thumb in the corners of his eyes and squeezed. "As good as," Frank said. "Apparently, one of my associates sent someone round to talk to her, and he became a little overzealous." He pulled his hand away and stared at his fingers, as if they held a mirror into which he could pick out the details of the past. "They wanted answers, answers about a man called Chaise. She didn't have them and she died ... because of him."

Kabac nodded, Frank's explanation seeming to strike a chord, his smile disappearing. "Revenge. Only right that it should be so. I hope that when your men find him they make him suffer."

"Oh, they will. They will."

. . .

"I would have liked her buried in London."

Frank shook himself back to the present and turned to look at Sarah's mother as she stared straight ahead, grim, stoic. "She loved it here."

Her eyes, black-rimmed where the mascara had run, burned into him. She sniffed. "Yes, well, I don't, and it's a hell of a trip to come and pay my respects."

He had no answer to that.

The funeral cortege wended its way through the narrow street to the little cemetery at the top of the village where Sarah was to rest.

"The only good thing about this bloody country is how they treat their dead."

He helped her out of the car and they walked slowly to the waiting hearse. The hired pallbearers lifted out the coffin and made the inchmeal trek to the appointed place.

No one spoke. Even when the priest opened up his prayer book, he incanted in little more than a whisper. Frank did not listen. Sarah was his wife, but no emotional bond existed between them. Like a fashion accessory, a piece of expensive jewellery to hang off his arm, she accompanied him to dinners and lavish balls at the mayor's sprawling villa just a few kilometres from Marbella. Everyone smiled and nodded in appreciation.

Sarah, that rare type of woman who simply oozed sex with every step of her lithe body, relished the effect she created. She slept with other men, which had ultimately been her undoing, but Frank did not care.

What riled him most was Ryan Chaise, the embarrassment and shame he had brought, something Frank could not afford to ignore, not even with the Ukrainians taking over. He'd thought about it long and hard after Kabac had left. He wanted an early retirement, a peaceful, uneventful one, and the Eastern European gangster's offer sounded tempting and quite decent. The money alone, however, would not bring him the peace he yearned for. Only Chaise's death would do that.

When the service ended, Frank thanked the priest, placed a small framed photograph of Sarah against the foot of the coffin, and watched as the assistants dressed in black sealed up the tomb.

Sarah's mother remained rigid, face set hard. "I'll stay here for a while," she said. "Then I'll go to the airport. My flight's at five, so ..."

"I can wait, drop you off if you wish."

She looked at him. "I think you've done enough, don't you?"

There was no reasonable answer to give, so Frank turned and went back to the car.

He saw the guy in the tracksuit and shades standing under the nearby lemon tree and should have known. If he had been younger, he might have been able to do something. If he'd been younger, he would have told Kabac where to go.

The man had a silenced automatic.

He shot Frank once in the chest, blowing him back against the side of the car, then shot him again in the head.

There were a couple of bystanders. No one moved or spoke, then turned away when the killer glared at them. He walked over to his car parked across the street and drove away, the day's work done.

When Sarah's mother came out of the cemetery and saw Frank's blood-spattered body, his eyes wide open and incredulous, she said nothing either.

THIRTEEN

He left some time after breakfast, with Emma still in bed, Reece sprawled on the sofa venting wind, and Darren at work. He closed the front door and went across the street to his car and looked back to see Emma in the window. He raised his hand, and she made the tiniest of responses, a mere flickering of the fingertips.

For a second he hesitated, the sight of her, her life, the simplicity and normality of it, it seemed to call him. He resisted and smiled. She did not return it.

As he turned to get in the car, he noted that some kind soul had run down the side with the edge of a coin, or the point of a key, a meandering white line cut deep into the paintwork. He hung his head and sighed. Not much changed. He opened the door and slid in behind the wheel, started the engine and took the Audi down the road, knowing Emma was watching him but not wanting to look back, to feel the tug at his heartstrings again.

He'd left her a note, and Darren might say something, Reece, too. The two men of the house would no doubt be pleased to see the back of him. Two nights he'd stayed. For them, it must have seemed like two weeks.

As he rolled the big car into the main street, something played at the back of his neck, the old sixth sense which always served him so well. This unerring early warning system, which alerted him to the close proximity of killers, first developed in the featureless desert of Iraq, saving his life on more than one occasion. Others soon began to realise it, and they stayed close, hopeful they too might stay safe, bask in his protection. Some benefitted; most did not. Death was forever at his side.

Now, it surfaced again. He pulled over and pretended to be looking inside the glove compartment. In reality, he took the opportunity to check the street. In this part of the town shops ran down on his left, a large public house set back in its own grounds to his right, with a wide terrace where anyone could sit, customers or not. A woman sat at a warped wooden table, with two small children running around her feet, any number of shopping bags sprawled on the ground.

Chaise smiled and spotted him. For the briefest of moments, but it was enough.

He adjusted the seat belt and took the car into the traffic once more, heading in the direction of the docks and the motorway spur. At the traffic lights, he spotted him again, a few cars behind. He strained to make out the driver's features, but he was too far back. Time would reveal everything, he knew.

The lights changed to green and he joined the highway. From there it was simply a matter of following the signs, as one motorway merged with the next. He settled down for the long journey, the route planned to cut across the country, using A-roads occasionally, and head east towards Norfolk.

After five minutes, he made a slight detour and left the motorway approach road. He had a visit to make, but first, he needed to have a small conversation. He drove towards a large roundabout and a supermarket petrol station. He parked in the forecourt, close to the service bay for air and water and waited. He didn't have to wait long.

The small Clio pulled into the service station. Chaise got out and walked towards the car, hands loose by his side, jaw set. Inside, he chuckled to himself. People stood around, filling up their cars, the weather dry, no one hurrying anywhere. A bus moved towards the entrance to the supermarket. A normal day. Ryan Chaise felt relaxed.

Colin sat behind the wheel of his Clio as Chaise strode towards him. He wanted to turn the car around, head back the other way, but the bus blocked his escape route. Other cars constantly came and went, his only choice to take the direction straight ahead and drive past Chaise who, no doubt, would block his way, lean in through the window, blow out his brains with the gun. Colin knew he had a gun. He could see the butt in the waistband. Of course, Chaise had placed it there on purpose, plainly in sight, so Colin had no doubts. The man's arrogance irked him. He remained still, slipped the Smith and Wesson out of its holster and put it between his legs. If he had to kill him, he would. London would not like a public execution of course, but if this was how it was to be, then so be it.

And now he was here.

Chaise smiled, stooped down on his haunches and tapped at the window.

Colin turned with infinite slowness and wound the window down.

"Are you new at this?"

Colin blinked a few times. "I beg your pardon?"

Another smile. Easy, broad, confident. Colin's stomach clenched. "Listen, I know you're following me, so I'll make it easy for you, okay? I'm going to East Anglia, a little market town called Beccles. I've applied for a job in an estate agency there, so you can save yourself a lot of time and energy, and report all of this back to Harper."

"*Harper*?" Colin gave what he believed was his finest questioning look. "Who the hell is Harper?"

"Just tell him, okay? I don't need all this bullshit. I'm being a good little boy, and I'm not going to embarrass anybody, unless ... unless, of course, they try to embarrass me first. Like you, with that gun between your legs. Careful it doesn't go *bang*." Chaise smiled, patted Colin on the arm and returned to his big, black Audi.

Colin's body went rigid, heat welling up over his collar. Damn the arrogance of the man. He stuck the Smith and Wesson back into its holster, reached inside his jacket and pulled out a packet of cigarettes. He noted with shock that his hands were shaking. How had Chaise made him? He'd been so bloody careful! Damn him.

He lit the cigarette, took in the smoke, wished to God he could stop, and watched Chaise drive off. Beccles. He punched the details into the sat nav and groaned. Suffolk. Something like three-hundred miles away. Jesus, it was going to take forever. He'd have to stop for petrol more than once, food too, he'd lose sight of him and then ...

He clenched his teeth. He was heading into a blind alley for all he knew. What if Chaise hadn't told him the truth? He leaned back, stared at the roof, blew out a stream of smoke. Something inside told him Chaise had not lied. He wasn't sure if that made him feel better, or worse.

FOURTEEN

Time moved on, and Brigit couldn't put off going to the shops any longer. The thought of trawling through the local shopping mall left her cold, but retail therapy might prove the order of the day after Chaise's visit. So, she gathered together the few things she needed, the most important being her credit card, and made her way to the door.

He'd always been able to unnerve her; something about his attitude, the way he held her with the mocking glint in his eyes. From the start, she'd done her best to steer Linny away from any sort of serious relationship with him, but since they'd made the decision to go to Spain, the distance didn't help.

That was her father's influence, of course. The Spanish blood, making Linny headstrong, impulsive, going to live abroad and loving every moment. Thumbing her nose at her mother, as she always had. Daddy's little girl. Bloody Daddy, not giving a thought about anyone but himself.

A lot like Ryan Chaise.

She snapped her purse shut and let out a sigh. Damn them all. Men. Linny's father had done his best to ruin Brigit's life, and now Chaise, trying to do the same to Linny. He'd called and she left him on the step, glaring. He looked so damned good in his tight t-shirt and chinos, his body hard and trim. She hated the way he made her feel, and this time, his eyes so kind, so pleading. She could have given over Linny's telephone number, but why on earth should she after learning what had happened in Spain? Linny, broken and distraught, but safe, needed time on her own to revaluate her life. The longer she spent away from Chaise the better everything would be.

Linny divulged little, leaving lots of gaps, causing Brigit to wonder what Chaise had done to cause her daughter so much grief. An affair? No, surely not, but he was a man and therefore weak; anything in a skirt, a flash of thigh, a smile and he would be hooked. They were all the same.

The morning hung grey and melancholy as she stepped outside and activated the central locking. The headlights flashed, the satisfying clunk followed. She loved her car, a Burgundy red MGB. During the summer, she loved nothing better than driving around town, top down, white headscarf and sunglasses, the nineteen seventies all over again. And as for those admiring looks ...

Men. Damn them.

Talking of which, a man crossed the street towards her, two others close behind, big, dressed in white t-shirts and blue jeans. Probably gay, but mean looking. Huge arms. Nothing sexual, however. Far from it. Once, Brigit would have allowed her legs to buckle at the sight of such beefcake, but not now. Now she could have the pick of the crop. And these guys were not for picking. The other one, however, seemed a much more tantalising proposition. Slim, athletic and tanned. Good chiselled features, soft brown hair, mature too. The sort of man to spend time with, get to know.

The way they strode with such purpose made her afraid. Without a pause, she broke into a run, reached the car and pulled open the door. Thank God the weather had turned cold and the top was up, because as she slammed the door shut and put down the lock, the slim one was already rattling the handle. He smiled. For a moment she wondered what it was all about, but within a blink one of the beefcakes had moved to the passenger door, pounding on the glass with a mallet of a fist.

Brigit stared into a face twisted and red with rage.

"Get the fuck out of the car, you bitch."

Always a staple part of the recipe for suspense in the movies, the car failed to start. The victim inside, the pursuers trying to get in, and the ignition refusing to fire. When the second beefcake threw up his arms before slamming them down on the bonnet, grinning like an ape, she gunned the engine and ploughed forward. She wasn't stopping for anyone and this wasn't the movies.

The car roared into life and swatted the beefcake to the side as if he were nothing, jackknifing him to the ground, floppy, like a marionette jerked backwards by invisible strings. She heard the smack of his body hitting the asphalt and a tremor ran through her at the enormity of what she had done. But she didn't stop, knowing with terrifying certainty they would kill her.

She glanced into her mirror as she shot the MGB down the centre of the street. The first beefcake knelt next to his friend, shaking him by the shoulders, as the slim one pulled out a gun. "Jesus," she spat, and wrenched the car down the first available left turn as the gun went off, and the bullet winged across the boot.

Her heart pounded and she bit down on her lip, racing along the side street to the far end, taking a sharp right. Putting as much distance between herself and those terrible men as possible, she worked through the gears and sped away.

This was all to do with Ryan Chaise. It had to be. Or maybe ...

It occurred to her there was another answer and her eyes narrowed. Maybe not Chaise at all. Maybe somebody else looking for Linny. She grunted to herself, the answer so obvious: associates of Linny's father.

"He needs a fucking hospital."

Johnny stood in the middle of the street, breathing hard, staring at where the car had turned out of sight. He put his gun back into his shoulder holster and glanced down at the first beefcake, who cried like a baby. His tear-stained face looked up at Johnny, those big eyes awash with fear and desperation.

"Did you hear what I said? That fucking bitch hurt him, man. We need to get him to a hospital."

"Did you get her number?"

Beefcake blinked. "*What?*"

"Her car registration. Did you get it?"

"No, I fucking well didn't, you piece of shit – help me get Lawrence into the car."

But Johnny wasn't listening. He stared down the empty street, keeping the frustration under control. "There can't be many MGBs around, certainly not that colour. It shouldn't be too difficult to trace." He turned to see the beefcake pointing a gun in his direction, hand shaking, crying uncontrollably, out of control.

"Help me, for Christ's sake. He's dying."

Johnny thought, thought about killing the beefcake. Then a neighbour came out of a nearby house and strode towards him. "I saw it all," he said as he approached. "Are you the police? That bloody woman, always so bloody superior." He stepped up close. "I saw it all," he repeated. "She's wanted for something, something serious? You had to use your gun, so it had to be serious. Yes, that has to be it. Damned woman, I always knew there was something, flashing her legs the way she does. Drugs, is it? Always bloody drugs these days ... if there is anything I can do ..."

Johnny noticed other people appearing, eyes wide, gesticulating, voices raised in concern. This wasn't going very well at all. He closed his eyes for a moment, wishing he were somewhere else.

"I can make a statement if you like."

Johnny opened his eyes and smiled. He really should kill this guy too, he mused, followed by the beefcake, then the whole fucking world. He wished he could, but knew such actions would be brainless. Sometimes, he reminded himself, guns did not solve every problem. He squeezed the man's arm. "Thank you very much," he said, "but that won't be necessary. Perhaps you could assist my colleague to put the injured victim in his car," he nodded towards his parked BMW. "That would be such a help." The man frowned, hesitating. "He's concussed, but nothing more."

The neighbour beamed, relieved. "Certainly," he said and waved to the other people milling around in their front gardens. "This man needs help. And quickly."

Johnny took a step back to allow three or four interested neighbours lift Lawrence and take him over to the BMW.

The beefcake stepped up next to him. "You fucking shit!" he whispered. "If that guy hadn't appeared you would have left us."

"Fuck off," said Johnny, through gritted teeth. "Get in the fucking car and get to the hospital, and keep your fucking stupid mouth shut. We're undercover police if anybody asks, you understand?"

"I'm going to break your fucking jaw when all this is over."

Johnny leaned into him, mouth close to his ear. "And I'm going to rip your balls off if you don't stop with the Superman bullshit, okay?"

For a moment, it seemed the beefcake might react, but just as his fists bunched, the neighbour returned, breathless but beaming. "He's in the back seat, officer." He frowned at the beefcake and Johnny led him away by the elbow.

"We're undercover," he said. "You're right. It is drugs. I'd like to ask you to keep all of this ..." He lowered his voice in his best conspirator's tone, "If our cover is blown ..."

"Say no more, officer. I understand completely."

From somewhere an aging, grizzled man appeared, face grim, eyes flashing with accusations. "Who the bloody hell are you, and what is going on?"

"Everything's all right, Norman," said the first neighbour, "it's a police operation. Everything's under control."

Norman shook his head, disbelief melded onto his features. "I'd say it's far from under control. A shooting in the street. Where's your warrant card?"

Johnny forced a smile. "It's like your friend says, we're under cover and—"

"Your two chums don't look like policemen to me. I'm going to phone someone."

"Norman, there's no need for that."

"There's every need, Stanley." He measured Johnny with an arctic stare. "I want to see some identification."

Johnny spread out his hands, "Look, if it'll help, we can go and telephone the station together. They'll vouch for me."

Norman grunted and strode off towards his house. Johnny went to follow when Stanley touched his arm. "He's a little on edge. His wife, she died a few months back. He took it badly."

"Don't worry. I'll have it sorted in no time."

Norman had already picked up the receiver when Johnny stepped into the hallway, took a quick scan of the interior, and quietly pressed the door shut. "Sorry to hear about your wife," he said.

Another glare, Norman hesitated before punching out the number. "I didn't know police carried firearms."

"We're drugs squad, Norman. Undercover. We don't operate within the usual parameters. But make the call, if it makes you feel better."

Norman turned his back and went to press the first button.

Johnny knew how to kill people, quietly and without fuss. He hit Norman in the kidneys, dropping him like a brick, put his knee into the small of the man's back, his hands under his chin, and jerked the neck around with a vicious twist. The audible snap of the spinal column sounded loud in the confines of the hallway, but Norman's senses wouldn't be registering anything from now on. Johnny let the body drop and stood up, took a breath and made a quick tour of the house to find what he was looking for.

After stuffing Norman into a bedroom wardrobe, he readjusted his tie and went back out into the street.

People continued to mill around, gaggling. Johnny waved to Stanley, who almost ran in his haste. Johnny beamed. "All sorted."

"Exactly as I thought, officer. Now, is there anything else you need?"

"The woman—"

"Brigit. That's her name."

Johnny made a show of remembering. "Yes, of course. Brigit ..."

"Spanish surname. Del Torro. Bull I think. Something to do with bulls ... weird."

"Brigit Del Torro. Perhaps you know a little more about her? Friends and family she might visit? We need to ascertain her whereabouts as soon as possible."

"You could put an APB out, couldn't you?"

Johnny frowned. He struggled for a moment, attempting to trawl up a memory of what the letters might mean. Before he sank even deeper into confusion, the neighbour took him by the forearm.

"All Points Bulletin. Get a roadblock organised, cut her off before she gets too far away."

"Yes, yes, of course. But we need to keep this low-key." The man looked at him. Johnny could hear the cogs of his brain whirring, giving life to tiny doubts. He forced himself to remain calm, convince this prick everything was above board. "She's part of a gang, you see." The neighbour's eyes widened. "She's armed and highly dangerous. So, if there's anything you can do, anyone you know of ..."

"I'll ask around," he said quickly. "No problem officer."

"Thank you," said Johnny and allowed himself to relax, the stress seeping away. "And now, I wonder if I could borrow you car?"

FIFTEEN

Sometime after five o'clock in the evening, Ryan arrived in the small market town of Beccles and found himself a small, nondescript hotel. His room was clean and plain, the view from the window uninspiring. Later, he ate a quiet dinner washed down with a single brandy, before returning to his room to change.

Afterwards, he spoke to the girl at reception, who pointed him in the direction of the river and a bar close by. He decided to ignore the chance for a drink and went to stand by the railings to watch the water meander by. The clear night sky brought a sense of peace, the countless stars reflected on the flat surface of the River Waveney, and romantic memories of Linny stirred from within, of long summer nights spent breathing in the heady scent of jasmine, stark mountaintops and walks through the busy streets of Torre del Mar, the sea lapping against the shore.

He sighed and turned around, leaned back and caught sight of a couple sitting snuggled up on the terrace, holding one another's hands, sharing smiles and the occasional kiss, not caring about the chill. Why would they? They were in love ...

He allowed his eyes to wander, noted the shadow and sighed again, aggravated. So, despite his best efforts, the tail had managed to find him. A slight tickle of annoyance in his stomach, nothing more, and he turned to go inside when a nagging doubt in the back of his mind caused him to stop. He'd driven fast, the Audi eating up the miles with ease, stopping once at a place called Diss to dump the car. A walk into town followed by a visit to a local car-hire, his plan worked seamlessly enough. He hadn't noticed the tail then, or at least he believed he hadn't.

He ran through each step again, like re-running a film. The tail had driven a Renault Clio, and Chaise had the number. At the service station back in Wallasey, he'd told the tail about Beccles, but how could the man's car outpace the Audi, arrive here before him and discover the hotel in which he was staying? Unless, of course, Chaise had misjudged how good he was at his job ... or ...

Chaise went inside the pub, which smelled new, furniture gleaming, the bar highly polished, soft piped music adding to the calm atmosphere. He crossed the room and ordered a brandy. He swilled the drink around the glass globe and scanned the tables, picking out the couples, some friends laughing, a group of office workers deep in conversation. No one sitting alone. He asked the barman where the toilets were, and the young guy nodded to a point over in the far corner. Chaise left the half-finished brandy and walked towards the door with the sign emblazoned on it.

He slipped inside and took a quick glance around. Three cubicles hugged the left wall with a row of four urinals facing them, washbasins and hand driers at the far end. Above these was a window, open on the first notch of the metal arm. He stood underneath and listened to the gentle lap of water and calculated the room's position in relation to the river. He went into one of the cubicles and pulled the toilet tissue from the roll. Being new, the unravelling took longer than he thought, but eventually a pile of tissue lay on the floor and the cardboard roll in his hand. He flattened then folded it and went back out.

Someone came in, barely gave him a glance, and he deftly put the card into his pocket and made as if he was struggling with his zip. He moved over to the washbasin and turned the water on. The man came up alongside, washed his hands, dried them under the electric wall-fan, then went out. Quickly, Chaise scooted over, dropped to his knees and wedged the piece of flattened card under the door, jamming it in as far as he could.

He stood, and tested opening the door. It would not budge. Satisfied, he returned to the basins and climbed on top, pushed up the window bar and heaved himself through, wriggling like a snake.

He kept himself fit, the morning ritual of fifty push-ups, squats and curls helping him maintain a modicum of muscle definition. A twice-weekly jog helped with his stamina. Even so, it proved a struggle to get out of the window. His belt jagged on the latch, and for a moment he floundered before managing to twist himself around, get his thumb under the leather, and pull it free with a jerk.

His body slid out into open-air, and he hit the ground with a roll, grunting with the shock of the impact. The knees of his trousers felt wet and he swore. In the half-light, he couldn't see much, but his fingers traced the tear in the material, and touched the stickiness of blood. He looked around. He had dropped into a back yard that probably ran the length of the pub. Keeping low, he pressed himself under the window and listened. No one had yet come to the toilet, but when they did, they would curse, push and bang before calling the barman. By that time ...

Chaise clung to the wall and groped his way along. With no lights, the darkness almost total, he moved by instinct alone until he came to a door. The rear entrance he hoped, and when he tried to open it, the heavy timber would not budge. He fumbled around and found the bolt. He thought about the back door at Emma's, the latch unhooked like a calling card. Chaise grinned because he now knew there were two of them. Two tails, the one in the Clio and another. And this one was very good indeed.

He eased back the bolt, slipped through the door without a sound, and felt for a light switch. He winced at the sudden glare, finding himself in a low ceilinged, whitewashed corridor, which wound its way in a gentle incline away from the pub and the river. A tradesman's entrance perhaps, from when the place was a hotel, or a great private house. Luck for once smiled, giving him a chance to lose the tail, if only for a moment.

More importantly, the tail would know he had been made.

The barman busied himself polishing a glass when a small cough from behind caused him to turn. "Yes sir, what can I get you?"

"The man who ordered this brandy," said the stranger, running his finger around the bowl of the glass, "do you know where he went? I'm here to meet him, you see."

"Yes sir, certainly, sir. I believe he went to the toilet. But I'm not—"

The barman stopped. Another man, red-faced, flustered and angry, approached the bar. "There's something wrong with the toilet door – it's locked."

The barman gave a little laugh, "*Locked*? But how is that ..." He smiled at the first man at the counter. "Sorry, sir, would you excuse me a moment?" He lifted up the counter hatch and went to talk to the irate customer who was gesticulating wildly with his arms.

As he ran Chaise's brandy around his mouth and scanned the bar, Esteban smiled. Harper had said this man Chaise was good, and so he was. A worthy opponent indeed.

SIXTEEN

Chaise finished his breakfast, checked his tie in the hall mirror and left. He had everything he needed, no need to go back to his room. At least it wasn't raining, so he took his time climbing a steep set of ancient steps towards the church. He paused to study the Norman exterior before strolling through the gardens and into the market town's square. Already shoppers milled about, so he slipped between them, checked for the tail, and took a coffee in a nearby café.

From his table, he had a good view of the estate agency on the far side of the square. A curious, sunken building, all awkward angles and ill-fitting windows covered with numerous advertisements for houses, many for sale, some for rent. The upper storey may have been flats. He sipped his coffee, checked his watch. The time for his appointment was ten-thirty, only a few minutes away, so he took in a breath and strode outside.

He paused at the entrance, checking for traffic and the tail.

He saw no one and crossed over.

The interview went well and the following morning, after he informed the hotel he would be staying for only a few more days until he found something more permanent, he met the assistant manager of the agency who took him on a brief tour of the properties they had on their books.

Chaise was part of the team now. His references had come through, and after a probationary period, he would have his own desk in the office from where he could build up a portfolio of clients. Until then, he would share the assistant manager's desk, all perfectly okay as far as Ryan Chaise was concerned. After all, he didn't know for how long he would be around. He never knew. Despite being in Spain for over ten years, no plan dictated what he did. Not to have a plan at all was the way he lived his life.

In Norwich, they visited another company office. Later, over lunch in an intimate little restaurant, Chaise listened, replied to questions, gave off an air of affability and good-humour. All the things he didn't feel, especially when he looked through the window to the car park. There sat the Clio. He almost smiled, a curious sense of comfort coming from the realisation that his tail was in open view. He wondered about the second one, of whom he had not caught a single sniff since the event at the riverside pub. The man must be good, very good. It was rare for Chaise to encounter someone who simply *disappeared.*

Whilst serving in Iraq they came to him and he thought it might be some sort of elaborate joke, conjured up by his mates. But no. This was serious. Three huge guys, flanking his bed in the middle of the night. He eyed them, their guns, and allowed them to take him to a nondescript training camp somewhere in Kuwait. They drove through the night and by the time they arrived, the heat was terrifying.

They gestured with their guns, forced him to stand in the middle of an open yard, where the sun's rays were at their most intense. He allowed the heat to wash over him, ignoring it, falling deep inside himself, Zen meditation stilling his soul, like a Buddhist monk, calm, silent, senses alert, but outwardly a statue. Made of stone.

Then he felt it.

That curious tingling, as if someone, somewhere, watched him.

He moved before the bullet smacked into the dust where only moments before he had stood. Chaise swerved, rolled, looked for cover as a second bullet streaked through the air inches above his head. Maintaining concentration, he raced over the hard, compacted ground, making for a stack of wooden packing cases. He scrambled behind them and felt his bowels loosen when he read the signs in black, smudged ink: *Danger. High Explosives.*

As he dodged left, the next bullet hit the side of the crates and he dived full stretch into the earth, arms protecting his head. A sudden flash followed by a low rumble, and the whole lot went off, the massive explosion ripping through the thick air, flinging bits of jagged, charred wood in all directions. He flattened himself, hands clamped over his ears as scorching splinters rained down, some of them hitting his back. None was big enough to cause damage so he took his chance, weaving to the left, then the right, pumping his arms, maintaining speed.

Ahead stood a tiny concrete blockhouse, the open door inviting him to enter. Too convenient perhaps, all of it so neat and well prepared. When another bullet whistled close to his head, he decided none of that mattered and flung himself through the opening like an arrow, hit the dirt with a jarring thud, rolled over and slammed himself against the adjacent wall, crouching beneath the single window.

He sucked in his breath, battling to calm himself, settle his heartbeat. Recovery came swiftly, his fitness level the envy of a professional athlete and as his breathing slowed, he glanced around the confines of the building.

Cool and tiny, perhaps nine metres square, it was a simple, empty space. Propped up in the corner a sniper rifle, with a telescopic sight. He grimaced. Bastards. A test and he, like an idiot, had fallen headlong into it. Anger rumbled deep and part of him wanted to stand up and tell them to fuck off. However, he did not. Those bullets were real and if his reactions had not been so well tuned, his brains would be decorating the sun-baked yard right now. Death awaited him anyway if he failed any part of the test, even if he somehow managed to stay alive, of that he had no doubt. The bastards had him cornered and he had little choice other than to follow the game through to the end.

Cursing under his breath, he scrambled over to the rifle and checked the magazine. A fully loaded L96 PM British Army sniper rifle, all he had to do was take an approximate bearing on whoever was shooting at him, try to force the assailant to move out into the open and loose off a few shots. Having survived the turkey-shoot, this, the second part of the test might prove more difficult but, who knows, it might even work; whoever it was might catch a stray bullet, get killed. Chaise, however, not a marksman, knew how difficult such an action might prove to be. So did they of course, whoever 'they' were. He ran his tongue over dry lips and wondered what he should do.

His mobile buzzed, bringing him back to the present. He noted the name and pulled a face. "I need to take this," he said. The assistant manager waved him away as the waiter appeared with dessert. Chaise got up, moving out of earshot.

"What the hell are you playing at, Chaise?"

"I'm doing as I hoped you'd want me to. Building a new, *normal* life."

"The infantile jest with the toilet door was not appreciated. Where are you?"

"Don't you know?"

Harper's breath rasped down the receiver. "No more bloody games, Chaise."

"I've got a job, and I mean to play no more games so long as you keep your man well away from me. Or should that be *men,* Mr Harper? I've clocked two so far."

A silence. Chaise counted the seconds, then turned off the mobile and returned to the table.

A curious frown from his lunch companion. "You look happy."

"Yes," said Chaise, staring down at his tiramisu, "why shouldn't I be?"

SEVENTEEN

Johnny pulled the car into a nearby side street and phoned Alfonso Calderon.

"Johnny," said Alfonso, chirpy as always. He sounded as though he had his mouth full, and a little too eager for Johnny's liking. "How the devil are you?"

"It didn't go too well," said Johnny.

"Oh, sorry to hear that. How do you mean, exactly?"

"I mean the bloody mother-in-law got away and one of your boys is hurt."

A silence. Johnny swore he could hear munching. Perhaps lunchtime came late for Spaniards. "I see. When you say 'hurt', what exactly do you—?"

"I mean he's gone to hospital. His brother's with him."

"*His brother*? Which of them do you talk about, my friend? Jerome or Lawrence? Who is hurt?"

"The other one told me, but I can't remember. They both look the fucking same, Al, but the one who got hit was the bigger one."

"That's Lawrence. And they're not brothers, Johnny. They're lovers."

Oh shit. "I see. Well, whatever he is, the other one's upset and he's taken this Jerome to the hospital. I think the police will be here soon."

"That's unfortunate. Can you get away without being spoken to?"

"Yes, I already have. I borrowed a neighbour's car."

"How clever of you. Listen, in that case, I want you to get back on the motorway and head towards the Liverpool Tunnel. You follow the signs for Wallasey docks, okay? Then you take a left, then the first left again. Keep going right to the bottom of the road, heading towards a roundabout. It is some way, so do not panic. From there you take another left and drive all the way to the very end. You will see an old lighthouse. You drive to it and wait. You got that?"

"Left, left, then left again. I think so, but I don't—"

"Just do it, Johnny. Tony will meet you there, in about half an hour, okay? He'll bring you in."

"Bring me in? Listen, I don't think it's all that serious. This neighbour, the one I borrowed the car from, he thinks I'm undercover – drug squad. I told him to keep his mouth shut. He believed me."

"Well, that's as maybe, but I want you back with us, Johnny. Nice and safe. Things have become a little ... *complicated.* Half an hour, you understand?"

Johnny was about to tell him about the other guy, Norman. However, some niggle inside, a growing unease, made him stop and reconsider. Alfonso seemed a little too eager, altogether too keen to 'bring him in' as he'd put it. And everything appeared planned, almost as if Calderon already knew everything. Nothing had surprised him. "Yes. I got it."

"Good. And Johnny ..."

"Yes?"

"Don't you *ever* call me Al again."

The phone went dead. Johnny frowned, but not because of Calderon's annoyance. Things had become 'complicated', he said. What did he mean?

. . .

In the end, the directions proved easy to follow, the journey straightforward with no deviations but it took a lot longer than half an hour. When at last he arrived, he took the car across the rutted wasteland that led up to the lighthouse, a grey, lonely looking place. Long abandoned, it stood against the elements, walls battered by aeons of harsh winds and torrential downpours. If it were night, the ghosts would skirt around the empty, blackened pinnacle where once a beacon had guided sailors far from the shore.

Now, with evening drawing on, it managed to present an eerie sight and, with Tony already waiting, menace. Arms folded, he leaned against the driver's side of a large, black limousine-type vehicle. The passenger door stood open. No one else appeared to be around.

Johnny stopped some twenty yards away and sat, hands on the wheel. The wasteland was a large, open expanse of scrub, dominated by the solidity of the lighthouse. Over to the right, the Irish Sea pounded against the concrete defences. A bleak place, perhaps secret lovers out to catch a few moments alone the only ones to venture close.

A perfect place for a private meet.

From over by his car, Tony grinned but didn't move.

Johnny had worked a long time for Frank down on the Costa. He'd seen a lot, met plenty of nasty people. He'd survived on his wits and his ability to act decisively when required. In the early days, when the place streamed with low-life gangsters from south of the River Thames, he'd helped Frank establish himself as the toughest, meanest bastard that Marbella had yet seen. Then came the Irish, and they were no pushover. A lot of ex-IRA, fuelled with a great deal of money, and all the equipment needed to mount a takeover bid.

But Johnny and Frank had ridden it out, done what they needed to and successfully retained control of their clubs, brothels and hotels. Recently, with the influx of Eastern European Mafia things had become hairy. Johnny and Frank often talked well into the night about retiring, going across the Med to Crete, or one of the smaller Greek islands, buying a couple of villas, living the quiet life. Something had always stopped them; perhaps it was greed, or perhaps the simple acceptance that no one ever retired from their line of business. Someone else always did the retiring for you. That's why he had to stay sharp.

Like now.

He stepped out of the car, keeping the door open as he stood, right hand on the automatic in his jacket pocket, the left raised in welcome.

"Hello, Johnny," called Tony, not changing position. He seemed relaxed enough, jovial even, despite his raised voice. "Leave the car there, and come on over here. Mr Calderon wants us to go back to Liverpool and talk over a few little things. We'll take you."

The waves smashed against the defences, catching Johnny's words and tossing them in the air. Already his throat felt hoarse as he shouted, "Why didn't he just ask me to go there himself, Tony?"

Tony shrugged. "Don't know. Something's happened, he said. But what it is," he shook his head, "I don't know."

"I'll follow you. This car isn't mine, it's been loaned to me. I'll need to take it back."

Tony shook his head. "I can't hear you, Johnny. Come closer."

"I have to return the car!"

"I think it would be best if we all travel in the same car, Johnny. You can leave that one here. We'll take you in, no problem. It'll be fine."

"*We*, Tony?"

Tony cocked his head to one side, "Eh?"

"You keep saying 'we'. What do you mean by that, Tony? Is someone else coming with us?"

Despite the distance between them, Johnny saw Tony's face go ashen. It might have been a mere slip of the tongue, not a trick to catch Tony out, but Johnny's question had opened up something disagreeable and Tony wasn't about to take any chances. Unfortunately for him, even before he managed to push himself off the car and unfold his arms to reveal two huge, black revolvers, Johnny had taken off way to the left at a sprint.

Johnny, moving fast but in perfect balance, shot Tony three times in the chest on the run just as a second guy appeared from around the front of the car. He must have believed he'd worked it out well, thinking he could use the door to shield himself from Johnny's bullets if Tony hadn't been successful in the initial fusillade. He was mistaken. Johnny recognised the Heckler & Koch MP5A3 the guy held, knew it was deadly at short range. So he ran like a whippet, and by the time the guy realised what was going on, it was too late. Johnny was already behind him. The guy tried to swing around, to let loose a blast from the little Heckler & Koch but the first bullet from Johnny's gun took him in the throat, throwing him backwards against the car door, his gun barking loud and fast but uselessly into the air. Johnny shot him twice more, once in the heart, the second in the head and the guy slid to the ground dead, the gun's magazine already spent.

Breathing hard, Johnny approached the limousine keeping his automatic trained on the machine-gunner until he knew for certain he wouldn't be getting up again. He kicked the MP5A3 away, turned and went to the other side and Tony, who moaned but did not move.

The big guy was on his back, smacking his lips, blinking up towards the sky, trying to understand what had happened. Blood spattered his shirtfront, the three holes small and black in the centre of red-rose blotches. Johnny got down close to him. "What the fuck was all that about, eh?"

Tony shook his head. "Don't know," he managed. Then the lights went out of his eyes and he said no more. Johnny swore, stood up, and launched a tremendous kick against the side of the limousine, denting the panelling.

He checked his gun. He had enough bullets, but he picked up one of Tony's revolvers just in case and put it in his waistband. It might come in useful for what he had in mind

EIGHTEEN

The estate agency building squatted wide and low in the town square, a sign across the entrance warning visitors not to crack their heads on the door lintel. People complained constantly but, as it was Grade II listed, nobody had the right to change anything. Dating back to the early seventeenth century, inside it was modern and well lit. Despite the narrowness, wide ranges of properties were displayed across the walls.

Chaise sat at the far end, going through the portfolios of unsold houses, thinking of a new approach to generate interest in a depressed, flagging market. Nobody was buying anything, unless offered at the right price. Persuading vendors to drop asking prices might encourage someone to put their hands in their pockets, but he doubted it.

He looked up as the door opened and a small ferret of a man came in, twitching his head around before beaming at the receptionist. "I need to talk to someone about my properties."

She smiled back and threw a look Chaise's way. "This is Mr Chaise, our new agent. Perhaps he can help."

Chaise came forward and offered his hand. The man took it. A feeble grip, and a little wet. Chaise had to suppress the desire to wipe his palm on the seat of his pants. Instead, he motioned the man towards his desk. "How can I help you, Mr ...?"

"Lomax. Christopher Lomax." He sat down, hunched up a little. His eyes darted around, agitated, unsure of himself. "I have a series of properties in Norwich. I rent them out to students and things are all right at the moment, but ... well, one of my properties, it's becoming a bit of burden. It's old, needs a lot doing to it and nobody seems particularly interested in renting any of the rooms, so ..." he shrugged, gave a self-conscious smile, "I want to sell."

He continued with the explanation, a whole string of reasons pouring out of him. Not that Chaise was interested. After a while, he allowed himself to drift off, thoughts going back to Spain, how different it all was there. The driving out to the pueblos and the villas, the weather, the pace of life. Funny how things turn around. To live like this, sitting in an office in an English market town, marking time, waiting for ... for what? Retirement? Already? The things he'd seen, the locations, the events, the death. To end up here, in the back of beyond, a place to fall asleep and simply wait ...

"... and that's the thing I've decided to do. So, what do you think?"

Chaise blinked, realising he had missed almost every single word. He grinned, leaned forward, rubbed his hands together and attempted to sound eager, "Well, first things first, we'll drive out there and I'll take some photos and a few measurements. I'll get the details in the shop window, do some mailshots and rustle up an advert for the papers. It'll be on the market by late this afternoon."

Lomax appeared shocked. He ran a hand through his sparse hair. "You can do all that, so quickly?" Chaise smiled and nodded. "Well, if you think that's ..." He shrugged. "Not sure what she'll think, but ... well, as long as you're sure, yes, let's proceed."

She? Who was 'she'? Chaise regretted not having listened now.

NINETEEN

By the time Johnny got back to the club, it was almost opening time. The bouncers stood at the door laughing and waitresses stalked around the dance floor as Johnny slipped through the entrance without a glance from anyone. Few punters graced the interior yet, but the music pumped as the DJ went through one last rehearsal. Johnny crossed to the far end of the main bar and lifted the hatch. The barman, doing what barmen do best – dry glasses – barely gave him a look as Johnny eased himself behind the counter and opened the private door to a rear corridor. He went along the murky depths until he came to a door marked *Private*. He pushed it open without knocking.

Alfonso, sprawled in a black leather swivel chair, had his jacket off and eyes closed, whilst between his legs a delicious-looking blonde girl in bra and panties engaged in a loud and enthusiastic blowjob.

She squawked when she caught sight of Johnny and shot to her feet, putting her right hand against her mouth. Alfonso, face red with outrage and embarrassment, hastily gathered together his now limp manhood and stuffed it back into his trousers.

"Get out," said Johnny.

The girl didn't need further encouragement and left the room at a run. Johnny shut the door behind her, locked it, leaned back and pulled out Tony's gun. He chuckled as he watched Alfonso struggling with his flies.

"You better have a fucking good reason for bursting in on me like this," said Alfonso, standing to allow himself easier access to his trousers. "And for pulling that gun at me."

"Oh, I have," said Johnny, "because I shouldn't be here, should I?"

Alfonso stopped and frowned. Johnny saw the lies, the intrigue written all over his fat face. First, the little tremor of uncertainty, the self-assuredness slowly draining away, replaced by fear. "What do you mean?" His voice sounded very small.

"I *mean* you sending Tony and some other idiot to take me out. Problem being they were both useless and now they're dead." He brought up the gun to emphasise the fact, not that it needed any emphasising, at least not to Alfonso, who emitted some fairly foul smells in response. He slumped into his chair and turned green as Johnny continued, smiling throughout, "So, why don't you tell me why you wanted me dead, Al. And don't try and come up with some nonsensical shite, or I'll blow out your fucking brains." He eased back the hammer and levelled the gun towards Alfonso's chest.

Alfonso threw up both hands, lips quivering, jowls wobbling, "For Christ's sake, Johnny, please don't fucking kill me."

"Tell me."

The Spaniard closed his eyes for a moment, took in a few rasping breaths. "All right. I got some news through. Bad news, Johnny. Really bad." He spread out his hands, the mercy plea developing into something of an exercise in overacting. "I didn't know anything about it until morning, I swear to God."

"What news?"

Another pause, a big swallow. "Johnny, they killed Frank. Shot him at his wife's funeral."

For a moment, Johnny wasn't quite sure what to do. Had he heard it right? The words seemed to him to be saying Frank was dead, but that couldn't be. Nobody could kill Frank. Not like that, a shooting. *"At his wife's funeral?"*

Alfonso nodded enthusiastically, "Yeah, I know. Terrible, isn't it. He was coming out after having laid her to rest, and they gunned him down. Right there. A dreadful thing."

"Who did?"

"Eh?"

Johnny took two quick strides and loomed over Alfonso, only the desk separating them. But that didn't matter, because he leaned across and put the barrel of the gun right against Alfonso's forehead and breathed through clenched teeth, "I said, who the fucking hell did it?"

"Ukrainians. They've taken over. All along the coast, mopped everyone up. The Brits, the Irish, all gone. Eastern Europeans rule the Costas now, Johnny."

Johnny squeezed his eyes almost shut, trying to stop the tears. Frank dead? No, he couldn't believe such a thing. They'd worked so hard, all these years. But, if it were true ... Johnny's automatic response kicked in, the animal instinct for survival. He leaned forward and glared at the snivelling wretch in front of him. "So why try to kill me, Al? What has Frank's killing got to do with me, over here, in Liverpool? Eh? Answer me that."

Alfonso appeared to shrink, his head sinking low into his chest, imploding. "Oh, shit, Johnny. Shit, they gave me no fucking choice."

"Who gave you no choice? Who the *fucking hell* are you talking about?"

"*The Ukrainians*. They want you gone, Johnny. You're a threat. And with you being so close to Frank and all—"

"You mean, you made a fucking *deal* with them?"

Somebody started pounding on the door. A voice, muffled, came from the other side, "Mr Calderon, are you all right in there?"

Johnny shook his head, "Ignore them, Al. Just answer the fucking question." He pushed the muzzle harder into Alfonso's forehead. The man whimpered.

"Yes," he gushed, "Yes, I made a fucking deal. What was I supposed to do? They're everywhere, Johnny. Ukrainians, Lithuanians, Russians. They're taking over the fucking world, and Frank should have realised and got out. They want control, and they don't care who the hell they squash in order to do it."

"So what did they offer you, you bastard? Let you keep this shit-hole, was that the deal?"

"Yes, exactly, Johnny. I'm sorry, I really am, I had no choice and even if I had, do you think they would have let you live? I had to say I would do it because if I didn't they would, and they'd probably come after me too. Oh, shit, Johnny, it was nothing fucking personal, it was just business. You have to see that, you have to try and—"

Johnny put his finger to his lips and stepped back. "Only business?"

Alfonso nodded, jowls wobbling.

Johnny shot him through the head.

Unfortunately for Johnny, because it was point-blank range, some of the skull fragments and bits of brain matter splashed over his jacket. He swore and spun around, angry now. "Fucking Ukrainians," he said and tore open the door.

Two bouncers stood there, together with the girl who had been giving Alfonso such a good time. All three gaped at him, probably because of the blood rather than the gun. Everything changed when Johnny shot the closest one, the blast throwing the bouncer hard against the far wall, and as he slid to the ground, the others broke into a run down the narrow, dimly lit corridor. Johnny shot the second bouncer in the head and he crumpled to the floor. The girl turned the corner, her screams disappearing with her. Johnny put the gun in his waistband, adjusted his jacket and walked back to the dance floor and out into the evening air.

Nobody stopped him. Nobody dared.

TWENTY

Chaise received the phone call early the next morning. Very early. He groped for the bedside lamp switch and peered at his mobile buzzing into life. The contact flashed as Linny's mother. Chaise groaned. Suppressing the tiny tickle of panic running through his gut, he picked up the phone and croaked, "Yes?"

"Ryan, I'm sorry," she began, voice quivering, frayed at the edges. "I didn't know who else to phone."

He rubbed his eyes, sat up and glanced at his watch. Four o'clock. "What's wrong, Brigit."

"Something ... I don't know where to start. I'm ... Ryan, *please* ..."

As the sobbing grew more pronounced, Chaise lowered his voice, trying to sound as caring as he could, "Take your time. Tell me from the beginning."

So she did. Everything. The three men who came for her, how she knocked one of them over, the gunshot, the quick getaway without knowing where to go or with whom to speak, not thinking of informing the police until two or three hours had slipped by. By then, she found herself at a friend's, drinking brandy. Then another, and before she knew it she fell asleep and now it was too late to contact anyone. "What am I supposed to do?"

"You stay there," said Ryan, swinging his legs out of bed, now fully awake. "Are you sure you weren't followed?"

"Yes, I'm sure."

"Are you *certain*, Brigit?"

"Bloody hell, they'd have needed a Formula One racing car to catch up with me."

"Well, that's good, Brigit. You've done okay. Listen, give me the address where you're staying and I'll come over."

"No, no, I'm all right. I wanted you to know but there's nothing you can do. I'm safe here, so please believe me, but the thing is, I've been thinking about it a lot – and I really can't come up with any other reason why it happened – I think they were after Linny. I could see straight away the sort of men they were. Dangerous thugs. That's why I ran off." She took a deep breath. "I believe if they want Linny, Ryan, they'll also want you."

He didn't go back to bed. How could he? So, in an effort to clear his head, he slipped into his tracksuit and went for a jog. When he passed the Clio he stopped, tempted to leave some sort of message in the grime of the bodywork. He stood and gazed for a long time before returning to his flat, anger brewing, the intrusion eating away at him. Under the shower he did his best to quell thoughts of finding the tail, grabbing his head and putting it through the windscreen of that crappy little car. Over a coffee, he managed to calm down before going to the office.

The appointment with Lomax wasn't until ten, so to kill time he trawled through the office website, trying to keep his mind occupied but with little success. He couldn't help but be disturbed by Brigit's words. Someone was after him, someone from Spain. Perhaps the guy in the Clio knew something, so Chaise decided the time had come to confront whoever the tail was and get some answers.

The door opened and Chaise glanced up and stopped, heart in his mouth. A tall young woman, hanging her coat from the nearby hanger, flashed him a look. She wore a sky blue pullover and short white skirt, with laced-up black shoes that accentuated the tan of her slim, well-muscled legs. He couldn't help but gawp, and when he noted her hard eyes, he felt the rush of blood to his cheeks and returned to his computer screen.

"You must be the new guy," she said and came over.

"Ryan," he said and took her slim, soft hand. He noted her beautiful, manicured nails, transparent varnish giving them more than a healthy glow.

"I'm one of the secretaries. Yvonne."

"Pleased to meet you."

A slight return of pressure from her hand before she flashed white, even teeth, tossed her tousled brown hair and moved over to her desk. "I hear you've been living in Spain. I've just got back from Gran Canaria. Lovely there. Have you been?"

"No. I was based in Malaga. Never really got the chance to go anywhere else. Property boom kept me busy."

"That's dead now isn't it?"

"Isn't it everywhere?" He sighed, logged-off his computer and pulled on his jacket. "Gran Canaria. I hear that's hot."

"The guys are hot." She smiled coyly, sifted through some papers. "Boyfriend didn't like it, said I was being too flirty."

"Hope it didn't spoil your time together."

She shook her head. "It's time to move on anyway. Going away with him made me see things a lot more clearly, if you know what I mean." Yvonne held his gaze. "What about you? Are you staying locally?"

"I'm living in the flat upstairs, for the moment."

A single arched, superbly sculptured eyebrow. "Until your wife joins you?"

He grinned, opened up his drawer and brought out a small, compact camera. "I have an appointment with a Mr Lomax, so I'm driving out to value one of his properties. I'll probably be with him most of the morning, I shouldn't wonder."

"Mr Lomax? Isn't he the guy who rents out to students?"

"I think that's what he said, yes."

She smiled and lowered her head. "Make sure you negotiate a low price. He's worth millions he is."

Chaise frowned. That was not an opinion he shared, given the man's scruffy appearance. "A millionaire you say?" She nodded. "He didn't strike me as one. A little eccentric, is he?"

"He fancies himself, I know that. Tried it on with me, and Cathy too. Thinks he can buy the whole bloody world." She shook her head, and Chaise noticed she was still smiling. "*Don't* give him my regards."

"I take it you don't like the man?"

"That would be an understatement. He ... never mind, you don't need the details. Just let me say he doesn't honour his commitments."

With her curious words ringing in his ears, he went out into the cold morning, unlocked his car and got in. A casual scan of the square reassured him that the Clio man was nowhere in sight, and he took his car out into the traffic and headed off in the direction of Norwich.

As Chaise stepped out of his car, Lomax came down the steps of the impressive-looking edifice he owned. He appeared changed, more agitated than before, his face taking on a hunted look, skin ashen. "Thank you for being so prompt," he said, pumping Chaise's hand.

Chaise followed him to the door, aware of Lomax's eyes constantly darting from left to right. He made no comment, focusing his attention on the job in hand. As he drew closer, Chaise realised the building wasn't so impressive after all. Tired, broken in places, former glory nothing more than a memory now, the cracked and chipped walls and steps a testament to years of neglect. Lomax too seemed to ooze fatigue, and something else. Fear, etched around his eyes, the hunted look Chaise recognised all too well, placing him on high alert. "Are you okay?"

Lomax gave a start, alarmed. "What the hell do you mean by that?"

The man's sharp, almost vicious response took Chaise by surprise and he held up his hands. "Only asking, Mr Lomax."

Lomax grunted, snapped, "I'm fine," and motioned him to follow. "Are you coming in or what?"

Chaise let the aggressive tone go. He had no time for altercations with this little man. He simply wanted the job done. Inside, take a few measurements, a handful of photographs and back to the office to get the details prepared before lunchtime. He smiled at the prospect of a light bite to eat and perhaps another chat with the lovely Yvonne.

He followed Lomax down the dark, depressing hallways, with its peeling wallpaper, threadbare carpet, and a thick, musty smell of stale sweat and urine filled his nostrils, clung to his clothes. Neglect ran deep and such places rarely sold quickly.

A steep flight of stairs on the right disappeared into the darkness above. Everywhere dark, drab paintwork contributed to the oppressive atmosphere and he noted the ceiling, streaked with yellow, which didn't help. Years of cigarette smoke stained every surface, the nicotine embedded within the very fibre of the building. To get this place up to scratch would require a lot of work.

"You say you've been having trouble renting out this place?"

Lomax rounded on him. They stood outside one of the rooms that branched off from the hallway and when Chaise peeped inside, he hated what he saw. Threadbare furniture, closed curtains, dirt-encrusted carpets. His stomach almost turned.

"I don't need your criticisms," spat Lomax, "I just need you to sell this place for me."

Chaise let out a long sigh. The man's aggressive attitude was proving too much. "Okay, but that might prove a little difficult. It's in a bit of a state, Mr Lomax."

"Don't you think I know that? I'm not an idiot, whatever your name is."

"Chaise." He reached inside his pocket and handed over one of the business cards with which the firm had supplied him.

The man's eyes grew moist and for a moment, Chaise thought he might faint. Lomax's voice, when he spoke, trembled, the sound of a man defeated, or very close to being so. His anger drained away, replaced by what sounded like despair. "I just want it out of my life.

I'm not sure for how much longer ..." He put the card, unread, into his trouser pocket. "It was my aunt's house. When she died five or six years ago, she left it to me. I have hardly touched it."

Chaise glanced to the ceiling again and ran his tongue over his teeth. He was about to speak when Lomax cut in, "Yes, I know," he said, his voice losing most of its edge, "It's filthy, isn't it. She was a smoker, sixty a day. Awful. She didn't care, not about herself, anybody, or this house. But it's a good house, big, with lots of potential. It has five bedrooms, three receptions and an attic, which could be converted. Outside, it's ... well, you'll see."

"Yes." Chaise pulled out a notebook and took some notes. He smiled. "Can you give me a few moments, to take some measurements?" Lomax nodded and Chaise went along the hallway and armed with a digital measuring device, went through each of the many rooms.

When he had finished, he found Lomax still standing in the hallway, back against the wall, eyes closed. Chaise coughed, the man's eyes sprang open, blinked, and darted this way and that, as if he did not know where he was.

"It was left to you, you say?"

"Yes. Sorry, I was ..."

"How much are you looking to get for it, Mr Lomax."

"Whatever it's worth."

"It needs a lot doing to it. Any potential buyer would probably have to spend more on it than the asking price. That's what you have to consider, if you want it to go."

"I want it to go." Lomax turned his head as if he had seen something. But when Chaise followed the man's gaze he saw nothing. "I want it gone, Mr Chaise. Out of my life. And I want it gone quickly. So tell me what the going price is for a place like this, and then halve it."

Chaise gaped. "What?"

Lomax met his gaze. "That's what I said. Halve it. I'll say it again – I want the damn place out of my life, you understand?"

The door swung open without warning and both turned as a tall, athletic-looking man came in. His hair cropped short and his body impressively filling the brown leather jacket he wore. He stopped when he saw Chaise and Lomax, their presence, by the wide-eyed look on his hard, flat face, taking him aback.

Chaise heard Lomax emit a tiny groan and when he looked he saw the man had grown even paler, if that was possible.

"What is this?" asked the stranger.

East European, Chaise guessed. Ukrainian perhaps, or Lithuanian; somewhere close.

"This is my friend," said Lomax quickly, gripping Chaise's arm as he stepped in front of him, as if shielding him from the stranger. "We're just leaving."

The stranger frowned, the beginnings of a smile developing across his thin mouth. "A friend? I see." His eyes settled on Chaise, but if the newcomer thought the challenge might unsettle him, he was wrong. Chaise held his gaze and returned a smile of his own for good measure. "Well, you will show your *friend* out because I have things to talk about, and they are important and for us alone. You were not home when I called. Your wife told me you might be here."

He stepped aside and pushed the door open wide. A gesture towards the street meant that Chaise should leave.

Chaise ignored the newcomer, turned to Lomax and said, "I'll write up the details as best I can. If you get in touch with the office, perhaps we could meet again." The hunted look in Lomax's eyes grew. Here was a man not simply afraid, but terrified.

"I'd like you to leave now."

Chaise nodded. "Well, you know where I am. I'll get it all sorted for you, and then I'll—"

"Are you deaf?" It was the Eastern European at the door. "He said for you to leave. So leave ... *now*."

Chaise sighed. He hated that. Bullies, arrogance, contempt. This newcomer was all of those things. Chaise had sensed it from the moment the man had burst through the door. It oozed from him like sweat, with almost the same smell. "Mr Lomax," he said quietly. The hunted face turned to him, and now there was something more there.

Pleading. A cry for help? Chaise lowered his voice, "If you need *anything,* then you've got my card, yeah? You understand what I'm saying? Anything."

"Hey, are you fucking deaf?"

The man strode down the hallway, agitated by something, his over-reaction, quick temper, all leading Chaise to suspect something was very wrong here. He faced the man as he drew up close, face twisted in anger, not used to being ignored. He thrust out a right forefinger to prod Chaise in the chest. "Get the fuck out of here, I said. And do it now."

Chaise took a look at the finger and smiled. It hovered perhaps a centimetre from his chest, ready for another poke. "You touch me again and I'll snap that in two."

Lomax gasped, the stranger gaped and Chaise's smile turned into a grin. He pushed past the Eastern European who seemed struck dumb, mouth opening and closing in total shock. At the door Chaise turned, nodding at Lomax who stood transfixed and ashen. "Remember what I said, Mr Lomax." Then he went out and slammed the door shut.

Back at the office, Chaise found the other secretary, Cheryl at the main desk. She handed him over a few sheets of paper almost as soon as he walked through the door.

"Where's Yvonne?"

She grinned. "All those messages came in within the last fifteen minutes, Ryan, and all from the same lady."

She arched a single eyebrow, waiting for further explanation. Chaise thanked her and went over to his desk.

"She must have phoned you at least half a dozen times," she said, a note of disappointment in her voice. "Have you had your mobile switched on?"

He frowned and pulled it out. It was dead, the battery run down. He cursed. "Damn it, no. Sorry."

"She sounded worried."

He looked at the sheaves of paper. They were all from Brigit and each call was two minutes apart from the previous one. He picked up the desk phone and punched out the number. It was out of service. He threw the receiver down and leaned back. He had no way of knowing where she was or how to get in touch. Whatever was causing her such worry must be getting a whole lot worse.

TWENTY-ONE

Johnny sat at the kitchen table, fingers wrapped around the coffee mug, staring down into the still steaming liquid. Behind him, Stanley busied himself tidying the cleaning things away, whilst his wife sat opposite, elbows on the tabletop, chin in upturned hands. "It must have been terrible for you, officer?"

Johnny nodded. He wore only his underwear; jacket, shirt and trousers tumbled around in the washing machine, the blood and brains rinsing away. He'd left the two guns in the car. He would need to remember them if things weren't to become even more complicated.

He'd rolled up an hour before, parked down the street, and watched the uniformed police officers moving from house to house. When they got to Norman's, they thumped on the door and waited. And waited. They spoke to another neighbour, who shrugged and pulled a face. Other officials milled around, taking measurements and recording findings in notebooks or on Dictaphones. They wore white coveralls and plastic gloves. One policeman peered through Norman's living room window, shook his head.

A radio crackled, and a stocky man in a grey tweed jacket stooped down in the road and prodded at something on the tarmac. Everything appeared efficient. Gunfire in a leafy suburban Wirral street was not a common occurrence, so every available piece of forensic evidence would be examined, catalogued and stored, every witness interviewed. Except for poor old Norman, of course.

Johnny took the car up to the driveway after the police left, checking nobody watched between net-curtains before he got out. He buttoned up his jacket to mask the majority of the bloodstains. When he'd knocked on the door, Stanley answered immediately, brought him in, sat him down, his wife fussing over him like a long lost son. She took one look at him, demanded he take off his clothes so she could wash them. No other questions. Both seemed so accepting, so kind.

He wasn't looking forward to killing them.

"Did you manage to find her?"

Johnny looked up. "Ah. No. Not a trace. I haven't been able to uncover a single scrap of information."

Stanley came over, drying his hands and pulled up a chair. He sat close, and he beamed, a triumphant look on his face. "I have."

Johnny stared at him, unblinking. "You have?"

"Yes. I've been doing a spot of detective work, officer." He brought out a small notebook and flicked through the pages. "I've spoken to everyone, and I've learned quite a lot about that woman."

"He's a proper little private detective, always watching those TV things. He loves Father Brown, don't you, darling? You should give him a job, Inspector."

Johnny smiled. "Yes."

"Too old for all of that, but it proved exciting. Made me feel like I was in one of those detective dramas."

"Don't watch those," said Johnny, leaning forward, "they'll give you nightmares." They all laughed, especially Johnny as the tension drained.

"Strange, but I couldn't get an answer from Norman's."

"Norman?"

"Yes, our next-door neighbour. I told you, his wife died. You went to help him when he phoned the station. I suspect that is why the police were here in such numbers, after what you said."

"Yes. Did you, er, tell them of my visit?"

Stanley sat back in his chair. "You told me it was undercover."

"So it is."

"You also told me not to say anything." A pause, added for dramatic effect. Stanley obviously relished this. "So I haven't."

Johnny grinned. "That's good Stanley. Now, tell me what you found out."

Later, he admired himself in the full-length mirror in the couple's bedroom. Not only were his clothes clean, but Mr Stanley had ironed them too. His wife was on invalidity benefits due to rheumatoid arthritis in both her hands and grew tired quickly. Poor woman, her once elegant fingers now nothing more than twisted claws. Stanley did everything, and proved bloody good. Johnny did the profile, then the twirl, pleased with the results.

At the foot of the stairs, Stanley's wife pressed a packet of sandwiches into his hand. "I know you won't be able to get much of a break, not with you being so busy. Following up all these leads." She smiled.

Johnny's heart melted at that point. How long had they been together? Forty, fifty years? They'd lived a life, done so many things. A normal life, but a good one. And now, here they were in the twilight, living out their last moments together. For how much longer would they wake up, eat breakfast and breathe in the fresh air? It was all so short, all so sad.

He knew he couldn't kill them. When they emerged from the fog of their misplaced public spirit, saw the reports on the television, realised how stupid they'd been and put two and two together, they'd inform the police. When, finally, they discovered Norman's body and their world came crashing in around them, Johnny would be on the run, his face all over the news. He needed to work fast, find Brigit, *persuade* her to reveal the whereabouts of Chaise's girlfriend and then, spring the trap. The consequences he would deal with later. He had a new determination to see it all through, whatever the outcome. Frank would have wanted it that way. He'd given him this job to do; the last job. He wasn't about to let his old friend down, despite the fact Frank was now dead.

Poor Frank. First Sarah, then this. Seeing his business dismantled by those bastards, all the years of graft for nothing, to end up shot down like a dog, with nobody there to do a damned thing to help. Fucking Ukrainians. They would pay, all of them. Somehow. And Chaise. Everything came back to him. The mess with Arthur Morgan, the deaths, everything Chaise's bloody fault. So he would pay first.

Johnny thanked them and stepped outside, checked the street before moving on.

"You can keep the car for a little longer if you want," said Stanley behind him.

Johnny stopped. "Thanks, but I don't think I'll—"

"I insist. Just drop it back tomorrow."

Johnny smiled, shook the old man's hand, went over to the car and got in. He lifted the newspaper on the passenger seat and stared at the guns. Tony's second revolver was fully loaded, and his own Smith and Wesson semiautomatic had a high-capacity magazine, with eleven bullets remaining. More than enough.

As he drove away, he caught sight of them in the mirror, waving from the doorway, Stanley's arm curled around his wife's waist, holding her close. Johnny was glad he hadn't killed them. The right thing to do, he decided, and a warm glow developed inside, causing him to smile.

In the ensuing days, smiling was to become something of an alien concept.

TWENTY-TWO

With the collection of papers in his hand, he sat down for lunch in the nearby pub. Not yet midday, few people were about, so finding a table proved easy. He chose the one in the corner, farthest from the door.

Long ago, before he'd even thought of a career in the armed forces, he'd read *Shane* and how the gunfighter always sat with his back to the wall. In those formative years, he'd developed an almost mystical image of the lone, silent warrior, drifting through life, righting wrongs, defending the weak and oppressed. Above all else, the notion of self-preservation, of being capable.

Now, all these years later he understood the wisdom of that description. Did Schaeffer know something that others did not, or had he spoken to men who had lived, and probably died, by the gun? With half a lifetime of death hanging onto his shirttails, here he was doing just that. Only he didn't have a Colt forty-five. He didn't have anything and when he saw the man from the Clio, he wished he had because the shadow must be carrying a gun. The idea troubled him but the Glock was in his flat and there was little he could do.

From the seat he'd chosen he had a clear view straight through the open entrance to the square beyond. By the door, the barmaid chalked up the specials for the day's lunchtime menu; across the street, the shadow peered into the estate agency window. Chaise sighed, put the papers down and tried to clear his mind of Brigit and Linny and why the hell her mother was trying to get hold of him so urgently. Perhaps Harper would know. Another telephone call might be necessary.

He saw the shadow turn. From that distance, the man could not see into the darkness of the pub so Chaise took the opportunity to sit back and study him. Older, perhaps late fifties, the years had taken their toll. But there was still something about him, an air of experience, certainly danger. Chaise noted the way he moved, lightly balanced on his feet; a fighter. Skilled. Despite his years, a difficult adversary. Again, he cursed himself for not bringing the Glock.

He flipped open his mobile and checked for any messages. None. He sighed, considered calling Harper, glanced up and swore.

The shadow had gone.

His appointment with the car salesroom was for two o'clock. A few minutes before then he parked the rental outside and strolled across the forecourt. The man in the blue pin-stripe strode towards him, grin set rigid on his broad face, hands clasped together. "Mr Chaise."

"Walk back inside."

The man frowned, then gave a little cry as Chaise took his arm and frogmarched him into the salesroom. He pushed the doors closed and nodded towards a nearby desk. "Sit there and tell me when you see a guy in a grey raincoat looking at the cars outside."

The man's face drained of colour, the frozen grin melting, his eyes wide with indecision. "I don't understand? A man in a grey raincoat?"

"Just do it. Sit down, shuffle some papers and make like you're talking to me about cars."

Chaise's eyes hardened when a second man came skipping down a winding staircase. Dressed in a white shirt, sleeves rolled up to his elbows, he whistled tunelessly, saw Chaise and almost tripped up. He grabbed the rail, taking in the situation at a glance. "Are you all right, Ted?"

Ted looked as if he wanted to squawk, and Chaise closed his eyes. Why couldn't people do the most simple of things? "I want something small but fast. Not too heavy on the juice, easy to handle. Two doors."

"Audi-TT," said the man on the stairs, and continued down, some of his previous self-confidence returning.

"You have one?"

"We have three. What colour."

"Silver."

The man nodded and raised an eyebrow at his colleague. "Are you sure you're okay, Ted?"

"He's fine," cut in Chaise. "I want to buy it."

Shirtsleeves moved up to the desk, frowning at Ted who remained stony silent. "We can arrange a test drive if you like. When can you come in?"

Chaise shook his head and reached inside his pocket, brought out his credit card. "I'll be back in a week. Take a deposit from this and hold the car for me until then." He handed over the card, which the salesman took between limp fingers and stared. "Take as much as you need."

"But we'll require you to—"

"I'll bring everything with me next week. Identification, references, everything." He leaned across the desk and stared at Ted. "Has he arrived?"

There was a pause before Ted blinked, realising the question was directed at him. His eyes grew wider as he looked over Chaise's shoulder and made a little whimpering sound. "Yes. Oh, shit. A grey raincoat. How—"

"You have a rear exit?"

"What the hell is this?"

Chaise turned to Shirtsleeves. "I just need to go out the back. The guy in the forecourt, the one in the raincoat? He's my girlfriend's husband. He wants to beat me up, possibly kill me. Do you understand?"

Shirtsleeves gave a gormless look, a little like Ted's. He gazed out to the forecourt and forced a smile. "I don't think he could kill anyone."

"He can. Believe me. Go and talk to him, would you? Sell him a car." Shirtsleeves frowned. Chaise pressed two twenty-pound notes into his hand. Again the stupefied look. "Just do it."

As Shirtsleeves wandered over to the entrance in something of a daze, Chaise turned again to Ted. "Now then, where is the rear exit?"

Chaise came around the side of the forecourt. Shirtsleeves was in conversation with the shadow, who appeared agitated and when he brought up his arms, Shirtsleeves retreated a few steps. Then he saw Chaise and his face lit up with relief.

The shadow turned, his hand already going for his gun. But Chaise was too quick, crossing the distance between them at a run and he hit the shadow hard across the carotid artery, sending him smashing into the nearest car. He crumpled to the ground, groaning. Chaise stooped and tore the snub-nose from the hip holster. He looked at Shirtsleeves who, ashen-faced, teetered on the brink of fainting. "You can phone the police if you like," said Chaise standing up, "but help me get this bastard into the back of my car first."

He drove out of town towards Lowestoft, making a turn down a narrow country lane, signposted for Gisleham. At a quiet, deserted spot he pulled over and got out. He checked nobody was around and opened the boot. The shadow seemed in a bad way, with blood trailing from his nostrils, his face chalk-white with purple blotches. Without a pause, Chaise took him by the lapels and heaved him into the road. He draped him over his shoulder, carried him to the other side and propped him up against a solid tree in the middle of a copse. He stepped back to have a good look. The force of the blow to his neck had almost taken the man's head off and a nasty red welt had developed across his throat. He continued breathing, however, so it did not seem he was about to expire. Reassured, Chaise used his tie to lash the shadow's hands together, returned to the back seat of the rental and rooted inside. He found the bottle, swished it around. Little more than a mouthful of water left, it would have to be enough. He crossed the road again, unscrewed the cap, and threw the contents into the shadow's face.

It had minimal effect.

Chaise went down on his haunches and picked up little stones, throwing them one at a time at the unconscious shadow. The first few brought no change, but after a dozen or so well-placed strikes on the man's forehead, he stirred. He coughed, moaned, shook his head and opened his eyes as a final stone struck him in the cheek. He growled, blinked a few times and realised his hands were tied. After a moment or two of fruitless struggling, he focused in on his assailant, recognised Chaise and fell back against the tree with a loud sigh.

"What's your name?"

A few laboured breaths, eyes closed, head lolling. "Colin."

"Colin? Pleased to meet you. I'm Ryan, but you know that already." He dangled the snub-nose from a finger stuck through the trigger guard. "Colin, I'm getting a little sick of being tailed now. I'm tired and I've got a lot to do, so I'll get straight to the point. I want you to tell me who you are and who you work for, or I'll kill you." Ryan smiled, twirled the snub-nose in best Western-roll fashion and pointed it directly towards Colin. "With your own gun."

TWENTY-THREE

The salesmen at the garage had done as expected and informed the police. Chaise's car proved easy to locate and by the time they arrived, Colin stood by the tree, rubbing his chaffed wrists. Of Chaise, there was no sign. The patrol car swung around in a tight arc, throwing up a cloud of dust and debris as it broke. Both the officers got out.

"Are you in some sort of difficulty, sir?"

Colin gave a wry smile and shook his head. "None whatsoever, officer. What seems to be the trouble?"

"We had a report, sir. Someone attacked you apparently, or at least someone answering your description. Can you confirm that for us?"

Colin shrugged. "It was nothing."

"An assault in a public place isn't *nothing*, sir," said the second officer, studying the rental car.

"Can you accompany us to the station, sir?" asked his colleague. "We'd like you to make a statement if you wouldn't mind."

Colin made a face, feeling the sweat beading on his forehead. "I don't think that's necessary, officer. I'm perfectly all right. I think there must have been some sort of mistake."

The other officer ran the flat of his hand across the bonnet of the rental. "This your car, sir?" he asked.

"No, it's my friend's. He's just gone over the way there," Colin pointed over to his right, beyond the rise. "Said he wanted to make a private phone call."

"And you're sure you are all right?"

"I'm perfectly fine, officer, as you can see."

The officer gave him a look, not believing a word Colin said. "The problem is, sir, the salesmen have lodged a complaint." He nodded towards the area Colin had indicated. "Over there, you say?"

"Yes, but there's really nothing to worry about officer. We had a little argument, but it wasn't serious."

"You were knocked down, sir. Is that what you call not *'serious'*?"

His colleague sighed. "The man at the car showrooms was told that you wanted to *kill* this other man. Then he hit you. Can you explain any of that for us?"

"No, but I can."

They all turned as Ryan Chaise appeared from over the nearby rise.

He'd phoned Brigit again; three times to be precise. Each time there had been no reply. He trawled through his brain for any memory, however small, of names, places, people they all used to know – Linny, Brigit, and him. Nothing. So, he spoke to Harper, eating the proverbial humble pie. Something was wrong, he could feel it. He telephoned and he waited, was re-routed, sent to various departments and asked the usual security questions.

At last Harper's wheeze came down the line. "I hope to Christ you're not causing trouble, Chaise."

"No, sir. I just have a small problem, that's all."

He heard Harper groan. "What is it?"

"There appears to be somebody after me, sir."

"The tail, you mean? This mysterious shadow who—"

"No, not him. This is something quite different. When I say 'after me' that is exactly what I mean, sir."

"Oh, for God's sake." Harper's voice sounded tired, but

unconcerned. Bored more than anything. "Isn't there always? I asked you to lie low."

"I have, so far."

"I don't like the sound of that, Chaise."

Chaise closed his eyes. "Sir, this is not my fault."

"It never bloody is. Just as in Spain, Chaise. You just *happened* to get involved with drug dealers." A longer pause; Harper clearly mulling over how to proceed. "Very well. So, have you any idea who it might be?"

"It's the same lot from Spain, at least I'm fairly certain. It can't be anybody else. They're over here, asking questions. They've been to see Linny's mother and now she's disappeared." Chaise took a deep breath. "This tail you put on me, he's told me quite a lot." A stony silence followed. "Would you like to tell me again why the hell you've had me followed?"

"I'm not having you followed, Chaise."

Chaise stopped and thought. Harper may have been the hardest, most unfeeling man he had ever known, but his integrity was beyond question. Almost. "Then who has?"

"Describe this person for me, if you would."

Interesting choice of words, *person*. Chaise remembered the second shadow, the back-up, the one he'd slipped away from near the Waveney River. Could there be a third, a woman perhaps? "He's an older guy, slightly built. Goes by the name of Colin."

Another pause. Chaise waited, wondering if perhaps Harper was indeed cooking up some sort of plot. "MI6."

Chaise stopped himself from laughing. "*MI6*? Are you insane? What the hell have they got to do with anything?"

"The Home Office, Chaise. It's outside their usual sphere of influence but they're paranoid that you might go out of control, start shooting people indiscriminately. So it is they who put a tail on you. I would have told you earlier, but ... well, you know how things are ..."

"The tail, this Colin character, he said it *was* you."

"He lied. You haven't ... you haven't *harmed* him, have you?"

"If you mean by that, have I killed him, then the answer is 'no'."

"Well, that's something I suppose."

"But I think the police are going to get involved, and that could interfere with what I have to do. I have to find Brigit, and I need help. She's missing and I need to find her before these bastards get to her, then Linny. You understand? I *need* your clout, sir, your influence."

"There are times when I *hate* you, Chaise."

"Yes, but can you help me?"

There was another, long drawn-out pause. "Very well, Chaise, but I want certain undertakings."

"Whatever you say, sir."

"Mm ... here's the deal. I'll make a few phone calls, talk to a few people, smooth your way a little. In return, Chaise, I want something from you."

It was Chaise's turn to remain silent. He hardly dared breathe until Harper told him exactly what the deal was.

And now, there they were. Two uniformed police officers, and poor old Colin looking sheepish. Chaise wondered if the officers knew how lucky they were to be alive still.

"Are you a Mr Ryan Chaise?" One of them read from his notebook. "You entered *Star Motors* salesroom this afternoon at approximately one-thirty and became extremely aggressive towards one of the salesmen. There followed an affray." He slapped the notebook shut. "You're under arrest, Mr Chaise. You do not have to—"

Chaise brought up his hand. In it was his mobile. "This is for you, officer."

The man frowned, looked at his colleague who shrugged. "For me?"

"Yes. Somebody wants to talk to you."

With some reluctance, the officer shuffled over and took the phone. He looked at it for a moment as if it was some sort of alien device before putting it to his ear and whispering, "Yes?"

Almost at once, he stiffened, his face drained of colour, and blubbered, "Yes, yes, sir. Of course, sir." He repeated this mantra a number of times, ending the conversation with, "Yes, sir, of course I understand, sir. At once, sir." Sweat broke out on his brow and he peered at the phone before meekly handing it back to Chaise, who spoke into the mouthpiece

"This is Ryan Chaise."

"I don't know who the bloody hell you are, nor do I want to know, but I will ask only this of you – that you do not cause me, or my constabulary any embarrassment. In other words, whatever you have to do, keep it bloody private."

"Yes, sir, thank you very much, sir, goodbye." Chaise closed his phone and grinned at the officer. He thought his impersonation of the servile sycophant had been quite effective. "And thanks to you, officer."

The policeman turned down his mouth, motioned for his colleague to get back into the patrol car and muttered, "I'll explain when we're out of here, Geoff."

Geoff didn't look convinced, but got in behind the wheel anyway, gunned the motor, and drove off.

Chaise looked askance at Colin.

"What now?"

Chaise shrugged, reached inside his jacket and pulled out Colin's gun. He sensed the man tense. "Don't worry, you're not dead yet. Harper told me he didn't send you, that it was MI6."

"That's a lie."

"That's *exactly* what he said."

"So what happens now?"

Chaise held his gaze. He brought up the gun and he saw the look, the ghastly change of expression when the victim knows with absolute certainty that life is about to end. In a blink, Chaise turned the gun around and presented it butt first.

For a moment Colin stood rigid, realising today was not his day to die and the tension went out of his shoulders. He took the gun, checked the chamber, and slipped it back into his holster. "You're an interesting man, Mr Chaise. Why aren't you going to kill me?"

"Because I need your help." Colin frowned and Chaise stepped closer, grinning. "You're going to help me sort out a little problem, Colin. It should be quite fun."

TWENTY-FOUR

They drove back to the car salesroom and picked up Colin's car. Chaise went into the reception area. Ted saw him, went white and stood up so quickly his chair toppled over. He held up both hands as if he were an extra in a very bad Western.

"Hold on there, *pardner*," said Chaise. "I've just come to cancel my deposit."

Ted didn't seem to understand, shook his head and began to shake.

"Listen, me and the hubby, we're getting on famously. So everything is all right now, you understand?" Ted nodded, but his hands were still in the air. "I've spoken with the police, and everything is all lovely and cosy. All I want to do is cancel the car."

Ted's arms came down very slowly. "That's, er, unfortunate. Are you sure I couldn't interest you in something else? A Mazda perhaps? That's not as expensive, and it's—"

"Thanks, but no." Chaise smiled and as quick as lightning snapped forward his hand in mockery of a gun, forefinger stuck out, thumb erect. Ted flinched, gave a cry and Chaise grinned. "Take it easy, *pardner*."

Ted let out a long sigh of relief and Chaise left, chuckling to himself.

Colin sat behind the wheel of the Clio and Chaise leaned in through the open passenger window. "Follow me to the car rental drop-off, then you can take me into town. I've got some business to attend to."

"What am I now, a sort of chauffeur?"

"You could say that, but it's not a lot different from what you were doing before, is it? The only difference is now we've been formally introduced."

"I'll have to call in at some stage. Check all this out."

"I understand. You've got your job to do." Chaise stood up and breathed in the air. "And I've got mine."

From his vantage point, Esteban observed the curious exchange and wondered what it all meant. He knew that the older man in the grey raincoat had been trailing Chaise since he had arrived back in the UK. He didn't know who the man was. A call to Harper would clear it up, but that was not part of his remit. He was to remain detached, do what was necessary, whenever it was necessary. For now, things appeared calm, but for how much longer he could not tell.

TWENTY-FIVE

Vladimir was not happy. He'd remained quiet so far, but the memory churned away inside and the more he kept it hidden, the worse things became. The man, the stranger, the one who had spoken to him, *nobody* spoke to him like that. Certainly not some arrogant shit, past his sell-by. He should have done something, a lesson on manners given. Annoyed at himself for not slapping the stranger for his disrespect, the man's arrogance galled Vladimir the most, such *contempt* taking him by surprise.

Now, mulling it over, he sat at the table drumming his fingers, frustration and anger mounting. He decided to take everything out on Chris Lomax.

Being a bully never presented Vladimir with any great moral dilemma. For him, to beat somebody senseless simply because they were weak, or because he wanted to, was not something he lingered upon. Cold, he allowed neither compassion nor conscience to undermine what he had to do. Such an approach kept him strong; the opposite course a sure-fire way to weakness. And Vladimir would not entertain such thoughts. Weakness was not an option.

He came through the door of the house and saw the students in the kitchen. They were laughing and joking, as always. Scrawny little shits. Vladimir hated them, hated their pale skin, their thin, stick-like arms, the way they paraded around in their underwear. Two boys and one girl. A fourth girl had moved out after Vladimir had put his hand between her legs. She'd slapped him, and he had broken her nose in return. Then the stupid slut decided to run away, telling Lomax she could not 'live in this atmosphere any longer'. What an idiot. In his homeland, women did as they were told, grateful to be fucked. He knew what they wanted and Vladimir always obliged.

The room grew silent when he entered, the atmosphere congealing. One of the boys stood up, came around the table with his hands outspread. "Please," he said, "we don't want any more trouble."

Vladimir cocked his head. "Trouble? Why do you say that? You have done something wrong?"

"Something *wrong?* What? No! No, we just don't want ..." He shrugged, forced a smile, but his lips were trembling, terrified.

Vladimir noticed a rank smell, turned up his nose and grimaced. "Don't shit your pants, you pansy. Where is Lomax?"

The boy, who couldn't have been more than nineteen, pulled a face. "He's not here. Not yet." Vladimir frowned, and the youth plunged on, "I think he's at the other house, doing his rounds. He usually gets here some time after eleven."

Vladimir reached over, hooked his fingers under the young man's underpants and pulled. "Get dressed," he breathed, and released the waistband elastic with an audible *thwack*.

The girl giggled. Vladimir shot her a sharp glance. "Make me some coffee. I'll be in the other room."

The 'other room' was a mess, magazines and bits of food strewn everywhere, half-empty glasses with what looked like white wine on the carpet, and in front of the gas fire various items of clothing. An ashtray sat brimful of cigarette stubs, and something else. Vladimir picked one up and sniffed. Cannabis. He nodded and threw it back into the bombshell of a mess and fell down on the sofa. He made a face, squirmed upwards and pulled out the television remote he had unwittingly sat on. He pressed it and the television came to life: a porn channel.

Vladimir settled back and watched whilst he waited for Chris Lomax to return.

Before five minutes had passed, the door opened and the girl came in with two cups of coffee, one in each hand. She smiled and Vladimir ran his eyes over her. Short, maybe less than five foot three, her body slim and taut and he liked what he saw. On her feet were pink slippers, with little teddy-bears on the top; she wore a man's shirt over a short black skirt. Her hair, in a modern style, cut short into the neck at the back, the sides flopping down over her cheeks. He didn't like it, preferring his women to have much longer hair. That way he could grab onto them as he took them from behind, riding them as if they were a mare.

He took the coffee. "What's your name?"

She sat down opposite him on a crumb-infested armchair. "Melanie."

He sipped at the coffee. "You like it here, Melanie?"

She shrugged. "It's okay for now. I'm looking for somewhere cheaper. Mr Lomax charges quite a lot."

Vladimir frowned, and a little alarm bell rang inside his head. "Oh? And how much is that?"

She told him and the alarm bell became very loud. Lomax charged the students something like one hundred and fifty more than had been agreed with Vladimir. The bastard was skimming off the top. "I see." He took another sip. "And what are you studying at university?"

"History and politics."

Vladimir twisted his mouth. "Whoa, that is something I know little about. Politics." He shook his head. "I prefer art."

"Really? What type of art?"

He shrugged, jutted his chin towards the television screen where a well-endowed black guy grunted between the legs of a slim girl. "That sort."

She giggled, cheeks reddening. "I see."

"How old are you?"

"Twenty-one. I'm in my second year now. I took a year out after school. Went to Turkey, visited Istanbul."

"Ah yes, I have been there. It is very ... beautiful, in a hectic sort of way."

She laughed. "Yes. You're Lithuanian aren't you?"

He nodded, took another sip. "I was born in Kaunus, which is a large port in Lithuania, but I left there when I was a little younger than you are now. My brothers, they were already here, and I decided to come and help them in their business." He leaned forward and put the empty coffee cup on the carpet. "You had a party last night?"

"Well, not a party as such, just the usual sort of Saturday night thing."

He smiled and nodded at the television. The scene had changed. A young girl was lying on a kitchen table on her back whilst a well-muscled guy lapped at her sex with his tongue. "You like to watch this sort of thing, Melanie?"

Her cheeks turned an even deeper shade of red, "Christ, no. Well ... not really." She giggled, finished her coffee, crossed her legs. Her skirt slid up her thigh. She didn't seem to notice and she turned to study the television. "It's for the boys really, but ..."

"But ... you like it?"

She looked at him. "It turns the boys on."

"And that's the part you like, yes? Them being turned on?" She didn't answer, and he smiled. "Ah." He reached inside his leather jacket and pulled out a packet of cigarettes. He offered her one and she took it, coming as far forward as she could on the chair without falling off. He flicked open his lighter and lit the cigarette for her, then his own. "So, what do the boys do when this is on?"

Melanie blew out a stream of smoke and shook her head. Her grin now a permanent fixture. "You know, the usual stuff." She looked at the screen. "But not like that. I mean, look at that guy. Shit."

"You like guys like that?"

She put her hand over her mouth and gasped whilst she held her cigarette up high, "God, I don't know."

"You don't know? You must *know* Melanie. You fuck these boys?"

"*My God,* how can you ask that?"

He laughed, more at the colour of her face than anything else. It was bright red now, glowing. If he put his hand against her skin, he felt sure he would burn himself. "How? That's easy, I just have." He flicked ash into the over-full ashtray. "So tell me. You fuck them both?"

She let her hand drop from her mouth and took a long pull on her cigarette. "Usually."

Her mood had changed, more brazen, confident; he liked that. He also noticed her cheeks grew a little less red. "So, you fuck them both at the same time, or separately?"

"Both at once."

"You prefer it that way?"

"They're young, not men. They get very *eager.* It turns them on, watching each other fuck me. Makes them do it more than once. The third or fourth time usually lasts longer."

He nodded, appreciating what she'd said. "And you like that?" She nodded, holding his gaze. "It would be different if you had a man? A *real* man. Someone who could fuck you all night long, pleasure you, not just with his cock? " He motioned towards the television. "Like him?"

"God, yes. That would be—"

The front door opened and Vladimir instantly snapped his head around and stood up. He smiled down at her. "Back to business. We must talk again, Melanie. And then, I can show you what a *real* man could do." He stroked her cheek and she tilted her head, pressing her skin against his fingers. He smiled again and went out into the hallway.

Chris Lomax had woken up early and left his wife sleeping whilst he went downstairs and made coffee. He hadn't slept well, the stress of the last few days taking its toll. The discoveries he had unearthed sent him into virtual apoplexy, and the knee-jerk reaction was to sell the house. Now, Vladimir had wind of it, and that Chaise character hadn't made things any better. It was a bloody mess and he could see no way out.

Except for one tiny light of hope.

Chaise had done something that Chris had never believed possible. He had threatened Vladimir, and the Lithuanian had not reacted. Was it through fear? If so, perhaps Chaise could offer some sort of escape route and not only through selling the damned house.

The more he considered this option, the more he realised just how stupid it was. Nobody in their right mind would stand up to Vladimir and his brothers. They had Norwich sealed up tighter than an Arctic winter, and they were vicious, calculating killers. Chris had got himself in deep, and he'd been an idiot to even attempt to cross them.

He looked up as Marianne came in, dressed in a see-through dressing gown, dishevelled hair hanging down to her shoulders. She looked amazing, even when she yawned loud and wide. She smacked her lips and went over to the window where the kettle stood, still warm. "You could have made me one."

"I thought you were asleep."

"I was." She yawned again, held onto the worktop and shook her head. "That was some night. I *need* coffee."

Chris gnawed at his lip and finished off his own cup. "I'm going over to check the flats. I've been to see an estate agent named Chaise who works in Beccles. He seems to think he can sell one of the buildings for me."

"He must be a miracle worker."

"Well, whatever he is, he seems to be full of confidence. Not the sort of guy you'd want to mess with. Anyway, I'll be gone most of the morning."

She turned. The sunlight from the window played around with her dressing gown, revealing her breasts with the nipples so brown, prominent. "I'm going back to bed. Don't disturb me when you get back."

"Quite a night you said?"

She smiled, closed her eyes, and let out a low sigh. "God, I'll say."

The lump in his throat almost cut off his windpipe. "Will you be going out again tonight?"

"I hope so," she said, looking at him. "That's why I need sleep this afternoon. I doubt I'll be getting much later on."

He stood up and went out, not giving her another glance.

During the car journey, he tried to keep the images of Marianne and Vladimir out of his head. As soon as they had met, the sparks had flown, and within a day, Vladimir had her in his bed. Truth be told, he'd had her everywhere. Kitchen, hallway, bathroom, on the stairs. Lomax knew it; she'd told him. What was he supposed to do, or even say? Vladimir muscled in, made the threats, the promises. All Lomax need do was give him fifty percent of the monthly rentals. That was all. Lomax objected and they took him down an alleyway and hit him several times. Mikhail, the older brother and as big as an ox did most of the punching, whilst Vladimir stood back and smoked a cigarette, laughing. Lomax remembered the blows, the humiliation as he dropped to his knees, blood leaking from his nose and mouth, whimpering like a baby.

Later, when he'd come home in the afternoon and heard Marianne moaning whilst Vladimir made love to her on their bed, the humiliation increased. What could he do? The cuts and bruises still hurt.

Everything still hurt.

He took the steps two at a time and went through the front door. Music played from the kitchen, so the kids were awake. The place stank of smoke, with a tang of dope at the edges. He'd have to bawl them out about that. He strode down the hallway in a determined manner, but when Vladimir came out of the front room, Lomax's bowels nearly evacuated themselves. He put his hand out against the wall to prevent himself from falling as his legs turned to rubber.

Vladimir smiled and lit another cigarette, blowing smoke. "Good morning, Christopher. Good to see you. Are you well?"

Lomax gave a tiny grunt.

"Good. I thought I'd call around, see how things are." He smiled, sending another blast of smoke into Lomax's face. "I think you and I need to have a little chat, don't you?"

At that point, Lomax could think of nothing else but how he was going to keep himself alive over the course of the next few hours.

TWENTY-SIX

They found a small, intimate bar in Beccles' town square and Chaise brought the drinks over and put them on the table. He sat down, took a sip from his glass of beer, and sat back to study Colin as he too drank. "Is your name really Colin?"

A thin smile. "Yes. I don't feel the need to use an alias. Never have."

"Never have? You've been in this business for quite some time, then?"

Colin shrugged. "You could say that. I joined the army back in sixty-eight. Junior Leaders, as it was called then." He laughed. "A bloody joke that was. Junior *thugs* it should have been."

"Is that what you were? A thug?"

Colin raised an eyebrow. "What is this, Sixty Questions?"

Chaise turned down the corners of his mouth and took another sip. "I like to know who I'm working with, that's all. If you don't want to tell me, that's fine."

A silence fell. Colin seemed to mull things over as he chewed the inside of his cheek. "Very well," he said after a long pause. "After three years I was summoned to undergo some aptitude tests. Some sergeant major had seen me out in the firing-range and made some complimentary noises to the staff officers. Less than a month later they transferred me to the Coldstream Guards. I was with them for another six years, became a sniper. I was never a thug, but I was a bloody good shot."

Chaise crossed his arms and studied the man across the other side of the table, a grudging respect developing. There were not many people in the bar, a few office workers, and a low hum of conversations. No one paid them any mind. "So how did you get into our game?"

"The same as we all do, I suppose. Men in suits approached me. My company major ordered me into his office one morning. I thought it was to do with my discharge, what I would do in civvy street. There was another guy there, very dapper, dark suit, like a business gent. He was all smiles, asked me to sit down, relax. The major left the room, and then I was made an offer."

"MI6?"

"It was called DI6 in those days. Before we all became politically correct, all open doors and polished grins. But it was the same thing, always has been. I'd served in Aden for two years, the arsehole of the world back then, and I had come to somebody's notice." He blew out his cheeks. "It's all a long time ago, Mr Chaise. I retired in nineteen eighty-seven. Or, a little more accurately, *they* retired *me*." He shook his head and took a large mouthful of his beer. He lifted the glass up to the light. "Nice pint."

"It's called *Gone Fishing*. One of the best of the local ales, I'm reliably informed." Chaise leaned forward and the tension escalated, an invisible electrical charge. "You told me what Harper said, about you working for MI6 was a lie."

"I did?"

"You know full well. So which is it, Colin? Are *you* lying, or was he?"

"Our business is full of deceit, Mr Chaise. You know that better than anyone."

Chaise nodded. "I guess so." He sat back, gave the room another quick scan. A big guy in a suit two sizes too small threw his head back and roared with laughter. The slimmer guy on the stool next to him looked crestfallen. Chaise took a drink. "So, if they *retired* you, what are you doing here?"

"I shot a UN delegate, simply put." Chaise raised his eyebrows, and Colin smiled. "By accident. I hit the wrong guy, and my superiors thought I'd lost my edge. I hadn't. The whole thing was a bloody farce. I was supposed to be on low-key protection duty, keeping an eye on a guy from Israel. Mossad were there of course, but they weren't supposed to carry firearms whilst in the UK, even though we all knew they did. Well, it was dark and it was late, and there was a party in a London hotel. Top class, penthouse. I saw this guy going in, and I knew, as we do." Chaise grunted. The infamous sixth sense, an early warning system for danger. "I followed him, but I wasn't quick enough. He went through the door like a banshee and nobody stood a chance. By the time I came in after him, he'd killed the Israeli guards and was about to do the same for the delegate when I shot him. Unfortunately," he raised his glass, "I didn't do it quite as well as I should, and the bullet went through him and into the delegate." He drained the beer and put the glass down very gently onto the table. "It was a fucking mess. All over the papers, the TV, questions asked in the House. There were plans for a documentary on ITV about it but then Gibraltar hit the airwaves and my little escapade was all but forgotten."

"*Death on the Rock*? I remember it. I was nothing more than a snotty-nosed kid at the time, but I've read about it since."

"Well, that little debacle proved fortuitous. A smokescreen, enabling my department to brush it all under the carpet. Apart from me, of course. They could have crucified me, Mr Chaise. Instead, they pensioned me off and sent me away with my tail between my legs, after I'd signed a pile of papers stating I acted independently, was solely responsible, and no government department had any prior knowledge of my actions. If I so much as breathed in the direction of the media, I'd be in Wandsworth prison before I could spit."

"They trussed you up nice and tightly, Colin. Lovely people we work for."

"By the nineties, I was living a normal life, signing on at the Job Centre, finally taking a little job as a school caretaker. I kept up my shooting, joined a club. The laws changed, of course. Strict as hell, tighter than a camel's backside, but I had all the papers, everything legal. I would shoot four or five times a week. I've never lost it."

"So what did they do? Call you in every now and then, when a job needed doing?"

"Something like that. They would contact me and I would do what was required. Nothing flamboyant, just in and out. Quick as you like. I killed people, Mr Chaise. Anyone they ordered me to. I'm not proud of that, but any choices I may have had, left me when I shot that Israeli. Simply put, killing is what I do best. Like you."

Ryan Chaise nodded and drank down his beer. He smacked his lips. "So, what's your job now, Colin? To kill me?"

"To *protect* you, Mr Chaise. Watch your back. There are people who want you dead. I don't know why, I haven't asked. I never do."

"They're paying you?"

"Of course. I don't do this for love of Queen and country. Fifty-thousand up front, with another hundred when the job is done."

Chaise whistled. "Jesus. That's more than I could earn in three – no, *four* years!" He shook his head, rolling the pint glass between his palms. "When the job is done ... that makes me a little nervous, Colin. It's a little too vague, all of that, because even I don't know when *the job* will be done. In fact, to be honest, I don't even know what 'the job' is."

"You and me both, Mr Chaise."

"So, you'll be around until ... until whenever. I don't think I like that, Colin. I work alone – when I used to work. Like you, I thought all of that was behind me. Gone."

"But then you crossed the line, Mr Chaise, didn't you? You killed one of their own over in Spain."

"They sent an operative to keep an eye on me, a little like you in many ways. But he went too far, tried strong-arm tactics, attempted to force my girlfriend to ..." He shrugged. "I've only ever killed those who deserved it, Colin. I'm not an assassin."

"Really? Is that what you think I am, Mr Chaise? A stone-cold killer?"

"Something like that."

"Well, I might be. All I know is, when this assignment is over, I'm gone. Buy a little house in Burgundy. Live a life, drink wine in the evenings, read. I'm almost sixty, Mr Chaise. It's time to close the book."

Chaise nodded, "One hundred and fifty thousand is a hell of a lot for a bit of babysitting, Colin. You certain they haven't given you something more to do?"

"Not as far as I'm aware, Mr Chaise."

"No, not as far as you're aware, like you not working for MI6?" He smiled, "Still, you're about to close the book, as you say." Chaise leaned forward and picked up Colin's empty glass. "I'll get us another, then perhaps we can begin the final chapter."

He went over to the counter and caught the barman's eye. As the young man pulled the drinks, Chaise looked over his shoulder and studied the mysterious, downtrodden Colin. He had no misconceptions. The man was lying, of that he had no doubt. Closing the book could mean a bullet in the back of the head. All Chaise had to make sure of was the bullet was his, and the head belonged to Colin.

TWENTY-SEVEN

After he'd seen Colin back to his hotel, Chaise took the Clio and drove to his flat above the estate agency. He made himself a cup of coffee and took it into the sitting room. It was only as he was about to sit that he saw the single sheaf of folded paper, which had been slid under his door. He sighed and thought he must be getting old.

It was a handwritten note with a telephone number and a signature. Marianne Lomax. Chaise frowned, pulled out his mobile and punched out the number.

She answered on the second ring. The sound of a street, motor cars, someone laughing in the background. "Mrs Lomax?"

"Is that you, Mr Chaise?" Her voice laced with fear, her breathing laboured. "I'm sorry I left the note, Mr Chaise, but I needed to get in touch. Christopher told me you'd been very kind to him." She gave an awkward sounding laugh. "I thought you'd never phone."

"How did you know where I lived?"

"What? Oh, I went to your office. They told me. Sorry, I'm not ..." More noise, a much larger engine sound. The squeal of a girl raised laughter. Marianne Lomax had to shout. "Sorry, it's a bus. Wait."

He heard her feet clacking across a road or a pavement. The sounds receded, so too the voices. "I'm sorry. Too much traffic. Listen, I need to speak to you."

"Is there something wrong? Tell me."

"I can't. Not here. I'm outside the bus station. Can I meet you?"

"You're *here*, in Beccles?"

"I have to see you, Mr Chaise. Please. I'll be five minutes."

That was a good estimation of the time needed to walk from the station to his flat. But Chaise wasn't about to wait. He went to his bedroom, took out the Walther, checked it and put it into his waistband. He pulled on his coat as he ran down the stairs.

It was a little after nine. Chaise crossed the street, went down the passageway next to the cake shop and dipped out of sight. His breath steamed, but nobody could see that. From here, he had a good view of the market square, the lights from the estate agency illuminating any approach.

She came around the corner, edgy, looking constantly over her shoulder. Chaise thought of the second shadow, knowing he was somewhere close, watching every move. It wasn't the shadow that concerned him right then.

It was Marianne.

He could see she was nervous, even from the distance of twenty or so paces separating them both. She pulled the collar of her coat closer. She wore a knee-length white raincoat, black boots and a dapple coloured shoulder bag. Raven hair cut short, hanging loose; slim, elegant, she attracted some admiring glances from two men who strolled past, talking and laughing loudly. She took no notice and pressed Chaise's doorbell.

A car came around the corner, travelling slowly. It crawled past and Chaise noted three shadowy figures inside. His hand crept towards the gun.

Marianne watched the car glide by, and she pressed the bell again and again. She might have been about to pound on the door, but the car accelerated and Chaise saw her shoulders relax. She waited before stepping back to look up to his window. She flipped open her mobile as he strode across the square and moved up behind her. He took her by the elbow, eased open the door and pushed her into the small, cramped entrance hall.

She twisted in his grip as he leaned back against the door to close it. "Jesus," she said.

"Who was in the car?"

There was barely room to move, and the stairs went straight up behind them at a steep angle, but Chaise wasn't going anywhere. Not yet.

She shook her head. "I'm not sure ..." Her hand shook as she pulled open her shoulder bag and fished out a carton of Marlboro.

"You're being followed?"

She tried several times to light up the tiny white Bic, but her hand trembled so much she couldn't do it. Ryan reached out, took it from her slim fingers, and ignited the flame. She leaned forward, cupped his hands, and took in the smoke. "Thanks." This close he had a good view of her smooth skin, the almond eyes, the full lips. She smiled, but when she did those same lovely lips quivered.

He turned the deadlock and slipped on the chain. "After you."

She went up the stairs and he tried not to gawp, but her backside pressed hard against the material of her coat and swung like a pendulum. He wondered how a weasel like Chris could keep a woman like her. Perhaps it was his bank account. He cursed himself for being so cynical and followed her into the flat. He left her standing in the middle of the room and crossed to the window. "Turn off the light, would you?"

"Do what?"

"The light." He motioned to the switch by the doorway. "I want to check the street."

She did so, and Chaise eased back a tiny gap in the curtain. He scanned every angle of the market square, checking for anything unusual or out of place. Satisfied, he turned around. "Thanks. You can put it back on."

Without hesitation, she did so, and drew on her cigarette, the smoke curling around those slender, elegant and manicured fingers. Chaise moved over to her, threw his coat across the armchair and smiled. He helped take off her coat and hung it from a hook behind the door. "Would you like a drink?"

Marianne blew out a stream of smoke and nodded. As he went to get the drinks, she sat down on the sofa.

"I only have brandy." He handed her a thick glass filled with a good measure of Courvoisier. As she took a drink, he settled a saucer down on the arm of the seat. "For the ash," he said and slumped into the armchair opposite.

She raised her glass. "Aren't you having one?"

"Just did, not twenty minutes ago."

Even here, in the safety of the flat, she seemed on edge, the cigarette waggling in her nerve-struck fingers. The glass clinked on her teeth as she drank and a thin glaze of sweat shone across her forehead.

Chaise waited, not wanting to force the moment. When she was ready, she would speak.

At last, she stubbed out her cigarette and stared directly towards him. "Chris is dead."

He blinked, the shock of her words stinging him like a slap. It took him a second or two to find his voice. "He's ... when?"

She shrugged. "This morning. I got a call, from the police. They'd found him on some wasteland in Diss. He'd been beaten to death." Her eyes flickered as they closed.

He shot forward, catching the glass before it smashed on the floor, and gently eased her back on the sofa. Her face drained of colour, taking on the pallor of a wax doll. She'd fainted. He adjusted her blouse collar, checked her pulse and went into the kitchen at a run.

When he came back with a damp cloth, she was still flat out, her breathing ragged. He got down on his knees beside her to dab away the sweat from her face. Little by little, the colour returned to her cheeks and when she opened her eyes, they shone bright and alert. She sat up, startled. "Christ, what the hell—"

"Take it easy," he said and lifted the glass. "I'll get you another."

"No," she said, voice sharp, and she grabbed at his hand. "I'm driving."

"Not tonight, you're not." She frowned at him. "You're staying here. Don't worry, the bed sheets are clean." He quickly held up his hand and grinned. "I'll take the couch."

TWENTY-EIGHT

It was almost six-thirty when Chaise heard Marianne getting out of bed, yawning, padding into the bathroom. The shower went on whilst he busied himself preparing coffee, together with bacon and eggs. By the time the fourth piece of toast had popped up she came into the sitting room, covered in his white bathrobe, rubbing her jet black hair with another towel, and she grinned. "Good morning."

"Did you sleep well?"

She nodded and walked over to the little glass-topped dining table, positioned under the window, and sat down. She looked out through the net curtains to the market square below. "It looks cold," she said in a faraway voice.

He put the plate down in front of her, placing the cafetière next to it. "If you're not feeling up to a full English, I quite understand."

"No, no, this is lovely." She bit down on a piece of buttered toast and leaned her face on her other hand. "I can't thank you enough for doing all this."

He sat opposite her and poured himself coffee. "You don't have to tell me anything you don't want to, Marianne. You can take as much time as you need."

As he watched her play around with the yolk of her egg, he

attacked his own. They ate in silence, the only sound other than the clink of cutlery against crockery the occasional car passing below.

The breakfast finished, Chaise pushed his empty plate away and studied her. Her own food had barely diminished. "I'm sorry," she said, shook her head and slurped at her coffee. "I'm not that hungry."

"That's okay. Listen, Marianne, there's one thing you can do for me before we go any further."

Her head came up, eyes wide, a ridge of fear forming underneath. "What?"

"Stop saying you're sorry all the time." He laughed as she blew out a loud sigh of relief. "Listen, as I say, you take your time, but I'm not exactly sure what it is you want from me."

Nodding, she finished her coffee and pulled out her cigarettes from the robe. This time when she lit one, her hand was steady. As she took in the first pull, her face took on a concerned look. "Christ, I hope you don't mind me smoking. I never asked, I'm so—"

He arched an eyebrow, then she laughed, and the tension was broken. "I don't mind at all," he said. "I've had a lot more important things to deal with than cigarette smoke."

She brushed a lock of hair from her face. "I honestly don't know why I came to see you. I guess because I've got nowhere else to go."

"The police perhaps?"

She gaped at him as if he'd said the most outrageous thing ever. "Dear God, *no*. If they knew that, they'd kill me."

"'They'? Who exactly are 'they'?"

"I'll need ..." She took another pull from the cigarette, turned her head and blew the smoke against the windowpane. "It was something Chris said, only just yesterday. He said he'd met you, over at one of his houses."

"Yes, he did. He was looking to put it on the market."

"Well, afterwards he came home and told me more about you." Chaise raised that eyebrow again. "He told me what had happened, how you'd come up against Vladimir."

"Ah ... *him*. Nothing major. The guy's got a bit of an attitude, that's all."

She blew out her cheeks. "An attitude? That's something of an understatement." She carefully stubbed out her cigarette against the side of her plate, brought out a tissue to wipe away the ash. She did this very methodically, with a good deal of concentration. Chaise waited, mesmerised by her long fingers, the tapered nails, her elegance. In another place, at another time … an image of Linny loomed up in his mind and he shifted uncomfortably in his chair.

"Do you know him well, this Vladimir character?"

"Christ." She pulled out her cigarettes and fumbled around for another one. He noted that the tremble had returned. "Know him? Yes, you could say that." She put the hand with the cigarette against her chin and looked at him. "I may as well tell you the whole damned, thing, Mr Chaise. Chris said he'd sensed something about you, a kind of strength. The way you had not been intimidated by Vlad ... and that you said that if he ever needed anything ... so ..."

"What exactly had he sensed about me?"

"He said you reminded him of somebody he'd met years ago. Chris may have not looked much, but he'd been around. He knew a lot about a lot of things, if you understand me. He'd travelled, all over the Far East, South and North America. It was there he met this guy. He told me. He was in a park, and there was some sort of political rally going on. Anyway, Chris was on a bench, eating a packet of crisps or something – chips, as they call them over there – and this guy in a dark suit and sunglasses came up to him. He took the glasses off and looked at Chris and said, 'I want you out of this park, *now*'." She shook her head and inhaled some smoke. "He may not be the toughest guy around, but he's bloody argumentative is Chris. But not with this guy. Chris said there was something about him, a menace, and he didn't argue, didn't even speak. He just got up and left." She nodded. "He said you were the same. You have a presence, he said. And being here, like this, I can sense that too."

Chaise nodded. "That still doesn't explain what it is you think I can do for you."

Another stream of smoke as she reached out and picked up the cafetière, poured herself a second cup. "I think I know who killed Chris."

Her words hung in the air for a long time before Chaise said, "How can you possibly know that, unless you were there when it happened."

"I wasn't. But I know Vlad, and I know what he's capable of. He killed Chris, I'm sure of it. Either him or his ox of a brother." She shuddered. "Mikhail. A horrible, horrible man. The police told me ..." She put down her cup and held onto it as the cigarette hand went to her mouth. It quivered like the aftershock from a minor earthquake. "They didn't tell me very much, but they said ... his head ..." She put her face into her hand and for the first time, he saw her cry. Apart from the obvious terror she must have felt, she'd shown little in the way of emotion for the loss of her husband.

"I don't need the details," Chaise said quietly. He leaned forward, brought out a paper tissue from his pocket and put it in her hand. "Listen, Marianne, let's just leave it for now, yes? It's too soon for you to be—"

"No," she said and dabbed at her eyes with the tissue, balled up in her fist. "No, I need to tell you. I'll be okay."

He nodded, sat back and waited.

She smoked, one leg jerking up and down quickly. "Vlad and I, we are lovers. It all happened very fast, not long after Chris introduced us. He needed some cheap labour to work on his flats, and Vlad was the guy he found. Well, when Chris brought him round to the house, he swept me off my feet. His smile, his easy manner. I was charmed I suppose. I was in a loveless marriage, and my needs were not being *satisfied* ... Chris and I, we haven't ... you know ... we haven't. Well, then he meets these Eastern Europeans, employs them to do some odd jobs in the houses he owns and rents out to the students. They work hard, and they're cheap. He even gives them a free room, in return for their labour. Well, it all seemed to be going okay until Vladimir tells Chris that all those guys, they work for him. But he will cut a deal. The deal ... Jesus ..." She took a pull on her cigarette. "The 'deal' was that they would carry on working, but that Chris had to pay Vlad fifty percent of his rental takings, each month. Can you imagine? Chris, naturally, wasn't having any of it. I remember it. We were in the kitchen, talking, and Vlad was smiling at me and I couldn't take my eyes off him. Chris was livid, but then Mikhail came in, and everything changed. That man, he's worse than an animal. He threatened Chris, told him all of his houses would be burnt down before the week was out if he didn't agree to what Vlad had proposed. And if Chris went to the police, he'd find me hanging from one of the bedroom windows. Nice guy, our Mikhail."

"Sounds like a barrel of laughs."

"Oh, he was. And it gets worse. Vladimir comes onto me really strong and idiot that I am, I feel ... flattered. He asks me out, and I accept. Chris didn't know at first, but a few weeks later he found out. By then Vlad and I were lovers, and it was ... well, he was *very* enthusiastic, let's put it that way. We'd meet up four or five evenings a week and we'd make love three or four times every night! He just couldn't get enough, and neither could I. He was insatiable, and I loved it. Of course, I'm under no illusions. I'm forty-three, how much longer is he going to want me? I already know he's eyeing up the students in the flats. But, no matter what, I simply can't stop. I have to have him."

"You're in love with him?"

She looked at the end of her cigarette, thought for a long time. "I don't think it's love. More lust, Mr Chaise. I'm 'in lust' with him. I know he'll leave me one day, perhaps soon. But for the moment, I'm content. Or should I say, I *was* content. Because the idea of him being responsible for Chris's death, that's turned my stomach, and I can't anymore. I won't. You understand? *I won't.*"

"But you don't actually know, do you?" She frowned. "You say you won't, but if he comes onto you again, you know you won't be able to resist. And then what? You'll forget about him murdering Chris? And how do you know he did? What if you're wrong, what then?"

"I'm fairly convinced."

"Proof, Marianne. That's the only thing that will stand up in a court of law, and you haven't got any."

"That's what I want you to do. Find the proof. Get to the bottom of it, find something that we can use to bring them to book."

"I'm not a private detective, Marianne. I wouldn't have the first idea where to start."

Her eyes filled up and she stabbed out her cigarette into the middle of her untouched egg. "So what am I supposed to do? Just sit back and let them get away with it, whilst Vladimir fucks me stupid?" She shook her head. "I'm not sure I can do that anymore, not knowing he killed Chris. So what am I supposed to do?"

"You could let the police do their job."

"Have you any idea how pathetic that sounds? It's fucking nonsense, Mr Chaise, to think the police can do anything. Vlad and Mikhail, they've got Norwich all sewn up. They control it, and they control the police too."

"I didn't know that. Sorry."

"They're gangsters. Drug dealers, pimps, prostitutes. They do it all. And they're vicious and ruthless and they'll cut down anyone who gets in their way. I went to a dinner party once, not nine months ago. I was Vlad's 'prize trophy', hanging on his arm. Grinning like a fucking ape he was. And do you know who was there?" Chaise shook his head and watched her put another cigarette between her lips. She lit it, blew out the smoke. "The fucking Assistant Chief Constable. Can you imagine?"

"So they're well connected."

"More than that. They've got dirt on anyone and everyone. And they'll spill it. That's the thing, they'll spill the whole lot and everyone knows it. So they keep their mouths shut and their eyes closed. In the meantime, the little people like Chris, are simply swept away. And now you're telling me there's nothing we can do."

"I never said there was *nothing*. Perhaps ..." He shrugged. "I'll think about it, Marianne, I promise. But if I don't have anything to go on, no clues or leads ..."

"I'm sure they're using the house. The one Chris took you to see."

"Using it in what way?"

"I don't know, but Vlad started getting agitated when he found out

Chris wanted to sell it. I think he's got plans for it, but I don't know what they might be."

"It's a starting point." He smiled, making it as easy as he could, despite not feeling very comfortable with anything she had said. Mixing it with gangsters would not sit very comfortably with his controllers down in London. "I'll go and have a look, see if there is anything going on, talk to some people."

She reached out and took his hand. "I don't want you to do anything risky, Mr Chaise. Don't put yourself in danger."

"Marianne, I'm a big boy. I can look after myself. And it's 'Ryan', not 'Mr Chaise'."

"Sorry."

They looked at each other and they both laughed.

Their laughter, however, held little humour.

TWENTY-NINE

He left Marianne in the flat and went round to Colin's hotel. He was not there. Chaise kicked his heels and stared up at the sky. It looked like rain. He could have done with the Clio. Where the bloody hell had he gone? Grumbling, he stuffed his hands in his pockets and went back to the office to let them know his plans.

At the corner, he thought he saw the same car that had cruised by the night before, but he couldn't be sure. Nighttime made recognising colours difficult, and he hadn't clocked the registration. It stood empty, parked a little way towards the end of the square, so he memorised the number before dipping his head under the estate agency entrance.

Yet another girl sat at reception. She hammered away at the keyboard, a pair of headphones clamped to her head, and flashed him a smile as he entered. She pulled off the phones. "Can I help you?"

"I work here."

She gave an embarrassed giggle and tossed her short-bobbed blonde hair. "Sorry," she said, her voice shrill. Young, no more than twenty, looking elegant in a white blouse, blue-spotted cravat and navy blue skirt. The perfect welcoming committee for any prospective customer. "You must be Mr Chaise?"

"I am. Could I ask you to phone a few numbers for me, and then patch them through if you get any replies?"

"Certainly." She beamed as he reached across, tore a Post-It from the pad and, using her pen, scribbled down some numbers. He passed it over. Her hands were long and slender, without a blemish.

He went to the other side of the long, narrow office and filled the kettle. He sat down behind his desk and switched on the computer, then gazed at the far wall, the rows of properties for sale and waited for the kettle to boil, his mind a blank. The computer came to life and he trawled through a further list of houses, trying to keep his mind off the fact that Marianne Lomax was just above him, smooching about in his flat, sitting in his bathrobe, limbs long and svelte.

Thoughts of Linny played around at the edges. Unconsciously he brought out his mobile and flipped it open. No messages. He sighed, rubbed his chin and went back to studying the screen.

The kettle came to the boil at the same time as his phone rang. He grabbed it a little too urgently and it nearly spilled out of his hand. He caught it before it fell, and breathed, "Yes?"

It was her, the secretary. He realised he hadn't asked her name, but before he could she said, "I have a Mr Harper on line one, Mr Chaise."

Chaise closed his eyes and waited for the line to connect.

"Ryan. Good of you to get your secretary to phone. How's Colin?"

"He's fine." Chaise didn't open his eyes.

"Nothing untoward has happened I trust? Nothing that might tarnish your burgeoning relationship?"

"No. Nothing at all."

"Glad to hear it. I don't want Home Office getting upset. Is everything else all right? It's always a pleasure to hear your voice, Ryan. Is it something serious?"

"I'm not sure."

"Not sure? I don't like the sound of that, Ryan. I do hope you are not meddling in things you shouldn't."

"I need you to run a number for me. Can you do that?"

"*Run a number*? For Christ's sake, Chaise, this isn't *The Rockford*

Files. I'm not your paid lackey, or your friend in the know! Besides, my department does not have the means to—"

"Just this once. I won't ask again." Chaise opened his eyes, "I promise."

"Pff ... is that supposed to make me feel more confident? Your promise?" A sharp breath. "If this is the precursor to any kind of trouble, Chaise, then I'm—"

"There won't be any trouble." He repeated the registration of the car he'd seen. "As quick as you can, dearest love," and he put the phone down.

He sauntered over to the receptionist, who was back in listening mode. She stopped again and pulled down the headphones. "I'm going out," he said. "If Mr Harper calls back, send me what he says on my mobile."

"You're going to make some viewings?"

"You could say that."

Outside, the cold bit into his face, and a slight sleet fell. Winter was set deep now and for a moment a vision of Spain filled his head before he zipped up his leather jacket and strolled around to the bus station. He waited for over ten minutes before a bus to Norwich arrived. He got on, paid the fare, found a seat towards the rear, and peered through the grime of the window.

When the bus drove past the car, he spotted a man leaning against the bonnet. A squat-looking individual wearing a thick donkey jacket, shivering and blowing breath into the hands cupped around his face.

Chaise eased himself back into his seat having mentally filed away the man's features. He blew out a long sigh. Angered at the way Chaise had stood up to Vladimir and perhaps wishing to seek some sort of retribution, he and his brother must have tracked him down after *persuading* Chris Lomax to give up his address. He really should warn Marianne, tell her to stay indoors, well away from the windows and not answer the door to anyone. He toyed with the idea of phoning his flat to tell her but decided to send her a text instead in case she was resting. When he got back, he'd have to make more permanent arrangements in order to keep her safe.

The bus bumped over some temporary road works, jarring his back. He hated public transport but had little choice with Colin and the Clio not available. It would be half an hour, perhaps more, before he made Norwich, then a taxi ride to where he had to go. He had a long day ahead.

He sank down, pulled up his collar, closed his eyes and slept.

Chaise remembered the address from the last time he'd met with Chris Lomax. The taxi pulled in just around the corner, just as Chaise had instructed. "I'll be about ten, fifteen minutes."

"It'll cost you," said the driver, a massive block of lard of a man who sported what he obviously thought was a classy looking fedora.

"Now why isn't that a surprise?"

Chaise got out and checked the street before setting off at a fairly brisk pace.

It was a quiet street, several cars parked up on both sides but with little sign of life. He went up to the door of the old, dilapidated house and looked for a doorbell. As there wasn't one, he tried rapping at the rusty knocker, which almost came away from the warped wood. So he used the side of his fist, stepped back and waited.

Something drew his eyes to the upper storey, and the grey, threadbare net curtains covering the windows. Perhaps fifty years of dirt and smoke fumes clung to the material and he shuddered. How did Lomax ever think he could sell a place like this?

After a few moments, he pounded the door again. Still nothing. He took a quick look around, checked both ends of the long, silent street, and pressed his palm against the door. It moved as he applied pressure, groaning on rotting hinges. One more look and he put his shoulder against the woodwork and pushed through.

He almost fell flat on his face as the door burst inwards, the wood splintering from the ancient frame. He drew himself upright, body tense, ready to receive an attack. None came. The place was empty, cold and still. He dusted himself down and explored.

Less than ten minutes later, he got into the back seat of the taxi.

"You were quick."

"I've seen all I need to see. Take me back to the bus station."

The man behind the counter peered over his mauve-tinted glasses as Chaise came through the door. Thick, bulletproof glass separated him from his customers. It was spotlessly clean, like everything else.

"Afternoon sir." The man put down the oily rag he had been using to lubricate the twin barrels of a beautiful, antique-looking shotgun. "What can I do for you?"

"I need ammunition, for my gun. Seven-point-six-five millimetre. Walther PPK."

The little man raised his eyebrows, readjusted his glasses and placed both hands on the counter. He looked as if he needed the support. "That's somewhat unusual. I supply mainly shotguns and their accessories. Mainly for farmers, and members of local shooting clubs. Such a firearm is a highly specialised piece of weaponry. I don't think I've ever had anyone asking about it."

"I'll be needing a shotgun as well. Twin-barrel, ten-gauge. I'm joining a club, you see."

"You are?" Chaise nodded. "And you, er, already possess a Walther?"

"Of course. I'm a licensed member of my club. But I've moved location, and I want to join one here. Pistol shooting."

"Pistol shooting? With a Walther PPK?" The man shook his head, pressing his lips together. "Sir, I have to inform you, that nowadays it is extremely difficult to supply any form of legal handgun in this country, or its ammunition, let alone one so diverse as a Walther." He let out a long sigh. "I might be able to manage it, but it will take at least a fortnight."

Chaise pulled a face. "A fortnight?"

"And I'll need all your documentation. Firearms license, shotgun license, passport, and a CRB."

"Criminal Records Bureau disclosure form? I have all of those things, and more."

"They'll all need to be verified, of course. That'll take another two weeks. All in all, we're talking about at least a month." He shrugged. "Sorry. The law's pretty tight on all of this now." He peered at something beneath the counter and clicked his tongue. "I'll have to register your name. If you want to continue, that is." His hands moved out of sight and Chaise heard the distinctive sound of a computer keyboard. "You do wish to continue, sir?"

Chaise shook his head. "I can't wait that long. I need the practise now."

The man spread out his hands. "What can I do? Sorry."

Ryan went outside and fell back against the wall of the shop. All right, he'd tried the legal route, he'd have to try something else. He had seven cartridges for the Walther and he felt sure they wouldn't be enough. If those damned Lithuanians had control of Norwich underworld he'd need a damn sight more than a handful of bullets, even if he made every single one count.

He considered waiting, letting things lie a little. Besides, what could he actually achieve for the moment? All right, so they might have murdered Lomax, and what they were doing down at the old house was an abomination, but did any of it really have anything to do with him?

He closed his eyes and let the cold air seep into his bones. It brought to him a sense of perspective. Harper would go ballistic, that much was for certain. And as for dear old Colin, he'd probably end up stopping Ryan with a bullet in the heart. No, best to wait. Think of an alternative.

He'd kept the Walther with him, not wanting Marianne to find it through a bit of casual snooping as she kicked around in the flat. Now, as he gently nudged his front door open with his fingertips, he was glad he had. He brought the gun out and waited a moment before he stepped into the cramped hallway.

They had forced the door, just as he had done over in Norwich. The chain hung loose, the metal slide ripped from the woodwork.

Someone big and strong had done that. He settled his breathing, mouth open, and listened out for any sound.

Nothing.

He eased off his shoes and began to ascend. He knew which stair creaked, and he took a large step over it and stopped. Again, nothing came. They had probably gone, but he couldn't be sure. The car he'd clocked earlier had moved. He cursed himself for not checking his mobile to see if there had been a text from the office. One day he'd get used to using the damn bloody thing. Not today. Today, he needed all his senses alert for whatever was waiting for him in the flat.

When he reached the top of the stairs, he flattened himself against the wall before taking a darting glance into the living room.

He gasped, and threw himself back against the wall, his mind reeling.

"Bastards," he breathed. The place was a mess, every single drawer, cupboard, cushion and bookshelf torn apart. He saw it all in that one fleeting glance.

A long breath, then he went through, arm extended, the Walther covering all the angles.

They'd been thorough but had clambered around like a herd of buffalo nevertheless. It was going to take him a long time to clear it all up.

Books with their broken spines littered the floor. A knife had sliced through the back of the sofa, stuffing strewn in every direction. The glass-topped table, where he and Marianne had taken breakfast, upturned and smashed. Jesus, didn't anybody hear this?

Still keeping the Walther ready, he moved over to the kitchen. It was the same. Cups, saucers, plates, everything thrown down and smashed. Cupboards hanging open, food everywhere, coffee granules mixed in amongst the debris. The fridge door yawned wide, the contents spilling out across the floor; already he smelt the faint tang of sour milk.

Finally, he edged towards the bedroom, with no idea what to expect. He nudged the door open with his foot.

It swung inwards very slowly and he saw the bed.

He blanched, felt his stomach twist and turn completely over. He had to force himself to look, fighting back the bile that rose into his throat.

It was Marianne.

She was naked and they'd put a noose around her neck and suspended her from the cross beams on the ceiling. Her neck stretched horribly. All that remained of her mouth was a gaping black hole, and her eye sockets looked like dates. They'd been gouged out, as too had her tongue.

It came over him quickly and he spun around, clawing forward into the kitchen, mindless of the mess, and he vomited into the sink.

Blindly, he groped for the tap and pulled on the cold water. Full blast. He put his head under the stream and left it there until the fug cleared and his senses returned.

The bastards had been and they'd left their calling card.

Now Ryan Chaise knew time really was a factor, the decision made for him.

He was going up against the Lithuanians.

THIRTY

Colin sat at the same table as the day before. He paused in the act of putting a ham sandwich into his mouth as Chaise came through the door and headed straight for him. Colin was already on his feet before Chaise made it to the table.

"What the hell's the matter with you?"

"I want a word."

Chaise strode off to the toilets and disappeared inside. Colin didn't pause for a moment and followed him in.

Colin walked through the door, not expecting anything more than a quick conversation.

What he got was the muzzle of a Walther PPK under his chin.

Chaise pushed him back against the door, teeth gritted. "Where the fuck were you?"

Colin brought up both hands in surrender. "Take it easy with that thing." His voice sounded constricted because it was. The gun was jammed into the area just under his chin and above his Adam's apple. He couldn't swallow.

"You said you were here to protect me. Your words, Colin. So where were you?"

"I had to report in," he managed.

"You were away for a fucking long time, Colin, old mate. I had to get a bus to Norwich because you had to *report in*. Fucking convenient, eh?" He pressed the gun harder and Colin gave a tight-sounding squeal. Chaise eased the gun back but kept it trained on Colin. He cocked his head. "Report in, you say? Okay, and that took you all morning?"

"Well … yes, it did actually." Colin rubbed at his throat, slipping two fingers under his shirt collar to release some pressure. "I got the call early in the morning so I had to leave Beccles, drive down to Ipswich, and …" He shook his head, now looking angry. "What the hell is all this, Chaise? You're too bloody free and easy with that gun, so tell me what the hell is the matter with you."

"Whilst you were out making your report to whoever it is you work for, I went to Norwich. Looked around a little, learned some interesting things."

"Such as?"

"*Such as* … last night, Chris Lomax's wife came to see me. Terrified. She told me some things, interesting things. So she stayed the night and this morning I went to see what was what. I needed your car, but it wasn't there, because you had to *report in*." His breathing grew unsteady, the anger rising. "She stayed in the flat. Her name was Marianne and she had come to me for help. And you should have been here, because when I came back … she was dead. Murdered."

"*What?*"

"I'll tell you later." Very slowly, he eased on the safety and put the gun in his waistband. He should have been ready, he should have expected it, but when Colin hit him, the shock sent him staggering backwards more than the power of the blow. And that was powerful enough. A corkscrew right, straight into his guts. He belched wind and folded, but managed to rock back to avoid the knee meant to crack into his face.

It was only a brief respite. The left hit him on the side of the head and the leg swept away his own. He hit the floor hard and Colin pounced, wrenching Chaise's arm up and back, almost ripping it from the socket.

"You've put that gun in my face twice now, Mr Chaise," he spat, putting the heel of his shoe into the side of Chaise's neck, keeping him down, applying the pressure on his arm. "You do it again, you better fucking well shoot me, because if you don't, I sure as hell will shoot you."

He released some of the pressure, perhaps the most stupid thing of all to do. Chaise rolled inside the arm lock, turning and twisting, bringing the heel of his hand up into Colin's groin. The space was tight, restricted, the blow delivered with precision and to good effect. Colin squawked and went down, but as he fell his head struck the edge of the sink unit with a sickening, heavy clunk. He grunted and crumpled to the cold tiled floor, eyes closed, mouth open, a nasty purple welt already developing over his eyebrows. Chaise didn't give a damn about that. His arm hurt like buggery and he gave it a few rotations to try to bring life back into the shoulder joint.

The door opened and a customer came in, took one look, and about-turned.

Chaise turned on the tap, splashed water over his face, and did the same with Colin, who coughed and spluttered before shaking his head and sitting bolt upright, his face white.

"Jesus."

"A little bit of advice for you too, Colin. You twist a bloke's arm, you make sure you break it."

Colin shook his head again and winced as he put his fingers against the welt on his forehead. "You could have split my skull."

"But I didn't."

Colin held his head with one hand, whilst groping for one of the sinks with the other. He found it, hauled himself to his feet and leaned his weight against the basin. He sucked in several breaths. "Jesus, Chaise, I feel fucking awful."

"Put some more water on your face and wake yourself up. When you're ready, I need you to do something for me."

He walked him round to the flat and waited at the foot of the stairs whilst Colin looked through the rooms. When Colin reappeared at the top a few moments later and descended, Chaise could see no discernible change to the man's features.

"That's quite a mess," Colin said, buttoning up his coat.

Chaise kept his own emotions closed. The man was cold, hard. Advantageous in the line of work they both pursued, but Chaise still would have liked something more, an indication of his shock, disgust. Anything.

"I need you to do something for me." Colin's face remained blank. "You've been in this game a long time, lived in this country, I haven't. I've been out of the loop for years. I don't want to lose my edge, so I need your back-up."

Colin rubbed the swelling on his face. "I'd say you've lost *none* of your edge, Mr Chaise."

"I'm not talking about that. I mean contacts, the right people."

"I don't understand what it is you're saying to me, Mr Chaise."

"I need some weapons. A handgun, and a shotgun. And I need them fast."

Colin frowned, then lifted his head to the ceiling and sighed. When his eyes again met Chaise's they were narrowed, hard. Unblinking. "My remit is to protect you, Mr Chaise, not equip you with an arsenal."

"It's either that or I go alone." He patted his hip. "I've got the Walther. I could take your gun too. It might be enough."

"Enough for what?"

"To kill the bastards who did this."

In the silence, the tension mounted; discernible, storm pressure building between them. Colin shook his head, "No, Mr Chaise, I can't allow that. If you start bringing attention to yourself, and killing off a bunch of violent psychopaths would certainly do that, my orders are to kill you."

Chaise turned his feet slightly towards the man not two feet away. In the confines of that small entrance hall, it wouldn't take long, and what was one more corpse to clear away? "Not if I kill you first."

"Mr Chaise, don't be so naïve as to think that I am the only person with those orders."

He did think, and had done for quite some time. The second shadow, invisible, but there nevertheless. "So, I cause a scene, and I'm gone, is that it?"

Colin nodded.

"And what about all this," he gestured vaguely up the stairs with his hand. "When I tell the police, all hell is going to—"

"No, Mr Chaise. No need for the police. I'll make some phone calls, have it all tidied away."

"You can do that?"

"My department, yes. They'll have this place back to how it was in no time." He glanced to the top of the stairs. "Why do you think they did that?"

"To send me a message – that they can."

"And the trashing of the place?"

"They want to know who I am, what I know. They're going to come back, Colin. And when they do, it won't be with an invitation to a dinner party."

"What the hell have you been getting yourself involved with?"

"I told you. Marianne came to me for help. Her husband had taken me to one of the houses he owned, and these people didn't like it, not one bit."

"These people? I don't get it. Who are they?"

"Eastern European gangsters. I've met their type before, and when Chris Lomax came up against them he paid the ultimate price." His eyes wandered up the stairs. "And so too has Marianne. They're people-trafficking, bringing illegal immigrants in from the Middle East, Iraq, Afghanistan, all around. No doubt they'll charge each one a minimum of twenty thousand euros, promise them a good job, nice flat. Then they end up here and they stick them in Portacabins and cream them for every penny they earn. It's a medieval slave market, and it's happening right here, right now."

"But what's that got to do with you, Mr Chaise?"

"Two people are dead because of it, Colin, and one of them right here in my flat. So I need your help. I want you to contact someone, someone who can get me those weapons. I'm going to finish those bastards, for what they did, and for what they are doing."

"I'm not at all sure about any of that, Mr Chaise. Even if I did agree, my contacts are somewhat limited."

"You'll know a friend of a friend. I know you do, Colin. All I'm asking is a little slack, because if they come after me, how are you going to contain that? By killing them, just as I want to?"

Colin thought about it, chewed his lip for a moment, then sighed. "Very well, there is someone ... but, Mr Chaise, I'm a little puzzled. Are you so angry because of the death of the girl, or because they invaded your personal space?"

Chaise gave the question long consideration. Unlike Colin, however, he kept his thoughts, and the answer, to himself.

THIRTY-ONE

Johnny was of the mind that if you did the opposite to what seemed obvious, everything would work out well in the end. Something of a fatalist, presented with a list or a set of cards, for example, he instinctively knew the last one would prove to be correct. So now, with the list of Brigit's friends in his sticky hand, he began at the bottom, believing success would follow.

Eleven names were on the list, but the eleventh proved not the one. Nor the tenth, the ninth, the eighth. Even as his theory shredded into tatters, he knew if he began again at the top, the seventh name would be the one. So he went for the middle, and it wasn't. Returning to the seventh, he slowly made his way up, moving from address to address, repeating the routine, asking the scripted, rehearsed questions. The answers came back the same; they did not know where Brigit was, hadn't heard from her for days, sometimes weeks.

When he parked his borrowed car outside the fourth house on the list, his heart soared. The little red MGB sat in the driveway, patiently and quietly. Three days of living in hotels, growing more desperate by the hour, driving from one address to another, scouring the whole of the Wirral to find the whereabouts of that damned woman, now resulted in success. Brigit was here.

He grinned as he went up to the front door.

It was mid-morning, the sun trying to shine. This meant people were about. To his left, a salesman of some description stood locked in an animated conversation with the next door neighbour. Johnny grew nervous but undeterred. There were ways and means of getting into a house.

The woman who opened the door was plump and blonde with the sort of face you immediately liked. Smiling, happy, bright-eyed, she asked him what he wanted. Johnny also smiled, flashed a calling card. "Hello, madam," he began, "I wonder if you've ever thought about how easy it might be for me to push you into the hallway, overpower you and rob your house?"

The woman's face fell, the fear coming quickly, sucking the blood from every line. She made a tiny, guttural sound and took a step back, hands raised as if to ward off the blow which she so obviously expected to come.

Johnny, however, merely smiled. "It's all right," he said, a slight chuckle accompanying the disarming smile, "I'm only here to sell you some high-security door chains, help you protect yourself a little more—"

"You scared the hell out of me." Her voice quivered, a frightened bird sound, high-pitched and very small. Her hand trembled, clamped over her mouth.

"Yes, I know and I'm sorry ..." Another smile, more concerned this time. He reached inside his jacket. "Listen, I've got—"

"I should telephone the police. Who the hell *are* you?"

"No, no, please, wait a moment. I have here an official letter from the local police station. It'll explain who I am." He searched inside his coat, shaking his head. He looked to the driveway. "That's a nice car you've got there. MGB isn't it? A classic?"

"It is ... it's not mine, Listen, you shouldn't *do* that. Christ, imagine if I had a heart condition or something." She had a tissue, and pressed it first on her left, then her right eye. "Jesus Christ ..."

"I'm sorry. I can call back. Really, I apologise. Stupid." He finished rooting in his jacket, but his hand remained inside. "How much does a car like that cost? You drive it every day?"

"It's not mine. Look, if you could—"

"Your husband's? Wow, I'd love a car like that. I'm a bit of a car freak myself."

"No, it belongs to a friend of mine. You have a letter you say?"

"Yes, yes. A notification. I should have given it to you straight away. It's here."

He checked the salesman next door. The neighbour laughed loudly. Johnny brought out the Glock, clamped his hand over her mouth and pushed her inside, slamming her hard against the hallway wall. He rammed the gun into her ample midriff. "Nice and quiet," he said and released his hand. She sucked in her breath, chest heaving, eyes not believing what she saw. Johnny pushed the door shut with his fingertips and turned her around, the gun at her right ear.

A large man appeared at the end of the hallway. He wore a white string vest and khaki work trousers, the braces dangling on either side. Unshaven, he looked as though he had only just that minute got out of bed, hair tousled, eyes red-rimmed. His mouth fell open as Johnny gripped the woman by the neck and pushed her forward, levelling the gun towards the big man. "Where is she?"

The man came awake, tensing up as if he were about to charge. Johnny seized the woman by the nape of her dress and yanked her backwards, the gun at her ear again. "Don't be a hero, big boy, or I'll plaster her brains all over your nice house." The man stopped, breathing hard. His eyes blazed with virulent intensity. Johnny gave him a smile. "Where's the owner of the MBG?"

"I'll kill you, you fucking bastard."

"No, you won't. Just tell me where she is."

"She's in the living room," interjected the woman, her voice sounding calm. "She's watching TV."

"Okay," said Johnny, and trained the gun on the man. "Let's all go into the living room, nice and quietly. Any sudden moves, or yells and I'll kill you both."

The big man let his shoulders drop and he moved towards what Johnny assumed was the living room door and pushed it open. The sound from the television became louder. As the man went inside, Johnny steered the woman down the hall to follow the man into the room.

Brigit sat on the sofa wearing a pair of tight-fitting jogging leggings and a blue, low-cut t-shirt, legs tucked under her, feet bare, chin propped up on a hand. She turned as they all trooped in, saw Johnny with the gun, gave a tiny squeal and moved to stand up.

"Don't say a fucking word," said Johnny. Brigit bit her lip and flopped back down on the sofa. Johnny still had the plump woman by the collar of her dress, with the gun pointing at the man. "Anyone else at home?" The man glared at him. "Any kids?"

"We don't have any children," said the woman.

"Well, that's a relief." Johnny gave the woman a violent shove. She stumbled forward, lost her balance, and almost fell before the man caught her around the waist and held her to him. Her tough exterior shattered at that moment and she started to wail. The man drew her closer, muffling her face into his chest.

Brigit sat rock still. Johnny waggled the gun in the direction of her feet. "Put some trainers on, we're going for a little drive."

The man growled, "Who the fuck are you?"

Johnny looked at him. "I understand you're upset, and that you want to hurt me, but I'll be gone soon, and you can sit tight, go back to your life and look after your wife."

"Sit tight? I'm going to fucking rip your fucking head off, you shit. *Who the fuck are you?*"

"I know who he is," said Brigit.

Johnny cocked an eyebrow, surprised at her defiant tone.

"You're the one who shot at me, aren't you? The friend of the one I ran over."

"Clever you. We're going somewhere quiet, where we can talk. So get some shoes on. Now." He swung the gun towards the man again. "You try to follow us, or phone the police and I'll kill her, you understand?" The man nodded. "Then I'll come back here, and I'll kill the both of you too." Brigit eased her feet into her running shoes, which were just a little way beyond the sofa. "When we've had our chat, I'll send her back. Then we can all get on as if none of this ever happened. Okay?" Another nod. "We'll take my car." He gestured for Brigit to come closer, and when she was within reach, he took her by the elbow and swung her out into the hallway.

At that moment, with his body turned away slightly, Johnny's gun moved from the general direction of the man, who took his chance and launched himself forward, throwing his wife aside.

But Johnny had been here before. He'd worked on nightclub doors, enforced Frank's business empire, killed men. The big guy was out of control, virtually foaming at the mouth, his great bear hands spread out to crush, and Johnny met him full on, relaxed and confident. He dipped low, used the big man's forward momentum, and threw him over an outstretched leg. As the man hit the floor on his knees and tried to get up, Johnny struck him hard behind the ear with the gun. The man went face down into the hall carpet and the plump woman, standing in the living-room doorway, screamed. Johnny took two quick steps and backhanded her across the jaw. The force of the blow cartwheeled her into the television, which collapsed under her weight. Her elbow went through the screen; it shattered with a sudden flash, and it smouldered and crackled as she lay amongst the debris, her mouth spouting blood, low whimpering sounds coming from deep inside her.

Johnny swung around. Brigit was already at the front door, about to tear it open when he took a bead on the back of her head and yelled, "Stop."

Fortunately for Brigit she did, her shoulders dropping, the fight leaving her in a rush.

Johnny stepped over the fallen man who had rolled over and stared upwards through glazed eyes. Johnny waggled the gun. "Don't forget, any heroics and I'll kill her."

He went down the hall, put the Glock in the back of his trouser waistband, and adjusted his jacket. With his hand gripping her elbow, he stepped out into the daylight with Brigit breathing very fast beside him.

"That was fucking stupid," he said and walked her to his car. "You do something like that again, and I'll ruin your pretty face. Understand?"

She nodded and he took her to the car, brought out his key and pressed the automatic locking. There was a heavy clunk, and the lights flashed once.

"Where are we going?"

Johnny gave a little laugh. "Oh, I don't know. Somewhere nice." He opened the door for her and she slid in. "You can decide." He slammed the door and went around to the driver's side. He glanced towards the house where the big man leaned in the doorway, back of his left hand pressed against a bleeding nose. "*Hasta luego,* big boy," Johnny said, touched his forefinger against his temple in a mock salute and stepped into the car.

As he gunned the engine and moved out into the road, he caught sight of the big man in the rear-view mirror falling to his knees.

Johnny's face split into a broad smile.

THIRTY-TWO

He took her to a corner café in the little seaside town of West Kirby. The rain beat down and the afternoon shopping brigade had sought shelter in the cramped space. The air was thick with voices and the smell of coffee and toast. Johnny edged through the tightly packed tables, bringing her a buttered scone, just to be different. She ignored it, choosing to gaze out of the misted window, occasionally brushing hair from her face. He sat down, noting the lines under her eyes and the tiny broken veins around her nose and cheeks. Despite the lack of makeup, she looked sensational. Every muscle of her lean body pressed against her tight-fitting clothes and he gazed at her, aroused, stirring his coffee mindlessly, engrossed.

"I bought you a scone," he said at last, and pushed her drink towards her a fraction. "And a coffee." He took a sip of his own, her indifference expected. He'd kidnapped her, driven at speed to this dreary place, and now attempted to engage her in small talk. He drank his coffee, and listened to the rain and the voices.

After what seemed an age, she turned and picked up the coffee, blowing over it with her soft lips. He became mesmerised by those lips, the lump in his throat growing. He coughed and she stared at him over the rim of her cup. "What's your name again?"

Steam rose up over her face, but not as far as her eyes, which blazed with such hatred they would have withered most men. Slowly she put down the cup and took a mouthful of the scone. She munched on it before answering. "Brigit."

"Ah, yes, I remember now." He smiled and looked around. Women mostly, armed with shopping bags, their constant natter not easing his developing headache at all. Her eyes, boring into him, didn't help. He tried not to squirm and wriggled uncomfortably in his seat. "God, I hate bloody places like this. I wish to God I hadn't come back."

"Back from where?"

He turned to her again, grateful for a slight softening of her glare. "Spain."

Her eyebrows went up. The penny had dropped and Johnny smiled.

"You're a friend of Ryan's?"

Johnny shifted position, leaned forward, voice low. "I just want some answers, that's all. It was never my intention to hurt you. It still isn't, and I'm sorry."

They stared at one another, unblinking.

"You expect me to believe that?" Her eyes burned.

"What?" A tingle of electricity ran through his lower abdomen. Her expression, the way the light played with the edges of her tumbled hair, sparkling with little flecks of gold and her mouth, which drew him in, so soft, so smooth. Before he knew it, he heard his voice as if in the distance saying, "God, you're beautiful."

From somewhere in the background came the sound of plates smashing on the floor. Someone cheered, and Brigit's eyes darted to the corner and Johnny, realising what he had said and grateful for the diversion, hurriedly drank his coffee, feeling his cheeks redden. He hadn't meant to say those words aloud; they sprang out of his mouth with a life of their own. Nevertheless, they were true. She *was* beautiful.

A long silence followed between them whilst customers continued with their conversations, a waitress moved between the tables, someone swept broken crockery away and tipped the pieces into a bin. Johnny finished his coffee.

"Why did you try to shoot me?"

He shrugged. "I tried to *stop* you, not shoot you."

"You've got a bloody weird sense of owning up to your crimes haven't you."

"*Crimes?* I haven't committed any crimes, I was only—"

"Yes, I thought you'd see it that way. You're like an open book, easily read. You're a thug, nothing but a vicious thug."

"No, I'm not. If you'd give me a chance to explain I'd—"

"Why did you do what you did back at Carol's? Charging in the way you did, with the gun, like some sort of lunatic."

"I did what I had to do."

She didn't look convinced. "So, I'll ask you again. Who are you?"

He blew out his cheeks and put his finished coffee down. "We can't talk here."

"I'm not going anywhere else – not until you give me some answers. And you can wave your gun under my nose as much as you want, but I'm not moving."

A large woman in a green raincoat pushed passed him and he knew, if he hadn't known before, this was not the place to be. His mind was in tatters, common sense ousted by overwhelming stupidity. He should never have used the gun in the street. He squeezed his fingers into his eyes. "All right. Answers." His head snapped up as the waitress passed, and he caught her by the arm and ordered two more coffees. He waited until she had cleared away their cups before he spoke. "I work for a man back in Spain. His name's Frank. This Ryan Chaise, he ... look, it's complicated and there's a lot to it."

"Tell me. I'm not going anywhere."

He nodded, knowing he had little choice. He could force her, drive her to a piece of derelict land and beat her senseless. He could. But here, with her so near, with that face ... he realised there was only so much he was prepared to do. Any sort of violence was not going to be part of it. "Okay, I'll tell you. Frank, he – I mean *we* had a business. It was doing well and had been for quite a while. Frank took some time to come over here and fix some deals. Whilst he was gone, this Ryan

Chaise got mixed up with some quite nasty characters. Gangsters I suppose you could call them."

"What would *you* call them?"

He shrugged. "Gangsters. They murdered Frank's wife."

Her face drained of colour and she gaped. "*Murdered*?"

Johnny nodded, about to continue when the waitress returned with their order. He smiled his thanks and she breezed away. Johnny watched Brigit stirring her coffee, no sugar. He leaned closer. Crows' feet spread around her eyes but they did not detract from her natural loveliness. How old was she, he wondered. Fifty? She looked more like thirty-five, but that couldn't be possible. Chaise's girlfriend was thirty-five. It didn't compute. He realised she was staring at him, those same eyes so unflinching. He sighed. "Frank blames this Chaise guy. If he hadn't involved himself, Sarah would still be alive and Frank's business would still be thriving."

"But ... you mean, it was Ryan who murdered this man's wife?"

"Not directly, but he was responsible. Ultimately. That's what Frank believed, and I do too. Frank and I, we weren't just boss and employee, we were friends. We started out way back, down in Portsmouth. Carved out a nice little business, made some money. Then, about twenty years ago, we went over to Spain. We were doing okay after we'd ironed out all the creases. Then this Chaise, he comes along and it's all gone haywire." He took a drink of coffee. "Frank's dead."

"But, but you said ..."

"I know what I said. Frank is dead, and there's the end to it. And with him, everything has disappeared; the business, the clubs, the investments. Washed down the toilet, and all of it Chaise's fault. So," he finished his coffee and brought the cup down with a bang, "what I want you to do is very simple." He leaned further forward, took her hand and patted it. "You're going to tell me where this Ryan Chaise is. Then I'm going to kill him."

THIRTY-THREE

Chaise came through the office door and went straight to his filing cabinet. The receptionist looked at him over the rim of her glasses but didn't speak.

He pulled out the details of Chris Lomax's properties and spread them out on his desk. There were five houses, all of them large Edwardian or Victorian edifices, with at least six rooms over three floors. No doubt they had cellars too, and all had sprawling gardens. Chris had invested wisely, most bought almost twenty years before, at knockdown prices. He'd renovated and converted them into studios or apartments. By letting out each room at around three hundred a month, he was making a tidy sum. Ryan calculated that each house would generate almost two thousand pounds a month, to bring in around ten grand. Even with the mortgage payments, Chris had cleared a decent profit. And then, there was the last house.

Chaise studied the details again. The sixth property was a crumbling monster of a place, in such a state of disrepair it would have served Chris better if it were demolished. He knew himself how dilapidated it was, but the garden proved the prize asset. It backed on to a field, a field which Chris had also purchased. Trees surrounded it, making the whole area very private and very secure.

The Lithuanians had thought that too, which made it the perfect base for their operations. When Chaise went and peered through the grimy window of one of the Portacabins, everything became very clear. The grubby mattresses, the clothes rails, the very basic cooking areas, the cramped conditions, the squalor. It all amounted to a very profitable human trafficking scam, and no doubt there were prostitutes and child labourers involved in it somewhere along the line.

So he'd decided to look at the other houses, try to find out the extent of the operation. He would be going up against brutal, violent men, but that was nothing new for him. He'd been down this road long ago.

It had all happened so quickly.

He squatted in the empty, bare-walled blockhouse staring at the sniper rifle propped up in the corner. Dust swirled across the floor, the hot desert breeze throwing up tiny particles of grit that caught in the back of his throat and made him gag. In that cramped place, the sensation multiplied tenfold. He took his neckerchief and pressed it over his nose and mouth before scrambling across to the rifle.

He checked it through, knowing it was all too neat and tidy. This blockhouse, the weapon. Too damned simple, but what other choice did he have?

He positioned himself in the corner opposite the small, glassless window and estimated the angle of fire. He knew full well the sniper had already moved. The classic mode of the sniper. Fire and move, fire and move. However, this far back from the light of the window, the sniper would not be able to see him, so there just might be a chance.

He brought the scope up to his eye and slowly scanned across his line of sight.

His strength had always been with handguns, and his ability in unarmed combat. Sniping was not something he had trained for. Rifle shooting was one thing, but this ...

He paused, ran his hand across his brow to wipe away the sweat, then looked again.

The sniper, if he was still out there, remained out of sight. Against the brilliant azure sky, everything appeared a drab brown colour, the tops of distant buildings all merging into one, heat haze blurring details. Nothing much broke up the view, no subtle shades, or curious shapes. Just the simple lines of ancient, Middle-Eastern houses; the same ones that dotted the landscape, perhaps for millennia. He blew out his cheeks and lowered the rifle, realising then that his throat was parched. He needed to drink, but apart from the rifle, the building was empty. He leaned his head back and closed his eyes.

A tiny shuffle, the minutest of sounds, but instantly Chaise knew what it was. The pressing down of rubber-soled boots into the sandy ground. Senses alert, he swung the rifle to the open doorway just as the man came through and Chaise shot him in the chest.

It was a quick burst, one that should have cut any man in half.

This one did nothing.

For a moment, everything froze. Chaise couldn't work it out, but his puzzlement gave his opponent all the advantage he needed.

The man had a knife, its large serrated edge curved slightly at the point and he charged, screaming like a fiend. Textbook style, Chaise rolled and knocked the man's feet from under him. He went down heavily, the air grunting out of him; now Chaise had the advantage and he struck once, twice, three times across the throat and the man went limp, the knife falling from lifeless fingers.

Chaise climbed to his feet, his head swimming, legs not as assured as they were. He picked up the neckerchief, wiped the sweat from his brow and kicked the rifle away. Damn thing had been loaded with blanks. All of it a bloody test, a deadly game of cat and mouse, to test him to the extremes.

Chaise reached down and took out the dead man's sidearm from his hip holster, checking the magazine, determined to be more careful this time. He worked the recoil and ejected a shell, examined it. Satisfied, he gripped it in both hands, dropped into a crouch and edged his way to the side of the open doorway.

"Are you all right, Mr Chaise?"

He gave a start and snapped his head around.

Yvonne, the receptionist, head tilted, lovely big eyes so full of concern, gave a slight smile. "You seem a little preoccupied. Worried maybe?"

"No, no, I'm fine." He gathered together the house details. "Just a few things to sort out, that's all."

"Mr Webster would like to see you, Mr Chaise."

Chaise stopped and looked at her. Webster. The company director. Mr Big. "When?"

"He asked me to tell you ... or should that be he *told* me to ask you?" She shook her head, the jewellery around her neck clinking slightly. "Anyway, whatever it is, would you phone him to arrange a time?"

"Sure." Chaise stacked the papers. "Listen ... there might be some cleaners coming around fairly soon, to clean my flat."

"Oh? But, it can't be all that dirty, can it? You've only been there a few—"

"I had a bit of an accident with a frying pan, that's all. Nothing serious, but, you know ... they'll probably park outside. I think they may have to change the carpet. Don't, er, don't tell anyone. Please." He flashed what he hoped was his most disarming smile. The lies came so easily, the embroidering of a story natural and unforced. Just another aspect of the kind of low life he led. "I burnt it, you see. The carpet. Knocked over the hot frying pan, and the fat set it alight. Stupid really."

She frowned and glanced upwards. "It can't be all that bad, can it? There's no smell, and I'm sure I'd notice, it being right above this place."

"Well, I panicked. Used that stuff, you know, the cleaning spray that takes away smells." He smiled again before becoming serious. The greater part of his previous life had been steeped in deception, lies, subterfuge, and rarely did his true self come to the surface. He couldn't allow it to, for there lay the path to questioning everything he did, and once the questions and the doubts grew, his defences would fall and danger would swiftly follow. Right now, however, in the confines of the estate agency with this girl looking so fine, none of that seemed to matter. He swallowed hard, reached over and brushed her arm with the back of his hand. "I, er, I wonder if we might ... you know, you and me, I wondered if perhaps ..."

"We might what?"

"Er, go out for dinner one night. You and me?"

She blushed, looked away, appearing stunned by the invitation. She took a moment to brush away a strand of hair. "Well, I'm ... I never guessed ... I ..."

Crestfallen, he couldn't keep the disappointment out of his voice. "Oh well, never mind. It's okay. It was only a thought after all. A hope."

"A hope?" She arched an eyebrow, but her eyes creased, amused.

"And you have to call me Ryan. As I asked you before. This 'Mr Chaise' business I can do without." His smile broadened. "So, what do you say?"

"Well ..." She pressed her lips together, then her smile broadened. "Of course, Ryan, that would be lovely."

"Cool." A massive wave of relief swept over him, and all at once, everything seemed brighter. Still smiling, he straightened up and put the papers into his briefcase. "We'll fix a time as soon as I get back."

"I'll look forward to it."

"Me too." He squeezed her arm. "I'm not always like this. The business in my flat, it's put me on the back foot, but ... well, the truth is, I meant to ask you out before it all happened."

"I'm glad you finally got round to it. And I hope they sort out the flat."

"I'm sure they will." He went over to the door, paused and looked back at her. "Remember, not a word, eh? I wouldn't want the boss to think I'm a pyromaniac!" She laughed and he went outside.

Images of Linny sprang into his mind and he grew angry, mainly with himself. The whole purpose of him coming back to the UK was to find her after she had run off and left him to pick up the pieces in Spain. Most of that debacle had been down to him and he wanted to tell her how much he regretted it all, how he wanted her back, as it once was. A moment's madness, innocently picking up a hitchhiker, and everything that followed; the danger, the deaths. Life changed the moment the gun went off and he'd never paused to tell her the whole truth. But now, he'd given himself up to other needs, and he despised his shallowness, questioning his true reasons for being here.

Linny, if only she knew. If she could see him now, surrounded by this shit, how he could so readily change from being charming and friendly at one moment to an absolute bastard at the next. Perhaps she was right, perhaps he didn't deserve her. All the deceit, the broken promises, it may well be better for her to stay away, to absent herself from his life.

How easy it had been for him to sidestep the situation, to put her to the back of his mind and ask Yvonne, the receptionist, to dinner. Did he really care for Linny? He functioned perfectly well without her. No lump in the throat, no emptiness in the pit of his stomach. Love. Was that something he had had with her, or was it all just a charade, another piece of play-acting, part of the day-to-day grind that is life? An integral part perhaps, but not the romantic, warm and essential ingredient we all think of as being 'happiness'. Perhaps he didn't love her. Sure, he'd come over here to find her, made an effort, but now the business with Chris and Marianne Lomax had taken over, become so much more important.

His old life, returning. And he knew, as Linny probably did, that it would never leave. So, she had. And right now, with everything building up around him, he had to accept her decision was the right one.

He stepped down off the pavement and was about to get into his car when thoughts of right and wrong, confusion and self-doubt left him. Across the street, the same vehicle which had cruised through the square not so very long ago, with three swarthy-looking individuals packed inside making no pretence of what their purpose was, all of them sneering, glaring. Chaise tensed, remembered what they had done to Marianne. To him.

He threw his briefcase into the back seat of the Clio and strode across the street.

It was almost closing time, blinds pulled down over shop windows, people thin on the ground, traffic virtually nonexistent.

The guy behind the wheel turned away as Chaise approached, pretended to doze, but not too convincingly. His companion poked him on the arm, but too late. As the man went to turn the ignition, Chaise tore open the door and dragged him out into the road by the collar.

One or two passers-by witnessed what happened next, but none of them could actually swear precisely what they saw as it all happened so quickly.

Chaise hit him, followed him down to the ground, rammed his knee into the man's windpipe and glared into his face as he squeezed his cheeks with thumb and forefinger. "You tell your boss, I'm coming for him. You understand?" The man whimpered, barely able to move his head. "And when I come, I'm going to kill him."

The rear door swung open and Chaise reacted, jumping up and kicking the door back into the emerging man's head, the rim of the door smashing him across the temple. He squawked, giving Chaise the few moments he needed, and he cut around the back of the car to catch the third as he struggled to get out from behind the wheel. A big guy. Chaise kicked him across the jaw with the flat of his shoe, pulled him out by the collar and threw him onto the pavement.

By now, the second one had recovered and Chaise saw him out of the corner of his eye coming around the rear of the car, face contorted, eyes bulging. Chaise kept low, put a three-fingered strike into the man's solar plexus, felt him go limp like a wet rag, and snapped his knee into the man's face. He spun backwards, squealing, clutching his broken nose, the blood spewing through his spread fingers.

"You're fucking dead," said the big guy, getting up from the pavement. He had a gun. A short stubby thing but Chaise paid it no mind. He moved faster than the gunman could ever have dreamed, the elbow taking him across the jaw, then the guts, and the wrench of his wrist caused him to retch and squeal.

Chaise smashed the same elbow into the man's throat slamming him back against a shop window. The pane quivered, almost broke and Chaise gazed at it, transfixed, holding his breath. But thankfully it held and he gave a long sigh of relief. Then he turned in a tight half-circle and chopped the edge of his hand across the big guy's throat. The man's eyes rolled before he sank to his knees, a dead weight, all resistance gone. Chaise became aware he held the gun in his hand. Feeling pleased, he put it in his waistband, brushed down his jacket and glanced around. All three men were down, two of them groaning, the big guy looking very bad. Chaise grunted and strode back to his car.

A number of people mingled close by, staring, faces agog. Chaise shrugged, "Tried to break into my car, then threatened me. Nothing's sacred anymore, is it? Not even here."

People nodded, muttered their loathing and threw disgusted looks at the men as they struggled to their feet, bent double, holding faces, clutching ribs. Nobody spoke as Chaise got into his car and reversed it out of the parking place just as a large black ford transit pulled up alongside. The men inside wore red overalls. Chaise grunted his appreciation. Efficient and quick. As he had been, dropping those three bastards in the street. A smile creased his face as he drove out of the town square.

THIRTY-FOUR

They drove out to the promenade at New Brighton, parked the car between the press of tourists' vehicles and wandered over to the sea wall. The tide was in and every so often the spray stung their faces and she shivered, hair lashing across her face. Johnny took off his coat and draped it around her shoulders, despite feeling the chill himself. His body had forgotten what the UK was like on a grey autumn day, how the cold bit down deep into the bones. He did his best to ignore it, and failed miserably. Too many years on the Costa del Sol had made him soft. She looked at him, said nothing, and drew his coat close.

"You have to understand some things," he said above the sound of the waves. "Frank and I, we were like brothers. When his wife was murdered, I was down in Marbella running the clubs. I didn't have a clue what was going on. Nobody did. There were problems on the horizon. The Eastern European cartels were making their presence known, and those bastards are lethal. There are just so many of them."

He took her arm and led her along the sea wall, passed Fort Perch Rock towards the area where once a pier had graced the seafront of New Brighton. Over to their left, across the River Mersey, the impressive sight of Liverpool stretched across the skyline. Not many ships now graced those waters, but the resonance of glory days still remained.

"I grew up here," she said as they strolled along. Anyone who gave them a passing glance would have been forgiven for thinking they were a couple. They appeared relaxed, almost content. "So much has changed since I was a little girl." She stopped, gazing across the river. "We used to come down here on our bikes, a whole bunch of us. I even remember the penny-slot machines on the pier."

"What the butler saw?"

She laughed. "And a lot else. If you know what I mean."

He chuckled, and they moved away again, their pace slow.

"So, you're a gangster?"

He took a moment to answer, but when he did his voice was light, cheerful. "Not in the strictest sense, not in the way those Eastern Europeans are, or the Chinese. A few dodgy deals, but ... we provide a service, Brigit. We run clubs, restaurants, bars, nothing major. Once, we used to dabble a little in drugs and prostitution ..." He saw the dark look descend across her features. "*Used* to, Brigit. The old days were different. We needed to be tough to survive and sometimes that meant we did things, things which today we would never even contemplate." He sucked in a deep breath. "I have a lot of regrets, but it's not like you see in the films, or read in the tabloids. We're not killers. We're businessmen."

"And what happens if someone steps out of line? You invite them into the office for a cosy little chat?" She shook her head and looked out across the Mersey estuary, the beaches of Formby so out of place in that vista of pulsating industry. Ships still plied their way in and out of Liverpool, a feeble reminder of when the ships were so many you couldn't see the water of the river between them. "You're all so bloody holier-than-thou, the lot of you. Ryan is the same. Always thinking he is above it all. But I knew. I told Linny. Christ, how I told her. I knew he was no good."

"Is that what you think of me? That I'm 'no good'?"

A puzzled expression crossed her features. "You tried to shoot me.

And what you did ..." She shook her head. "I don't know. Why are you being so nice to me now?"

"Why are you being so nice to *me*?"

A slight colouring of her cheeks, some of the assertiveness seeping away. "I don't know."

"I've tried to explain. Frank's death came as such a shock, and when I saw you ... those other guys with me, the big ones? They were not part of what Frank and I had, Brigit."

"So who the hell were they?"

"Bouncers. Doormen. They work for a guy in Liverpool, an old friend of Frank's whom he owed money. They want to get to Chaise for the same reasons I do, to beat the truth out of him. He hurt some of their people over in Spain. The only difference being, for me it's personal, for them it is purely business."

"And shooting at me was part of that?"

"That was before I knew you."

"You don't *know* me, not at all. You know nothing about me."

"I'd like to."

She stopped, her mouth opening slightly. "Jesus, you know how to charm a girl, don't you?" She looked away, angry now. "You'd like to? That your usual chat-up line, is it? After the gunshots and the slaps?"

He swung her around by the arms and glared at her. "Why can't you accept what I've said? Why is it so difficult for you to believe me? If I wanted to, I could have killed both your friends, driven you away to some forgotten place and broken your neck after getting the truth out of you."

"Why didn't you?"

His breathing came in short gasps. In truth, he didn't know the answer himself. None of this was in his plan, a plan which originally consisted of him finding Chaise, killing him, and returning to Spain. He never envisaged meeting someone like her. Now he had, all of his thoughts tossed around like clothes in a tumble-dryer. "Because as soon as I saw you, I knew I couldn't."

She tore herself free of his grip and marched over to the railings, mindless now of the sea spray, the wind and the cold. He studied her back, the leggings, the swell of her buttocks against the tight Lycra and the lurch in his guts almost made him rush over and grab hold of her.

He squeezed his eyes shut, forcing himself to calm down and he joined her to watch the waves rolling in. "Tell me what you know about Ryan Chaise. Who is he?"

She sighed and moved away again from the river. He took her arm and walked with her. She didn't resist. "God knows. We were in Spain, Linny, myself and Tony."

"Tony?"

"My ex. We thought a new beginning in Spain might put the spark back into our lives." She chuckled. "It didn't. He took to drinking cheap wine and before long, I had the yearning to come back home. Linny, she'd met this guy, Ryan Chaise. An estate agent he told us, when she brought him round one evening. But I could see there was something not right about him. I watched him. He's fit. Super fit. The way he carried himself, a particular confidence. As if nothing could touch him. He frightened me."

Johnny nodded. "You think he had a past? A troubled past?"

"Almost certainly." She gave him a sharp look. "You're the same. You're no businessman, no matter what you say. You're a thug, and you know it."

"A thug? That's the second time you've called me that."

"It fits you well. The way you hit ..." She shuddered. "I've only ever seen such things on TV. You come from a different world, a world of violence. It comes easy to you. You have no conscience."

"I did what I had to do. What would you have preferred, that I simply stood back and let them both attack me?"

"I would have preferred it if you'd never arrived." She sucked in a breath. "No, it's the coldness, the way you did it, almost as if it was natural. Nobody I've ever known has done what you did."

He hunched his shoulders. The wind cut through his thin shirt and he wished to God he had another coat. "I think we should go somewhere else. Maybe a bar or something."

"A bar? This is an autumn day in New Brighton, not bloody Malaga. We'd be better off in front of a log fire somewhere."

"That would be quite nice, actually. I can't remember the last time I sat in front of a real fire."

"I know a pub, a little way away. *The Magazines*. We can go there, if you like."

He studied her face. A lovely face. A face he would like to wake up to in the mornings, kiss, caress. "All right," he said. "We'll have a drink by the fire."

"Then you can tell me exactly what you want, Mr Businessman."

The fire sputtered in the grate, and he bought the drinks. At this time in the early evening, the customers were few but the barman was cheery, and the atmosphere welcoming. A few men in the corner shared jokes and friendly banter, warm-hearted claps on the back. Johnny realised such a place held so many charms, so much he'd like to become accustomed to.

Brigit smiled as he sat opposite her. "Lager and lime for the lady." He picked up his glass. "Real ale, so the barman informs me. Jesus, I've forgotten what this tastes like." He took a sip and closed his eyes for a moment, savouring the flavour. He smacked his lips and took a long draught. "This is nice. Homely."

"It's a pub," she said and pulled Johnny's coat closer around her. "No need to become all poetic."

"I'm not used to it, that's all."

"Would you want to?"

"I might. Yes. I haven't got anything to go back to in Spain, that's for sure."

She sat back and folded her arms. "I'm not sure what I'm doing here, sitting opposite you like this. I must be fucking nuts."

He drank his beer, at a loss what to say. Being here, in Brigit's company, caused much to change in his head. Changes he found attractive. If there was a chance ...

"I'm sorry for Frank's death. He meant a lot to you."

He studied her face for the slightest sign of sarcasm or cynicism, but there was none. "Yes," he said at last. "Gunned down, visiting the grave of his wife. They shot him outside the cemetery."

"My God!"

He shrugged. "It happens. I suppose I always knew it would."

"Your world, it's so ... so unlike anything. Tony, when I was with him, I never actually knew what he did. Can you believe that? Sounds bloody ridiculous I know, but he'd go off for days on end and I never stopped to think where. We ambled along, had a nice house, cars, holidays in the sun. Like I say, we'd bought a villa in Spain and Tony fell into the life very easily and I never once questioned anything. I'm shallow, and I believed as long as I had a pool and a good social life, everything would continue. But when he started drinking, it soon fell apart. I re-examined my life, who I was, what I wanted. You understand?"

"Yes. Yes, I do."

"So I made the decision, for myself, to come back to the UK. I don't want to make any more stupid mistakes. A relationship with someone like you would be a big mistake."

His stomach twisted. "We didn't exactly get off to a good start."

"That's an understatement if ever there was one!" She reached for her drink. "Maybe you are telling the truth, but I'm not sure. I'm not sure about anything at all."

She sipped her drink and he watched her in silence.

Someone in the other room selected a song from the jukebox and Johnny grinned. "Bloody hell, this takes me back."

"You're an enigma, you know that?" He frowned. "You seem so ... casual, relaxed. And yet, what you did."

"Can't we get over that Brigit? Put it away somewhere, somewhere very far?"

"I don't think so. I can't forget the look on your face."

"Well ... I suppose you're right, but I don't know what will happen to it all, the clubs and everything. The Lithuanians or Ukrainians or whoever the fuck they are, they'll take it all over. And then they'll have to face up to the new world order." He took another mouthful of beer. "The Chinese. It's all them now. They're taking over the Costas, undercutting every business there is. Not just the cut-price bazaars they run in every bloody village and town, but my line of work too. They make the East Europeans look like puppy-dogs in comparison."

"So you must be relieved to be out of it, in a way?"

"I guess, although I would have liked for a somewhat different reason. Frank's death ... that wasn't right. They could have bought him out. No need to do that."

"Do you think they'll come after you?"

He shook his head, pressed his lips together, frowning deeply. Should he reveal all concerning his visit to the Liverpool nightclub? The killing? By now the police would be all over the lighthouse, linking the two incidents. How much longer could he keep it hidden? He sighed. "There's no reason for them to want to kill me. Why the hell should they? I'm here, they are there. 'Never the twain shall meet'. But if they do, I'll take a lot of them with me, you can be assured of that."

"I don't doubt it. You're a dangerous man."

"Only when riled, Brigit."

"Or when you are ordered?"

"What Frank asked me to do, that was not an order. It was a request, from a friend. Now that friend is dead, but I intend to see his wishes through."

"By killing Ryan?"

"By killing Ryan. Correct." He finished his beer and noted she had not touched hers. "You're not thirsty?"

"I'm scared."

He leaned forward and unconsciously took hold of her hand. She didn't resist. "Brigit, I'm not here to hurt you. I don't want to hurt you, but you have to know ..." He closed his eyes and lowered his head for a moment. When he brought his head up again, he could feel the moisture accumulating in his bottom eyelids. "Listen ... this is something I have to do."

"Honour? Is that it? I've heard a lot about the *code*. The Mafia."

"If you like. I will do what I have to do, no matter what. You know where this Chaise is, and you're going to tell me."

"I don't know where he is."

"That's a lie, Brigit."

"No, it's not. I have his mobile number, nothing more. He came to see me, to ask me about Linny, but I told him nothing – because I don't know. Linny phones now and again, but she never tells me very much. I have no idea where she is staying or who she is with, and that's the truth."

"All right. Then I want you to phone *him*, tell him you want to meet up, that you have news about Linny."

"He won't believe me. He'll want to speak to Linny herself."

"Then you phone her. Tell her it's a matter of life and death and she has to meet up with Ryan. I'll think of something, but you're going to bring Ryan Chaise to me and I'll kill him. Then we can all get on with our lives."

"And if I don't?"

She glared at him and he held her gaze, squeezed her hand tight. "You have to understand this. If you refuse, I'll become that guy again, the one you saw at your friend's house, and you don't want to see that guy again, do you?"

"Jesus Christ, but you are one evil bastard."

"That I may be, but I'll do anything I have to in order to avenge Frank."

She wrenched her hand free and sat back in her chair, breathing hard. "What a bastard you are."

He pulled out the folded sheet of paper in his back pocket and pressed it down on the table. He jabbed at the list of names. "They're all here, Brigit. All of your friends. I've already been to see a few of them, so it shouldn't be too difficult to go back to the others. I could make all of this so very difficult."

She grabbed the paper and scanned it. "Where the fuck did you get this?"

He snatched it back and refolded it. "One of your ever-so-friendly neighbours. Nice bloke, very publicly spirited. Thought I was a policeman. And who was I to shatter his fantasy?"

"Shit." She put her fist in her mouth and bit down hard on her knuckles. Her eyes were squeezed shut, and a single tear ran down her cheek.

"Look, I only want Chaise. Once he's dead, I'll disappear. I promise you."

Her eyes sprang open. "Promise? Why the bloody hell should I believe any of your fucking promises?"

"Because I mean it. Like you said, I'm a man of honour."

"Yes, and like I also said, you're a bastard."

"Maybe. But only in this. Once Chaise is dead, you'll never see me again. That's my word."

THIRTY-FIVE

They walked down an aisle in one of the larger out-of-town supermarkets, and Johnny bought her some toiletries, toothpaste, toothbrush. Once through the checkout, they strolled across to the car and he held the door open for her. She got in without a word and searched through the shopping bag whilst he went to the other side and got in.

"Thanks," she said without looking up.

"I'm sorry for all this," he said. She turned her face towards him. "Truly. If there was any other way, believe me, I'd try it."

"*Believe you?* You said those terrible things to me. Your threats. How am I supposed to trust you?"

"I'm sorry."

"But you're not. You meant every word."

"If you ring Chaise, I'll go away."

Her mouth twisted and she rifled through the bag again for something to do. "I've never liked him, true enough ... but *killing* him. Does it have to be that way?"

"It's no more than he deserves. He's responsible."

"But he's not a Lithuanian, is he? Perhaps he just got sucked in. Have you ever considered that?"

He hadn't, accepting every word Frank had spoken. If it proved to be the case that Chaise was nothing more than a victim of circumstance, did he still deserve to die? Johnny rubbed his face. Everything used to be so clear and uncomplicated before she came along. He said he'd walk away when it was done, but could he? Something changed inside when he saw her, and now ...

Brigit pulled out a chocolate bar and unwrapped it. "I'm starving."

"We'll go for a meal. Somewhere classy."

"How can you be so dammed normal in one breath, and then in the other say such terrible things?"

"If I'm to get what I want, I have to, understand? In the world I live in, it's what I do. Who I am. I've had to survive, Brigit, in a world that will not tolerate weakness."

"That's a world I don't want anything to do with."

"I'm not asking you to get involved. Just to help. That's all."

"Help you in killing another human being?" She shook her head, munching down the chocolate. "You could be anybody, anybody you wanted. You don't have to do this."

"It's the only thing I know."

"I don't believe that. If you wanted, you could turn away from this life, this path you've chosen. I'm sorry for your friend, I truly am, but if he is dead, and the things you had in Spain have all been taken away, why not step away yourself? Start again."

"Doing what exactly?"

"I don't know, *anything*. Normal things, that normal people do."

"I wouldn't know where to start. You don't understand my life. It sucks you in, deeper and deeper and before you know it you don't even recognise yourself anymore." He moved closer. "I've done terrible things, things I'm ashamed of. I wish to God I could step away, join the rest of the human race, find a job, a little flat, sit in front of the TV and eat hot dogs and ice cream. Have you any idea how attractive that is to me?"

"Why don't you do it then? Leave it, Johnny. Come back home and start a new life, before something awful happens."

"You sound as though you care."

She pursed her lips. "Care? I don't *care* for anyone, Johnny. And you haven't exactly enamoured yourself to me, have you?"

"No, I suppose not." He sat back and looked out through the windscreen, at the shoppers emerging from the supermarket. Young and old, couples, families. Sane, normal lives, full of problems and difficulties, but *normal.* Like she said. It would be so good to go to sleep without feeling afraid, to wake up with nothing to worry about except missing the bus for work. And work, good God, what was that? An office, a warehouse, a shop? Did he care, would it matter? Perhaps if he lived such a life, someone like Brigit might be interested. Perhaps even Brigit herself.

He became conscious of her stare, and he shifted position uncomfortably. "You honestly think I could do those things? Start afresh, begin a new life here? A different life?"

"Of course I do." She gripped his arm. "You could do so many things. You're intelligent, quick-witted, handsome."

He arched an eyebrow. "Handsome?"

Her cheeks reddened slightly. "Yes. You know you are."

"You're not so bad yourself, Brigit."

Her voice sounded far away when she said, "You said I was beautiful."

"So you are."

He leaned across and kissed her very lightly on the cheek, which reddened even more deeply. Then he turned the ignition and took the car out of the car park without another word.

They booked into a hotel and they took their dinner in the restaurant. It was a good meal, well cooked, and the service was prompt and efficient. They followed it with a couple of drinks in the bar then went back to their room.

Brigit excused herself and took a shower. Johnny stood at the window and gazed out across the sweep of the river. The lights sparkled brightly along the Liverpool seafront and he thought how much it reminded him of New York, only on a much smaller scale.

She came out, drying her hair with a small towel, a larger one wrapped around her body. He felt his heart thump and he tried not to stare. “I’ll have one now,” he said.

“You don’t think I’ll run off?”

He shrugged. “I’d find you again.”

“Yes. You probably would.” She sat down on the edge of the bed and rubbed her wet hair. “That was a lovely meal. Thank you.”

“I don’t want you to think I’m some sort of monster, Brigit. I’m not.”

“No. I can see that.” She glanced at the bed.

“I’ll sleep on the floor.”

She looked at him and smiled.

In the morning he woke feeling cramped and sore but made no mention of it as she applied some light makeup, fixed her hair, and together they went down for breakfast.

They didn’t talk very much. The sun had come out and they took coffee out on the terrace and watched the birds playing on the branches of the trees.

“You’ll phone her,” he said, his gaze never leaving the tree.

“Yes.”

They spent a lazy day, driving through the tunnel to Liverpool where they shopped. She looked through some clothes and, without being prompted, he bought her almost everything she picked up. She soon ceased to look at anything, and he took her to a bar he knew and they had lunch, she a prawn salad and Johnny a cottage pie accompanied by crusty bread. Afterwards, they went down to the Pier Head, then Albert Dock.

“I don’t often come to this side of the water,” she said, leaning against the railings, studying the murky depths of the river.

He took in her features, her swan-neck, the high cheekbones, the way the muscles rippled along her forearms. “Do you go to a gym by any chance?”

She grinned. “Only about five times a week. Why, is it noticeable?”

"Only slightly." They laughed, and as the day progressed any lingering tensions seemed to slip away.

Later, she phoned her daughter, but when she received an automated reply, she left a voice message, asking her to get back as soon as she could. Johnny, satisfied that she had least tried, allowed himself to put it to the back of his mind. For now. Ryan Chaise, Frank, the Lithuanians, they could all take a back seat.

They got back to the hotel late and she flopped down onto the edge of the bed whilst he took off his jacket and hung it up in the wardrobe.

"It must have been awful on the floor last night," she said, her eyes drifting over him as he stood there in a loose-fitting shirt and chinos.

"It was okay. I had a couple of blankets, so ... I'll be okay again tonight, but tomorrow I really have to—"

She shook her head. "Go and have a shower. Then we'll talk some more."

After his shower, they went downstairs and waited in the bar for the waiter to come with the menu. They barely talked at all. The waiter showed them through to the bright, airy dining room, they made their selections and settled down to another very tasty dinner. Over coffee, she checked her phone, found Linny had not replied and looked annoyed.

"Don't worry," he said. "We'll do what we can tomorrow. Let's try and not think about any of that tonight."

Back in their room, he slipped the chain across the door, turned and there she was, with her face so open, her eyes taking on the slightest hint of mockery. "What do you want to talk about?"

He stepped into her, and they were kissing, mouths rolling around each other's, desperate, eager. His hands went to the buttons of her blouse whilst hers tore away his belt and pulled down his zip. Her breasts were full and soft, and he kissed them but then she pushed him away and for a moment, he thought she meant to slap him. Instead, she wrenched free his trousers and pulled him out. She saw him and released a tiny moan before she pressed him down onto the bed. With deliberate slowness, she stepped out of her jeans and he gazed at her skin, the tanned flesh, the hard muscles of her abdomen.

He grew harder and grinned, but soon the grin turned to a grimace of unbearable pleasure as she straddled him and lowered herself onto his erection. She started a slow rhythmic grinding, soon building up in speed and aggression, controlling, dominating him. She threw her head back, mouth open and rode him for a long time, varying the pace, bringing him to the very edge before pausing to allow him to recover. Then, she would begin again, repeating the process until she herself came, screaming out loudly, clawing at the matted hair on his chest. When finally she became quieter, she lifted her face, awash with perspiration, and began again, this time not stopping until he too came. It didn't take long, and she gripped him with her sex as he flooded into her, cursing, shouting out obscenities through clamped teeth.

She rolled off him and lay on her back, breathless. "God, Johnny. What the hell are you trying to do to me?" She turned and smiled at him.

He shook his head, mesmerised, put his arm over his eyes, tried to come to terms with what had happened. In all his life, he'd never had a woman like this, one who dominated him, brought him to the peak so gloriously and repeatedly. He laughed softly, felt her get off the bed and he took a sly glance as she went to the dressing table. He took in the slim waist, the muscular legs, her well-rounded buttocks. Every inch of her flesh glistened with a sheen of bronze. The body of a thirty-five-year-old for sure, the muscles in her back hard, no excess flesh. Lean, young. It must be true that she visited the gym so often. Many men may have found it something of a turnoff, those muscles, that strength. But not him. He relished it, the sight of her so lithe and so cut, he was in heaven. He grinned to himself and put his head back in the soft pillow and basked in the after-glow of probably the best sex he had ever had.

Then he realised what she was doing.

He sat up, rigid, not daring to breathe.

She had his gun and pointed it straight at him.

"I know how to use this," she said quietly as he swung his legs around and stood up.

"Don't be a fool," he said. "You shoot me, they'll put you away for six years. Maybe longer."

"Yes, but you'll be dead."

"You want that?"

"You want *me* dead."

He gaped at her. "No, I never said that! For Christ's sake, Brigit."

"You don't need to say it. I can sense it."

"But ... listen, what we talked about, the day we had ... Brigit, I told you. Chaise. It was all about him, but now, after this ..." He glanced down to the bed, the crumpled sheets, the stains from their love-making spreading grey across the material. "I'm no longer sure."

"I don't believe you."

"Brigit," he took her in, that body, the way she stood there so assured. He felt himself stirring, despite the gun. "God, Brigit, how the hell do you think I could kill you after what we just did?"

The gun lowered ever so slightly. "You mean that?"

"Of course I do."

"You're going to put all these ideas about killing and retribution to one side?" He nodded. "And in the meantime, you're going to ... what? Wine and dine me in a series of fancy restaurants?"

"I only want to talk to him. Get it straight. And warn him too – there are other people out there who have grudges to bear, and a lot of them are directed towards me. Even more so when they find out I want to leave the fold."

"You do? Are you sure?" He nodded once. "And me?

He frowned. "What about you?"

She smiled and nodded to his abdomen. "I can see how much you like me."

"Shit." He looked down at his semi-rigid cock. "Sorry."

She slowly put the gun down on the dresser and came towards him, and took hold of his manhood in her hand. "In another place, another time, we could be really good together."

"Who's to say we still can't be?"

She titled her head to one side. "You want to convince me?"

So he did.

THIRTY-SIX

Over a light breakfast of rolls and coffee, Brigit spent most of the time watching him. When he had put the last piece of buttered bread into his mouth and swallowed it down, she leaned over the table and took his hand. "Last night, Johnny. The things you said. Did you mean them?"

Johnny looked down at her hands, the way they held his, and he liked what he saw. "I only need to talk to him, that's all."

"I'm not talking about that. I'm talking about what you said about us."

He looked up at that point. "*Us*?"

"You said you'd like to get to know me better. Outside of bed."

She laughed and Johnny felt the relief lifting him up, lightening his spirits. "Yes. Yes, I would."

"Are you sure?"

"Of course I'm sure. Brigit, I haven't … I haven't got anything pulling me back to Spain and … and my life, it's …" He didn't know what to say, how to explain. Two days ago, everything seemed simple, so cut and dried. Now, with this woman, nothing would ever be clear again.

"So, let me just get this straight. You won't be going back?"

He shook his head. "They killed Frank outside the cemetery, and now they'll try to take over the entire business. But there are others, as I said, who won't simply stand by and let that happen. There's a war coming, Brigit, and I don't want any part of that. I'm glad I'm out of it."

"A war? What do you mean by that?"

"The Chinese want control, and they won't find it easy. Russians and Lithuanians, they are crazy people, Brigit. I don't want any part in it. Times have changed. I've changed."

"And you promise me you're not going to kill Ryan, or anyone else?"

"How can I say that? There are people out there, Brigit who ... the two guys who were with me when I ... people like them."

"The two gorillas? I knocked one of them over." She put her head in her hand, "Jesus. I'd forgotten about that. What happened to him?"

"Hospital. But as far as I know, he's okay." He lowered his eyes. "I'm not sure if I'll be able to convince them to back off, not in any way you would understand." He reached over. "Brigit, even if I decide not to kill Chaise – and I'm not saying I've decided anything yet – I have no way of controlling what others might do. Whatever he did out in Spain, it was massive. You understand? He did things, things which can't be ignored or forgotten."

"That old code of honour bullshit again."

"Something like that. These people, they are unpredictable and ..." He blew out his cheeks.

"Well," she poured herself the last few dregs of coffee from the silver pot on the table, "I don't care either way. It's Linny I'm concerned about, how it will affect her. If there is some way I can cushion the blow ... Johnny, I know you're a dangerous man, that you are probably very capable of doing everything you say, and I'm wondering if there is some way you could ..." She shrugged, swilled the coffee around the bottom of her cup, then drank it down. "Maybe you could convince these others to ... I don't know, make them see sense?"

"I can try."

"That's all I need to hear." She reached forward and took his hand again. "I loved last night, Johnny. The second time …" She closed her eyes. "I think, if we can get through this, we could be good for each other."

"I think so too."

"You mean it?" He nodded. "Because I … listen, I'm not young anymore, Johnny. You were very flattering, but the truth of the matter is the years keep rolling on and I'm not going to look this good for much longer. I visit the gym every day except Sunday. I'm fitter now than I've ever been, and I know I'm vain and shallow, but it's all I have, apart from work. I haven't had happy times, not with men. I run my own business, which takes up all of my time. Men have not featured very much, not since Tony, and even Tony, I soon realised what a loser he was, so ... I've not been interested for a long time, Johnny."

"So what's changed?"

"I don't know. Something. You, you're … I don't believe you are as cold and as callous as you make out. There's a need inside you, a fragility. I like that."

Was it time to tell her? The spectre of the lighthouse loomed huge in his mind.

He enjoyed the sensation of her fingers as they played around his own. If he allowed himself to, falling for this woman would be so easy. And why not, he asked himself. There was nothing left for him anywhere else, no family ties, only himself to worry about. With over four hundred thousand in the bank, there really was no reason not to make a new start. With her …

She gave his hand a small squeeze. "Despite what you think, last night was not something I usually do." He raised an eyebrow and she blushed. "I *mean,* leaping into bed with someone so quickly! Jesus, you've got a dirty mind."

"I wasn't thinking of that part ... although it was *very* nice."

"Well, that's ... *kind* of you to say, but ... oh God, I'm not explaining myself very well at all, am I?"

"You mean to say that it normally takes you a few dates before you ... before you ... have sex."

"Yes. I'm not some sort of sex maniac, Johnny."

"That's a pity."

She laughed, slapped his hand and sat back. "If you must know, I'm something of a recluse. I don't go out much, preferring my own company. Except for the gym, I tend to stay at home. My friends are close, and we meet up now and then but as far as men go, well ..." She let her voice trail away.

"You don't have to explain anything to me, Brigit."

"No, but I want to. I don't want you to think I do this a lot."

"I never thought you did. Look, if what you're trying to say is you'd rather not get any further involved with me, then let's leave it at that."

"Is that what you want?"

Her eyes looked moist, but surely they were not tears ... "You say such a lot of things, so full of contradictions. I honestly don't know what—"

"We had a good time? Nothing more?"

"Christ, Brigit, I didn't mean to sound as if it meant *nothing*! It was the best I've ever had." He turned his face away, the heat rising to his cheeks. "But if you're not ready to trust me or—"

"All right, listen. There was someone else before Tony, *long* before. I was sixteen when Clive came into my life. I worked in a hairdressers and when he came in, looking so fine and handsome, my jaw just dropped. The look in his eyes when he saw me, the thrill that ran through my body, I can't describe. I cut his hair and we chatted. Before I knew it he was asking me out. There I was, a little girl. A few months before, I had been sitting behind a classroom desk, now I was being wined and dined by a real gent. And he was a gent. He never forced himself on me. We went out for drives, meals, the cinema, it was all very gentle and slow. Then he took me away for the weekend, and we made love for the first time. It was wonderful. I loved him and

I believed he loved me. From that moment, we couldn't keep our hands off each other. We did it everywhere. The car, alleyways, the park, hotels. I asked myself why he never took me back to his home, and he told me he only had an apartment above his office. He was the manager of a large corporation that sold parts to the aircraft industry. Silly things like 'fasten your seat belt' signs, all of that."

She picked up a teaspoon and played with the sugar bowl, lost in her memories. "I fell pregnant, of course. I had fears, but Clive was wonderful. Looked after me, even when my father was raging, threatening to throw me out. Clive got me a flat, and when my time came he took me to the hospital, stayed with me, even helped me with the birth. I was floating. He'd come and see me most evenings, and he'd help me. Then ..." She stabbed at the sugar. "A woman called at my place. Very attractive, stern. She told me she was Clive's wife, had long suspected something was going on but with no idea how far it had developed. She came in, held the baby, cried. It was awful. She stayed all afternoon and when Clive arrived ..."

She blew out a breath. "He left me, of course. After that day, I never saw him again. Not even a bloody phone call to ask me how the baby was. I probably cried for about five years."

"And the baby?"

"She grew up into a beautiful woman. Linny."

The silence stretched out and Johnny didn't know what to say. An old story, nothing surprising, but it proved she trusted him, wanted him to know more about her, what made her the person she was. If this had happened a year ago, six months even, he would be sprinting away as fast as his legs could carry him. Commitment, caring, words which did not belong in his vocabulary. But now, life had become very much different. He reached over, and took her hand in his. "I don't know what's going to happen, to you or me, or anything. I only know that last night was the best night of my life and I want to repeat it, many times. Sometimes I think it's best not to make too many plans. Simply let things take their own course."

"That's very Buddhist."

"Is it? I wouldn't know. All I do know is I'd like us to make love again. And again."

She arched a single eyebrow. "How old are you, Johnny?"

He frowned, wondering where this might lead. "Forty-two."

"I'm *fifty*-two. I won't always look like this."

"Right now, you look amazing, Brigit. I've never seen anyone as beautiful as you."

"This side of forty you mean."

"This side of anything. Don't be so hard on yourself."

"I'm a realist. I've had other men, I've heard all the bullshit. Eventually, after the pain of Clive became less, I took lovers. Not many, but enough. None of them could compare. Not that I consciously compared, but that was inevitable I suppose. I'd never been with anyone for more than two or three months until Tony came on the scene, and he found it hard living with me. And since the break up, I haven't been with another man – for over three years now. And I didn't think I wanted to be."

He smiled, and a few tiny needles of heat begin to prick at his jowls.

"But there's this thing about Ryan, and I don't know how to reconcile it."

Johnny sighed, released her hand and sat back. "I feel obligated, Brigit, to get to the truth."

"To a dead friend? Johnny, it's not going to change anything, is it? It's not going to bring him back."

"No, but at least I'd know."

"And if he was wrong? What if Ryan just happened to be in the wrong place at the wrong time?"

"Yes, but I remember you telling me you thought there was something different about him. You told me he frightened you."

"Even so, I can't believe Ryan would do any of those things. To kill a man's wife? He's an estate agent for God's sake."

"I think he's something more. Whatever he is now, that is not what he was."

"There is only one way. Listen," she leaned forward, "if I speak with Linny, she must know the truth of what happened. She'll tell me, and when we have the truth, will you let it go?"

Johnny became agitated, shifting position. Perspiration broke out across his brow and he pulled away and turned in his chair, looked through the large panoramic windows towards the hotel gardens, the birds skipping on the grass, streaks of blue struggling between ribbons of white clouds. It was going to be a beautiful day. "You haven't listened to anything, have you?"

"Please, Johnny. We can put this behind us. You're a good man, I know you are."

He turned to her. "Brigit, you have no idea who or what I am. I told you, there are other people involved and it's not as simple as you make out."

"You told me—"

"I didn't tell you everything."

Her face grew serious, her mouth hard. "You told me about the two gorillas, that they would take some convincing, so is there more?"

"A lot more."

"I don't think I like the sound of that."

He watched the birds again. "All right. Speak to your daughter. But I know what she'll say – she doesn't know anything. You'll have wasted your time."

"But if I get hold of her, she might know something. She might even know where Ryan is. Then you could talk to him, and maybe ... Johnny, whatever it is you've done, I'll understand."

"No, you won't, Brigit. Because it's beyond understanding and the longer we hang around the more danger we'll find ourselves in."

"I don't understand. Danger? What sort of *danger*, and who from?"

He'd said too much, so he spread out his hands, "Who knows?" Soon, perhaps in a day or so, Chaise would be nothing more than a sideshow when the witnesses told their stories and the police began to close in. The 'gorillas' too. So far he'd been lucky, but he knew it couldn't last.

She stood up and came round to his side of the table, cupped her hand around his neck, drew him close and kissed him. "What time do we check out?"

"Eleven."

She glanced at her wristwatch. "It's just gone nine." She smiled. "That gives us two hours."

"God, Brigit." He ran his hand up her thigh and settled on her firm buttocks. "You're amazing." His stomach turned to liquid and he pulled her to him, a charge of electricity building.

"Promise me, Johnny. Whatever happens, we'll get out of this in one piece."

He closed his eyes and nodded. He liked the feeling of submitting to her, something he'd never known before, but welcomed nevertheless. "Yes."

She gripped his hand and pulled him to his feet. "Two hours. Think we can make the most of it?"

"Almost certainly."

Later, stepping out onto the balcony, the chill of the early morning cutting deep through the thin material of his shirt, Johnny fished out a cigarette and lit it. He had tried many times to give them up, but now, his willpower in tatters, he smoked and listened to the sounds of the river.

Over in the far distance, the view of Liverpool brought no comfort. Uncertainty and confusion raged through his body, shredding his senses. This woman had come into his life, unplanned, unlooked for, and he no longer knew what to do. It had been so easy before, his course of action set. Chaise had to die. Alfonso's treachery had been one thing, but Brigit's presence, and the effect she had on him, proved too much. Killing Chaise was the goal, the one unerring desire, now he was unsure.

If Brigit's words proved true, and Chaise's actions were nothing more than the accidental responses of a man drawn unwittingly into a cycle of violence, would taking his life solve anything? Perhaps the opposite would be the case, and Johnny's need for justice and revenge would prove meaningless. Alfonso may have known the truth of it, but he was dead. The brothers, wherever they were, were nothing more than mindless grunts, following orders, Perhaps his energies should be focused on them, for they were the true danger now, their revenge being the one threat which could undermine everything. If there was a future for him and Brigit, then the grunts stood in the way of it.

He blew out a stream of smoke and the knot in his stomach twisted ever tighter. He didn't know what to do and that frightened him more than anything else. The only certainty remaining was the knowledge the killing had not yet come to an end.

THIRTY-SEVEN

Chaise made a log of all the houses, noting their size, how many people came and went, whether the streets were busy. He didn't notice anything suspicious, nor signs of Vladimir or his brother. Chaise had only Marianne's vague description of the man to go by, but he felt he would know him, given his size. Those who did arrive were typical student types. By eight o'clock, he had enough details to devise a plan.

His last call took him to the old house where Lomax had taken him. As he approached, he saw the door open and a light shining from the hallway. He hesitated. It has been a long day, so he decided enough was enough and turned to go.

The Jeep came down the street and for a moment Chaise pondered on making a run for it, or a stand. The Walther pressed against his waistband, but this was not the time. Not yet. He pulled up his collar, lowered his head, and continued, hoping they would ignore him or mistake him for yet another passer-by.

The Jeep pulled up hard and the doors sprang open.

Chaise stopped, letting his shoulders drop. The driver, the same one he had hit in Beccles Market Square, stood at the door of the car whilst the other came around and stepped onto the pavement to block Chaise's path.

It was Vladimir.

The street lamps gave his face a ghastly colour, highlighted his hard features; Chaise noted the maniacal grin and the gun in his hand. No surprise there.

"We meet again," Vladimir said and took a step closer, but not too close. His companion over at the car must have given him a full rundown of what Chaise was capable of.

"Seems that way."

"You will get into the car, we have things to discuss."

"I don't think so."

Vladimir smiled, the gun coming up a little more. "I'll kill you if you don't."

"You'll kill me if I do."

Vladimir pursed his lips. "I just want to know who you are, that is all. My father actually, he is the one who would like to talk. He is a little intrigued and would like some answers."

"Your father?"

Vladimir nodded, and motioned with the gun. "Please. I would prefer it if you did as I ask. If you refuse, I'll shoot you. In the knees." His grin grew wider.

Chaise looked back at the Jeep. The other one had a gun too. That made it difficult, out here in this deserted street, the houses black, empty. "Very well. But you have to know something." He looked back at Vladimir, held his gaze. "I'm not alone."

A slight rise of the eyebrows. It was enough for Chaise to realize that Vladimir knew little if anything about Colin, or the second shadow, wherever he was. "I had thought of such a possibility." He nodded. "Perhaps he is close?"

"I would certainly think so. Probably got his gun trained on you right now."

A slight tremble on the cheek, a moment of uncertainty. Vladimir let out a long sigh. "Very well. But we will still go and see my father.

Afterwards, I shall bring you back here to your car. Hopefully that will be the end of it."

Chaise didn't say anything. He had no intention of this being the end of anything, but he wasn't about to reveal such thoughts to Vladimir. So, he shrugged and went over to the Jeep.

The other guy glared at him, "Give me the gun."

Chaise weighed up the options, shrugged, and handed the Walther over. The guy pulled open the rear door and Chaise got in.

They drove him out of town and nobody spoke. Chaise watched the houses as they blurred by, and he thought of all the people inside, living their lives, unaware of the vicious dramas played out in the streets around them.

Cosseted, cocooned, call it what you will, the world of violence and criminality touched few of them, and that was how it should be. Chaise trod a path of danger, and right now he faced the consequences. He longed for normality sometimes and believed he had found something close in Spain. How wrong he had been then, how wrong he still was to give these thoughts even the briefest consideration. There was no point. He was who he was. As the car continued, the images of houses grew more blurred ...

He threw himself out into the scorching heat, hitting the dirt in a roll, and sprinted low to the first piece of cover he found. He slammed himself against the stack of crates and gulped in his breath, sweat rolling down his brow, stinging his eyes. He put the back of his trembling hand against his face and wondered how long he had left to live. If other snipers lurked in the surroundings, now was their chance. There was nowhere else to go, and thirst became more than just an annoyance. Water was a necessity. His throat burned with the need to drink.

The tannoy, crackling into life, drove all such thoughts from his mind as a detached, ephemeral voice cut through the dry heat, "It's over, Chaise. Throw down your weapon and step out into the open."

He'd taken the handgun, leaving the sniper rifle full of useless blanks behind. However, the handgun would serve him well, and more of the bastards would die before the damned test was through. If it was a test. Perhaps they had always wanted to kill him.

He chanced a quick look across the open compound and swore.

There were at least eight men walking through the dust, full combat gear, automatic rifles ready. Chaise calculated how many he could drop before the bullets ripped him open, and he knew it was hopeless. The weight dropped from his shoulders, decision made, and a strange kind of peace settled over him. He stood up, hands held high, the handgun dangling from his right index finger.

"On the ground," the mechanical-sounding voice from the tannoy barked.

Chaise waited, considered his actions. In the distance, a Humvee braked hard, sending up a cloud of broken ground. More voices, lots of agitated people. Chaise saw armed men disgorging themselves from the vehicle, spreading out to form a tight circle. The man in the centre, covered by this small defensive ring, must have been a high-ranking officer of some description. Chaise neither knew, nor cared.

"*On the ground,*" said the voice, more urgent this time, adding to the atmosphere of danger. "Do as you are told, and throw the weapon away."

The first line of soldiers before him tensed and he nonchalantly allowed his handgun to fall to the ground. At once, they rushed forward, one soldier kicking away the gun whilst a second pointed his rifle straight at Chaise's head. "Get on the ground, you piece of shit."

Chaise dropped to his knees without comment and someone came behind him, put their boot between his shoulder blades and kicked him face forward into the dirt. A rifle muzzle pressed into his temple whilst hands ran over his body.

"You move and I'll kill you."

He closed his eyes, allowed more hands to turn him over onto his back. The sun burned through his eyelids, seared into his brain and he felt grateful when they yanked him upright and nudged him forward with their rifles.

When he reached the Humvee, the officer had his hands on his hips, gnawing away at his lip. Chaise held the man's burning gaze for a few seconds before someone put a rifle stock into his back and knocked him down to his knees.

The officer leaned forward and spat into his face, "You're a fucking murdering bastard."

Chaise blinked, wishing it was water instead of spit. "Thank you, sir."

It was the wrong thing to say, and Chaise knew it. The officer winced, nodded his head once, and it began, the blows raining down on Chaise's body, slamming into his ribs, the wind rushing out of him and he fell, tried to curl up, but nothing could stop them as he wriggled and struggled. They kicked and punched and soon the world became filled with pain, scalding, searing, crippling, pain. From somewhere he dragged up some inner strength, some desperate urge to survive, and he rose, arms fending off the blows as best he could. Then something heavy cracked into the nape of Chaise's neck; the pain ceased and the sun stopped burning.

The Jeep ground to a halt and Chaise's door opened, and he blinked, took a moment to regain his bearings and got out. He stood in a large, semi-circular gravelled driveway, a sprawling house looming over him with broad steps leading to the large double doors. Lights blazed from virtually every window.

Vladimir was still smiling, but the gun was no longer in his hand. Chaise saw the butt sticking out of the man's waistband. "Are you surprised by what you see?"

Chaise took another look at the house. A fine, grand mansion, well over a hundred years old, possibly more. As well as the steps, marble pillars flanked the fine entrance. "Should I be?"

"Perhaps you thought you were dealing with mindless thugs, eh? Low lifes, opportunists. Rats in the pack."

"You speak good English, Vladimir."

His eyes could not hold back the surprise this time. "You have me at a disadvantage. We met in the hallway with Lomax, but I do not *know* you."

"Not even after going through all my things?"

"You're a secretive man. Even the girl would not tell." He grinned. "She was pretty."

In a blink, Chaise hit him. It was so fast that neither Vladimir nor the other guy had time to react. Even as Vladimir crumpled forward, the air gushing out of him, Chaise took the gun, and twisted him round to form a barrier between himself and the driver. The gun made the driver stop. "Throw over the keys."

Without hesitation, the man delved into his jacket pocket, and came out with the keys. He tossed them onto the ground.

"Now, put the gun in the front seat." Chaise watched him do so. "Okay, you go tell your boss to come outside, or I'll kill his beloved little boy right here, right now."

The driver's mouth opened and closed a few times, the shock petrifying his limbs.

Chaise let Vladimir fall to the ground where he stayed, taking in rasping gulps of air. The blow, a three-fingered strike to the solar plexus, was sufficient to drop any man. It might have killed him and a part of Chaise regretted he hadn't followed through and wiped the bastard out for good. He took in a breath. Time enough for all of that. He narrowed his eyes at the driver. "I've given you an order, now do as you're fucking told."

The man-made a sound like a wounded animal and broke into a run, tripping over the steps in his eagerness to get away.

Chaise put his foot on Vladimir's head and pressed down slightly. "You be a good little boy for a moment, Vladimir. Daddy will soon be here."

"I'm going to kill you," he said, words muffled as his contorted lips moved amongst the gravel.

"Not today you're not," and Chaise grinned, a new direction forming in his conscience. Why wait for 'later'. Why not let it begin *now.* "In fact, not any day soon, you piece of shit. Because I'm going to fucking crucify you, and every one of you miserable bastards. You think on that as you go bye-byes."

Then Chaise drew back his foot and brought it down with tremendous force onto the side of Vladimir's skull, not once but three times.

THIRTY-EIGHT

The light that spilled across the driveway gave Chaise a perfect view of the huge double oak doors. He crouched behind the bonnet of the Jeep and took a bead with Vladimir's automatic. It was a Russian-made Stechkin variable automatic, a weapon he was not too familiar with; he would have preferred the Walther, but time was pressing.

He knew enough about the gun to alter the fire-rate, then blazed away at the door, bullets smashing into the solid wood, sending up a mass of broken shavings in all directions. Moving fast, he ripped open the car door, scrambled inside and started it up. He swung the Jeep around the driveway before anybody had the courage to come out of the house, and gunned the engine, flying out of the drive and down the winding approach road.

He had no idea where he was going, having missed the drive to the house. He let his instincts dictate as he peered through the windscreen, the headlamps cutting through the encroaching night. Around him woodland formed an impenetrable wall and afforded him effective cover from any guards lurking in the dense undergrowth; he knew instinctively they would be waiting somewhere and somewhere close.

He reached the bottom of a slight incline and hoped he was heading towards the main entrance when he took a bend and the headlights from a parked car momentarily blinded him. He hit the brakes hard, slewed the Jeep across the road to the right and rolled out across the ground, leaving the engine still running.

He slithered over to the trees and waited. The Stechkin was almost out of its twenty-round magazine, and the Walther was back in the Jeep. He cursed under his breath.

"Mr Chaise?"

The tension faded, the raised voice bringing a smile to his face. He blew out a breath, climbed to his feet and shambled forward, holding up his hand against the glare from the parked car. "Colin? Turn the damned lights off."

There was an instant response and Chaise allowed himself to relax. He watched Colin coming forward out of the gloom. He had his hands thrust inside his raincoat pockets.

"That's far enough," said Chaise, bringing up the Stetchkin.

"I hope you haven't caused too much excitement, Mr Chaise. That would be unfortunate, given my remit."

"Stuff your bloody remit, Colin. Where the fucking hell have you been?"

"Here and there. Trailing you. Like I told you, I'm here to protect you."

"And yet you let them take me away in that fucking Jeep?"

"That puzzled me – why *you* allowed them to do that."

"I wanted to know who the father was, where he lived. I've got the second piece of information."

"And the men who brought you here?"

Chaise smiled. "I did a little something for Marianne." He walked over to his car, leaned through the open window, switched off the engine and scooped up the Walther. "We'd better go, they'll be coming after us fairly soon."

"Fairly predictable response. Tell me, did you kill anyone, Mr Chaise?"

"What the fuck do you think?"

"I'd like to think that whatever you did can be contained, Mr Chaise. You know what my employers think of you racking up these problems. They're already pig-sick about what happened in the flat."

Chaise thought for a moment, went round to the boot of the Jeep and opened it. Chaise whistled when he pulled back an oily grey blanket, the interior light revealing what lay inside. "Did you get in touch with your dodgy friends for me, Colin?"

"I did. But they are somewhat reluctant to deal with you in your own territory, so to speak. They prefer to meet you in London."

"It won't be necessary, not now." Chaise lifted a Kalashnikov AKS-74. "I think I have all I need right here."

He picked up an accompanying holdall stuffed full of magazines, slammed the boot shut before taking a step backwards and shooting out the two rear tires with the Stechkin. As the air exploded in a great hiss, he hurled the Russian handgun into the woods, pulled out the Walther and brushed past Colin. "Come on, we've things to sort out."

"I'm not happy," said Colin as he accompanied Chaise to his Clio. "You are placing me in an impossible position." He squeezed in behind the wheel and got the car into reverse. As he did so, a series of lights dipped and jabbed through the night from the direction of the house. They were moving closer, very quickly. "Looks like we've got company."

"Let's delay them for a moment."

"Mr Chaise, *please.*"

But Chaise was already hanging out of the window, and he let go a burst from the AKS that peppered the front of the lead car as it came in to full view, hitting the engine and igniting it into a thundering blast of flame and smoke.

Swearing, Colin battled with the steering wheel as tyres screamed in the soft ground, sending up a shower of wet soil. He gunned the engine, driving the little Clio hard, putting distance between them and the other, blazing car. The knuckles in his hand glowed white, his face set hard, teeth gritted.

"Lighten up, Col," said Chaise, "the fun's only just beginning."

Colin snapped his head around. "Mr Chaise."

"What?"

"Don't ever call me Col."

THIRTY-NINE

Earlier the same day, Johnny drove Brigit back to her friends' house. She needed a change of clothes, she said. He told her he needed to ditch the car, as soon as possible. So he waited and watched her walk down the road towards the house where she had been staying.

He trusted Brigit. Honesty permeated from every square inch of her taut, lean body, a body that stirred his memory of the previous night. She'd run her hands over him in a way he had never believed possible, making him so hard he thought he would explode. If he allowed himself to dare to believe what she said was true, perhaps there was a chance for them. Two days ago such considerations did not feature in his thoughts, but now ...

He opened his eyes and peered through the windscreen. He'd fallen asleep and a sudden stab of panic caused him to wince. He checked the dashboard clock and swore. She's been gone for over twenty minutes. Without another thought, he reached for his gun and stepped outside.

She came round the corner in the MGB, drew up close and got out. She'd changed, a plain skirt and hooded zip jacket. In the back of the open-topped car sat a large suitcase.

Her smile brought a tinge of shame. How could he have doubted her?

She leaned into him and kissed his cheek. "You'd better put that away before I start thinking you're planning on hurting someone. Possibly me."

He laughed and deftly dropped the Glock into his pocket. "Sorry. I fell asleep and panicked." The MGB looked superb this close. "We're going in this?"

"Don't you want to?"

"My God, yes. It's beautiful."

"I'll drive," she said, getting into the sports car. "I thought we could go down to Chester, find a place to stay before I get in touch with Linny."

"She's in Chester?"

"I've no idea. I think she has friends there. Either way, Chester is a good idea, don't you think?" He smiled in agreement and clambered in next to her. "Will your car be all right here?"

"The police will pick it up sooner or later. I've put the keys under the sun visor. By the time they arrive, we'll be long gone." He pulled a face. "Unfortunately, this car is a little conspicuous. We'll be easily spotted."

"I'm not trading it in, if that's what you're thinking. And why worry about that? No one's looking for us, are they?"

"No, I'm just ... your friends. What if they tell the police?"

"They won't. I've convinced them." She reached over and squeezed his knee. "Let's hope I can convince you."

"I think perhaps you already have."

"You're a big softie, aren't you?" She grinned, turned the ignition and took the car out into the street.

Throughout the drive, she stopped at almost every lay-by to stab out Linny's number and wait whilst the phone buzzed away. She sent texts and voice messages, but nothing came back. When they checked into a hotel just outside the City of Chester, she took a shower and lay down on the bed and tried once more, before Johnny got between her legs and spent a long time probing her with his tongue.

As waves of pleasure washed through her, a voice came down the phone.

"Mum?"

It was a small voice, sounding far, far away. Brigit moaned, gripping both edges of the mattress.

"Mum, is that you?"

Brigit sat upright instantly, pushing Johnny away. She swung herself around and stood up, breathless. "Linny? My God, where the hell have you been?"

She selected 'hands free' and laid the phone on the bedside table.

"... and just trying to get things a little clearer in my head."

Brigit pressed a forefinger against her lips as Johnny came to her and sat down on the edge of the bed. "But darling, I've been so worried."

"Me too. Christ, Mum, I've been calling you forever, but there was no signal. Haven't you seen the news?"

"No signal, but ..." She frowned at Johnny. "What news?"

"There was a shooting, in your street for God's sake. Didn't you know? It was on the television and witnesses mentioned a red MGB. Mum, that's you, isn't it? What the hell have you been doing?"

Johnny made as if to cut his throat with his finger, but Brigit held out her hand, palm outwards. "Lovey, things have been a little *strained*. I've been staying with some friends, that's all. But I'm all right, I promise."

"So you weren't there when everything kicked off?"

"No. I'm fine, I promise."

"I was certain ... Christ, I've been so worried. So, what happened with your car? Was it stolen?"

"Yes. Yes, it was." Johnny frowned. She ignored him and continued with the lie, "The police are looking for it."

"Well, that's something I suppose. But Mum, make sure you get your phone fixed, or whatever the problem is because I've been sick with worry."

"I will, lovely. I will. And what about you? I've left you so many messages. Where have you been?"

A pause, the only sound her breathing over the speaker. Finally, a sudden rush of words, "Mum, I'm all right. I've had time to think, and I've decided ... shit, listen. Ryan. You must think I'm the most terrible, heartless bitch, but—"

"I don't think that at all, darling." She sat down next to Johnny and held his hand. He snaked his arm around her waist and held her naked body close.

"I should have explained to him before I took off but ... Mum, he's ... he's so *cold.* I love him, that hasn't changed, but I had no idea ... no idea at all about who he is. He kept everything hidden and when he finally started telling me, I freaked out."

A loud sniff followed by the rustle of material or something came down the line. Brigit said slowly, "No idea about what, my love?"

"His life, his *real* self, what he was capable of – *is* capable of. All through these years ... Lies ..."

Brigit felt Johnny stiffen beside her. She shot him a glance, pressed her forefinger against her lips again. "Capable of what exactly? Linny, I don't understand." Another long silence, followed by the distinct sound of Linny blowing her nose. It was clear she was crying. "Please, Linny. Just take your time, tell me what's been happening."

"Christ Mum, I don't know how to even start. One minute we were living this normal, simple life and then ... it was awful. There was this guy and ... shit, listen. Ryan got himself involved in something. A friend had found some drugs and everyone seemed to want them. Horrible men. Truly horrible. They ... they murdered a girl, shot and killed a local man up in the mountains, put another poor man inside a fridge ... Jesus, it was ghastly. And Ryan was in the thick of it."

"*Ryan*? But, why? What did it have to do with him?"

"I'm not sure. He picked up someone, a hitchhiker and there was a struggle. A gun went off and the guy died. Turns out he was some sort of gangster and Ryan just happened to be in the wrong place at the wrong time. The police pulled Ryan in for questioning and the whole thing snowballed from there."

Brigit looked Johnny squarely in the face. "You said a girl, Linny? Ryan killed a girl?"

"Christ, Mum. *No!* Not Ryan. The police found her in a burned-down house. Arson. The girl was inside when they set it on fire, but it had nothing to do with Ryan. Some horrible, disgusting men from Estepona did it, as a sort of gangland revenge thing, so the reports said."

"You're absolutely sure Ryan had nothing to do with it?" She locked her eyes on Johnny's.

"Mum. I told you, no. Ryan was just an innocent bystander, dragged into it because of the hitchhiker. But soon it all got totally out of hand. A man came to the house, a strange man. Not a gangster like the others. Worked for the Government. He spoke with Ryan and that's when I began to suspect Ryan hadn't been entirely honest with me. And later ... Christ, Mum, this man ... he tried to rape me. *Force* himself on me, you understand?"

"Linny, what the hell are you talking about? He tried to *rape* you? *Who?*"

"I told you, the guy from the Government. Don't you ever *listen* ... Jesus."

"I had no idea about any of this." It was Brigit's turn to be shocked, and all at once, the tears rolled down her cheeks, unchecked. "What happened?"

"Ryan shot him. Right there, right in front of me. Took out a gun as if it was the most natural thing in the world and ... Mum, it was terrible."

"He shot a man? *Ryan*?"

"Point-blank range."

"Dear God." Brigit fished for a tissue, but realised at once she had nowhere to keep one. Without a word Johnny went over to the dressing table and returned with a wad. She smiled and dabbed the tears from her eyes. "So, what happened to him? The police, they arrested him?"

"Nothing happened. Some more men came and they cleaned up everything. Not police, British guys. They took everything away, the body, the bullet, blood, clothes, everything. It was as if none of it had happened by the time they left. That's when I snapped. Because then I knew who Ryan was, and what he'd always been. And all those years of us living a normal life, it was all a charade. A lie. I can't live like that anymore, Mum. I just can't."

"But Linny ... a charade? What does that mean?"

"Mum. Ryan works for the Government. He's a special operative."

"For the government? You mean, like a *spy?*"

"Mum, he told me everything, who he is, what he does. He said he had told me too much, that he'd signed papers and if they ever found out they would kill him. I can't live my life with him, not anymore. Christ, Mum, you have no idea."

"This sounds so *outrageous*, my love. A special operative?"

Linny took a deep breath. "Mum, he's ..." Her voice came ragged and fast. "Ryan is an assassin. The man I thought I knew is a professional killer."

FORTY

Later, Chaise returned to his flat to discover Harper's men had visited and cleaned everything, leaving no trace of Marianne or any evidence of the appalling things the Lithuanians had done. He stood and stared at the sanitised interior, knowing if he tried hard enough he could stir up the memories, but he didn't want to try so hard; he wanted to keep the hate buried for now, the burning rage.

He quickly gathered together a change of clothes and went to Colin's hotel, aware of time pressing; Vlad's compatriots would arrive soon with murder uppermost in their thoughts.

Colin met him in the hotel foyer and took him through to the quiet bar, background music playing softly to fill in the silences. Chaise was in no mood for talking and he sat and sipped at his drink whilst Colin stared into space.

For over ten minutes they sat in silence. At last, a single cough broke the silence and Colin shuffled in his chair, sheepish, uncertain. "I called it in, Mr Chaise, and I have to tell you, no one is very happy. They are anxious you don't create a situation that may involve the authorities. They feel you are already out of control, and they have ordered me to kill you."

The atmosphere changed, charged with danger as Chaise's mood grew menacing. He nudged his glass away, leaning back into his seat. "And what did you say, Colin?"

"I told them I could contain the situation."

"That was kind of you."

Colin squeezed his mouth together, exasperated. "Please try to take this seriously."

"That's exactly what I am doing, taking it all very, *very* seriously."

"Yes, I know. I've seen how *serious* you can be. I'm not so sure I will be able to contain anything anymore, not now."

"So what do you suggest? Guns at dawn?"

"Mr Chaise, I'm in a difficult situation. I've grown to respect you. *Like* might be pushing it a little too far, but I can see you are a man of scruples. Your sense of justice is clear to anyone, and is to be commended. You wanted to help that woman, and they came and they killed her. Now you want revenge."

"I want to crush them, Colin. I can't sit back and let them get away with what they've done, what they continue to do."

"This is what drove you in Spain, yes? The desire for personal revenge?"

"I'm not a one-man crusade, Colin, but I won't be threatened or attacked by anyone. And when mindless thugs come into *my* house and ..."

Colin held up his hand. "I understand. I do. I'm not excusing them, for Christ's sake, but it's your actions, your responses which cause the problems, Mr Chaise. Your methods."

"I fight fire with fire. It's not simply Marianne. They are trafficking people, Colin. Destroying people's lives, desperate people, with no hope. They prey on them, take advantage, then rob them blind. No one does a fucking thing about it and what they did to Marianne ..." His voice trailed away and he took a long drink.

"So what will you do?"

"Tomorrow, I'll go to the abandoned house. I'll leave early, get into position. Then I want you to do me a favour."

Colin frowned. "These *favours* are mounting up, Mr Chaise."

"I'll remember you in my will, Colin."

"Mr Chaise, I don't know what you're planning but we can't have a gunfight in the street. That is exactly what Whitehall does not want."

"It won't be in the street. Not if you do as I ask."

"I'm at a loss as to what I can do for you, Mr Chaise."

Chaise smiled. "There were other things in that holdall, Colin, not just magazine clips. We're going to send those bastards a message, very simple and very direct. Then they'll come to me, and I'll finish it. You don't have to be a part of any of it after that point, Colin. I promise."

"I'm not sure ... Mr Chaise, you have to understand, I have my orders."

"Fuck your orders, Colin. This has gone way beyond any sense of duty towards faceless, nameless government departments."

"Duty?" He shook his head. "I'm not like you. I am detached from any of this. I've never allowed myself to get too close. I do my job, then walk away."

"Your job is to kill me."

"Only if it gets out of hand, Mr Chaise. I can't allow you to become a sort of Doc Holiday, gunning down the bad guys."

"As they have, you mean?" He leaned forward. "If we don't stop them, they'll get away with it."

"The police will deal with it. Send them what you know and leave it to them."

"They have the police all sewn up, Colin, and you know it. I'm going to help those immigrants, the ones cocooned up behind that old house. What those bastards are doing is worse than slave-trafficking and I'm not going to allow it to continue."

Colin shook his head. "It goes on in every city in the country. A massive trade in human livestock. What can you – one man – possibly hope to achieve?"

"Not much, but it will do something. And, more importantly," he raised his glass and drained it, "it'll make me feel a damn sight better."

The air bit through his thin coat as he sat huddled in the darkened alleyway. He'd checked his watch a hundred times since he'd positioned himself there not two hours previously. It was almost three in the morning. The streets were empty and still and, apart from the lamps that sent out arcs of sickly yellow light, the only other glow came from his bedroom window, shining like a beacon, inviting them in. But they hadn't come, and now his limbs ached and his fingers were numb with cold.

He closed his eyes and settled himself back against the wall. Another hour, then he would return to Colin's hotel, shower and set off for Chris Lomax's abandoned property. His mind drifted to the past, returning to his time in the desert.

They bundled him into a small room and threw him to the ground, stripped him, thrashed his buttocks, soaked him with a power hose. Disorientated, confused, desperate, he put up a pitiful defence and they beat him, hard fists smacking into his abdomen and ribs. By the time they finished, he felt as if he had gone ten rounds in a world championship boxing match. And lost.

Manhandled into the Commander's office, his feet trailing across the dirt, they dropped him in front of the desk. Someone swivelled a lamp and shone it into his face, the light burned into his brain and he moaned, tried to bring up his arm. The effort proved too much, so he squeezed his eyes shut, kept his mind a blank, breathed through the pain, ignored the tightness of his throat, the sandpaper coating on his tongue. He desperately needed to drink.

"You'll tell me your name," said a voice from somewhere behind the scorching lamp.

His lips were too thick to form coherent words and someone kicked him, forcing him to mumble, "You know it."

"Humour me."

A hand grabbed his hair, yanked back his head. A face came close. "Tell us, you piece of shit."

They punched him again, the first blow sending stars racing across his eyes, the others so swift he no longer knew where he was, the fists seeming to strike someone else. He tasted the sand in his mouth, mixing with the blood and believed he was going to die. One thought dominated everything: the need to drink.

All he desired, all he ever wanted – water. A single mouthful would be enough.

"What unit are you with?"

Chaise grimaced, forcing himself to get to his knees, to glare at the man in the neatly pressed uniform, the man with the pips on his shoulder. "You know that too."

"Answer me, and all of this will stop. Name, unit. Who sent you here?"

A tiny tingle of fear ran through his stomach. Had he got it wrong? Where these people from another force, another sector, or the enemy? No, that was stupid. They'd brought him to the compound and subjected him to a test. The ultimate test of survival. To be shot at, attacked and ... and now this. The interrogation.

He knew they were not the enemy. They hadn't crammed shit into his mouth or stuck truncheons up his arse. They hadn't raped him. No, they weren't the enemy. This was still the test.

"I need water," he managed.

"What's that you say? *Water*? You'll get all the water you need if you tell me your name and unit, and who sent you."

"Water first."

"No. Information first, you bastard."

"I can't think. Please."

Someone behind him moved. He sensed there were three of them altogether. The two who brought him in, and the officer asking the questions, whoever he was.

One of them thrust a canteen into his face and he took it and drank. The water, cool and clean, cut through the dust and the grime, brought new life to his limbs, and his brain. It was the most delicious thing he had ever tasted.

They believed they had almost broken him. The self-control almost broke more than once, but Chaise had forced himself to submit, to surrender to the punches, the kicks. He'd waited, knowing the moment would arrive. And now, with the help of the water, his thoughts clarified, senses returned to high alert. With renewed focus, eyes registering where he was, he handed over the canteen to the first soldier, who reached out to take it.

Chaise struck, as fast as a praying mantis, grabbing the man's wrist, twisting it, flipping him over onto his side. The second soldier reacted, brought his rifle around, but too late. Chaise moved into him, elbows striking hard and fast, breaking his nose with a frightful crack, slamming him into the corner, dazed and bloody. Chaise took up the automatic rifle, spun around and aimed it towards the officer, who gaped, ashen, terror written over his face.

The first soldier climbed to his feet, rubbing his wrist and Chaise grinned, "Don't do anything stupid."

Leaning forward with his hands planted on the desk, the officer did his best to appear vexed. "You're the stupid one, Chaise. Have you seen yourself? Naked as a babe?"

Chaise arched an eyebrow. "You bastard. You've known my name all along – all of this was nothing more than part of your fucking, pathetic little test."

"One that you have passed."

Chaise frowned and considered the officer's words. As he did, the heat rose from deep within, set his teeth on edge, caused his hands to shake. How dare they, these bastards? To subject him to all this crap. If they wanted to know if he could kill, they only had to ask.

The officer stood up straight. "Put the gun down, private."

"If I do, you'll kill me."

"Don't be bloody stupid. You're the finest candidate we've ever had. You've passed. It's over. Put the gun down, please."

He wanted to, he truly did. He lowered his eyes, focused in on the rifle and tried, tried so hard to drop it, but he no longer had any control over his limbs. The heavy, cold metal of the weapon seemed welded to his grip. If he let it go, death would follow. And he so wanted to lie down, sleep. Wake up from this nightmare. So tired now …

"You'll receive some further training, to refine your natural skills. You have a flair for violence which is very agreeable." Chaise gazed into the man's eyes. The officer smiled and for a moment he looked almost human. "It's all over, Chaise, so you can relax, get yourself cleaned up. I'll be talking to your CO. Get the ball rolling."

The first soldier, still rubbing his wrist, took a step closer, grinning. "I'll look forward to your training. Give you a little more to think about."

Chaise's head reeled, relief washing over him in a huge, sudden wave. He lowered the rifle and threw it sideways towards the soldier, who caught it, took out the magazine and dropped it on the desk.

"What do you want us to do with him, sir?"

"Do with him? Get him dressed, for one thing, Reynolds. The first act of the play is closed."

Nobody laughed and Chaise merely frowned before the strength drained from him and he pitched forward into blackness.

A car's headlights hit him in the eyes and he pressed himself back into the shadow, flat against the wall, the desert sand replaced by the cold of a British morning. He shook his head, brought out the Walther PPK and slowly eased the slide backwards and forwards. He'd chosen the Walther for its lower velocity, knowing if he needed to shoot the noise would be less than the Russian armoury he had acquired.

He watched as the car stopped in front of the estate agency. A man got out, tall, well built, wearing a suit as if turning up for work at the office. He paused to check both ways before stepping up to Chaise's flat and pressing the doorbell.

From his position, Chaise could not make out the man's features, but it was clear he was no East European gangster. He seemed relaxed and casual, as if it were three in the afternoon rather than morning.

The man pressed the bell again, stepped back and craned his neck to peer towards the flat window. He turned, bringing out his mobile, and Chaise got the first decent look at his face.

It was the guy from the car park all that time ago, the one from whom Ryan had lifted the Walther. Mellor's man. Simms.

What the hell was he doing here?

FORTY-ONE

He cursed himself for allowing his mind to wander. Cracks had appeared around the edges; too many years in the wilderness making him grow soft. Angry now, he peered keenly towards Simms who stood, hands on hips as if pondering what to do next.

At that moment, another car came around the corner.

Chaise saw it all as if in slow motion.

Simms, of course, was not prepared. Why would he be? When the car pulled up and the doors opened, four men got out, dressed in identical clothes; black balaclavas, leather jackets, combat trousers. Nevertheless, there could be no mistaking Mikhail. The man was a monster, making Simms seem like a schoolboy in comparison.

They circled Simms, gaggling away at him. He put up his hands, and that was his first mistake.

Mikhail punched him hard in the abdomen, probably harder than he had ever been hit before, the force of the blow enough to smash through a barn door. Simms staggered and crumpled, spluttering, fighting to catch his breath. Mikhail kicked him under the chin and Simms no longer moved, leaking blood over the pavement.

Chaise remained still. He had no feelings for Simms, merely curious about what would happen next.

Mikhail stepped over Simms and gestured to his compatriots. One brought a package from the car. By its shape, Chaise instinctively knew what it was and he felt his stomach knotting. Semtex.

As one of them fitted the detonators, the others dragged Simms into the doorway. They were going to blow the place to kingdom come, and Simms with it.

Chaise's choices became simple. He could either run in the opposite direction, get into his car at the far end of the alleyway, and leave it all behind him or step out into the lamplight and kill them all.

He made his decision, hoping Colin had already delivered his part of the bargain.

Under the trees, along a rutted trackway, Colin parked his car. He'd disengaged the locking mechanism of the main gates, feeling pleased his old skills still had their uses and checked there was no alarm system before continuing. Now, in the silence, he pulled out the sawn-off shotgun and the canvas shoulder bag from the boot and made his way through the woodland towards the house. He did not think there would be any guards, the Lithuanians confident in their own strength, but if he came across any, he knew exactly what to do.

He reached the gravel driveway and bent down on one knee. The house was in darkness, a solid, massive behemoth looming before him in the black, silent morning. He took a quick glance around and moved forward.

This was the most critical part, and he knew it. Anyone watching would be able to pick him out clearly, despite the night. And, as expected, when he drew closer the sensors came into play and the security lights went on.

He winced at the sudden glare, but took aim anyway, and loosed off both barrels towards the entrance.

The doors shuddered and splintered from the blast and Colin fed in two more cartridges as lights came on inside the house. Without a pause, he fired again and the doors groaned inwards, one of them torn from its hinges. It yawned open and Colin put two more shots through it, shattering its already fragile surface.

Voices cried out from within. Frightened, confused voices. Within ten feet now, Colin took out the smoke grenade from the bag, gripped it in his right hand and pulled out the pin with his teeth. He hadn't done this for a long time, and his heart hammered in his chest. He had one chance and the voices were coming closer.

He brought his right arm over in a wide arc, sending the grenade sailing through the air towards the door. It hit the top step, bounced forwards, and clattered through the shattered doorway.

Colin moved away in a half-crouch, counting the seconds in his head. When he reached thirty, the grenade exploded with a deep, heavy *whump*. He whirled to see a rapidly developing cloud of thick, grey smoke belching from the house entrance. He got down on his knee again, put the shotgun aside and brought out the snub-nose.

The security lights gave him a grandstand view.

Two men came out, hands in front of their faces, blind men blundering around as the smoke billowed around them. He shot the first in the knee and the man fell, writhing on the top step, hands gripping the wound. His companion swung around in a wild sort of flamenco, screaming. Colin fired again, but the bullet zinged harmlessly by. It was enough to send the man scuttling back inside.

Colin took out the second object from the bag and looked at it. He wasn't sure if Chaise's plan would succeed. Chaise had wanted Colin to use fragmentation grenades, of which there were three in the back of the Lithuanians' car, but Colin did not agree. He was already in a dilemma about everything but knew this was no time for soul-searching. The line already crossed, he looked at the rock in his hand, with the message secured and covered, held in place by clingfilm.

He swore and threw the rock towards the door.

It made the centre of the steps and tumbled back down to the ground to rest next to the writhing man.

Colin ran.

He was not used to this. Within perhaps a few dozen paces, a tightness around his chest increased, a burning in his lungs, searing pain in his ribs. By the time he staggered to the car, sweat covered his face, his breathing laboured. He held onto the driver's door, gulping in the air, forcing down the growing sense of dread threatening to overwhelm him. He was too damned old; too many fried breakfasts and not enough exercise. His heart couldn't take it. He should be in Burgundy, sitting in his farmhouse, relaxing, drinking a good, full-bodied red, not playing at soldiers for Ryan fucking Chaise.

He pulled open the door and got in, wiping his face with the back of his hand. With the car in reverse, he went back down the trackway to the main road.

It proved difficult, the taillights worse than useless, the fog lights not working. He put the indicator on for extra illumination and concentrated on keeping his speed down.

Sweat dripped into his eye and he blinked, momentarily blinded. Before he knew it, the car veered off to the left and crashed through the undergrowth, tree branches screeching across the bodywork. Colin cursed, fought to keep the car straight, and braked hard.

Silence, ominous and huge, an invisible monster looming over him: crushing him. He held on, breath rattling his chest, more sweat running down his face. Nothing to do except wait, recover. He let his forehead rest on the wheel. Time meant nothing now.

Time. Too much time. Racing away time.

His eyes sprang open and he slammed the car into first and shot forward, clearing the thick vegetation with a great scream of churned-up undergrowth, tangled bushes, leaves and earth. The tyres whirred, the steering wheel spun through trembling fingers and he braked again as the first man came running down the track, picked out by the Clio's headlamps.

"Shit!"

Colin got the side window down and leaned out. The man was running fast, a big, heavy-looking automatic rifle strapped across his chest. He skidded to a halt and dropped down to his knees, levelling the rifle towards the car.

Colin shot him in the chest, dipped back inside and rammed the car into reverse again.

He kept his eyes fixed on the rear windscreen, jaw set, determined to ignore any distractions. He had to keep moving before any more of those damned lunatics appeared.

The gateway came into view, the street lamps beyond the most welcoming sight he had ever seen. He swung the car out into the road and gunned the engine, foot slammed down on the accelerator all the way to the floor.

He glanced into the rear-view mirror, saw nothing and allowed himself a moment to relax, letting out a long breath. The trees on either side blurred by, and ahead he saw the first streaks of the grey dawn spreading across the horizon. He fumbled inside his pocket for the mobile, almost letting it slip through his wet fingers. But he held on, managed to bring up Chaise's number and connected.

The phone vibrated in Ryan Chaise's pocket and he lifted it out.

"It's done."

He snapped it shut without a word and slipped it back into his trousers. He took another look towards the estate agency. The guy with the Semtex adjusted the detonator as Mikhail whiled away the minutes by lifting Simms to his feet, cuffing him across the jaw, then slamming his knees into the man's crotch. Simms howled, going limp in the big ape's grip. Mikhail backhanded him with nonchalant ease, sending Simms pirouetting to the ground. The others looked on and laughed.

Chaise calmed himself and moved.

He crossed the road briskly, making a direct line towards Mikhail.

Nobody noticed him until he was within spitting distance.

"That's enough, Mikhail."

They all froze, even the guy with the detonator. All of them must have been sporting looks of absolute incredulity because not even the balaclavas could mask their utter surprise.

"I want you to put any guns you've got on the ground. Very slowly."

For a moment, he wasn't sure if any of them had heard him, the silence almost total. He jerked the Walther. "Do it."

"I'm going to kill you," grunted Mikhail, and he flexed his massive hands.

"I'll kill you first, Mikhail." Chaise pointed the Walther at the big man's head. "This little baby may look small, but it's got enough power to blow your fucking brains all over this street. So put down your guns and get in the fucking car."

"You had better kill me now you bastard, because I promise you—"

"This isn't a fucking movie, Mikhail. This is real life, and yours is about to end if you don't do as you're told. Get in the fucking car and drive away, back to Daddy. He's got a message for you."

Mikhail pulled the balaclava from his head. "What the fuck are you talking about?"

"Like I said. I've sent Dad a message. He'll want you to follow what it says, so be a good lad and go and see him."

"You put my brother in hospital, you bastard."

"Did I? Pity, I had hoped he was dead."

"He's brain damaged, you piece of shit." His hands came up, clenching and unclenching, "I'm going to make sure you suffer before you die, you hear me? I'm going to make you beg me to kill you."

"Like Lomax's wife, eh, Mikhail? The way you made her suffer? I'm in the game of evening up scores, Mikhail, and this one has not yet made the final whistle." He motioned with the Walther. "Get in the car. You," he pointed to the guy who had been busying himself with the detonator. "Leave all of that there. Now, all of you, guns on the ground."

Slowly, one by one, the men brought out their handguns and put them on the pavement. They moved to the car and began to get inside. No one spoke until Mikhail stopped at the passenger door and turned, grinning, the streetlights picking out his big teeth. "The wife? She pleaded for her life. You know that? She begged me to stop."

"But you didn't stop, did you, Mikhail?"

"She had guts. A brave girl. A good girl, too. You understand me?" He winked. "I enjoyed her before I killed her."

The Walther came up, with slow and calculated intent.

"Chaise. Leave it. That's an order."

Simms's voice broke through the night, splintering the tension, hauling Chaise back from the brink. He glanced across and saw Simms sitting up, pressing a handkerchief against his shattered nose. "I'm ordering you, Chaise. Back down."

Chaise narrowed his eyes to mere slits, controlling his natural desire to blow the big man's brains out as he turned once more to confront Mikhail. "I'll be seeing you. Don't think I won't."

"I'll look forward to it." The big man grinned, got in and slammed the door. The car drove away at speed.

For a long time, Chaise watched the taillights disappearing into the night.

Simms groaned and Chaise gave him a swift glance. "Are you all right?"

"Just fucking dandy. What the hell do you think?" He put his back against the wall and pushed himself upright. "Jesus, he was a fucking ox."

"Thanks for stopping me. The plan would have gone to shit if I had killed the bastard."

"Plan?" Simms looked at the blood on his handkerchief. "What plan?"

"Never you mind. Did Harper send you?"

"No."

That was a surprise and Chaise considered the options. He couldn't think of any. "Well, whoever did, you may as well tell them that I've almost finished up here."

"They're nervous, Chaise. They haven't been informed of anything."

"Who? Harper, MI5? Who?"

"That's for me to know," he said and winced as he took a breath. His hand pressed against his stomach. "I've never ever been hit like that in my life. Which reminds me," he nodded towards the Walther, "that's my gun."

"So *that's* the reason you called, eh?" Chaise shook his head, turned the gun in his hand and presented it butt first to Simms. He nodded towards the automatics strewn across the pavement. "I've got a good selection to choose from. No hard feelings, eh?"

"What am I supposed to say to that?" He took the gun, checked it, and slipped it into his waistband. "I think you just saved my life."

"Don't flatter yourself." He pointed to the Semtex. "It was all about that."

FORTY-TWO

Sometime before breakfast, Brigit punched out Chaise's number and waited for it to connect. She stood by the dressing table of the hotel suite and studied Johnny as he lay asleep on the bed, sheets entangled between his legs. She trawled her eyes over his body and a tiny flutter ran across her belly. The night had been one of the best of her life, Johnny a generous and caring lover, taking time with her, ensuring her needs were met. They'd made love three times, something she'd never experienced before. Insatiable, his passion seemed to grow with each thrust of his delicious loins. If she continued to chip away at his hard edges, perhaps he would stay with her; a long-forgotten warmth bathed her, telling her she had found it in her heart to forgive him for the man he once was.

"Brigit?"

She gave a tiny gasp. "Oh, Ryan. Sorry. Yes, I'm—"

"It's Linny? Has something happened to her? Is she hurt?"

Even now he could turn it on, the consummate actor. Pretending he cared. "She's fine, Ryan. I've spoken to her, and everything is perfectly okay."

She heard his sigh. "Thank God."

She wanted to say something, reveal the truth to him, but she held back knowing her time would come. "Ryan, we need to meet. Talk."

A prolonged pause. Did he sense, perhaps, that his false charm had failed this time? Had her voice been too sharp, too full of the anger she felt for this man. Or, more simply, she wondered if he had disconnected.

"Brigit, it's kind of complicated right now."

"Ryan, it can't wait. Maybe not today, but tomorrow. It's important and I wouldn't have telephoned you except I—"

"All right. Listen. I'll text you an address and we can meet. Where are you?"

"At the moment I'm staying in a hotel. Outside Chester."

"*Chester?* I can't come there, Brigit, there're too many things I need to sort out here. I'm in Norwich."

A stab of panic pierced her throat and she fell down onto the edge of the bed. "Jesus, Ryan, that's bloody miles away."

"I can't come there, Brigit, not now. In a few days, perhaps."

"Not even for Linny?"

She heard the sharp intake of his breath. "Fuck, Brigit, you said ... what the hell has happened?"

"Nothing to get anxious about, but we need to sort things. And you need to be here."

"She's upset, isn't she?"

Self-control disappeared in an instant, and she blurted, "*What the hell do you think?*" She bit her bottom lip, cursing herself for allowing her anger to reveal itself. A part of her wanted to continue, to tell him exactly what she thought of him, but then he would probably become tetchy, throw down the phone and she would never see him and Johnny might again suspect his guilt. "Yes," she said, struggling to maintain the even tone in her voice, "she's upset. I hate seeing her like that, so if we could meet up I'm sure we can straighten everything out."

Another, albeit smaller pause. "Yes. You're right, Brigit. All right, I'll be in touch. Just give me a couple of days."

The phone went dead and she sat and looked at it for a long time.

Not until Johnny's fingers ran up her spine did she put Chaise out of her mind. She smiled down at her lover.

"Who was that?"

"Him." She rolled over into his arms and he held her close, kissing the top of her head, whilst his hand continued to flutter up and down her spine.

"You've fixed a meeting?"

"In a couple of days."

He tensed, the fingers stopping their journey. "A couple of days? Brigit, I'm not sure we can wait that long. If what your daughter says is true, and what happened is all over the news, they'll be looking for me."

"It'll be all right, Johnny."

"How do you know?"

"Trust me." She snuggled into him, his arms strong, warm. If only they could stay like this forever, not in a hotel room but in their own place. Waking up next to one another, so close, so safe. She closed her eyes as his fingers gently fluttered over her skin again and she felt his cock begin to stir. She sighed, her hand moving down between his legs to feel him, engorged, pulsing with desire. "Just before we have breakfast, I want you to remind me what you can do with this lovely big thing of yours."

Chaise tapped his bottom teeth with the mobile, going over what Brigit had said, sounding so anxious, so angry. In the past, she'd never made her feelings known, yet Chaise always knew. He saw it in her eyes every time they met. He wasn't good enough, and now, if Linny had told her the truth ...

He glanced at his watch. It was almost seven. He hadn't slept a wink, and today would be tough. Simms was busy making yet another batch of coffee and Colin had returned to his hotel to shower. Soon it would be time to leave, and Chaise didn't feel prepared. He rubbed the grit from his eyes. The unexpected appearance of Simms could well tip the balance, if Chaise could persuade him to help. The bottom line was that Chaise needed him.

"I made it strong," said Simms, coming into the room with two mugs of steaming coffee. "You look like shit."

Chaise took the coffee and stared into the cup. His body already buzzed with an overdose of caffeine, nevertheless, he still felt weary. "Thanks."

"We need to sort things, Commander." Simms sat down on the chair over by the window. "I didn't come here for a social call."

"I've got things to do, things that can't wait, and might mean you coming along."

"I'm not sure I understand. Has it got something to do with those characters I met last night?"

"It's got a great deal to do with them, but I'll tell you on the way." He took another drink. "Then you can tell me what *you* want."

"I can do that now."

"On the way, Simms. On the way."

They met up with Colin just off the square. "We should go in two cars," said Chaise, and nodded towards Simms. "Mine stays here as it's a hire car. You can take me, Colin can follow us."

"Commander, I'm not at all sure about any of this," said Simms."

"Join the club," said Colin with a wry smile. "Are you sure you've thought everything through, Mr Chaise?"

"Colin, stop being an old woman, and stay close." Chaise walked over to Simms's car. He hefted the holdall and waited until Simms had opened up the doors then threw the bag into the back seat and got in.

They drove through the streets, heading out of the market town towards Norwich. Chaise knew the route by now, and Colin still had the sketch map provided by Chaise the night before. He glanced at his wristwatch. "I reckon they'll be in position round about now."

Simms kept his eyes straight ahead, "*They?* The goons from last night?" Chaise grunted. "So what's the plan?"

Chaise rubbed the stubble on his chin. He wished he'd showered. "Deadly simple, but first, what is it you've got to tell me?"

"That's rather simple too, Commander. You're to go to the Middle East."

Chaise snapped his head around. "The Middle East?"

"Yes, Commander. Major Mellor has given me the instructions." He patted his jacket. "I have everything here for you. Passport, identity papers, money."

"It may have escaped everyone's notice, Simms, but I'm no longer a field operative."

"I think you'll find that your situation has changed."

"Has it, by God?"

"I'm sure Major Mellor will answer all of your questions when I take you to see him."

"And what about Harper? Is all of this his idea?"

Simms shrugged, "I take my orders from Major Mellor, Commander. I tend not to ask questions."

Chaise blew out his cheeks and looked out across the rolling countryside, colours washed out, the dawn grey, weak and unpromising. "I can almost guarantee Harper is at the bottom of this. Shit, the Middle East?" He closed his eyes, determined not to conjure up any more painful memories. "I hoped I'd never go back there again as long as I lived."

"Well, sorry to say that's not the case. A British diplomat has become involved in a little indiscretion, and you're to extract him before it all becomes rather embarrassing. Major Mellor seems to think you are perfectly suited for the assignment, so ..."

"And where exactly is this British diplomat?"

"At present, he's under house arrest, in Tel Aviv."

"And you want me to bring him home?"

"Not me, Commander. Control."

"But Israel ..." Ryan squeezed his lips together. "That's the Mossad, Simms. They don't take kindly to outsiders coming into their backyard."

"Which is exactly why Major Mellor put your name forward,

Commander. He seems to think you have all the qualities required for a successful outcome."

"Jesus." Chaise leaned back against the headrest and closed his eyes. "Keep following the signs for Norwich, Simms and wake me when we get there."

"I have to report in to inform them of your acceptance."

"Do I have a choice?"

"Not really, no."

"As I expected. Let's hope I don't get killed in the meantime."

"You think that's a possibility? With what we're going to do today?"

Chaise opened his eyes and gave Simms a sideways glance. "I think there is every possibility, yes."

Then he turned away and slept.

FORTY-THREE

At the first student house, Chaise walked up to the front door and pressed the bell, not releasing pressure until he heard someone stomping down the hallway, uttering a string of profanities.

The door creaked open and a derelict-looking young man, dressed in a grubby t-shirt and blue shorts, yawned and scratched his mop of wild, unkempt hair. "What the fucking hell do you want?"

"I want you and all your friends to get out of the house in five minutes."

"*What?*" The young man shook his head, frowned deeply. "Who the fucking hell are you? And what fucking time do you—"

"Five minutes." Chaise brought a handgun and waved it under the young man's nose. "What's your name?"

"Stefan."

"Well, *Stefan*, you've got five minutes, or I'll come back and blow your fucking head off."

A little under seven minutes later, a mixed bag of disorientated and half-dressed young people stood shivering on the pavement, clutching various bags and personal effects. Chaise nodded to one of them. "And who are you?"

"Stowell. Peter Stowell."

"Well, Peter Stowell, you've got a little job to do. I want you to go over to that phone box," he gestured across the road, "and call the fire brigade. The rest of you, I'd get well away if I were you." He waved to Stefan, got down on his haunches and pulled open the holdall. Stefan shuffled up close, frowning. "There's enough high-explosive here to make a nice little bonfire of this place," Chaise said and stood up with the Semtex and the detonator. He grinned. "Any time you're ready, Stefan."

Mikhail stood at the top floor window and looked down both ends of the street. He massaged the back of his neck, flexed his shoulders and turned away. He grunted at the man by the door and went downstairs.

He found his father in the back kitchen sitting on a rickety chair, next to a dilapidated table that leaned grotesquely on its uneven legs.

"Any sign?"

"Nothing."

"The bastard has made idiots of us," said Mikhail's father, and slammed his fist down on the table with such power the legs gave up their futile efforts to keep it upright, and the whole lot collapsed. He kicked away the debris and stood up, his face red, veins pulsing at his temples. "You find him, wherever he is, and you bring him to me." He clenched his fist and shook it. "I'll castrate him before I slit open his belly and pull out his entrails."

Mikhail remained impassive. "Sending us that message, telling us he was coming here, it's some sort of trick, I can feel it."

"Like you felt it at his flat, when he took your gun away?" Mikhail took in a breath but said nothing. "Maybe you're right. He's playing us for fools, whoever he is. I will not tolerate it, Mikhail. So, you will find him and you will bring him back to me, and this time, you will do *exactly* as you are told, or I'll make sure—"

He stopped, held his breath as without warning, the house shook. A slight trembling of timber and masonry, followed by a distant rumble, deep and concussive. Plaster drifted down like snow from the ceiling.

Mikhail whirled, gawping towards the window. "What the hell was that?"

His father pushed him aside. "A gas main, who gives a fuck? Get the men together. We'll go back to his flat, set the place alight as I first wanted and smoke the bastard out. He wants to play his games, then we'll oblige him, but we won't be playing by his rules, you understand?" He slammed his fist into his palm. "What he did to Vladimir, Mikhail, I'm going to make him pay, and I'm going to watch him as he—"

Mikhail cut him off with an upheld finger, but before his father let his fury rip, the sound of a fire engine's siren drew closer and he froze and frowned.

"Mikhail."

The man from upstairs burst into the kitchen. He had his mobile with him and his face was rigid with fear.

"What the hell is it?"

The man blanched at the sound of the father's rasping voice. "Forgive me, Mr Chenko, but it is Stefan. There's trouble at one of the other houses."

"What the hell do you mean, *trouble?*"

"I mean, it's on fire."

Mikhail was already moving towards the main door as his father shouted, "You find out what the hell is going on then you get back here, Mikhail, because I want that bastard hung out to dry."

Mikhail stopped at the door and glared back down the hallway. "It's as good as done, father. I'll bring him to you on a plate."

He slammed the door.

Chenko looked at the other man, who cringed in the kitchen doorway. "How many men have we got here?"

"Me, and two others."

"And what is your name?"

"Ivan."

"Well, Ivan, send the others with Mikhail and you stay here with me." He pulled out a gun from inside his coat and checked the magazine. "I have a feeling our English friend will come calling."

. . .

Chaise took the mobile from the trembling hands of the young Lithuanian he had pushed into the back of Simms's car at gunpoint. "Good lad, Stefan," Chaise said with a grin. "Now, I want you to go and talk to those fire brigade boys. Tell them there's been some trouble with the gas, all right? Anything you like, but just keep them busy. That way you'll stay out of it, and that way you'll live, you understand?"

Stefan nodded. His lips trembled. "And Mikhail?"

"When he arrives, you tell him I'll be waiting for him back at the old house."

"He will kill me when he finds out what I have done."

Chaise leaned forward and squeezed Stefan's shoulder. "No, he's the one who's going to get killed. When he goes to Lomax's old house, he dies."

He stepped back to allow the young man to scramble out of the car. Without a moment's hesitation, Stefan ran over to the fire crew, who were busy putting out the minor fire that had erupted in the rear of the students' house.

Simms, who sat behind the wheel, and had witnessed everything, shook his head. "Control isn't going to like this, Commander Chaise. Using that explosive isn't exactly what you'd call 'low-key'."

"I know." Chaise peered across the road to where Colin stood in the middle of a bunch of onlookers, staring towards him, features set hard. "I think I may have overstepped the mark, ever so slightly."

"I beg your pardon?"

Chaise shrugged. "Just a little trouble brewing on the horizon, that's all. Listen, when this is over, I have to go to Merseyside, so tell your bosses that I'll be in touch when I get back."

"I thought I might tag along with you."

"No, I don't think that's a good idea, mate. Not today."

Simms looked at the dashboard and sighed. "I wanted to kill you, Commander Chaise. For what you did to me. But ..." he looked at him, his eyes softening, "you *did* save my life. I just want you to make me one promise."

"What's that?"

"Kill the gorilla who beat the shit out of me."

Chaise grinned. "I'll see you very soon, Simms." He crossed the road and went up to Colin, apologizing as he squeezed through the press of people gathered watching the smouldering remains of the blast.

Chaise watched Simms take the car down the street. "He's taken all the weaponry," Chaise said quietly. "Just as a precaution."

"I'm still not happy."

"Colin, stop worrying. Those students are so terrified they won't be telling anyone anything. Nobody is going to cotton on to what any of this is all about."

A cloud came over Colin's face and he took Chaise by the elbow and led him out of earshot of the little crowd. "I have my orders, Mr Chaise. I've already delayed calling in, out of some misguided allegiance to you."

"It's not misguided, Colin. I appreciate it, I honestly do."

"That's as maybe but the simple fact is, I have my orders. I'm to protect you, but if things get out of control ... well, you know what I'm supposed to do."

"But you're not going to, are you? One, because it's not going to get out of control, and two, you like me."

Colin's eyes closed for a moment. "'Like' has got nothing to do with it. Listen, what you're planning on doing, is sheer lunacy."

"Is it? I don't think so. I'm ridding the streets of vermin, Colin. There are people in those Portacabins living a shit-miserable existence, with no hope, no money, and no future. And whilst they scratch together what they can, those bastards take them for every penny they earn. It's not the immigrants, Colin, it's the mindless gangsters who deal in human traffic that are the real scum of the earth. I couldn't give a flying fuck where they come from, all I know is I'm here to help. They butchered Marianne and her husband. They came into *my* flat and violated my possessions, as well as violating her. I won't tolerate that, not from anyone."

"So, what are you going to do? Kill them all?"

"If I have to. I don't really give a fuck, Colin. For me they're already dead, so you needn't worry too much, okay? I'm not going to cause too much of a scene and afterwards, all you will need to do is make your phone call and have some people come along and take them all away in body bags."

"You make it sound all so simple."

"It really is, Colin. That's what you fail to understand. There's nothing difficult about death." He smiled. "Let's go, before Mikhail arrives with all his merry men."

FORTY-FOUR

Chaise cut across the open fields behind Lomax's old house, moving fast, darting from one piece of cover to the next. He'd already been on the move for well over five minutes. Colin stayed in the car, satisfying his conscience. Being so far away meant he would not witness anything, and what he didn't know wouldn't hurt him. At least, that was the hope.

Crouching behind a clump of trees, Chaise checked both his automatic pistols and fitted them with silencers. He had more clips in his pockets, enough ammunition to deliver hell to the bastards who waited inside the house. He had debated whether to bring the AKS, but the added firepower may have brought the unwarranted attention of a passing police officer, something Chaise did not want.

He sprinted across the field, keeping low, making a zigzag path to a further sprinkling of trees and bushes. From here, he had a good view of the house, silent and grim. A dark, sinister edifice, plucked from a scene in a classic horror movie. Dead ivy clung to the walls, trailing around rotted window frames, and overgrown steps led from the unkempt lawn to a patio, cracked and chipped, everything speaking of decay and neglect. Once glorious, those days long gone, only the vaguest of memories remaining of its former grandeur. A sad and lonely place, and inside were the miserable shits responsible for bringing so much misery to so many. Chaise gritted his teeth and ran forward.

Only a broken-down old fence needed negotiating before he moved into the large back garden, with the row of Portacabins standing so innocuous yet containing such horrors. If the outside world knew what went on here the ensuing outrage might force the authorities to do something. Chaise was under no illusions: this was the tip of a very nasty, very seedy operation, other gangs in other cities plying the same trade. Once, booze and later drugs lined the gangsters' pockets; now people, desperate, disposed and frightened people, made the cash registers ring. It turned his stomach.

Crouching close to the fence, he put his shoulder against the flimsy wood and leaned inwards. With little pressure, he broke through the rotted timbers and took off to the right. Within a few strides, he was in amongst the Portacabins, staying low and moving slowly, one Glock held in both hands, the second in his waistband.

At the first door, he bent down, breathing lightly and listened out for any raised voices. The low rumble of snoring was all he heard. He checked his watch. Ten o'clock. The men inside must have been working a night shift.

That suited him fine for what he had to do.

He looked across at the other buildings. Everything quiet, a few birds singing from the nearby trees.

Ten o'clock.

He frowned and the first niggling doubt crept through his guts. Night shift or not, why was the place so utterly deserted?

Chaise scanned the house for any sign of movement. Windows, black and lifeless, glared out at him. Perhaps everyone had gone to check out the explosion at the other house. That had to be it.

He eased down the handle of the first Portacabin and slowly pulled open the door. After a brief pause, he put his head inside.

A single man lay spread-eagled on one of the camp beds, chest slowly rising and falling, a heavy, thick rumble escaping from his throat. Around him was a mess of jumbled clothes, CDs, leftover food, empty beer cans. Something wasn't right.

From behind, a noise made him swing around, the Glock ready.

Across the lawn, a cat appeared from the narrow alleyway, which ran along the side of the house to the backdoor and gave him a glance before jumping silently onto the fence which ran the length of the garden. Chaise allowed himself a long sigh and lowered the gun.

The solid, cold metal of another gun pressed against his head.

"You move and you die," said a voice, barely above a whisper, unmistakably Eastern European. "Very slowly, put your weapon on the ground and turn around."

Without hesitation Chaise complied, placing the Glock carefully on the grass. With his hands raised, he stood and gazed into the hard face of the man who had, up until recently, lain snoring on the camp bed. The gun in his hand looked very large from this close up.

"Put your hands behind your head and step away."

Chaise did so, watching the man scoop up the Glock and slip it into his pocket.

"Walk towards the house. Any attempt to run, I will kill you."

As Chaise took the first few steps, something moved to his right. He glanced over and sucked in his breath. Bunched together in the doorway of the farthest Portacabin, a gaggle of immigrant workers watched in wide-eyed fascination. There must have been at least twenty of them, young girls, tiny children. The whole, stinking operation right here, waiting to be taken down, and he had made a bloody mess of everything.

They crossed the grass, the man with the gun never far behind, and when they reached the patio steps the kitchen door swung open and a squat, wide bull of a man appeared, grinning like he'd won a million on the lottery. Immaculately dressed in a tailor-made pinstripe suit, his belly strained against his shirt, whilst his head – which seemed ridiculously small for such a large frame – bobbed on a thick tree-trunk neck.

"Welcome to our humble abode," he said, stepping aside to allow

Chaise to enter. He leaned forward and quickly frisked Chaise, found the second Glock and weighed it in his hand. His grin widened as he pressed the gun against Chaise's temple. "You're going to die, my friend. But before you do, I'm going to cause you a great deal of pain. I will listen to your screams and they will please me. When you call out for your mummy, then I shall end it for you. Now, take off your trousers."

Chaise frowned and shot him a glance.

"Your trousers. Take them off, then bend over the table." This was not something Chaise had prepared for. Staring deep into the fat man's eyes, he saw something there which he had come across many times before. The wild, uncontrolled glare of the sadist.

He considered his options but knew there was little he could do. Even if he could take out the fat man, there was still the other guy who had positioned himself expertly on the other side of the door, well out of reach. By the time Chaise seized the Glock, he'd be dead. He had no choice; holding the fat man's gaze, he unbuckled his belt.

The fat man took a step backwards and gave Chaise an admiring glance as the trousers fell to the ground. "You're very tanned." He gestured with the Glock. "Underwear too, my friend."

Chaise stepped out of his trousers then slowly slipped off his boxer shorts and stood upright.

"Very nice. Now, your jacket and shirt. No sudden movements or I'll kill you."

Memories of days back in the desert flooded into his mind, how they tried to humiliate him, prodding him with guns, whistling and clicking their tongues as he stood, naked as the day he was born. And here it was again, the same sad old piece of shit.

With the last piece of clothing discarded, he stood ramrod still whilst the fat man delicately ran the muzzle of the handgun over Chaise's chest and down his abdomen. "You have many scars on your body," he said, "all of which tells me that you are not merely an estate agent. The way you move, the way you hold your gun, your body," he lowered the gun to Chaise's cock. "Who are you?"

Chaise took a breath and looked at the man. "I could ask you the same thing."

The fat man arched an eyebrow. "Yes, it is only right you know the name of the man who is going to make you scream." He smiled. "My name is Chenko. Now, what about you?"

"As you said, I'm just an estate agent."

Chenko laughed. "I don't think so, my friend." He tapped Chaise's flaccid cock with the muzzle of the gun. "You are a policeman, perhaps? Undercover, is that it? I think that is what you are, sent from an outside Force, yes, to infiltrate our operation? Yes, I think that is what you are, a cop who is *clean*, eh? One of the few not on our payroll. Well, let me tell you something, my friend. You may believe your badge, or whatever it is you have, will protect you, but ..." he leaned forward, greasy jowls wobbling, "... it won't! So, tell me, how did you learn about our business here, my friend?" Chenko lifted Chaise's cock with the barrel of the gun. "I am going to cut this off," he said, a tiny ripple of delight at the edges of his voice, "I'm going to cut it off very slowly, to maximise your pain, then I shall stuff it into your mouth as you bleed to death. Such a shame to destroy a thing so wholesome. You must have given much pleasure to a great many women." He lowered the cock and brought the gun to Chaise's face. "But now, its days of fornicating pleasure are done. For today, my friend, I will castrate you. Not just your balls, but everything. As you scream and beg me to finish you, I will cut open your stomach, with all those lovely muscles, and pull out your intestines. And you will see it all, before you die. Medieval in its horror, my friend. Your pain will be greater than you can possibly imagine, and it will not stop, my friend. It is going to last forever."

Chaise swallowed hard and when he looked into the fat man's face, he believed the truth of his words. "Can't we make some sort of a deal?"

"Oh yes," Chenko said, with a wide grin, "yes, of course we can. My friend, I am not an animal. I will not do any of those terrible things if you tell me who you are, and who you work for. It is quite simple."

"If I do, you'll still kill me."

Chenko licked his lips, and ran the gun over Chaise's pectoral muscles, circling each nipple with the muzzle. "Of course, but in a kinder way. And not until I have had my pleasure with you."

"So, I either don't tell you anything and you castrate me, or I do and you fuck me? Is that about it?"

"Perceptive, my friend. Very perceptive."

Chaise expelled air loudly through his nose. "You're a sick old bastard, aren't you?"

"Ah, you see, already we are beginning to know one another. So, how would you like to play this?"

"I'll tell you."

The man's grin grew even broader. "I knew you would, my friend. Now, I want you to bend over what is left of that damned table, because my pleasure will start right now. I'm going to screw you, nice and slowly, then you will tell me what I need to know. Agreed?"

Chaise looked away as Chenko put the gun down and unbuckled his belt, and then he studied the table, which leaned dramatically on its three legs. He doubted it would take his weight, certainly not when the fat man pressed over and rammed his cock into him.

He squeezed his eyes shut. So, it had come to this. The final ignominy. Sodomised by a fat, greasy old man, then dispatched.

Images of Linny came into his head. Her smiling face, bikini-clad body, the nights they had spent at nightclubs, restaurants, village fiestas, the laughter, the drinks, the love. Strolling along the beach with the early morning sun peeping over the horizon, the sea lapping against the shore, time stretching endlessly before them. It played across his mind, like a moving picture show of memories.

To end up here, like this. The bile came up from his stomach, burning the back of his throat. Mistakes, miscalculations, the wrong path chosen. Why in the name of Christ had he picked up that hitchhiker back in Spain? If he hadn't, life would have carried on and his past remained buried. Instead, from that point on, all his choices had been wrenched from him until he stood here, in this woeful place, waiting for the final movement to be played out.

A hand pressed down on the nape of his neck and pushed him forward across the table. He squeezed his eyes tight shut.

"Just relax, my friend," he heard the fat man say, voice thick with desire, accompanied by the sound of a trouser zip opening.

A thought, a hope sprang into Chaise's mind. "Think of your son," he said quietly.

He sensed Chenko hesitate, penis going flaccid, his voice trembling when he said, "What did you say?"

Chaise straightened, turned and bored his eyes deep into the fat man's. "Think of your son lying in a hospital bed, brains like mush and think of the man who put him there ... me."

Chenko's face crumpled, tears welling up, a Tsunami of emotion building from deep within.

Chaise looked beyond Chenko's shoulder and grinned.

A single gunshot rang out, sounding like the chime of the Great Bell of Bow in the close confines of the kitchen. Chenko's body quaked, confusion and fear screwing up his features. In a blur, Chaise slammed his elbow across the fat man's jaw, rammed his knee into the ample gut and chopped him across the mastoid, each blow delivered with terrifying precision and power.

Chenko expelled air in a gust, and even before he toppled, Chaise swept up the Glock from where it had fallen and trained it on the open kitchen doorway.

The snoring man who had marched him to the house would never snore again, his head blown apart like a ripe melon, his body splayed out across the patio, lifeless. Beyond stood Colin, the snub-nose smoking in his hand.

"Jesus Christ," hissed Chaise, lowering the Glock, "You took your time."

Colin clicked his tongue. "Get some bloody clothes on, Mr Chaise. You're making me blush."

Chaise needed no further prompting, reached for his clothes and tugged them on. He looked at the fat man, whose open eyes stared unseeing towards the ceiling. "You think he was the father?"

"I would guess so. A right sick old bastard, that was for sure." Colin stepped over the body and moved into the kitchen, breaking open the snub-nose to replace the spent cartridge. "What a dump." He gestured outside. "Do you want me to let the people in the Portacabins go?"

"Not yet," said Chaise. "First of all, we have to deal with Mikhail."

Colin nodded. "Are you all right?"

Chaise took a moment to answer. His life had put him into many difficult situations but this one was right at the top of the list. "Thanks, Colin. For what you did."

"Don't mention it, Mr Chaise. I'm here to do my job, that's all."

"Well, I won't forget it."

"I'm wondering what you would have done if I'd have stayed in the car as you wanted me to?"

Chaise shook his head. "Waited for the right moment. Taken him down. I may not have made it though, not with the other guy standing by." He shrugged. "At least I would have had the satisfaction of finishing off that old git." He prodded the body of the fat man with the toe of his shoe. "If he was Vladimir's father, this is a job well done, Colin, old mate."

Colin opened his mouth to speak, then tensed, face growing rigid with concern. He crossed to the door that led into the hallway. "There's a car pulling up outside."

"Quick," said Chaise, pulling on his jacket, "help me get the welcoming surprise ready.

FORTY-FIVE

For a moment, the sun came out from between the clouds and they strolled along the banks of the River Dee, crossed the bridge to the far side, sat on a bench and said nothing. Brigit closed her eyes and rested her head on his shoulder and Johnny smiled, the sensation stirring in his loins pleasant and welcome. He couldn't remember the last time he felt so emotionally close to someone.

Of course, he knew it couldn't last. What had happened was all because of the upheaval and heightened passions of the past days. Adrenalin, fear, they do strange things to the body. The physical aspect of their relationship, the almost violent coupling of their bodies, was all down to the suddenness of it all – inner tension needing release.

It couldn't be anything else.

The recurring problem of Ryan Chaise caused Johnny to vacillate between Frank's wishes, and what Brigit had told him. It seemed that Chaise was as much a victim of circumstance as anyone. Would it be right to kill him, to assuage Frank's belief in the man's responsibility for his young wife's murder? If Frank had known the truth, the reason for Johnny's visit to the UK would not exist and Frank may well still be alive. Fate, working to save us or damn us.

"What are you thinking?"

He kissed the top of her head. "Not much."

"You're thinking about it all, aren't you? What Linny said, the rightness of going through with your dead friend's wishes, wondering why I don't want you to kill Ryan. All of that."

"No, I'm not."

"I know you are, Johnny. You can't balance it out, can you? Well, to be honest, neither can I. Why should I give a damn about Ryan Chaise, or what happens to him? " She sat up, rotated her head a few times to ease any tension she might be experiencing. "My main concern is Linny. I know she left him because of his lies, his web of intrigue and deceit, but she still loves him. If you killed him, and she found out I knew, she'd never forgive me. She'd hate me for the rest of her life."

Johnny reached across and massaged the back of her neck. She purred, arched her back, eyes closed, lost in the ecstasy of his touch.

"I've made some decisions," he said.

And he had. He'd mapped it out in his head, examined every turning, every twisting road. He'd made mistakes in his life, so many he'd lost count. Now was the time to do something right for once.

She looked at him and his hand dropped from her muscles. "I know you feel loyalty to your friend, I understand that, I really do. But Johnny," she squeezed his hand, "we have a choice – *you* have a choice. I can't begin to understand what's happened these last few days, but meeting the way we did and everything that has happened since it's made me think of so many things ... and the one thing I'm absolutely sure of is that I don't want it to end. " She turned her head away to stare out across the river.

Johnny followed her gaze. A family of swans glided towards the weir. They lived such uncomplicated lives, oblivious to the torment and anguish played out all around them. She pressed the back of her other hand into her eyes as tears rolled down her cheeks. "Jesus, I wish I was like them," she said.

Johnny smiled. "Yeah, that would be cool, wouldn't it? No worries, except finding enough food. Every day the same. There's a lot to be said for that."

"Johnny." The name came from her lips, soft, and it hung there between them for a long time. He held his breath. She blew out her cheeks. "What are you going to do?"

"Before I met you Brigit, everything was as simple as the life those swans have. Now ... now, I'm not so sure. I've never met anyone quite like you."

"I'm not so wonderful, Johnny. You don't know anything about me."

"I know enough. I'd like to think we could ..." He left his thoughts unfinished, and shrugged his shoulders. He put his own hand over hers. "I'd like to see more of you, Brigit. And I don't just mean more hotel rooms."

"How are we going to do that, Johnny? You saw the police report on the News this morning before we left. How are we supposed to carry on as *normal* people?"

Johnny sat back. She had turned on the TV after they had made love, and there it was. Gunshots in a Wirral street, dead bodies found near Moreton shore, and a gang-related killing in Liverpool clubland. Police claimed the incidents were not linked, but a doubt remained and until the ballistic reports came back, no one could be sure. It was only a matter of time until the truth became known.

"I'll turn myself in. I had nothing to do with that nightclub, nor the lighthouse." He looked deep into her face. "All they have is me shooting at you. And you know I would never have done that if I'd known ..." He squeezed his eyes shut. "I'm so sorry, Brigit. I was lost. All I knew was I had to find Chaise. Nothing else mattered."

The lies bit deep and he wondered how much she believed. If she harboured even the slightest doubt, she would abandon him and leave all his hopes dashed. Maybe one day he would tell her but for now, the pretence of innocence had to continue. But he knew time was his enemy; the police were not idiots. They would find those two gorillas, and tie him to the other killings. It was all such a fucking mess.

"What are you thinking now?"

He opened his eyes and studied her face. Such a face, one to gaze at in awe, to never grow tired of. "Now? Right now, I'm thinking differently. I've woken up from the nightmare. I want to leave the old life behind me, well behind me. It may have been good to me, but I don't want it anymore. I have money stashed away, enough to live a comfortable life. I'm not going back, Brigit, not to Spain. I can't. All that's waiting for me there is a bullet in the back of the head. Like they did to Frank."

"But isn't that what you still want to do, Ryan? A bullet?"

He shook his head. "No. No, Brigit. I don't want that. Not anymore."

She gaped at him. "Are you sure, Johnny?"

"As sure as anything. When I first arrived here, that was *all* I wanted to do. To avenge Frank, his wife's death, the death of *my* life too. Because that is what happened when they gunned down Frank. So it became my one focus, my reason for carrying on. To kill Ryan Chaise. And then, I met you, and slowly ... what your daughter said, that proved everything. His innocence. I've been looking in the wrong place, blaming the wrong people. Frank was wrong, and so was I."

"What will you do if you find the real culprits, Johnny? Kill them instead?"

If only she knew. He turned his gaze to the ground. "There's been enough killing."

"I wish to God I could believe that."

"You can," he said. "I want to take a chance with you, Brigit. If you could give me the benefit of any doubts, trust me just a little more and are willing to take a chance on me too."

He waited, hardly daring to breathe.

Her eyes appeared blank, with only tears spilling from those beautiful, big eyes of hers.

Mesmerised, it dawned on him how much life had changed over the past few days, how his heart, every ounce of logical thought had become ensnared by her, so much so that even his memory grew more and more hazy. How much had he told her, how much did she know? Confusion and anxiety fought their battle inside as the heat rose up through his collar and he stood, breathing hard, wishing it would rain, or snow or both. Anything to cool him down.

"Johnny ..." He looked down as her tears rolled unchecked. "You tried to kill me."

He fumbled for words, the explanation. If he made an error now, everything would collapse, all his hopes, his altered state of mind. "Remember when you aimed my gun at me? You chose not to pull the trigger. You made a decision, took a gamble, whatever you want to call it. Something happened between us, Brigit. I can't explain it and I don't even know if I want to, but meeting you ... I'm not a great one for religion or fate or any of that, but there's a feeling inside me which I didn't even know I had. A need, something buried so deep it's scary, Brigit. You chose not to shoot me. Well, I've chosen too, Brigit."

He knelt in front of her, placed his palms against her cheeks. "You're so beautiful." He leaned forward and kissed her very softly on the mouth. "I'd be a fool to let you go without a fight." He dropped his hands. "I'm willing to do the best I can."

She smiled and at last found a tissue to dab away the wetness from her face. "Me too."

"I'm not going to kill him, Brigit. I think we should still meet because sooner or later he'll find out who I am, why I came here. And when he does," he shook his head, "he'll want to kill *me*. He's not who he appears, Brigit. I can feel it."

"After what Linny told me, I don't think there's any doubting who he is. So, we will meet up with him, as we said. We can end all of this, peacefully."

He nodded. "Yes. Yes, we can."

She pulled out her mobile and stared at it for a long time. "I'll phone him to confirm what we planned. Afterwards."

"Afterwards? After what?"

Brigit looked down, her cheeks reddening slightly. "After we've gone back to our hotel, Johnny. I want to show you my appreciation."

He squeezed her hand and helped her to her feet and both of them strolled back to their hotel, smiling at the swans as they drifted by.

FORTY-SIX

They parked the car and got out, tense, checking every direction, guns concealed under their jackets. Mikhail didn't want any unexpected faces raising questioning brows. He studied the front of the house, the old door replaced with a new one, solid, strong and secure. Nobody was going to put a shoulder against it and break inside ever again.

He knew, however, something wasn't right.

Ivan was not at the window and Mikhail rubbed his chin, uncertain, nervous. His hand slipped inside his jacket. "Go around the back, Sergei."

Sergei came up to the big man's shoulder and craned his neck to stare at him. "What's wrong?"

"I don't know. A feeling. Ivan is not watching the street as I ordered him to. It could be nothing, but go around the back and check the sheds. I want to know everything is all right. Pyotr, you stay here by the car."

Pyotr leaned back against the bonnet and saluted with an index finger touching his temple. "Right you are, boss."

Mikhail rotated his shoulders. "Go now, Sergei. When you've checked out the sheds, come back and—"

The front door creaked open ever so slightly. They all froze, waiting. But for what? Mikhail, the chill growing inside, groped for his handgun and dropped to his knee. He gestured to Sergei, urging him to move left. Pyotr crouched down behind the car for maximum cover.

A car rolled by but no one paid it any heed. Mikhail extended his arm, aiming the gun as Sergei, pressed up against the railings adjacent to the steps, stared, wide-eyed. The gap in the doorway yawned open barely ten centimetres.

Mikhail's heartbeat throbbed in his neck. Fear never featured in his makeup, the emotion alien. He dismissed such weakness, contemptuous but now an unknown sensation ran through his gut. Perhaps what some called fear? Perhaps, but whatever it was, control had to remain with him. Strength. Power. Domination. He twisted his head, hawked and spat into the tarmac. There could never be any other way.

Bent double, he moved towards the house steps and mounted them two at a time, Pyotr and Sergei dropping in behind him, guns extended and ready.

Two paces away and the door creaked open further, as if by its own volition. Mikhail stood rigid, eyes adjusting to the gloomy interior. If what he experienced a moment ago could be called 'fear', utter despair now consumed him. A tiny moan grumbled from his throat as his knees turned to jelly and he groped for the door surround for support.

His father sat in a chair, a little way inside, facing the street. He was naked and his eyes were open.

Nothing moved. No sound. A deathly cold hung from every part of that terrible house.

As if in a dream, Mikhail took a step inside, eyes growing more accustomed to the dark. He sensed his two companions step close and heard their low, disbelieving gasps.

"What the fuck ..."

Anguish numbed Mikhail's fingers, the gun dropping from his grasp. It clattered to the ground and he blinked, looked down and noticed something, something which brought his senses back into sharp focus. A piece of cord trailed across the floor to the door handle.

He followed its course back down the hallway, beyond his father and into the interior.

Now everything was clear.

At the end of the cord stood a man.

Chaise strode past Chenko towards the three men in the doorway, none of whom reacted. Mikhail, slightly ahead of the other two, stood transfixed, and even when Chaise moved past him and attacked his companions, hands striking at vital points, obliterating any resistance with frightening ease, the big man did not flinch.

Chaise shoved Mikhail farther into the hallway. The big man teetered forward, turned, eyes lifeless, disbelieving. Chaise stepped over the bodies of the others, pressed his back against the front door and closed it.

He smiled. "Hello, Mikhail."

The big man seemed to react to his name and a light flickered on in his eyes. He frowned, glanced again to the body in the chair and breathed, "You did this?"

"He's your father, isn't he?"

Mikhail continued looking at the corpse. "More than a father. A mentor. A teacher." When he turned again, his face was a pale mask of violent intent. "I'm going to tear you apart, and feed your flesh to my dogs, you son of a whore."

Chaise tilted his head. "Remember Marianne, Mikhail? Remember what you said to me, what you did to her? You remember telling me how she begged you to stop? Your father was the same."

"You *lie*!"

Chaise smiled. "Sorry, but the simple truth is, your daddy couldn't take it. Especially when I stuck a poker up his puckered arse."

Mikhail's whole body trembled, his fists coming up to a face contorted into a red ball of fury, the sweat trickling down to drip onto the floor. "You murderous *dog*! I'll crush you like an insect!" He moved.

Something blurred in Chaise's hand.

With few implements to choose from, he'd found an old, rusty knife amongst the clutter in the kitchen, its blade thin. He knew it would take a lot to put someone of Mikhail's size and strength down and he could have shot him, but he wanted it personal. He wanted to see the look in the big man's eyes when death gripped him and Chaise wanted him to know why he was dying.

Mikhail charged like a bull, his massive frame filling the cramped confines of the hallway. Chaise slipped to the side, hoping to catch him, flip him forward. The tight space allowed for no such manoeuvre and all he managed was a reverse chop to the man's throat, with as much effect as a fly swat against an elephant.

Mikhail bellowed, huge hands reaching out to destroy. Chaise parried, hit once, twice, three times, the blows going in hard and fast, pressure points struck with expert precision. He swung into the big man, pressing the advantage with an elbow to the solar plexus, another to the jaw. Mikhail's mouth spewed blood and he crumpled against the wall, the house shuddering with the impact. A snap kick to his knee, knuckles in his throat, the big man swayed.

Chaise, overconfident, sensed victory, went for a haymaker and Mikhail caught the arm, grabbed Chaise under the chin and spat out teeth before hoisting the ex-SBS operative off his feet to smash him against the opposite wall.

The air exploded from Chaise's lungs. He shook his head to clear the fog swirling in front of his eyes and heard Mikhail roar before a solid foot slammed into his ribs, followed by a vicious punch across the head that made Chaise's jaw rattle.

The floor loomed towards him and for one bizarre moment, he found himself admiring the pattern on the tiles before he became vaguely aware of powerful hands lifting him with frightening ease. The knee slammed into his groin, bile erupting in his mouth, burning his throat. He went limp, whimpering and Mikhail laughed before tossing him down the hallway as if he were nothing more than a small, unwanted toy.

Chaise hit the ground with a jarring jolt, rolled into a foetal position, hands clamped around scalding testicles. He'd given the man everything he had and nothing had made the slightest impact. He truly was inhuman and Chaise knew he was in serious trouble.

The nausea eased and he rolled over, senses out of sync, muscles useless, alerts going off in his brain ordering his body to respond but nothing worked, except a pathetic scurry backwards. Through blurred eyes, he saw the horrible monster pounding towards him, with only the chant of 'fee-fi-fo-fum' missing. When his back hit the far wall, Chaise realised there was nowhere else to go, his options disappearing fast. The one thing left to focus on being Mikhail's maniacal grin, the look of victory.

Mikhail must have sensed it too. He broke into uncontrolled, cackling laughter, throwing his head back, shouting, "I told you, *I TOLD YOU!*"

He reached down and hoisted Chaise to his feet and Chaise used the one remaining option and rammed the knife directly into the big man's throat, right up to the hilt.

Mikhail's mouth worked open and shut, eyes blazing in disbelief. Staggering backwards, his hands clawed at the handle but it may as well have been a wet fish as blood gushed out, and his fingers slipped, unable to find a grip. He gagged and floundered, wild and desperate, but the blade remained buried deep. He toppled and fell, body going into uncontrolled convulsions.

Chaise watched, bent double, breathing hard, the relief washing over him like a warm bath. Exhilaration too. Glee. He chuckled as the man died.

He'd been asleep for a long time. But now he was fully awake.

FORTY-SEVEN

They waited and watched as the big black transit rolled up and the men came into the house, silent, faces blank. Nobody reacted. Not even a cursory nod.

Chaise sat at the broken table, hands resting on his lap, fingers intertwined, staring into nothing.

Colin, having spoken to the people in the Portacabins, stood, arms folded, leaning in the doorwell. It had begun to rain. He didn't speak.

The men in the blue overalls worked quickly; even so, it took them the best part of an hour to get the bodies into black zip bags, clean up the blood with solvents, check all of the rooms were as neat as they possibly could be. They'd found Ivan on the landing, his neck broken. Mikhail and his father were in a terrible mess and of the other two, one groaned when they picked him up.

"What do we do with this one?"

Chaise shook his head and Colin stepped up, put his fingers into the man's larynx with nonchalant ease and applied the appropriate pressure.

They put the body into another bag.

"And the people outside?" asked one of the men.

Chaise stared at the big man in the blue overalls standing in the kitchen doorway. "We phone the police. And the local TV station."

Colin wiped his hands on an old dishcloth. "Why the hell would we want to do that?"

"Make it official. To send a message. This is happening right across the country and we can't do a damn thing to stop it, but at least we can make them *think*."

"What's this," interrupted the big man, with a sneering laugh, "you some sort of crusader?"

"You can go and fuck yourself," said Chaise and stood up, and immediately regretted it. He clutched his side and winced.

"Mr Chaise," said Colin, easing Chaise down onto the chair again, "I think we've had enough for one day."

Chaise looked at Colin, recognised the sense of his words. He shot a glance at the big man. "You just do your job and leave the eulogies at home for your armchair, all right?"

The big man in the blue overalls nodded, turned and went. The tension went with him.

Colin took hold of Chaise's elbow. "You should see a doctor, get those lumps and bumps looked at." Chaise made a face. "All right, you know best. But listen, try to think ... do you really believe it's wise to let the police in on this?"

"What are you worried about, Colin? That your bosses in Whitehall will think I've brought too much publicity to the situation? That you might have to fulfil your obligations?"

Colin let his hand fall away, mouth becoming a thin line. "Mr Chaise, I think we've already gone way beyond that."

"So what are you going to do?"

Colin tilted his head slightly. "I'm going to talk to them and await instructions."

"Like the good little soldier you are?"

"Like the good little soldier I am."

Chaise let out a sharp laugh. "And you expect me to wait for their decision? To sit around wondering whether you've been given the go ahead to blow my fucking brains out?" He sneered. "Don't underestimate me, Colin."

"That's something I will never do, Mr Chaise."

"As long as we understand each other."

"We do."

Chaise nodded. "Do what you have to do, Colin, I'm past caring. I have a few loose ends to tidy up and I'll see you back in Beccles."

"Are you sure you are able, Mr Chaise? You took a fearful beating."

Chaise sneered. "I'm fine."

"I'll need the car, Mr Chaise."

"I'm catching the bus. I *need* time alone. You're not going to try and stop me, are you Colin?"

"Wouldn't dream of it."

"I hope we can reach some sort of mutual understanding. Killing you is not something I would particularly enjoy."

"Same here, Mr Chaise."

Chaise went down the hallway and nudged past the men who were busy finishing off the cleaning of the floorboards. Outside, the rain had eased a little and a little bunch of onlookers stood and stared. Chaise put his hands deep into his pockets and headed off down the street, not giving any of it so much as a sideways glance.

The countryside streamed by as he sat towards the back of the bus, next to the window, his mind a blank, no thoughts meandering through. He preferred it so, always able to detach himself from the carnage and any subsequent fallout. His ribs thumped, the bruising spreading, fire bursting across his whole body. Pain, his old companion. He closed his eyes, the motion of the bus rocking him into a kind of sleep.

When they finally stood him in front of three officers and told him he had 'passed' his test, they sent him to Hereford to train with the

Special Air Service. Halfway through, more officers came, and they talked to him and he answered their questions, kept his natural rebellious streak well and truly buried, and they attached him to the Special Boat Service. He first saw action with an American Marine unit in Iraq, but a big guy with a goatee beard had annoyed him, and he reacted. Five or six were needed to pull him off the big Yank, but by the time they did, Chaise had broken the man's neck.

The fallout occurred soon afterwards.

Air brakes hissed and Chaise opened his eyes. The bus pulled up in Beccles's town square and Chaise got out and hobbled up the road towards the estate agency, every step sending a new stab of pain through him. When he went through the door, Yvonne's jaw almost dropped to her chest.

"Dear God, have you been in an accident?"

Chaise hadn't checked himself in a mirror, but when his hand went instinctively to his cheekbones he felt the swelling and knew he must have looked terrible. "Nice to see you too."

"Where the bloody hell have you been?"

He grinned and immediately regretted it, his hand caressing the bruising around his jaw. "What a lovely welcome."

She was on her feet, coming around the desk at a rush. "Are you all right?"

Her concern seemed genuine and when she touched him on the arm, he didn't flinch. In fact, given everything that had happened, he welcomed the sensation.

"I was worried," she said. "You didn't phone the boss."

"I know."

Her smile broadened. "And you never called back for our date."

He allowed his eyes to drop to the floor. "I know that too, and I'm sorry." His own smile played around at the corners of his mouth. "Perhaps later?"

"It's almost five o'clock now, Ryan. The boss is livid."

"Well, let's say seven?"

"Seven? This evening? Are you sure?"

Chaise nodded. "I'll go and get showered, then maybe I could pick you up?"

A slight colouring of her cheeks. She was small, or *petite* as they say in the best etiquette journals, her dark hair parted to the left, tiny flecks of grey at the roots. Almost the complete opposite to Linny. Perhaps that was why he found her so attractive. Or perhaps there was something else.

"Are you sure you're all right?"

He blinked, aware he had been gazing just a fraction too long. "Sorry. Yes, yes, I'm fine. So, is seven okay?"

"I'd prefer eight."

Her smile showed off perfect, even teeth. He realised how much he missed the closeness of a woman. Marianne had stirred something inside him. Marianne And now Yvonne ... He'd avenged Marianne's death. He'd killed them all.

"Ryan?"

Her hands gripped his shoulders, her huge eyes filled with concern.

"I'm all right."

"You'd better telephone the boss. He gave me such a hard time over the phone, thinking I hadn't told you."

"I'll put him straight."

"Ryan, I'm worried ... I'm not sure if—"

He put his finger over her lips and she stopped, eyes growing moist. "It's all right," he said, voice very low, and he leaned forward and kissed her mouth. "You're so beautiful."

Her eyes seemed to become liquid, and he took her around the waist and drew her close. She giggled, and he kissed her, much more deeply this time. He felt her body grow soft. As she coiled her arms around his beck, all the pain became nothing more than a memory, distant and vague, and he ran his tongue around the inside of her mouth and consumed her totally.

FORTY-EIGHT

Johnny came back into the room, rubbing his hair with a towel and saw Brigit closing her mobile. When she turned, she smiled. "Who was that?" he asked.

"Belinda. She just telephoned me, wanting to know if I was okay."

"Belinda? Who's Belinda?"

A dark look came over her face. "Remember how you burst into the place where I was staying? You nearly killed her husband?"

The memory flooded back and he nodded, feeling awkward and returned to rubbing his hair, turned, and stopped. A tightness developed inside, his throat becoming dry. He looked back at her. "Why would she call now?"

"I don't know. She just wanted to know if I was all right."

All of a sudden, the early warning went off inside his brain. "She didn't say anything else?" He tried to keep the edge from his voice, but he failed.

"Johnny, if it's the police you're worried about, she won't say anything. I told you. We're friends, and I've convinced her everything is all right by telling a few white lies. I said you were an old, jealous lover, but we'd had a lovely time in Chester, things had been sorted and she didn't have to worry."

She came towards him, gave him an admiring look as she ran her hand over his stomach. "I love the way you're so confident about your body."

His mind, for once, was not on what her fingers were doing. He gripped her hand and lifted it up to his lips. "Brigit. You told her we were in Chester?"

"Johnny, don't be so bloody paranoid."

"Did she ask you where we were? I mean, *specifically*."

"Johnny." She tore her hand free of his grip. "What the hell's the matter with you?"

His face loomed close to hers, and the rage and the panic mingled together to almost pitch him into violence. "*Brigit,* did you tell her where we are?"

"Johnny, you bloody lunatic, she wouldn't tell the police. I told you."

"It's not the police I'm worried about." Her crossed to the dresser and reached inside his jacket hanging on the back of the chair. He brought out his gun and checked it.

"Jesus Christ, Johnny. What the hell is wrong?"

He turned around and looked at her for a long time. "You told her, didn't you?"

He could see by the way her face changed it was true.

"Get dressed," he said without emotion, "then go and wait in your car in the car park. Telephone Ryan Chaise, set up the meeting. But do it now, Brigit. And do it quickly."

Jerome stepped away, the silenced gun in his hand, the grin on his face. On the other side of the room, Lawrence had Belinda's husband by the throat.

"Well done," said Jerome, his voice as oily as a slick.

"We'd better leave," said Lawrence, and slammed his fist into the husband's guts. He whooshed out air, Belinda screamed, and Jerome cracked the gun across the side of her head and laid her out flat. "I fucking hate hysterical women." Then he put the barrel against the back of her head and blew out her brains.

Lawrence made a retching sound, "Shit, Jer, you could have warned me."

The husband, on his knees clutching his stomach, saw it but couldn't move, his eyes registering fear, despair. "Get ready," said Jerome, put the gun between the husband's eyes and blew out the back of his head also.

Lawrence threw up despite the warning.

It didn't take long.

Johnny stood under one of the trees skirting the car park. From his vantage point, he had a clear view of anyone driving through the entrance. When a car finally did arrive, he bent down on his knees and brought out the gun.

They both got out. They weren't wearing their signature skin-tight t-shirts this time, both in dark blue tracksuits, with broad white stripes down the legs. Lawrence limped along with the aid of a single crutch, the legacy of his encounter with Brigit's car, whilst his friend stood scanning the hotel.

Brigit, sitting behind the wheel of the MGB applying some lipstick, didn't appear to notice them as they walked past. Neither did they spot her as they moved towards the hotel.

Johnny checked nobody else was close and came out from under the trees, striding across the car park.

He was some half a dozen paces away when another car appeared. Johnny gasped and turned, the sound of wheels crunching over gravel taking his attention. He knew he'd made a mistake as Brigit screamed and he whirled around, keeping low, to see Lawrence producing a machine pistol from inside his tracksuit, an Uzi by the look of it. Other voices cried out as Jerome rushed forward in a zigzag pattern, an automatic in his fist.

The car engine roared. Tyres spun across gravel, urgent desperate voices, confusion mingling with terror. The driver knew this was not the place to be. Johnny gaped as the stranger grappled with gears, desperate to make a hasty retreat. Brigit's high-pitched squeal, nothing making sense; everything happening too fast.

A strange buzzing grew in Johnny's head and he knew he'd lost the edge. "I'll kill her, Johnny."

The words rang out across the car park like bullets, pulling Johnny up sharper than the Uzi ever could.

Jerome held Brigit by the throat. Far away, tyres whirred as the car shot out into the street, accelerating fast and Johnny caught a flash of white, terrified faces peering out from behind the glass. Something smashed him hard in the kidneys. A sickening swell of pain and lights flashing across his eyes. He'd been hit before, but never with such venom, such crippling power. He crumpled, knees cracking against the gravelled ground. How could it have gone so wrong, so quickly?

"Don't you fucking hurt him."

Brigit's voice, as distant as a far-off planet. Through a thin mist, she struggled in Jerome's arms. Johnny noticed the bulging bicep, the way a thick, throbbing vein strained against the skin.

Another blow centred just below his ear, metallic, hard and vicious, setting his teeth on edge; a single point of agony spreading outwards, enveloping him, turning everything black.

"I'll do a deal," he said.

After they bundled him into the back of their car they drove down a winding track away from Upton-by-Chester towards the zoo. Lawrence took great pleasure in revealing how they'd found Brigit, a plan almost identical to the one Johnny had followed, the irony of which brought pain as well as surprise. Jerome pulled over into a lay-by and Lawrence laughed. "We'll kill you here, Johnny old fruit. In front of her." He grinned, waggling the gun before Brigit's streaming eyes. "Don't worry, we'll dump you together."

"Listen," Johnny said quickly, trying to gesticulate with his tightly bound hands, "there's a guy, the bloke Frank told me to come over here and kill."

"There's no fucking deal we're going to do with you, Johnny," said Jerome, leaning over the driving seat to aim the automatic with deliberate slowness.

"Wait," breathed Lawrence, frowning. "What about this guy? Who is he?"

"A rival, from over in Spain. He's got money. Lots of money. He'd run off with it, made his way over here. That's why Frank wanted him found. He'd taken the money, you see and Frank sent me to get it back."

"Frank's dead."

"Yeah, but the money isn't. This bloke, this Chaise, he's still got it."

"It's a load of fucking shite," said Lawrence, who sat beside him in the rear seat, his crutch propped up next to the door. The lines around his eyes etched deep, Johnny assumed he was in pain. The cramped confines of the vehicle didn't help.

"No, it's not," said Johnny, wincing as he rubbed the raised flesh around his ear with his bound hands. His mind raced, the pain focusing his thoughts. "He took drugs from Frank, caused all sorts of trouble and then sold the lot to a bunch of Ukrainians. Frank lost face, making him appear weak. The Ukrainians moved in, killed Frank, took over. It's all down to this Chaise. I want him dead, and we," he nodded towards Brigit who gawped at him, "we were going to run away with the money. Make a new life, start again."

Jerome pulled a face and squinted over to Lawrence. "What do you think?"

Lawrence shrugged. "I still don't know what the fucking deal is."

"I'll tell you," said Johnny. "We set up a meet. Brigit here, she's his girlfriend's mother. It's perfect. She'll arrange it all, we kill him, then we share the money."

Lawrence screwed up his mouth. "No, that doesn't sit well with me, Johnny."

"It's almost a million."

Not a flicker crossed Lawrence's face. "No. You see, there's a fundamental flaw in your plan, me old fruit."

Johnny tried to prevent his mouth from falling open. He'd given it his best shot, but now life was about to end, in this lane, in the middle of nowhere. Brigit and Johnny, together for eternity. He closed his eyes for a moment and tried to swallow.

"What flaw?"

Johnny's eyes sprang open and he looked at Brigit, who held Lawrence's gaze. "What he says is true. We can do it. I'll tell Chaise to come, and we'll make the deal. The money was going to be for my daughter, you see, and we—"

"The fundamental flaw is not that, sweetheart."

"What the hell is it then?"

"It's the part where he said we can share the money." Lawrence grinned. "We won't be sharing anything. The deal is this, Johnny, and it is perfectly simple. It's the money, *all* of it, in exchange for your life." He nodded at Brigit. "And hers. Are we agreed?"

Johnny almost blacked out with relief. "Yes," he said. "We are, but maybe you could spare us enough for the taxi fare home?

FORTY-NINE

After dinner, they strolled down to the river and stared out across the black, mirror sheen of the Waveney as it gently rolled by, both of them lost in their thoughts. He snaked his arm around her waist and they went back to his flat. They made love and afterwards, they sat up in bed and he held her close. She didn't seem fazed in the least by exposing her fine body to him, and he liked that. He liked her.

Earlier, Brigit had phoned him, her voice sounding subdued and staccato as if she were reading lines from a script.

Linny wanted to meet him. There were things to sort out, things to finalise. Brigit assured him everything 'was fine' and they set the meeting for tomorrow at around six o'clock and she told him where. Chaise changed the time to four, not liking the idea of meeting anyone, even Linny, in a strange place in the dark.

Brigit had paused. Six o'clock would be better. Chaise insisted.

"You're worried," said Angela, running her fingertips across his pectoral muscles.

"No. It's all OK." He leaned down and kissed her and her hand dropped to his crotch.

"You're like no one else I've ever met," she said, slowly pushing away the sheet, her fingers rolling over the tip of his stiffening cock. “There’s a danger about you. These scars.” She ran her tongue across his abdomen, tracing the course of where knives and bullets had once pierced flesh. “God, your body ... you’re so fucking yummy!”

He threw her over onto her back and entered her without ceremony.

The following morning they came through the office door together to find the boss standing arms folded, grim-faced. Angela strode over to her desk without a word, averting her eyes. Chaise offered a smile, receiving a deep frown for a reply. “I asked you to phone me, Mr Chaise.”

“I was a little busy. Sorry.”

The boss jutted his jaw forward like a bull, hands on hips, a man used to giving orders, to having them followed. “You should have left a message.”

“Yeah, I know.” He shrugged. “What was it you wanted?”

“I’ll come straight to the point. You’ve been here for two weeks and in that time you haven’t made one solitary sale, despite spending most of your time out of the office.”

“Following up some leads.”

“And when might these leads become genuine sales? You came highly recommended, Mr Chaise. I need results.”

“You’ll get them, soon enough, before the day is out. I’m cutting across country to finalise the deal.”

“Across country?”

“Yes. I suspect by the end of the day, we’ll have at least half a dozen houses right across Norwich sold.” Chaise grinned, reached out and seized the man’s arm. The boss tried to pull away, but the grip proved too strong and his face took on a more blanched hue. “Trust me. By five o’clock you’re going to thank your lucky stars you hired me.”

. . .

Chaise spoke to Harper from his mobile as he slid behind the wheel of his car. His superior was not in a good mood. "You're treading on thin ice, Chaise. That bloody pantomime in Norwich saw you coming within a whisker of being compromised."

"I've got the good Colin to help me through," replied Chaise and looked across to his passenger who stared straight ahead, his mouth a thin line. "Thank his boss from me."

"Mr Mellor is an understanding gentleman, Chaise, but even his patience is running thin."

"I'm sure you can *persuade* him, sir."

"You're pushing things to the limit, Chaise. To the absolute wire."

"I know, but ... you can take care of the houses, sir? Now that they are vacant I think they could generate quite a bundle."

"It may have escaped your mind, Chaise, but I'm not an estate agent – I leave that nonsense to the likes of you."

"But you have sorted it all out, sir?"

"As we speak."

"Then there can't be any complaints, surely? By rubbing out those bastards we've done the community a service."

"It's going to be on the six o'clock news, Chaise. Concerned neighbours, swallowing their fear of retaliation."

"There won't be any, will there, sir? Not now."

A silence, followed by a long breath. "No. You took care of that particular concern. Where are you going now, Chaise? Mellor's man told you of your next assignment, so I'm assuming ...?"

"I'm going to the Wirral, to tie off some loose ends. Then I'll be with you."

"You keep your head down, Chaise. I don't want any more bloody super-hero nonsense."

"No, sir. Absolutely not, sir. There won't be any trouble at all. I promise you."

Promises are often made in good faith. Occasionally, however, circumstances erode good intentions.

Sitting in the back seat of the car, a gun trained on them as they motored along the country roads of South Wirral, Johnny pressed his thigh against Brigit's and wondered how the hell it would all pan out. He'd finally meet up with Ryan Chaise, but it wouldn't be Johnny doing the killing. The plan, for what it was worth, had worked so far but as soon as the two knuckle-heads realized there were no drugs and no money, the shooting would start.

Falling for Brigit had made him soft, slowed his reactions, blinkered his mind. And now he was in deep shit. He looked across at her and forced a smile. She didn't respond.

He wondered if any of it was worth it.

FIFTY

During their second stop at motorway services, Chaise knew someone was following them. After coffee, he and Colin strolled back to the car and Chaise, a few paces ahead, stopped without warning. As Colin collided, almost tripped and called Chaise 'a bloody ass', Chaise, amongst a flurry of apologies, chanced a quick sidelong glance towards the silver Seat. He'd spotted it in Beccles and again at the first break. He didn't say anything to Colin, who appeared oblivious, a strange, dark mood pressing over him, seemingly weighing him down with some sort of inner conflict. Conscience perhaps. Killing never proved easy. Even when the bastards deserved it.

He'd made a phone call at the first stop. Chaise guessed it was a quick report to his superiors, whoever they were. When he came back, Colin appeared different, distant. Chaise didn't ask. He'd already guessed.

Chaise drove slowly through the sprawling car park. Before the exit, he pulled up sharply and, before Colin could say anything, got out and went to the boot. He opened it, pretended to rummage around for a moment or two, then went back to the driver's door in time to see the Seat moving out from between parked cars. Chaise got in, continued to the exit and joined the motorway. He said nothing to Colin and if his companion noticed anything, his lips remained firmly sealed.

The Seat held back, well over a hundred metres to the rear, but Chaise knew he was there, and the first trickle of unease ran through in his stomach.

The second shadow had broken cover at last.

They made good time. Chaise estimated five hours for the journey. Four and a half hours after leaving Beccles they came off the M56 and hit the M531 to the Wirral. Chaise pulled in at the Moreton bypass and telephoned Brigit.

Her voice held an edge, and something else too. A degree of friendliness so far beyond anything Chaise could believe, he almost laughed. "Ryan, *darling*. How are you?"

Chaise glanced askance at Colin, who sat rigid as always. "I'm good, Brigit. And you?"

"I'm wonderful, darling. Ryan, my love, we're at Thurstaton Hill. You know where that is, don't you?"

"I think I can remember, yes."

"You're a treasure, you really are. We'll be waiting for you, my love."

"*We?* You mean Linny's with you?"

"Yes, my darling, of course, and she's eager to see you again, after so long."

Chaise shifted position and frowned. "Is she?"

"Yes, of course she is. You know she is, you little tease. How I love you, the way you tease."

Chaise almost told her to stop. Something was very wrong, their usual neutral, often icy exchanges replaced by a new, forced friendliness. "Brigit, are you all right?"

"Never better, my lovely. I've missed you, so much. But you know that, don't you darling?"

Chaise paused, exchanged a glance with Colin who frowned. "Yes. Yes of course," he said slowly.

"And you, my love, everything is well with you? You have the stuff? You do have the *stuff,* don't you darling?"

Chaise's own frown now deepened, and he continued on a cautious note. "Oh, yes, Brigit, I've got the stuff."

"You are lovely. Now, text me when you arrive, won't you? So we all know you're here."

"I will. And Brigit?"

"Yes, my love?"

It was Chaise's turn to play the game, if only to reassure himself that it really was an act. "Kiss-kiss."

"Yes, my love. *Kiss-kiss.*"

The phone went dead and Chaise slipped the mobile back into his pocket.

"Sounds all very lovey-dovey."

Chaise threw Colin a much longer look. "Didn't it just."

"What do you mean by that?"

"I mean Brigit never calls me 'love' or 'darling'. And she's never sent me kisses. She hates my fucking guts."

"So what did all of that mean do you think?"

"It's obvious – we're heading into something very bad."

"A trap?"

"Almost certainly."

Colin put his head back and closed his eyes. "Why is it that whenever we go anywhere, or do anything, Mr Chaise, it always ends in trouble?"

"Would you have it any other way?"

Chaise didn't wait for a reply and rejoined the link road that would eventually put them in the direction of Thurstaton Hill.

He took Brigit's mobile from her and looked at it. "That was very cosy."

"We're close."

"I could tell," said Lawrence. "He didn't seem to suspect anything."

"Why should he?"

"I just get a bad feeling about the way he so easily accepted everything, that's all. Almost as if you had already planned it."

"Planned what? *This meeting*? How could I do that?"

He shrugged and looked across to Johnny who sat peering through the window. "She's really turned your head, hasn't she?"

"What would you know about it?"

Lawrence sucked in his breath. "You're a dead man walking, Johnny, so I'd shut the fuck up if I were you."

Johnny released a long, low sigh. "So that's still your plan is it?"

"If this guy doesn't turn up with the money, or if he can't put us in touch with it, I'll shoot you dead. And him, and," he winked, "her too. This guy, who is he?"

"I told you," said Brigit, no trace of fear in her voice. "He's my daughter's boyfriend."

"Yeah, but who *is* he?"

"An estate agent."

Lawrence gaped, turned to Jerome, his face splitting into a wide grin. "Shit, I thought he was something to do with your good friend Frank, Johnny."

Johnny shook his head. "No. He just got lucky finding some dope back in Spain, that's all. He sold it for a fortune, then came back home."

"Lucky you say? Well, looks like his luck is about to run out."

The car continued down the lane to the main junction, then headed towards the M531. Soon they would reach Thurstaton.

Chaise and Colin cut across the open ground, finding a concealed vantage point overlooking the approach to the Hill at Thurstaton. A country park and natural beauty spot popular with walkers, today the steady drizzle kept everyone away, apart from Chaise and Colin who pulled up their collars, crouched down behind an outcrop of rock and waited.

"You're sure she will come?"

Chaise nodded. "She said so."

"Yes, but you also know it is a trap, don't you."

"Well, something's not right. She's a bloody good actress, is Brigit. All that false banter ... I don't know what's going on, but something is."

"I hope this woman hasn't made you forget all of your training, Mr Chaise."

Chaise squinted across to him. "I haven't forgotten anything, Colin. You'd do well to remember that."

"Oh, I do, Mr Chaise. I just think your judgment has become somewhat blurred, that's all."

"Blurred? No, not at all. We'll wait until they arrive, check everything is okay, then I'll talk to Linny. I have a lot of explaining to do."

"You don't seriously think she is going to take you back? That you can pick up your life from where you left off?"

"Why not?"

"Because they won't let you. You're their property, and you always have been."

Chaise gave a slight, dismissive laugh. "Where did you go when we made the last stop, Colin?"

Colin blinked, frowned, and looked away, a slight colouring of his cheeks giving away his sudden discomfort. "I had to call in, nothing more."

"Why don't you have a mobile?"

"I'm not comfortable with technology, Mr Chaise."

"Really? Maybe it's more a case of you not wanting me to see who it is you called?" They held one another's gaze for a moment. "And what instructions did they give you this time?"

He shrugged. "The usual. To watch, protect."

"Nothing more? Nothing about what happened in Norwich?"

"That was dealt with, you witnessed it yourself."

"Yes, but someone might have seen. There was a body, lying in the street. Dead. I saw it, but I didn't mention it. Others will."

"In the street? But ..." Colin put his finger and thumb into his eyes and squeezed. "Mr Chaise," he continued without looking up, "let's just say my remit has not changed. That's all you need to know. And besides, if—"

The conversation froze as a car rolled into view. Both men focused on four people, their shapes indeterminate due to the distance. They could be four men, or four women. The engine cut. Even the birds grew silent.

FIFTY-ONE

Johnny took in the surroundings. A wide, semi-circular car park adjoining the Hill, dark sandstone rocks jutting upwards and outwards, forming a natural amphitheatre, with well-worn pathways leading into the expanse of natural parkland, where any prospective assassin could easily conceal themselves. Johnny wondered if Chaise was already there, watching.

He felt sure someone was.

Lawrence struggled out of the car, taking deep breaths whilst he scanned the surroundings; Johnny held Brigit's hand as they both waited.

"If there's any nonsense, kill him," said Lawrence.

"It'll be my pleasure," said Jerome and pressed his gun against Johnny's temple.

Lawrence leaned on his crutch and tore Brigit loose from Johnny's grip. "You can come with me."

"We made a deal," she said through clenched teeth as she stepped outside.

"And the deal still stands, so long as your friend delivers. Jerome, keep loverboy here until we get back."

Johnny tried to catch Brigit's eyes, but she had already turned away, and his stomach rolled over, a sickening chasm opening up deep inside. He was a pawn now, a minor player in a game gone disastrously wrong. Perhaps Chaise might win through, but putting trust in a stranger was an alien concept. The fight went out of him and he slumped into the back seat and wished he could curl up and die.

Lawrence led her away from the car. She struggled in his grip, to no effect. "We'll go to the top of the brow." He breathed hard, face screwed up with the effort of holding her whilst negotiating the path with his crutch.

"You should have stayed at the car."

His eyes flashed. "Jerome's a donkey, darling. No brains, just a big dick. I'm the only one who knows what to do." He nodded towards the top of the rise. "From there we can see your pal when he arrives, and he'll see us. That way no one will be taken by surprise."

"I'll need to talk to him."

"Yeah, and you will. But if you make any stupid moves, or say anything suspicious," he patted the revolver in his waistband, "I'll kill you. You understand?"

She nodded, unable to tear her eyes from the black menace of the gun. She swallowed hard. "You really are a bastard, aren't you?"

"I just want the money, lady. I couldn't give a fuck about you or your friend." He nodded back to the car, "You almost killed me when you knocked me over, I hope you realise that. But, I blame Johnny, little shit that he is. Alvaro sent us, to talk to you so Johnny could find this guy, but I didn't know the reason. I wish I did, but the whole bloody thing went pear-shaped the moment you ran off. And now Johnny's gone soft, which is down to you. Like a fucking circle, going around and around. The both of you. Fucking stupid, the whole fucking lot of it."

"He hasn't gone soft, just changed."

Lawrence grunted and swung her round close to him. "Soft or not, the money should see everything right. Alvaro's dead. Johnny killed him." Brigit's eyes bulged. "Oh, didn't he tell you? Your new golden boy?" His nails dug into the flesh of her arm. "You stupid fucking bitch. He hasn't fucking changed, not really. He blew Alvaro away, together with Big Tony. The guy's a fucking killer, and when he's snapped out of this daze you've put him into, he'll kill again. If he's still alive of course." He grinned and pushed her away. "Now get up that path and stand at the top. I'll be right behind you."

Rain, falling gently at first, now hammered down and Brigit stumbled along the narrow pass that twisted between heavy gorse and heather. She tried to clear her mind of Lawrence's words, forcing herself forward, ignoring the ever more treacherous pathway, concentrating on keeping herself from slipping over.

She groped for outcrops of rock to prevent herself from falling, her designer trainers nothing more than a fashion accessory. She slipped, hit the ground with her knees, swore, took a breath and continued. By the time she reached the top, her trousers sported wet, brown patches of dirt across the knees, and her jacket soaked through with sweat and rain.

Dragging her sodden hair from her face, she scanned the expanse of coarse heathland which rolled far away before her into the distance. Through the rain, she spotted the many tiny paths criss-crossing between rocks and thick gorse, a haven for wildlife. Away to her left, the Dee Estuary, and beyond, the mountains of North Wales. At any other time she would take time and admire its beauty because even in this curious half-light, with the rain sweeping across in thin wisps, the view was breathtaking. But her only thought now was for Johnny. And how he'd lied.

Lawrence came up beside her, breathing hard. She raised an eyebrow. "You want to be careful with that leg. You might fall and hurt yourself."

"Fuck off," he snapped. "Move over to that flat piece of ground. From there we'll get a good view of everything."

She smiled, a tiny surge of triumph bolstering her. To see him like that, labouring under the strain, it almost made her want to dance.

But as she walked, dread took over. Outwardly calm, inside she was in crisis. And not only about Johnny. She had tried so hard to warn Ryan, but had she succeeded? Had he picked up on her outrageous familiarity, the lies? He knew she despised him, but had it worked, would he come? And then what? Perhaps when all this was over, they could sit down and come to some understanding. Linny needed to move on, and Ryan needed to leave them all well alone.

As for Johnny, that too would have to be resolved. His dark past. Would he change, *could* he change? Was anything Lawrence said true? She sat down on a large flat boulder, no longer mindful of the wet, the discomfort.

Lawrence leaned on his crutch, his breathing ragged, the flesh around his cheeks ghastly pale, eyes yellow and watery, a trail of snot hanging from his nostrils.

"You look like shit," she said, unable to keep the joy from her voice. He didn't respond and that too gave her a glimmer of hope for a conclusion that might still prove favourable.

FIFTY-TWO

Colin watched Chaise take a wide route across to the far side of the heath, moving stealthily from one outcrop to the next before dropping out of sight completely. The man knew what to do, old skills never far away. Colin had watched him with Mikhail's father, knew his capabilities, his single-mindedness.

Few people had the means, or the desire, to deal out death with such precision. Chaise had such capacity. Even when confronted with someone as massive as Mikhail, he'd never given up; despite being battered and bloodied, the determination to kill remained. A formidable adversary in every sense and an admirable one too. A shame to end his life, but orders were orders ...

Colin blew out a breath, stood up and began his cautious ascent to his car, parked out of sight on the far side. He took his time, confident Chaise would be safe.

When he reached the vehicle he pulled out one of the cushions from the parcel shelf. It was small but plump and would serve his purpose well. He glanced at the sky, various hues of grey indicating the rain had set in for the day. He sighed again, gathered his coat collar closer around his throat and set off towards the main car park.

. . .

Chaise crouched down behind a large lump of sandstone and peered out towards Brigit and the big stranger. The man filled his tracksuit impressively, but the sight of the crutch was curious. And where was Linny?

He rolled back behind the boulder and considered his options. Colin told him he would take out the second stranger in the car, bring Linny to him if she were there, but what if Colin fucked up?

The guy was old, probably past it. He had resolve, but perhaps his reflexes were not as they should be. Chaise had discovered that back at the car salesroom when he had floored him with surprising ease. And hadn't Colin intimated that he no longer had the heart for this kind of thing, that he longed for retirement? A farmhouse in Burgundy, and red wine in the evening. He was shaking after the night at the Lithuanian's house.

Too late now for second thoughts. Too late for anything.

Chaise ran a hand over his face. Linny turned his life around, brought him normality, but how quickly the old ways returned and all because of a chance meeting with a drug pusher back in Spain. They'd struggled, and the man had died. Everything changed from that point, all the hopes of a normal, average life.

He loved Linny, but he'd let her down and the ties that bound him to his true nature had tightened. The lies ran deep, too deep for Linny to ever forgive him. Perhaps if he offered to leave it all again, tell Harper to shove his bloody job?

He checked his gun for something to do. Who the hell was he kidding? Harper would never release him. And if not Harper, somebody else. He'd end up like Colin. Embittered, disillusioned, hankering for a life he could never have.

Making no effort to conceal himself he put his gun in his waistband and stepped out into the open, hands swinging loosely by his side. A normal guy, here to meet up with his girlfriend.

As he drew closer, he saw the big guy's gun for the first time and his guts tightened. Neither the man nor Brigit noticed him, as they faced the opposite direction. Chaise slowed, conscious of not making any sudden movements. The guy gripped the crutch hard, leaning his full weight onto it.

And then he turned and saw Chaise for the first time. Immediately he pulled Brigit close, threw the crutch aside and pressed the gun against her head. She went white and Chaise stopped, raising both hands above his head.

Colin strode towards the rear of the car. He could easily see the two men inside, one very big. Neither appeared to be talking and Colin came round to the left side of the vehicle.

For a moment, everything stopped. The seconds stretched out and Colin waited, hands behind his back. He was an innocent passer-by, nothing more, and when the big guy finally turned and saw him his face grew taut with alarm. Clearly, he had not expected to be disturbed.

The door opened and he got out.

Colin couldn't help but gasp. The man was a superb physical specimen, muscles taut and strong, exposed skin glistening with health and strength. A body-builder and a damned good one at that.

"Can I help you?"

Colin smiled, hands remaining hidden. "Sorry," he said. "I'm a little lost. Well, my dog is to be honest. Have you seen him?"

"Dog?"

"Yes. I was taking him for a walk, and he ran off in this direction. Have you seen him? Liver and white Welsh Springer spaniel. Name of Jess."

The man cocked his head. "Are you for fucking real?"

"Sorry?"

The man took a step forward, jaw jutting out. "I haven't seen your fucking dog, you moron. Now fuck off before I rip your fucking head off."

Colin blinked and allowed his mouth to hang open. "Sorry, I didn't mean to—"

The big guy leaned closer and said very softly, "*Fuck off.*"

Colin forced a smile, nodded and took two steps backwards. "Yes, yes of course. Sorry."

The big guy gave him a last dismissive glare, turned and made to get back into the car.

Colin brought around both hands, the snub-nose buried inside the small cushion and he shot the man twice in the back of the head, the gun making tiny, damp, muffled sounds as the bullets sent out two plumes of stuffing into the air. With no silencer, Colin had to improvise, but the results proved equally as good. There was no chance of the gun snagging in the material as it was hammerless. Perfect for this type of kill.

Before the big man crumpled lifeless to the ground, the other clambered outside, eyes wide with confusion. Colin pointed the gun straight at him and smiled. "Now then, you sit nice and quiet until I explain to you *exactly* what the bloody hell is going to happen."

Without any hesitation, the man did precisely that.

FIFTY-THREE

The handgun pressed hard against Brigit's temple. She appeared stricken with terror, the man holding the gun grinning like someone possessed. Chaise's anger raged inside and he fought to remain calm, knowing any sudden movements would end with Brigit's brains splattered all across the heath. So Chaise waited for the right moment, straining like a spring fit to snap.

Brigit whimpered, wriggled in the man's grip. He applied more pressure, his free hand clamped around her mouth, her screams muffled. He was strong, determined, eyes narrowed as he spoke through clenched teeth, "I'm going to kill her, you bastard, but I'm going to kill you first, for her to enjoy." She squealed and again he squeezed harder.

Chaise held his breath. The Walther pressed against the small of his back but by anyone's estimation, before he made the slightest movement death would come as quickly as a blink of an eye. Brigit's death, perhaps even his own.

He looked straight into the man's eyes. "We could make a deal."

The man laughed. "A deal? I'm not making any more fucking deals, not with you or with anyone. Whoever you are, you've caused a lot of pain, and the only way you can make any of this good again is by giving me the money."

Chaise darted his eyes towards Brigit, who sagged in the big man's arms. Seconds trickled away. There was no money, nothing to barter with, but a way to prolong things, and give Colin the time to arrive and save them, needed conjuring up. "I have the money," he said quietly. Voice calm, unrushed. "It's in my car. Just let her go, and we can bring all of this to a close."

"I'm not letting her go. She's my guarantee of you doing as you're told, and I'm not so sure you'll do that. Because you're not just a fucking estate agent, are you?"

"What else am I?"

The man smirked. "You stole drugs belonging to Johnny's boss, and you sold them. You must know some people, bad people. That makes you something of a player, and I don't trust players. How much did you make on the deal?"

Chaise didn't hesitate, confidence returning as he played out the game. Every second wasted talking brought the moment when Colin put a bullet in this ape's brain closer. "Quarter of a million."

The man nodded, impressed. "I thought it was going to be more, but no matter, it'll do nicely. *Very* nicely." He pressed the gun harder and Brigit winced. "So, you go back to your car, get the money, and then I'll go away."

"For good?"

"For good. You can go and do whatever it is you do, and I'll buy an air ticket to somewhere nice and warm." He tapped the gun barrel against Brigit's head. "You fail to come back in five minutes and I'll kill her. You understand?"

"Perfectly."

"Good." He frowned. "I've met a lot of tough guys, but you ... there's no fear in your eyes and that makes me nervous."

"Oh, I'm very afraid, I promise you."

"No you're not. I can *see* it. You're no more a fucking estate agent than I am a traffic warden."

Chaise let his eyes wander over the man's bulging frame. "You'd have no problem collecting fines if you were."

Another smirk. "So what exactly is it you do?"

"I told you, an estate agent."

"Estate agents don't make deals over drug money."

"True enough." He took in a deep breath, wondering how much longer he could make his story believable. "I worked for the Spanish police. Undercover. I'd infiltrated some gangs along the coast, got them to trust me. But then, as with everything, I got a little greedy. Decided to branch out on my own."

"That figures. And now you're on the run, is that it?"

Chaise shrugged, trying not to look too smug. A few more minutes, Colin would be here. "Things have changed over there. It all hit the fan, people fell out, got themselves killed. I decided to make a break, that's all."

"Yeah, but you made some silly mistakes, didn't you? Upset the wrong people. You ruined a lot of people's lives, and Johnny came over here to kill you."

"I didn't ruin anything. All I did was protect my own and I've every intention of continuing doing so."

"Not today, my friend. Because today is the day you die if you don't bring me the money."

"Please. Just think about this. If you kill us, the police will hunt you down. They won't stop. So let's bring this to an end, but without the violence. You can do that. You really can."

"I just want the money. I couldn't give a flying fuck about anything or anyone else. Johnny's caused me a lot of grief and I have a personal score to settle with him, but you, you can make all of this right for yourself and this bitch. Go and get the money."

Where the hell was Colin? For one of the few times in his life, Chaise didn't have a clue what to do next.

Colin watched as the man who had introduced himself as Johnny, bundled the dead guy into the back seat of the car. The sweat glistened across Johnny's brow as he strained to drag the heavy corpse across the upholstery. When he eventually succeeded, he stepped out into the rain and took in some deep breaths. "What next?"

"Why don't you tell me?"

Johnny pressed the door shut and leaned against it with both hands. "What do you want to know?"

"All of it. Who you are, what you're doing here."

"It's a long story. It all goes back to Spain, what happened over there."

"You want Chaise dead, is that it?"

"Chaise, yes, I wanted him dead. For sure. He caused it all, my partner Frank's death, the loss of our business, clubs, bars, restaurants, all gone because of him. Frank sent me here to settle it all, but ..." He peered at the ground. "I met Brigit. She's his girlfriend's mother and everything has changed since we got together. Now I just want a life. With her."

"You seriously want me to believe you'll simply walk away once this is over, hand in hand into the sunset? Forget about all the wrongs, the deaths? Don't make me laugh."

"That's exactly what I'm telling you." Johnny's voice took on a note of desperation and he turned and faced his interrogator. "Listen, I've been a close friend of death, seen friends and enemies die in a hail of bullets. It never caused me a moment of anxiety, not until now. Brigit has changed everything and seeing her manhandled like a terrified child, for the first time in my life, I feel afraid. *Please.* Just tell me what I have to do and I'll go away, leave. Brigit too. We will never trouble you or Chaise again. It would be as if we were dead, and you can forget all about us."

"Sounds reasonable. Only problem is, I don't believe you."

Johnny's face crumpled. "I swear to God it's true. I'll get Brigit to tell Chaise where his girlfriend is and it'll end. I don't want any part of this kind of lifestyle, not anymore. Besides, I have no choice. Where am I supposed to go, eh? Frank's dead, the organisation broken, wrecked. I'm on the run from the police, and there's nothing waiting for me in Spain. Brigit knows, we've talked and I believe she wants to make a go of it with me. I'm not going to turn my back on such a chance, am I?"

Colin nodded towards the distant expanse of rock and heathland. "And the other guy? The big one with the crutch. What's he going to do?"

Johnny followed Colin's gaze. "He thinks he's here to get money. Brigit fed him some crazy story, and he swallowed it all. He's on the other side of the hill, waiting for Chaise with a gun against her head. I need to go and help her."

"No. You stay here. I'll go and get it sorted. Try not to do anything stupid."

Johnny moved to come around the car, but Colin brought up the gun. "I said, *you stay here*. I'll bring your Brigit back to you. Trust me, I know exactly what I'm doing."

Johnny sighed, and his shoulders went slack. "Do I have a choice?"

"Not unless you want the other guy to kill her."

Johnny's eyes filled up, and he hung his head down. "All right. But please, be careful."

Colin shook his head, wishing his orders covered every eventuality. Killing a monster in a white t-shirt was one thing, but a pair of lovers? He moved away towards the path that led to the area beyond the rise.

"I need to be certain you won't kill us when I return with the money."

The big guy's arm flexed around Brigit. "You'll have to trust me unfortunately." He grinned, enjoying the situation, relishing his domination. "Now, you've wasted enough time so go and get the money, or I really will hurt her." He squeezed harder against Brigit's nose and mouth and Chaise saw her eyes roll up into the back of her head as she clawed at the man's hand with little effect.

Colin must have failed. Chaise's mind raced, knowing time had run out. He made as if to walk away but instead narrowed the gap between him and the big guy with a sideways step. Six feet, maybe five. He heard Brigit's moan, knew the grip had relaxed and seized the moment. "I haven't got any money, you fucking idiot."

Indecision swept over the man's face, solidifying muscle, petrifying thought. He shook his head, "*What?*"

"I haven't got any fucking money. It was all a fucking lie. I've never had it, never worked for the police, or anything remotely similar, you dickhead. I'm a government operative with MI5, and you are fucking nicked."

Within a blink, everything erupted. The man bellowed, his face twisting into uncontrolled rage. He hurled Brigit to the ground. She bleated as spittle and blood dripped from her torn mouth. The gun whirled. Chaise had to act now, charge forward, take the bullet, try to keep the momentum and hit him hard and sure. The guy was big and strong, but nothing like Mikhail. It would only need one blow, and Chaise might succeed before the bullet did its job.

There was no need.

Colin came over the rise, the Smith and Wesson an extension of his hand, the shots smacking into the big man's chest, one, two, three, hurling him back against a solid, massive clump of sandstone rocks.

The big guy's mouth hung open in horror. His strength proved formidable, as his hand came up, the gun levelled at Chaise.

The gun barked once, but Chaise was already rolling, the bullet scorching the air above his head, missing him by a fraction. He came up on one knee, prepared to move again and saw the big man's eyes dimming, the gun slipping from fingers unable to respond.

Colin strode forward, reloading the gun, snapping the cylinder closed, and point blank put a bullet through the big guy's head.

In the space of a few seconds, the tables were turned. The big guy slid down the boulder, eyes lifeless, a wide smear of dark blood trailing behind him, a wide red paint stroke of life. He crumpled and died in the dirt, hunched up, the rain beating down over his corpse.

Chaise's breath hissed as he leaned towards Brigit and took her in his arms, cradled her, slowly rocking her backwards and forwards, mouth pressed against her ear, tiny kisses bringing a sense of comfort. She was safe. It was over.

Colin blew out a breath. Chaise looked up at him. "Jesus, you certainly know how to bloody well string it out, don't you?"

Colin stood silhouetted against the dark sky, the Smith and Wesson smoking in his hand. He didn't speak, merely stood a silent, solid statue.

"Thank you," Chaise said, pulling his face away from Brigit's. She hung in his arms, limp, barely conscious, relief giving way to shock.

"*Thank* me?" Colin shook his head, dragged the back of his gun hand across his forehead. "Don't you bloody thank me, *Mister* Chaise. I've done nothing for you to be thankful for."

Chaise frowned and glanced past Colin to see another man coming over the rise at a run.

Colin spun and watched the newcomer draw closer. Brigit, tearing herself free of Chaise's embrace, got up, stumbled forward and fell into the man's arms.

Chaise stood up. "What the bloody hell is going on? Who's he?"

"His name's Johnny," said Colin in a low, detached voice. "He came over from Spain to kill you. Because of what happened."

Brigit, her face smothered in Johnny's chest, sobbed uncontrollably whilst Johnny kissed and stroked her head. At last, she turned to look at the others, her eyes streaming. "It's true, Ryan. He came here to kill you." She reached out a hand and stroked Johnny's cheek. "But all of that has changed now. There'll be no more killing." He went to speak, but Brigit stopped him with an index finger pressed over his lips. "I know all about what you did. The parts you didn't tell me. You hurt me, Johnny, but if you are truly willing to make a new start, I'm willing to put everything aside and trust you."

Oblivious to everyone and everything, Johnny clamped her to him, squeezing as tight as he could, laughing with a mix of relief and happiness. Brigit smiled over his shoulder at Chaise

Confused, Chaise struggled to understand even a fraction of what was happening. "But what about Linny? Where is she?"

"At a friend's. Don't worry Ryan, she's safe. None of this has touched her. I'll get her to phone you, now all of this over. No promises, but perhaps the time has come for you to consider changing."

"If only it was all so easy," said Colin and stepped away so his gun could cover them all.

Tension resurfaced, the air growing chill. Something wasn't right and Chaise stared into Colin's steely eyes and knew. The look, the one he'd seen so often in the past. The look of a killer. He bunched his shoulders. "What the hell are you talking about, Colin?"

"You're a bloody bastard, Mr Chaise, and I have my job to do. It's been nice knowing you." He turned the gun. "Don't fret, my remit does not include the woman." He winked. "Only you."

Chaise moaned. A massive weight pressed down over him and he closed his eyes. From elation to despair, in a matter of a few seconds. The only good thing to take to his grave was the knowledge Brigit would survive. Linny might even thank him. Chaise's own death, of course, bearable, perhaps even coming as something of a relief.

Chaise still possessed the Walther. He flexed his fingers, determined to make whatever happened as difficult for Colin as possible.

Nothing ventured.

He reached behind him.

A muffled *thwack* stopped them all. Colin gasped in surprise.

The steady fall of rain lent a strange, preternatural air to the surroundings, with Colin blinking, confusion and bewilderment spreading over his features. He swayed slightly, body twisting, mouth moving open and shut. Open and shut.

Chaise gawped, incredulous. Another muffled, solid thump thrust Colin forward with a powerful shove; he pole-axed forward onto his face and lay still. A bloom of thick blood seeped out around his head.

For one awful elongated moment, nothing made sense. Colin was dead. Two holes in his back: one between the shoulder blades, the other higher at the point where the cerebral cortex meets the brain stem. Someone had shot him from a distance. A sniper.

Chaise gaped, no clarity of thought possible for a moment, not until it all clarified in his head. "Get down," he roared, hurling himself flat to the earth, scrambling amongst a scattering of boulders. Johnny, reacting from habit, pulled Brigit down without a pause, getting her behind some cover.

"What the fuck is going on?" screamed Johnny.

"There's someone else," hissed Chaise from behind the boulders, "but who, or where, I haven't got a bloody clue." He remained concealed, life on the edge now, knowing at any moment everything could end.

He was alive, Brigit too, but for how much longer and how the bloody hell to get away? The sniper was good. To remain hidden, like a ghost, and nail Colin took a level of skill way off the scale. The first shot slightly off the mark, but the second proving deadly. He was out there, waiting. With all the patience of the hunter. If any of them raised their heads, it was lights out.

He looked across to where Brigit lay huddled in Johnny's arms. All of them safe. For now.

His mobile shrilled into life and he yelped, heart leaping. He ripped the phone out of his jacket pocket, glared at the display and groaned. "You pick your moments," he said.

"Are you all right?"

With his heart pounding in his throat, Chaise struggled to string words together, coherent thought a maelstrom. He mumbled, "I'm ... I'm here."

"*Ryan?* Are you hurt?"

Chaise swallowed hard, lubricating his throat a little. "I ... Yes. Yes, I'm all right."

"Listen to me. The sniper, he won't kill you. He's there to protect you. You understand?" Chaise sucked in his breath, fighting to calm himself. "Can you hear me, Ryan? Do you understand what I've said?"

Chaise pressed the back of his hand against his forehead, stopping the sweat from dripping down into his eyes. "Yes. Yes, I understand. Harper, what the *fuck* is going on?"

"You are not injured in any way? You don't need medical assistance?"

"Harper, what the ... yes, I'm all right." The fog cleared a little, brain returning to work. He sat up and stared across to Brigit, her eyes closed, breathing regular. She seemed to have slipped into unconsciousness, perhaps for the best. "Do you want to explain to me what this is all about? Colin's dead. He was going to kill me, then somebody—"

"Yes, I know, Ryan. I've just received the phone call. My man shot Colin. I told you, Ryan. Colin was a freelance working for the Government. They wanted you dead, and I had to prevent that. I have other plans for you, my friend."

"Other ... what the hell are you talking about?"

"The sniper, Ryan. He saved your life. He was following *my orders,* so try to show a little gratitude."

"*Gratitude*? You mean, you've had this guy trailing me all this fucking time, and you wait until now before you give him the order to—"

"No, Ryan." Harper sighed loudly. "Try and bloody well think. He's *totally* autonomous, works in his own way, in his own time. I had no control over any of it. I merely gave him the order. To protect you."

"Protect ... Jesus, Harper, you really are a bastard."

"As I said, Ryan ... a little gratitude? A simple 'thank you' would be nice."

"You wouldn't have done any of this if you didn't have something in mind, Harper. So what the hell is it you want?"

"Ah good, you're finally thinking straight. For a moment I was worried things had got to you, made you vulnerable." He gave a small laugh. "I'm relieved. Because, what I'm asking requires you to be at the top of your form, Ryan."

Chaise closed his eyes, allowing his body to slump, accepting life's inevitable journey along a one-way street, controlled by Harper. "Tell me."

"I could have you put away for thirty years, Ryan. What you did in Norwich, many would congratulate you, put you on a pedestal. The press certainly. The law, however, they would take a different view. But you didn't care, did you? Your only thought was to do what you believed needed doing, regardless of the consequences. Such actions, however, cannot achieve success in isolation. You needed help, someone to assist and watch over you. A friend."

"You?"

"*Exactly*. And I have looked after you, Ryan. I've saved your ungrateful life, allowing you to go and catch up with your precious girlfriend."

A rush of expectation made Chaise almost lightheaded. "You know where she is?"

"Ryan. I want you to listen to me. You're mine now. I've taken care of the shit you caused, here and in Norwich. No one will ever know. Soon, a black Ford Transit will arrive, with people to tidy up the mess. Linny's mother will be required to sign some papers, so wait until they are finished. They will then drive you to a safe house for debriefing. Afterwards, you can recoup. I will look after the tiny details, square things with the police, the media. You understand what I'm saying?"

"What is it you want from me in return, Harper?"

Again, that small, infuriating laugh. "Always the cynic."

"Tell me, you bastard."

"Every once in a while, Ryan, I'll send you a job to do. A job ideally suited for your particular skills. There are not many like you, my friend, and I need to keep you close. Ready. When the call comes, you will respond in the way only you can. I think Simms has already given you some details of your next assignment. More will follow. No questions asked, no answers given. Money will be deposited into your bank account on a regular basis. You can live a comfortable, normal life. But when I ask, you do. Clear?"

"Perfectly. And my protector, what about him?"

"He's the best there is, Ryan. An assassin, but unlike you, he works from a distance. What I need is a man who gets up close and dirty. *You*, my friend."

Chaise squeezed fingers into the corners of his eyes. "I want your word you'll give me time to sort things out with Linny."

"Your kind heart does you credit, Ryan. I hope it is not developing into a weakness."

"I just need to talk to her, get everything straight and in the open."

"I understand. Of course, I'll give you time, but not a great deal. Certain things can't wait."

"Can't wait? Jesus, you really are pulling all the strings aren't you."

He heard the approach of a large vehicle, the distinctive sound of tyres crunching on gravel. Chaise peered across the heath, searching for the silent sniper. "You have told your man not to shoot?"

"He knows what to do. I wouldn't worry too much. If he wanted to kill you, you'd already be dead."

"Comforting thought. Thanks. Wait a moment." He let his arm fall to his side and turned to Brigit and Johnny. "It's finished. There's no more danger."

Johnny's eyes narrowed as he gently cradled Brigit's head in his lap. "I came here to kill *you*. I wish to fuck I had now."

"You're not the only one, mate. Listen, tell Brigit I'm sorry, all right? I never meant for any of this to happen."

"What, just like with Frank?"

"None of that was of my making. None of it."

"Bad luck follows you around like a faithful dog, is that it?"

Chaise ignored him and put the mobile against his ear again. "If this is some sort of sick joke, Harper, I'll—"

"It's no joke. Nor is it a trick. Like I said, if I wanted you dead ..."

"And what about Brigit?

"What about her?"

Chaise held Johnny's eyes. "She has a friend, and I believe he might be in a spot of trouble too. Police."

"I'll fix everything, have no fear. Your girlfriend's precious mother and her new love can disappear. I know all about him. I don't live in a cave. You just make sure you follow my instructions, that's all I require."

"I don't suppose I've got much choice?"

"No. I'm afraid you haven't, Chaise. It's like I told you – you're mine now." Harper's laugh grew louder, setting Chaise's teeth on edge. "*All* mine."

THE END

Dear reader,

We hope you enjoyed reading *Whipped Up*. Please take a moment to leave a review, even if it's a short one. Your opinion is important to us.

Discover more books by Stuart G. Yates at https://www.nextchapter.pub/authors/stuart-g-yates

Want to know when one of our books is free or discounted? Join the newsletter at http://eepurl.com/bqqB3H

Best regards,

Stuart G. Yates and the Next Chapter Team

CPSIA information can be obtained
at www.ICGtesting.com
Printed in the USA
BVHW081930190321
603030BV00003B/339

9 781034 35946